BLOOD RELATION

ARCANE CASEBOOK 6

DAN WILLIS

Print Edition – 2020

This version copyright © 2020 by Dan Willis.

All rights reserved. No part of this book may be reproduced or transmitted in any form or by any electronic or mechanical means, including photocopying, recording or by any information storage and retrieval system, without the express written permission of the copyright holder, except where permitted by law.

This novel is a work of fiction. Names, characters, places and incidents are either the product of the author's imagination, or, if real, used fictitiously.

Initial Edits by Barbara Davis
Edited by Stephanie Osborn

Cover by Mihaela Voicu

Published by

Dan Willis
Spanish Fork, Utah.

1

NEW ADDITIONS

"I have just about had all I'm going to take of your nonsense, Lockerby," the detective in the dark green suit said as he entered the opulent office.

Detective Michael Crookshank was a lean man with the kind of gaunt, sunken expression and red face that spoke to long hours, poor habits, and hard drinking. He definitely wasn't New York's finest, but he was the detective in charge of the Phillip Asher murder, so Alex had to play nice.

But only for another minute or two.

The office of Phillip Asher was on the ground floor of his palatial home. Banks of glass windows rose to a height of twenty feet behind the massive desk, revealing the immaculately manicured grounds and the skyscrapers of the Core beyond. Empire Tower, the titular symbol of wealth and power occupied the center window, standing far above its fellow towers.

As impressive as the view was, the office was even more so. Along the side wall ran a bank of polished oak shelves packed with leather-backed books, rising up to the room's high ceiling. A brass ladder hung from a rail that ran the length of the shelves and curved around at the back of the room until it met an immense hearth with a mantle of polished marble. The fireplace below yawned open, revealing a decorative grate fronted by gleaming brass andirons. A Persian rug adorned the floor, and art by the old masters covered the walls. It was impossible to stand in the opulence of this office and not feel the weight of Phillip Asher's wealth and power.

Or at least it would be if he hadn't been bludgeoned to death with a poker from the fireplace while he sat at his massive, intricately-carved desk. Since Phillip had been in the process of changing his will to leave his vast fortune to charity, Detective Crookshank had assumed one of his progeny had committed the murder to prevent the loss of their inheritance. Since son Ben was actually in the house the night of the murder, suspicion naturally fell on him. To make matters worse, his brother and sister had both been out of the city that night. As far as Crookshank was concerned, it was an open-and-shut case.

Benjamin Asher sat on a large couch with his legs crossed and his fingers steepled in front of him. He was a man in his late thirties with a pencil mustache, intense eyes, and perfectly slicked-back hair. His clothes were elegant, his shoes were polished, his shirt was pressed, and his cufflinks shone in the light of the late morning sun streaming in through the windows. It was Ben who had hired Alex to find out what had really happened to his father.

On the couch next to Ben sat Leah Asher Halverson, Ben's younger sister, and Richard, her husband. On the other side stood Lionel Asher, the middle child, wearing a casual shirt with slacks and sporting a tennis racket. The last person in the room was a young blond man in a moderately nice suit who had an attaché on his lap. His name was John Taylor, a junior partner from Phillip Asher's law firm, and the man who had written up Phillip's new will.

Crookshank stood by the desk where Phillip Asher had met his end and thumped on the mahogany top.

"The evidence in this case couldn't be clearer, Lockerby," he declared. "Phillip Asher was killed by his son Ben when the old man threatened to cut him out of the will." The Detective turned to cast an accusatory glance at Benjamin. "Now if we can dispense with any more theatrics from your PI, I'll be taking you in now." He motioned to the two uniformed officers who had followed him into the office.

"Just a minute," Alex said before the policemen could respond. He'd been standing on the opposite side of the massive desk and he moved around to where Detective Crookshank stood.

"I have to admit, Detective," he said, pasting a friendly smile on his face, "you are absolutely right about the motive."

Crookshank gave him a half-smile and a raised eyebrow.

"Really?" he said. "How magnanimous of you. Since Lionel and Leah were both out of town, I guess that only leaves your client."

Alex nodded sagely and waited for the detective to raise a beckoning hand to the officers.

"But," he interrupted, "Ben is the president of his father's shipping company. And Lionel started his own far east import business, supplying silk for his brother-in-law Richard's textile mills." He turned from the siblings back to Crookshank. "They're all worth a fortune, so why would they care if their father gave away his money?"

Crookshank gave Alex a look that implied that the question was self-evident.

"For some people, there's no such thing as enough money," he said, emphasizing his words as if it were an aphorism. "Besides, as you just admitted, no one else had a motive."

"Unless there's another heir out there somewhere," Alex said.

"Really, Mister Lockerby," Lionel Asher said as his sister covered a gasp with her handkerchief.

Alex continued as if he hadn't heard the protest.

"I discussed the terms of Phillip Asher's existing will with young Taylor," he nodded at the junior partner from Phillip's law firm. "And he tells me that the existing will has a provision in it that covers the possibility of bastard heirs."

"Is this how you plan to get yourself out of trouble?" Lionel demanded to Ben. "By tarnishing Father's good name?"

"Mr. Asher," Alex interrupted before Ben could answer. "I don't wish to be indelicate, but there's only one reason your father would include such a clause in his will."

"You mean to say that he feared there might be an heir he didn't know about," Leah said, her voice full of challenge.

"Even if that's true," Crookshank said, "why would this heir kill Phillip?"

Alex shrugged.

"He was about to change his will. Once the money was gone, there'd be nothing to inherit."

"Yes," Lionel spoke up again. "But what would prevent them from just coming forward before he changed the will?"

"Simple," Ben said, speaking for the first time. "Father might not have acknowledged them."

"Exactly," Alex said. "It would be much safer for them to come forward after your father's death. With the proper documentation, they could pursue a legal remedy, but with Phillip alive to denounce the claim it would be much harder."

"You're saying that this mystery heir intended to wait for Mr. Asher to die, then make their claim," Leah's husband Richard said. "But when Phillip wanted to divest himself of his fortune, they had to move to prevent that."

"Exactly," Alex said, giving Richard a sly smile. From what Alex had seen of the man, he was deviously intelligent, an observation backed up by how quickly he picked up Alex's train of thought.

"All of this is speculation," Detective Crookshank said in a voice that indicated he wanted this conversation to be over. "Unless you can prove this heir exists, Lockerby, it's just a wild story."

Alex turned to his client.

"I read somewhere that your father used his shipping business to smuggle supplies to the British and the French in the early days of the Great War," he said. "Is that true?"

"I know the Captain likes you, Lockerby—" Crookshank began in an exasperated voice, but Alex waved him silent.

"Yes," Ben said, confused at the change of subject. "The government asked for his help and he was happy to oblige. He even went to Europe several times to coordinate with our allies."

"And on his second trip," Alex continued. "The one he took in 1915, wasn't he stuck in Belgium for five months?"

"Yes," Ben admitted. "We were just children at the time, but I remember being worried sick."

"You were concerned because your mother had passed away the previous year," Alex said. "Your father was only supposed to be gone a few weeks, but you were alone for almost half a year."

"Well, not alone," Ben said. "We had a nanny and Horace was with us." Horace was Phillip's aging butler. Alex had considered him a suspect, but Phillip Asher had provided a very generous sum to the man as a retirement several years ago. Horace, however, refused to retire, so Phillip kept him on.

"Are you suggesting our father had a fling while he was stuck in Brussels?" Lionel asked, some of the previous hostility fading from his voice.

"Yes, that's what he's saying," Detective Crookshank said, irritation in his voice and on his face. "He's trying to muddy the waters, but it's just idle speculation. We checked to see if any claims of kinship had been made against Phillip Asher and there aren't any."

"Ben," Alex asked. "When the government asked your father for help, they were worried the Germans might catch on to who he was. They gave him an alias, didn't they?"

The color drained from Ben's face and he nodded.

"Yes," he said, his voice horse. "He went by Friedrich Schneider."

Alex turned back to Crookshank, who had begun to look a little green himself.

"Did you look to see if there were any claims against a Friedrick Schneider?" he asked. Crookshank's lips split into a scowl but before he could answer, Alex pulled a folded paper from the inside pocket of his suit coat. "Fortunately, I did," he said, handing the paper to the detective.

Crookshank opened the paper and scanned it.

"What is it?" Leah Halverson asked, her voice barely a whisper. She clutched her husband's hand so tightly her knuckles went white.

"It's a birth record from Belgium," the detective said. "According to this a baby boy was born to a Friedrich Schneider and Leslie Bardo Schneider. The boy's name was Johan."

"And this," Alex said, pulling another document from his pocket, "is a claim by Johan Schneider, saying that his father, Friedrich Schneider, was an American. Johan is seeking citizenship, but I suspect that's just a ruse. You see, this paperwork was filed two years ago."

"That doesn't make any sense," Richard Halverson said. "According to that birth record, Friedrich Schneider was married to the boy's mother. If he has a marriage record, that would be proof of his paternity. He could have just come forward."

"Even with a marriage license, there wouldn't be any way to prove that the Friedrich Schneider on the form was actually Phillip Asher using his wartime alias," Alex said. "Johan's best chance was to wait till Phillip couldn't deny the marriage, then let a judge decide."

"So who is this Johan Schneider?" Lionel demanded. "Is he the one that killed father?"

"I think I can answer both questions," Alex said. "Johan most certainly killed Phillip. If your father had managed to change his will, Johan would have been left with nothing. As to where he is?" Alex shrugged. "As far as I can tell, no one with the name Johan or Schneider is associated with this case in any way. But names are curious things. Did you know that in English, the name Johan becomes Jonathan?"

"I think everyone knows that," Crookshank said. "But there's no Jonathan Schneider mixed up in this business either."

Alex looked at the man and gave him a patient smile.

"Young Jonathan would be about twenty-two," he said, turning to the wing-back chair. "Right about the age of our ambitious junior partner."

All eyes turned to the attorney, who looked startled.

"Well, my name is John," he protested. "But—"

"And as the low man on your firm's totem pole," Alex pressed on, "you had the job of writing up Phillip Asher's new will."

"But my name's not Schneider," he insisted. "It's Taylor."

"As I said," Alex went on, "names are funny things. A lot of immigrants came to New York after the war. Thousands of them flooded through Ellis Island, and sometimes the officials working there couldn't pronounce their names. It might interest you to know that many people lost their original surnames on that island. A small price to pay to become an American. The name Schneider was one of those that was routinely changed. Like Johan, it was translated into English. Literally it means cutter, but in practical application it was changed to—"

"Taylor," Crookshank growled, staring hard at the young lawyer.

"Very good, Detective," Alex said.

"I'm sure that would be a fantastic story," Taylor said, shaking his head. "If you could prove any of it."

Alex pointed to the claim of parentage that Crookshank still carried.

"That's just a copy," he explained. "But I had a look at the original down at the Hall of Records. It was undoubtedly submitted by Johan Schneider personally, and I managed to lift several fingerprints from it." Alex pulled an envelope from his pocket and held it up. "You may remember that I asked you for some particulars of Phillip's will and you obligingly sent me a letter containing the answers."

Taylor's face blanched.

"I was careful to open that letter with gloves," Alex went on. "You'll be shocked to learn that your fingerprints are a match for the ones on Johan Schneider's citizenship petition."

"I think you'd better come with us," Detective Crookshank sighed as he took the envelope from Alex. One of the uniformed officers stepped up behind Taylor and placed a restraining hand on the young man's shoulder.

"Is he really our brother?" Leah asked as Taylor was marched out in handcuffs.

Alex shrugged.

"I don't know," he admitted. "It's possible, but he might have just been taking advantage of having the right last name."

"Did he kill Father?" Ben asked.

"It certainly seems that way," Alex said. "Right now the evidence against him is circumstantial, but once the police search his home and his office, they might find a more direct link."

"Thank you, Mr. Lockerby," Ben said, rising and sticking out his hand for Alex to shake. "Andrew Barton said you were the best, and he was right."

Alex shook his hand, and when no one else had any questions for him, he saw himself out.

"I bet you think you're real clever," Crookshank said, falling into step beside Alex as soon as he left the office. "Making me look like a chump in there."

"I was just doing my job," he said, not stopping. "I was hired to prove that Ben Asher didn't kill his father. Unfortunately the best I could do was provide you with a much better suspect. Making you look the fool was just a bonus."

Crookshank grabbed Alex's arm and jerked him to a stop.

"I know you're the Captain's pet dick," he snarled, still clutching Alex's arm. "But a lot of us are watching you. Sooner or later you're going to make a mistake, and on that day we're going to come down on you like a ton of bricks and not even the Captain will be able to save you."

Alex fixed a bored expression on his face. Crookshank wasn't the first policeman to threaten him and he suspected he wouldn't be the last, but the man was right about one thing. Captain Callahan had his back. He helped get Alex work with the department, so if anything went south on one of Alex's cases, cops like Crookshank would drag Callahan down with him. That was something Alex couldn't allow, so instead of berating Crookshank like he wanted to, he just smiled at the man.

"Nice to know I'll have you looking over my shoulder," he said, tugging his arm free of the detective's grip. "Makes me feel safe."

Crookshank snarled something unintelligible as Alex turned and walked out the Ashers' massive front door.

Fifteen minutes later, an open-top skycrawler scuttled up to the platform at Empire Station. Sparks of white-hot electricity arced from its blue energy legs as it skidded to a stop, swaying slightly before it lowered the car onto the support blocks by the platform. Alex waited for the lower deck to clear before descending, since the September weather was pleasant and mild.

His heels clicked on the marble floor as he made his way to the far side of the station where the beverage counter stood. Marnie was away, but one of her helpful young women handed Alex a thermos full of coffee without him having to even ask for it. She also gave him an interested smile, which Alex ignored on account of the girl being at least ten years his junior.

He thanked her and set out for the building elevators in the center of the back wall. In former days, when Alex had gone up to the top floors of Empire Tower, he'd had to go through the security station and take Andrew Barton's private elevator up to the offices of Barton Electric. These days, however, Alex only rode up to the twelfth floor.

"How are you Mr. Lockerby?" a wizened man in a red velvet vest with gold embroidery greeted him.

"Doing well, George," Alex responded as the man flipped the switch that would close the doors.

"Up to your office?"

Alex nodded and George pulled the large lever that started the car moving upward. When they reached the twelfth floor, he centered the lever and opened the doors.

Alex wished George a good day, then stepped out onto the landing. To the right were the offices of a law firm and an architect, while to the left were a Broadway talent agency and the new offices of Lockerby Investigations.

It was hard for Alex not to grin as he went to the end of the hallway where a burnished cherrywood door broke up the vellum-colored wallpaper of the hallway. Frosted glass windows ran out on each side of the door, giving vague hints about what lay beyond, but revealing nothing. This door didn't have a window like his previous one, just a solid panel with the name of the business and the Runewright symbol in gold lettering. He'd given up the "Runewright Detective" name when he'd moved offices though; it just seemed a little crass, considering his new surroundings.

After the disaster with Bradley Elder, Alex had agreed to work for Andrew Barton on an as-needed basis, helping him link up his power relay towers. Instead of money, Alex got the Lightning Lord to pay him with this office and with an apartment up on the residence floors of Empire Tower.

Taking the gleaming brass doorknob in his hand, Alex turned it smartly and walked in.

It took Alex a minute to square what he was seeing with all the years he'd spent in his mid-ring office. Back then, the door opened on a room with two old couches across from it, and his secretary's desk off to the left. Now the desk sat directly opposite the impressive front door. The old desk had been made of some cheap wood and painted grey. It had been serviceable enough, but it was nothing compared to the massive oak number with brass accents that occupied the new waiting room.

Gone were the old couches, replaced with two new ones, one on either side of the door. They were upholstered in an elegant art nouveau pattern and the arms and top had polished wood runners.

Behind Sherry's desk were a bank of windows that completely covered the back wall, filling the room with light.

"Hey boss," Sherry said, looking up from her desk as he entered. "Everything go okay with the Asher case?" Sherry Knox had tan skin, dark, shoulder-length hair with eyes of deep blue, and a perpetual grin. She had been Alex's secretary for almost two years now and she'd fallen into the role with ease. It didn't hurt that she was an Auger, possessed of an all-but-unknown ability to see the future. Or rather to see the future when the future felt it was convenient.

"Mornin', Sherry," he said, hanging his hat on a row of pegs by the door before crossing to her desk. "I think Ben's in the clear. It'll depend on what they find at the lawyer's house, but at least I've established enough reasonable doubt that a jury should have a hard time convicting him."

"I'll get his bill ready and send it over then," she said, scribbling a note on one of her various pads.

"Anything in the cards for me this morning?"

She looked up at him with a disgusted look on her face.

"Same old, same old," she grumbled. For over a year, Sherry had been getting the same reading when she dealt her cards for Alex.

You're not seeing what isn't there.

It was a maddeningly unspecific message and he'd long ago stopped trying to work out what it meant. He'd just have to wait for it to come to him in its own good time.

"Any other messages?" he asked, pushing the riddle from his mind.

Sherry nodded.

"Mr. Barton wants to see you at the Brooklyn Relay Tower. He said it's ready."

Alex glanced at the heavy door on the right side of the office. Behind it was a short hallway that led to his private office, his map room, the records room, and another room he hadn't figured out a use for yet. Over the last week, he'd used up many of his standard cadre of runes and he needed to spend some time in his vault to write new ones.

"Duty calls," he said with a sigh, then picked up his hat and headed out the door.

2

CONNECTIONS

It had been four years since Andrew Barton partnered with John D. Rockefeller to take his ground-moving crawler buses and run them on rails mounted thirty feet above the street. That was before Barton had expanded his power network with a relay tower in the Bronx and now one in Brooklyn. Back then, skycrawlers only ran from north Harlem down to the south side docks. Now the electrified rails that carried the insect-like skycrawlers ran all over Manhattan, up to Westchester, down to Brooklyn, and out to Long Island City and Queens.

Alex sat in the front of a skycrawler, watching the city fly by as he finished a cigarette. Normally Alex read the paper on a long crawler trip but when he had to visit Barton's relay tower in Brooklyn, he always waited for an open-topped car and sat up front. The Brooklyn crawler line started from the City Hall station and ran across the Brooklyn Bridge. It wouldn't have been too difficult to run the skycrawler track over the street on the bridge, just like it was in town, but Andrew Barton was nothing if not flamboyant. He'd insisted that the rails be run to the side of the bridge, out over the water. Newspapers and others had screamed it was dangerous, but Barton had already shown that skycrawlers couldn't fall off their tracks even if they lost power, so the line was built the way he wanted it. Some people still refused to ride it, but Alex absolutely loved the trip. When the ground fell away and there was nothing below the crawler but its electrified rail, Alex felt as if he were flying without an airplane.

Not that he'd ever been on an airplane.

It only took a minute to cross the East River. After that, it was only a few more stops until Barton's power relay tower came into view. It rose up just south of Prospect Park towering over the surrounding buildings, or what was left of them. Just like Empire Tower in Manhattan, the more affluent residents and businesses wanted to be close to the tower and its constant flow of energy. The tower had only been operational for two weeks at half capacity, but already many of the surrounding structures had been demolished and new, more expensive buildings were going up.

Alex flicked his cigarette butt away and settled back in his seat as he waited for his station.

Ten minutes later Alex stood in front of the relay tower. Unlike Empire Tower, the relay was a ten-story structure that only looked like a regular apartment or commercial building. It had a ground-floor lobby with a security office and an elevator that appeared perfectly ordinary. The only giveaway that the tower was not what it seemed was the large, doughnut-shaped power distribution ring sticking up from the roof. Originally the Brooklyn Relay Tower had been built to house etherium generators, the massive machines Barton used to convert magical energy into electrical power. Thanks to linking runes and Alex's plan to connect each tower directly to the main generator in Empire Tower, the Brooklyn Relay didn't need any generators at all. As a result, the building was just an empty shell with the power room on top, the lobby on the ground, and an elevator connecting the two. All the floors in between were empty.

Alex pushed open the heavy glass door of the lobby. Empty or not, the Brooklyn Relay was one of Andrew Barton's properties, and the door was suitably impressive. The glass had been etched to show a likeness of Empire Tower with waves of electricity radiating out from its top. Heavy brass handles adorned the front, and the hinges and frame were made of polished steel.

As Alex entered the building and crossed the tiled marble floor in the direction of the lone elevator, a paunchy security guard peered over his newspaper at him. Alex knew his name was Bill Grady and he hailed from Ireland originally.

"Mornin' Mr. Lockerby," he said in a polite but disinterested brogue.

"Good morning, Bill," Alex returned as he pushed the elevator button. "How's the wife?"

Bill's eyes had already drifted back to his newspaper and he shrugged.

"Not good a'tall," he said with a sigh.

"Still with you, I see," Alex said in a somber voice...but he couldn't suppress a grin.

"Aye," Bill confirmed. "The old battle-ax."

"Well, better luck tomorrow," Alex said as the automatic elevator car arrived.

"From your lips to God's ears," he said, not looking up.

Alex stepped into the car and pushed the lone button for the top floor. When the doors opened again, Alex stepped out into a short hallway then turned left, emerging into the large open space that made up the building's top floor. In the center of the room was a heavy cement pillar with a protective glass case covering the top. Inside were three marble slabs that had been cut to hold three square plates of pure silver.

Around the table in the center, there was a curving row of electrical fuse boxes, laid out in a circle. Heavy insulated wires ran from the boxes up through holes in the ceiling, attaching to the metal doughnut above. Behind the fuse boxes, a metal stair spiraled its way up through the ceiling as well. Windows ran around the walls, giving a view of Prospect Park to the north and Brooklyn proper to the south. Alex could even see the spot where The Narrows met Gravesend Bay in the far distance.

Blood Relation

"Lockerby!" Andrew Barton's voice called from the top of the spiral stair. "Is that you?"

Alex answered in the affirmative and Barton came skipping down the stair like a kid at Christmas. He wore a silk suit made of some deep red fabric with black satin lapels, a dark shirt and a tie that matched the suit. He was clean shaven, having shorn off his short beard some months previous, but he still sported a fashionable pencil mustache.

"It's about time you got here," he chided as he reached the bottom of the staircase. "I've been waiting over an hour."

"Didn't Sherry tell you I was wrapping up a case?" Alex asked, knowing full well that she would have.

"Yes," Barton grumbled. "When I agreed to let you only work for me part-time, I didn't imagine you'd be this hard to get a hold of. Aren't you supposed to just sit in your office and wait for people to come to you?"

"Sometimes," Alex admitted. "But usually after that happens, I have to go out and do actual investigating."

Barton gave him a scrutinizing look as if he thought Alex might be lying and evidence of it might be found on his face.

"Maybe we need some kind of signal," he said at last. "You don't have some kind of rune that I could use to get your attention, do you? Let you know to call me?"

Alex shook his head. While such a thing would be incredibly useful, it simply didn't exist.

"Are you sure?" he said, eyes half closed in a suspicious glance. "You didn't tell me about your linking rune idea until I'd already hired that lunatic Bradley Elder. You wouldn't be trying to get out of your job working for me now that I put you up in that nice new office, would you?"

"No," Alex said with a chuckle. He knew Barton well enough by now to know that he was only half-serious. "I'm not hiding some secret radio rune from you."

Barton shrugged in a gesture of resignation, then the bright, enthusiastic smile returned to his face.

"Well, you're here now anyway." He rubbed his hands together in anticipation. "Did you bring your kit?"

Alex hadn't, but he fished his vault key out of his trousers pocket and held it up. The linking runes he made for Barton were both secret and expensive and he didn't like to carry them around.

"Fine," Barton said. "Get your bag while I open the case."

Alex went to the wall near the elevator where he'd chalked the outline of a door during one of his many visits to the relay tower. Tearing a vault rune from his red-backed book, he licked the back and stuck it to the wall. A few moments later he pulled the heavy door to his vault open and went inside.

The drafting table where he wrote his runes sat at the far end of the massive space inside the door. Hallways ran off to either side, but Alex ignored them, heading instead for the half-height filing cabinet on wheels that stood next to the drafting table. Opening the top drawer, he withdrew a yellow-backed version of his rune book and dropped it into the outside pocket of his jacket.

When Alex returned to the power room, Andrew Barton was standing by the glass case. The massive glass top of the case had pivoted up on hinges and was held at an oblique angle by small chains that kept it from falling all the way back.

"It's finally ready," he said as Alex stepped up beside him. Inside the glass were three marble slabs, each one with a square depression cut into it. Inside the depression was a heavy silver plate, and on each plate Alex had carved a rune. Originally he'd thought that linking runes didn't actually deteriorate like all other runes, but after months of testing, he'd determined that linking runes simply deteriorated much more slowly than normal. To combat that, Alex had used silver to hold the master runes. After he'd engraved them with a diamond-tipped stylus, he'd filled the lines with ink that had been infused with diamond and sapphire powder. They weren't permanent, but they'd last for over a decade before having to be replaced.

The silver plate in the center of the glass case held the rune that linked back to Empire Tower. All of the electrical energy Brooklyn would need flowed into the relay tower from that single point of contact. The rune on the right sparkled as Alex looked at it, pulsing with colors that shifted from yellow to blue-green. Energy from the central rune flowed into this secondary plate and from there to each of the breaker boxes on the right side of the room.

The plate on the left was exactly like the one on the right, but it wasn't connected to the central node. Without power, it just appeared to be an elaborate symbol etched in the silver surface of the plate. Alex couldn't see them, but he knew that linking runes had been attached to the outer edge of the inert plate, connecting it to the left-hand breaker boxes.

"Okay," Alex said, pulling out the yellow book. "All the links are in place, all I have to do is connect the transfer plate," he indicated the one on the left, "to the main and you'll be in business."

Barton nodded, rubbing his hands together in eager anticipation.

"Go ahead," he said. "I've checked and rechecked everything." He reached out and patted the side of the glass case. "She's ready."

Alex tore out the top page out of the yellow book, along with the one behind it. He didn't have to check to be sure, since the only runes in this book were linking runes.

Licking the back of the first rune, he stuck it to the transfer plate on the left. He repeated the process with the second paper, but instead of sticking it to the main power node, Alex dropped it carefully onto the plate. There were no sparks and no hum of electricity, but millions of volts were moving through the innocuous-looking square of silver. If Alex had touched it, he would have been electrocuted instantly. That said, the rune wouldn't link properly if the paper wasn't in firm contact with the plate.

Leaning down, Alex peered through the glass. Before he could ascertain whether or not the rune was making good contact, Barton reached into the glass and pushed the paper down with his finger.

"Show off," Alex said, standing up straight. Barton grinned.

Taking out his lighter, Alex lit the paper on the transfer plate. As it burned away, the paper on the central node caught fire as well. Both vanished in a fraction of a second, leaving a sapphire-blue rune hovering over their respective plates. After a moment the runes popped, like a soap bubble hitting a needle, and the rune on the left-hand plate began to pulse with light.

Indicators on the left side breaker boxes lit up and Alex could hear them humming as current began coursing through them. Barton moved to the box on the end of the left side and began walking around the curve, reading the power meters set into each box.

"They're all reading full power," he said, turning to Alex. "Let's see if the antenna is working." He turned and headed for the spiral stair, motioning for Alex to follow.

Up at the top of the stair was a landing and a door that led out onto a small balcony that jutted out from the roof and gave an incredible view of the city to the south. Above them, the massive doughnut-shaped antenna hummed and crackled as it projected its energy through the air. When Barton led Alex out onto the balcony, he reached into thin air and pulled a tripod into his hand. He set it up and then reached into nothingness again to retrieve a heavy brass telescope which he fastened to the top of the tripod.

Alex had done magic for most of his life, but nothing he could do compared to this dimensional pocket trick that sorcerers did. Worst of all, they made it look so easy, so casual. It simply wasn't fair.

"I have a boat stationed out in Gravesend Bay," Barton explained as he focused the telescope. After a minute he clapped his hands together with a fierce, toothy grin and stood back so Alex could look.

The telescope was focused on a small boat, bobbing in the gentle chop of the bay. A large electric lantern with a green filter was mounted in the back of the boat, and it glowed with an intensely bright light.

"How is that light so bright?" Alex asked, stepping back from the telescope.

"It's an arc lamp," Barton said. "Very bright but it takes a fair amount of power. The fact that it's working so well means we now have full power projection all the way down to Fort Hamilton and the river. That's all thanks to you," he went on. "It took that nutcase Bradley almost two months to connect the Bronx Relay, but you did it in just a couple of weeks."

"I'll have Sherry remind you of that the next time you call and I'm out on a case," he said with a grin.

Barton reached into his inside jacket pocket and pulled out two cigars, passing one to Alex.

"Don't get too comfortable in your fancy new digs," he said, pausing to bite the tip off the cigar. "The Jersey City Relay broke ground last week, so there's lots to do."

"Speaking of lots to do," Alex said, flicking his lighter to life and holding the flame to the tip of his cigar. "I need to get back to my job."

Barton rolled his eyes and shook his head at that.

"I've got at least three other projects I could put you to work on right now," he said, blowing a perfect ring of smoke. "I'll even find a place for that pretty secretary of yours so you don't have to worry about putting her out of work."

"I like my job," Alex said, and he meant it. Figuring out how to link a bunch of separate breakers to a single node and then link that back to Empire Tower had been fun, but it wasn't especially taxing. If Alex had to do that for the rest of his life, he'd go mad from boredom.

"Of course," Barton said, somewhat magnanimously. "But if you work for me, I'll pay you fifty thousand a year. You'd have to solve a lot of cases to make that kind of scratch."

It was tempting. Barton was offering more money than Alex would make in ten years, and he was absolutely serious. Sure, cases like Ben Asher's paid well, but those only came along every couple of months. It had been a long time since he'd been unable to make rent, but he could live very well on fifty large a year.

"Sorry," he said after a pause to think about it. "I'll help out whenever you need, but I'm honestly just a detective."

Barton held his gaze for a long moment, then he shrugged and puffed his cigar.

"My offer still stands," he said. "Whenever you're ready."

Alex thanked him, then descended the spiral stair back down to the control room. Since his vault was still open, he just went inside and shut the door behind him.

3

EASTERN ALCHEMY

Alex opened the plain wooden door that covered the entrance to his vault and stepped into the little hallway that connected his back office rooms to the waiting area of his new office. Once he'd learned to open multiple doors into his vault, it was fairly easy to put a semi-permanent one wherever he wanted. The trick was that the plain wooden door that covered the opening wasn't actually part of the vault. It was attached to the wall and only served to prevent anyone but him from entering. The actual vault door opened inward and was concealed inside the vault itself.

As Alex pushed the cover door closed, he felt the protection runes engage. They were the same ones that secured the front door of the brownstone, meaning it would take a team of men and a battering ram to get the simple wooden door to budge. Even then they might not be able to get inside.

His new private office was immediately to his left behind a cherry-wood door marked *private*. The next door along the hall led to an empty room that was big enough for a meeting table, though Alex didn't usually meet large groups in his office, so that room was currently empty. Furthest away was his map room where a focusing rune had been painted on the hardwood floor under a table with an enormous map of Manhattan mounted on it. At the far end of the hall was the door that emptied out into his new waiting room. As Alex started forward to check in with Sherry, he noticed a glimmer of light shining from under the map room door.

Taking hold of the handle, he opened the door to find a short, stumpy man in a grey suit laying out several items on the map table. He had a bushy blond mustache, a weathered face, rosy cheeks, and a pointed, sloping nose under dark eyes. As Alex opened the door, the man looked up from what he was doing and grinned.

"Hello, Mr. Lockerby," he said with just the hint of Irish.

"Hi, Mike," Alex said, giving the man a smile. Mike Fitzgerald used to work on Runewright Row selling minor mending runes, barrier runes, and a finding rune that, while not up to Alex's standards, would work if the lost object was close. Sherry had convinced Alex to start a side business finding lost pets, so he'd recruited Mike. Since he already knew how to use a finding rune, Alex supplied his more advanced ones and Mike handled the legwork.

"Sherry's got three cases for me this afternoon and I did two this morning," Mike said, holding up a pair of what looked like dog collars and a fancy silver brush. It always amazed Alex how devoted pet owners were to their furry companions. He hadn't considered pet finding worth doing, but Sherry had been right, it brought in a surprising amount of money.

"Do you need anything from me?" Alex asked.

"Nah," Mike said with a shake of his head. "There's plenty of finding runes in the box." He pointed to a wooden box with a lid that sat on top of an elegant sideboard. "If this keeps up, though, we'll need more by next week."

Alex made a mental note to prioritize writing more finding runes, then wished Mike good luck and closed the door. When he entered the waiting area, he found Sherry sitting at her desk making notes in a case file, and she wasn't alone. Two Oriental men stood in front of the desk with their hats in their hands. The older of the two wore a fancy embroidered jacket, loose fitting trousers, and carried a black Chinese-style hat with a tassel attached to its top. He had long hair braided into a tail that hung down his back, and he wore a pair of wire-framed spectacles. The younger man was dressed in a brown suit and carried a bowler hat. His hair was cut short, very similar to the way Alex wore his, and it was slicked back.

"Oh, Alex," Sherry said, rising. "I didn't hear you come in."

"I just arrived," Alex said, giving her a smile. They had agreed to pretend that the office had a private entrance to explain how Alex could come and go without passing through the waiting room.

"Are you Mr. Lockerby?" the young, suit-wearing man said. His features were Asian, but he spoke without any trace of an accent.

Alex stuck out his hand and the young man took it.

"Call me Alex," he said as he shook the man's hand. "How can I be of service?"

"Alex," Sherry interjected, pointing to the young man. "This is Lung Chen, and this is his Uncle Su Hi. Mr. Su is an alchemist," she went on. Alex gave Sherry a quick smile, he was impressed that she knew about Oriental surnames being given first. "He just received a shipment of rare ingredients from China, but they were stolen from this warehouse." She tore a paper off the top of one of her pads and handed it to Alex.

"It's very important that we recover our property, Alex," Chen said, remembering to call Alex by his name. "My uncle needs them for his work, and they were very expensive."

"If they came from China you probably had to wait a long time for them too," Alex said.

"Exactly," Chen confirmed. "We're depending on those ingredients and the potions they'd make to keep the business running. We don't have the time or the cash on hand to order more. Can you help us?"

"What kind of ingredients are we talking about?" Alex asked. He didn't know much about Chinese alchemy, but he knew that it differed greatly from the Western style. Jessica had explained it to him once, saying that the way alchemists worked depended on the ingredients they were used to using.

"They're mostly herbs," Chen said. "Ciwuja, red and black reishi, Chinese ginseng, that sort of thing. There are a few more exotic ingredients as well, powdered chiru horn, tiger teeth, and a jar of spleens from the Yiwu salamander. Nothing dangerous or illegal."

Alex nodded along, but his stomach soured at the report. While he was unfamiliar with the list of ingredients, it didn't sound like anything terribly rare or special. That would mean that neither Chen nor his uncle would have any personal connection to the missing shipment. Without that connection, using a finding rune was out.

"Did anyone beside yourself and your uncle know that this shipment was going to be arriving?"

Chen turned to his uncle and said something to him in one of the Chinese dialects. After a moment, the uncle shook his head and answered.

That explains why Mr. Su had been so quiet, and why he brought his nephew. He doesn't speak English.

"My uncle says that a lot of his customers were waiting for the potions the ingredients would have made, but no one knew when they'd be arriving."

"All right," Alex said, looking at the name on the paper Sherry had given him. He didn't know the warehouse, but it was over by Grand Central Terminal. To reach New York, a shipment from China would have to arrive in California and travel by rail from there. That was bad news as well; most of the warehouses by the rail terminal saw goods and people coming and going all day, meaning that it was unlikely anyone would have noticed something suspicious.

"I'll go over to the warehouse and see if I can learn anything there," Alex finished.

"I thought you used a powerful finding rune to locate this kind of thing," Chen said.

Alex took a minute to explain the ins and outs of finding runes, then gave Chen and his uncle a reassuring smile.

"There may be something the thieves left behind at the warehouse that I can use to track them," he said. "Even if there isn't, I can still investigate the old-fashioned way. If I haven't located your property by Thursday, I'll call you and let you know where I am with the investigation. Does Sherry have a number where I can reach you?"

Chen looked a bit crestfallen, but he nodded. Clearly coming to Alex had been his idea.

"I realize how important this is to you," Alex added. "I'll give this my full attention."

"Thank you, Alex," Chen said, sticking out his hand again. "And good luck."

After a brief, whispered discussion in Chinese, Chen and his uncle departed.

"Was that as bad as it sounded?" Sherry asked.

Alex just shrugged.

"It would have been better if Mr. Su's herbs had come from a relative's garden in China," he said. "Then he would have had a connection to them. Without something like that, the finding rune has nothing to grab on to. I think Mr. Chen was counting on me finding their missing ingredients today."

"How did it go with Andrew Barton?" Sherry asked, changing the subject. "I see you didn't take his job offer."

Alex turned to Sherry and found her smiling at him.

"How is it you know stuff like that but not anything about Moriarty?" he said, more than a little exasperated.

Sherry just shrugged, sending her dark curls bouncing.

"My gift works how it works," she said. "I have no say in the matter. Though I can tell you to grab a sandwich at the lunch counter in the terminal before you go. You'll be at that warehouse for a while and it's already two o'clock."

Alex narrowed his eyes at her, but she just shrugged again and gave him a winsome smile.

"Anything else I should know?" he asked as he put his hat back on his head.

"Dr. Bell will want to discuss the news with you over dinner," she said with no trace of a smile. "So you should probably buy a newspaper when you get that sandwich."

Half an hour later, Alex took his third skycrawler trip of the day. The warehouse he sought was close to Grand Central and there was a crawler station right in front of it. As he waited for his stop, he ate a ham and cheese sandwich with piccalilli, which turned out to be chopped gherkins in a mustard sauce. It wasn't bad, but he wasn't used to it, so he was left tasting it well after the sandwich was gone.

The warehouse where Mr. Su's ingredients were stolen went by the imaginative name of South Terminal Storage and occupied a worn-looking building near a rail siding. Alex asked after the foreman and was directed to a beefy looking man with coal black hair and no discernible neck.

"I'm very busy," he said after a secretary in the office called him in from the floor over a P.A. system. "So make it quick."

Alex introduced himself, passing the neckless man one of his business cards.

"You're here about the robbery," the man said, handing the card back. "I'll tell you what I told that Chinaman, whoever broke in did it right under the night watchman's nose. They hunted around till they found what they wanted, then they left, presumably the same way they got in."

"Presumably?" Alex asked. "Do you mean to say you don't know how they got in and out?"

The big man looked sour and Alex could hear him grinding his teeth.

"I just need the details, Mr—"

"Anthony Lockwood," he supplied. "Look, I'd like to help you, but I just don't know what I could say. We've got two night watchmen here and they make their rounds every hour. Whoever got in managed it without breaking a window, jimmying a door, or making a sound."

That seemed unlikely to Alex. A much more plausible scenario was that the guards had fallen asleep on the job. If that was the case, though, it would mean the burglars had gotten lucky, and Alex didn't believe in luck.

"I know what you're thinking," Lockwood said. "And the guards weren't drinking or playing cards instead of working. When they start their rounds, they punch a card at the time clock. I checked their cards and they both punched in on time the whole night, right up to the burglary."

Alex tried not to look worried at that. Thieves who could get in and out with the level of precision Lockwood was describing would have to be pros. That meant they either already had a buyer for the alchemy ingredients, or they knew they could easily sell them. That didn't jibe with what Chen had told him. According to Chen, the supplies weren't especially rare or valuable. If a professional thief had taken the trouble to steal them, he must believe they were worth quite a bit.

"Did the thieves take anything besides the Chinese herbs?"

Lockwood shook his head.

"They made quite a mess, but the only thing taken was the parcel from China."

"How did they make a mess?"

Lockwood sighed and motioned for Alex to follow him. He left the office and led the way out onto the warehouse floor where row after row of shelves were stacked up, each piled with boxes, crates, and parcels of all description. Gangs of men with wheeled carts appeared to be swarming all over the warehouse. Some were taking boxes from a stack on the loading dock and distributing them to various shelves, while others were taking items down and relaying them to where people in cars and trucks were waiting to pick them up.

Alex whistled as he surveyed the chaos.

"How did they know where to find what they were looking for?" he asked.

"That's what I mean by they made a mess," Lockwood said. "They opened a dozen crates looking for that one from China. There were pieces of crates and shipping straw all over the floor. That's how the night watchmen knew we'd been robbed."

"How could they do all that and still not be seen or heard by your watchmen?"

"Must have been a gang," the foreman said with a shrug. "I can't see any other way it could work."

This made even less sense to Alex. The herbs would have to be valuable indeed to inspire an entire crew to attempt such a heist. Either Chen had lied to him about what was really in the container, or the thieves had grabbed the wrong thing.

"Are there any other shipments from China in the warehouse right now?" Alex asked.

"Sure," Lockwood said. "You can get that list from our secretary. Now, if there's nothing else, I've got a warehouse to run."

Alex was sure he'd have lots more questions at some point, but right now he couldn't think of any, so he thanked Lockwood and headed back to the office. True to the foreman's word, the secretary came up with a list of everything currently in the warehouse.

Sitting down on the ratty waiting room couch, Alex went through the manifest page by page. It took over an hour, and when he was done, he had a list of seven containers that had come from China. Alex tried to find the containers himself, but the warehouse's system of organization confounded him. As far as he could tell, it was impossible to find anything once it had been shelved. He was reduced to asking Lockwood to assign one of his men to help track down the shipments.

It was nearly five o'clock when Alex examined the last of the seven parcels, a sealed hatbox that was decorated with Chinese art and bore a shipping label covered with pictographic characters. He'd visually inspected all seven of the remaining Chinese shipments and they were all untouched.

"Find what you were looking for?" Lockwood asked as the whistle blew for his men to go home.

"I don't know," Alex admitted. "Your thieves seem to be real pros, but if that's the case, why didn't they know exactly where to find what they were looking for? Why did they have to break open a bunch of other crates? Are you sure nothing was missing from those other shipments?"

"Nope," Lockwood said. "I called the owners of the opened crates and they came in to pick up their goods. All of them confirmed that nothing was missing."

Alex had been hoping that the theft of the herbs had been a ruse designed to throw authorities off the track of whatever the thieves were really after, but that was looking more and more like a dead end.

"I've got to get home to the wife, Lockerby," the foreman said. "You can stay and talk to the watchmen if you like, but I'm locking the doors, so you'll have to talk on the loading dock."

Alex followed the big man out and found both the night watchmen waiting. He'd assumed one of them must have been in on the theft, but if that was the case, why was he still showing up for work? Now that the thieves had what they came for, it was only a matter of time before they got paid.

The night watchmen were both older men with quiet, serious demeanors. Both of them corroborated each other's stories and the more Alex talked to them, the more convinced he became that they had nothing to do with the theft.

Frustrated, he thanked the men and headed back to the crawler station. He had no idea what he was going to tell Lung Chen and his uncle. Right now he had exactly nothing, no clues, no suspects, and no idea how to proceed. Still, he did have a day to figure it out so he resolved to ask Iggy about it and get his mentor's advice.

One crawler ride later, Alex rode the elevator up from the security station in Empire Terminal to the residence floor of Empire Tower. His apartment was one of the smaller ones, but it still had a front room, kitchen, office, and two bedrooms. It was by far the nicest place Alex had ever lived.

He had a key for the front door, but he never carried it. The door was protected by the same runes on his vault cover doors and the brownstone's front door. All he needed to do to pass was to open his pocketwatch and the door would yield easily.

Once inside, Alex headed through his front room and down the hall to the office. Another of his rune-protected cover doors stood against the back wall and led into his vault. He used to have two more-or-less permanent openings into his vault; one in his old office, and one in his bedroom in the brownstone. Since he'd moved to Empire Tower, Alex had also moved the office door and added a third, here in his apartment, to make it easy to get to the brownstone. Most nights Alex had dinner with Iggy and slept at the brownstone; still, it was nice having his own place, even if he didn't use it much.

Alex was just pulling out his pocketwatch to open the vault door when the phone on his desk rang. He contemplated ignoring it, but that was a bad precedent to set. Detective work required a lot of odd hours and contact with people who kept odd schedules, so he picked up the candlestick phone, pressing the receiver to his ear.

"Is this Alex Lockerby?" a familiar voice asked. When Alex admitted that it was, the man went on. "This is Detective Derek Nicholson, of Division Three."

Alex remembered him. He was one of Lieutenant Detweiler's men, a decent enough fellow though not terribly bright.

"I remember," he said. "What can I do for you?"

"I hate to bother you, Alex, but I'm looking at a dead woman and I think she was into some kind of strange magic. I could use your help."

"Officially?"

Even with Frank Callahan filling the job of Captain over the detectives, Alex still had to get approval to work a police case if he wanted to get paid.

"I cleared it with Lieutenant Detweiler."

Alex considered saying no; he was hungry and frustrated by his failure at the warehouse. Still, the cops always paid his bill on time, and keeping them happy came with other dividends.

"All right, Detective," he said. "Give me the address and I'll come right over."

4

CALCULATIONS

The elevator bell rang and Alex stepped off onto the carpeted hallway beyond. A placard on the wall opposite had the number ten emblazoned on it. The address Detective Nicholson gave Alex was for a relatively new apartment building squarely in the east-side middle-ring. Turning left, he made his way toward the end of the hall. A large window occupied the wall at the end and Alex could see the last rays of the setting sun painting the tops of the skyscrapers in bands of yellow and orange.

A young policeman in a blue patrolman's uniform stood by the open door to apartment 1017. He had an earnest expression on his face, and he eyed Alex nervously as the latter approached along the hallway. Clearly he was new on the job and Alex couldn't help feeling old. The cop still looked like a kid.

"Can I help you?" the patrolman asked as Alex stepped up to him.

"I'm Alex Lockerby," Alex said, handing him a business card. "Detective Nicholson asked me to come by."

The young man stared at the card with wide eyes. Apparently he'd been on the job long enough to know the official police position on private detectives, which meant he should tell Alex to beat it. On the other hand, Alex clearly knew which detective was in charge of the scene, which meant Alex probably belonged there. The indecision on the young man's face was almost comical.

Before he could instruct the cop to ask his superior, Detective Nicholson's voice emerged from the apartment.

"Lockerby, is that you? Let him in."

Relieved, the patrolman handed the card back and stood aside as Alex stepped around the door frame and entered the apartment. From where he'd stood in the hallway, he couldn't see inside, but now he found himself in a modern, well-appointed apartment. The furniture was all relatively new and the front room was neat and orderly with a pair of chairs that bookended a reading table and a couch opposite. The table supported a lamp and a radio. Along the back wall of the front room were several shelf cabinets all filled with books.

Alex could see a kitchen area off to the left and a hallway disappeared into the rear of the apartment. The table in the kitchen was bare except for a vase containing flowers and a set of salt and pepper shakers. Beyond the table, the counter supported an electric toaster and a teapot but was otherwise bare, and there were no dishes in the sink, or none that Alex could see, at any rate.

Everything in the apartment was as it should be...with three exceptions. Standing in front of the couch in the front room were two large blackboards on wheeled stands, and lying beneath them on the pale blue carpet was a large, round bloodstain. What looked like a handprint was off to one side and there was evidence of smearing near it, no doubt from the victim's ultimately futile struggle for life.

Standing around the bloodstain were two uniformed officers and Detective Nicholson. The Detective looked exactly as Alex remembered him, a somewhat dumpy, disheveled man with a broad face. His suit was a dark gray color and it looked like the man had slept in it, his white shirt had a mustard stain where his paunch bulged out and his hair appeared several weeks overdue for a barber.

"There you are," he said as if Alex had kept him waiting for hours. He looked down at the bloodstain, then ran his fingers through his unruly hair. The expression on his face was one of both frustration and relief. "I think this case might be right up your alley."

Alex refrained from either smiling or rolling his eyes.

Nicholson wasn't the sharpest knife in the drawer; in fact, Alex was certain he had some relative in a position of authority in city government that got him his job as a detective. That said, Nicholson had some serious street smarts. He knew an opportunity when he saw it and he'd make the most of it if he could. That was why he'd called Alex in on this case. As far as Alex could see, nothing in the room spoke of rune magic. There might be an alchemy lab set up in back, but he doubted it. Alchemy had a certain smell that tended to permeate the spaces in which it was practiced.

"This place is rented to Alice Cartwright, age forty-two, now deceased," he nodded at the bloodstain on the carpet.

"Coroner already come for the body?" Alex asked.

Nicholson nodded and continued with his notes.

"She was stabbed in the chest and fell here," he indicated the bloodstain. "A neighbor found her when he noticed the door open."

"Did you move anything?" Alex asked, looking around. Other than the bloodstain, there were no signs that anything was amiss.

"No," Nicholson said. "And there aren't any signs the killer broke in."

"So she let him in," Alex said. "Maybe she knew him."

"Or he coulda been a salesman," Nicholson offered.

"Is there a Mr. Cartwright?"

"No," Nicholson confirmed. "Alice was a spinster."

"What did she do for a living?"

Nicholson looked at the uniforms but they only shrugged back at him.

"We're still working on that," he said. "I've got men canvassing the building."

"I thought you said there was magic involved," Alex said, taking another look around.

Nicholson grinned at him and held up his finger in a theatric gesture. He turned, grabbed the top of the nearest blackboard and pulled, causing the board to flip over to the back side. The front had been blank, but the back was covered with chalk markings. Strange words and symbols adorned it, radiating out from a central sentence in the middle. The sentence was circled and lines ran out to other groups of the unintelligible text but none of it made any sense.

Before Alex could ask a question, Nicholson grabbed the second board and flipped it over as well, revealing more of the nonsense. Clearly he'd turned them around in anticipation of Alex's arrival so he could have this dramatic revelatory moment. Part of Alex resented him for it, while the rest recognized a fellow showman. Alex was fond of doing this exact kind of thing when revealing the solution to an especially difficult puzzle.

"After that incident with the Harper boys, I figured this might be more of the same," Nicholson said. "I didn't want to take any chances."

Alex didn't believe that for a second. If that were true, he never would have stood that close to the chalkboards. The Harpers were brothers who robbed banks using explosive runes, something that shouldn't have existed. Alex learned that Roy Harper had developed them under the influence of a drug known as Limelight.

On the other hand, everything Roy had written while under its influence looked like nonsense to everyone else. Alex looked at the blackboards again. The things written on them were clearly nonsense, but Roy's nonsense had been mostly illegible, the nonsense on the board had been written with an almost mathematical precision.

Mathematical.

The word rang in Alex's head like a bell and he stepped up to examine the board more closely. After a moment he found what he was looking for and took out the piece of chalk he always kept in his jacket pocket.

"What are you doing?" Nicholson demanded as Alex drew a line under what looked like a malformed letter 'T.' He was understandably nervous. If it had been a rune that had been drawn on the board, it might be activated just by touching it.

"Don't worry, Detective," Alex said. "This isn't magic, at least not the kind you're thinking of." He pointed to the circled text in the middle of the first blackboard. "I thought this was written well, but it turns out it's actually pretty sloppy."

"Who cares how it's written?" Nicholson asked.

Alex shrugged at that and started writing in the space below the sentence.

"If this had been written better," he said, "you wouldn't have called me because you'd have realized that what you have here isn't magic, it's math."

When Alex finished, he'd written what looked like a math problem, if math problems didn't have numbers. What had looked like the word 'ant' before was actually the letter 'A' with an 'N' next to and slightly above it with a plus sign coming next. It had been written in such a way that Alex had assumed it was the letter 'T.' More letters and symbols went out from that ending with an equals sign and more letters.

"I'll be damned," Nicholson said, rubbing his chin. "So what does it mean?"

Alex just shrugged at that, dropping his chalk back in his pocket.

"No idea," he admitted. "I know magic, not this stuff."

Nicholson gave him a hard look, as if he thought Alex was lying, then stepped back, over to the blood spot.

"Then I guess you don't know what this means either," he said, indicating the smears near the bloody handprint.

Alex stepped closer and peered down. What he'd taken to be smears at first were clearly symbols. Taking care to avoid the blood, he knelt to get a closer look. Unlike the letter-based math on the boards, these were clearly numbers. Two digits, written over one, with two more below.

"I make it nineteen, seven, and eleven," Alex said, looking up.

"Yeah, I can read too, Lockerby," Nicholson said with an edge in his voice. "Any idea what it means?"

"Is there a safe or a lock box in the back?" he asked. "Three numbers all under thirty, it could be a combination."

Nicholson looked up at the officers, who had stood quiet during Alex's examination.

"Either of you mugs find a safe?"

They both shook their heads.

"There's a bunch of files in the back office, but they aren't even locked," the shorter of the two said, jerking his thumb in the direction of the hallway.

Alex was torn. The case of the dead Miss Cartwright was definitely intriguing, but he had plenty of work to keep him busy. Still, it was clear that Nicholson was at a loss and Alex could always use more billable hours.

"Tell you what," Alex said, setting down his kit. "Let me look around with my gear. If there's a safe hidden somewhere, I'll find it."

Nicholson nodded sagely, as if it had been his idea all along.

"I'll go talk to the building manager and catch up with the boys doing the canvass, he said. "See if I can find out what Miss Cartwright did for a living."

Alex watched him go with the two officers in tow. He took a moment and copied down the hieroglyphics from each blackboard, doing his best to transcribe them into his notebook. When he finished, he tucked the notebook back into his shirt pocket and opened the battered valise that served as his kit bag.

Alex got out his oculus and set it aside, then took out his egg-shaped multi-lamp. The lamp had four curved sides, each with an oval crystal lens mounted in it. Three of the lenses were covered with a leather cap, so the light from inside only had one direction to shine. Each lens was inscribed with runes and there were runes all around the bottom of the lamp.

The front of the lamp opened by folding the side down from the top on a hinge, which allowed Alex access to its interior. He removed a brass reservoir from a row of them clipped into his kit bag, and snapped it into place in the bottom of the lamp. The reservoir had an alchemical solution in it that would burn with a bright silver light. When viewed through the oculus, the light would cause biological traces to fluoresce, making them easy to spot.

Alex lit the burner with his brass squeeze lighter, then closed the door to the lamp. His oculus consisted of a leather pad that went over the right side of his face and was held on with a leather strap. A brass tube, not unlike a telescope, was mounted to it, positioned over his eye. There were several focusing rings and colored lenses that could be used to change the sensitivity of the oculus, and he fiddled with them briefly before starting his investigation.

The home of Alice Cartwright wasn't just orderly to look at, it was clean as well. Alex found fingerprints in the usual places; icebox, kitchen cabinets, office drawers, and her nightstand. There was evidence that she'd cut herself in the bathroom and had cleaned up the blood. That probably meant that she shaved her legs, which could mean there was a man in her life.

If such a man existed, however, Alice had not had him in her bedroom. Nothing there indicated anything untoward had occurred.

All in all, Alex's search of the apartment had been both frustrating and fruitless. Determined to be thorough, he extinguished the silverlight burner and clipped in the one that made ghostlight. With the greenish light emanating from his lamp, Alex went back over the apartment, taking extra time on the blackboards in the front room and in Alice's office. The office was simple and straightforward, just a desk with a phone on it and four filing cabinets full of papers. He swept it twice, but nothing showed as magical.

Defeated, he blew out his lamp and set it on the desk to cool. As far as he could tell Alice Cartwright had led an average, somewhat boring life, yet someone had hated her enough to stab her to death. Her apartment was nice, but nothing in it spoke to money, at least not the kind you'd kill to get.

There was still the matter of her job. She might have been a kept woman or had a small amount of family money, but the four file cabinets full of papers spoke to some kind of work. With a sigh, Alex opened the top drawer of the first cabinet and pulled out the first three file folders. He had just sat down at Alice's desk to go through them when he heard raised voices coming from the front room. One of them was clearly the young policeman from the door and, after a moment, Alex heard Detective Nicholson as well.

Setting the files aside, he stood and packed his lamp and oculus back into his kit.

"I don't care if you're investigating the murder of the Arch Duke Ferdinand," an unfamiliar voice was saying as Alex made his way out of the office. "This apartment is under my jurisdiction until I say otherwise."

Alex emerged from the back to see Nicholson standing nose to nose with a man in a light blue suit. He was a little taller than the

Detective, but otherwise was the man's polar opposite. Where Nicholson was dumpy and unkempt, the newcomer was thin and immaculate. His suit was pressed, his tie was straight, his hat had been blocked recently, and Alex could see the crease in his trousers from across the room. The only thing out of place about the man was the ring of dark brown hair around his head that didn't quite match the bit on top. Clearly he was wearing a toupee.

"On whose authority?" Nicholson demanded, getting right in the man's face.

Alex had to admit, Nicholson might not be much of a detective, but he made a great guard dog.

The immaculate man reached inside his suit coat and Alex pressed his thumb against his flash ring. He didn't figure the man would pull a gun in a room with three policemen in it, but dumber things had happened.

When the man's hand came out again, he clutched a folded piece of paper which he shoved into Detective Nicholson's chest.

"I have authority from the War Department," the man growled. "You can read it right here in black and white. Assuming you can read," he added.

Nicholson ground his teeth so hard Alex could hear it from across the room and he was starting to turn red.

"What interest does the War Department have in Alice Cartwright?" Alex asked, raising his voice to cut off an outburst from Nicholson. Alex's curiosity had been piqued by the man's claim and if Nicholson exploded, that would probably ruin his chance to fish for information.

The man in the blue suit jumped a bit and turned. Clearly he hadn't heard Alex's approach.

"Who are you?" he demanded.

Alex plastered on his friendly smile and stuck out his hand.

"Detective Lockerby," he said. "And you are?"

The man looked like he wanted to tell Alex to go jump off the roof, but he mastered himself and took the offered hand.

"Earnest Harcourt," he said. "Now if your friend here is finished," he nodded at Nicholson, "I need you all to clear out of here."

DAN WILLIS

Alex didn't look at Nicholson to see if he'd finished reading the paperwork, he just smiled and nodded as if he agreed.

"Well if that paper says what you claim, we'll go," Alex said. "We're only too happy to help the government." Harcourt took a breath to argue, but Alex had anticipated that and rushed on. "Of course, a woman was murdered here, so we can't just take your word for it, you understand. You might be in league with the killer."

Harcourt gave Alex an annoyed look.

"And what would I possibly want here if I was involved in Alice's death?" he asked.

So he isn't just some official, he actually knew Alice.

"You could be here to destroy vital evidence," Alex explained in the voice one might use to calm an unruly child. "We have to be careful, criminals these days are getting very clever."

"I assure you, Detective Lockerby, I am who I say I am," Harcourt growled.

"And I believe you, Mr. Harcourt, but my Lieutenant would have my hide if I just turned the crime scene over to you without checking first."

Harcourt had no rebuttal to that, but he clearly didn't like it.

"I'll tell you what," Alex said, putting a conspiratorial arm around the man's shoulders. "Detective Nicholson will use Alice's phone to call this in, and the officers will wait out in the hall, how's that?"

Harcourt considered it, then nodded.

Nicholson shot Alex a look of pure venom, but he nodded for the other officers to wait in the hall. Once they were gone, he took the paperwork Harcourt had given him and stalked back in the direction of Alice's office.

"How long did you work with Alice, Mr. Harcourt?" Alex asked, wondering if this was the man Alice shaved her legs for.

"About three years," Harcourt said. The irritable tone in his voice had receded, though he still wasn't happy. If Alex could get him to relax just a bit more, the man might start talking.

"She was stabbed," Alex said. "We think by someone she knew."

"Well it wasn't me," Harcourt said, the irritation returning to his voice.

"No," Alex said with a chuckle. "I was wondering if you knew of anyone who might have wanted to kill her. Was she seeing anyone? Did she have debts? That sort of thing."

"I'm sure I don't know," he said. "Alice worked for me as a computer, I wasn't privy to her private life."

Alex turned to look at the blackboards.

"Is that what this is?" he asked.

Harcourt had been too busy arguing with Detective Nicholson when he came in and he clearly hadn't observed the room. The second he saw the blackboard, the color drained from his face.

"That's it," he shouted. "I want you out of this apartment right now."

Alex started to protest, but Nicholson cut him off.

"Let it go, Lockerby," he said. "I just got the word from Captain Callahan. We're to turn over this crime scene to Mr. Harcourt for as long as he likes."

Alex wasn't too surprised to hear that. Harcourt had been throwing his weight around as if he believed he had the authority.

"Good," the government man growled. "Now get out."

Alex just smiled, picked up his kit, and followed Nicholson out into the hall. As soon as they were gone, Harcourt slammed the apartment door and Alex heard the lock snap into place. He almost laughed, but Detective Nicholson grabbed his arm and walked him quickly away from the door.

"You want to explain what all that was about?" he growled.

"He wasn't going to talk to you," Alex said with a shrug. "I just gave him an alternative and stalled for time."

"And?" Nicholson demanded.

"And Harcourt said that Alice has been working as a computer for the government for the last three years."

Nicholson looked confused at that.

"What's a computer?" he asked.

"Detective," Alex said with a sigh. "I have absolutely no idea."

5

FEDS

The incessant ringing of his alarm clock pulled Alex from sleep at seven the next morning. There were many reasons Alex enjoyed being a detective, but one of his favorites was not having to be at his office exactly at eight AM. Still, he had a gang of professional thieves to find and only one day to do it, so he felt guilty about just going back to sleep.

Alex slept in his bed at the brownstone, which was his usual habit, so he showered and dressed, then headed downstairs to see if Iggy was up. They hadn't spoken the previous evening as Iggy retired early with a headache, so Alex was eager to talk.

"Morning, lad," Iggy said when Alex entered the kitchen in search of coffee. Having anticipated his need, Iggy handed Alex a steaming cup on a saucer.

"Thanks," Alex said, dropping heavily into one of the massive oak chairs that surrounded the kitchen table. In the days after Alex had spent the bulk of his life energy to move Sorsha's falling castle, coffee had been one of the things that kept him going. During that time, he almost couldn't function without it. Now his relationship with the brown elixir was more like greeting an old and cherished friend. Alex didn't want to start the mornings without it, and he wanted the occasional visit throughout the day.

"Are you feeling better?" he asked Iggy as he blew across the top of his steaming cup.

"A bit," his mentor admitted.

Now that Alex had a few sips of coffee, he observed that the old man was looking a bit run down.

"I think I'm due for a trip to the spa," he said.

Thanks to his recent work, Alex now traveled in much more exclusive circles than when he was younger. He knew that rich men and women would often travel to exotic spas to eat strange foods and bask in the reputed healing properties of natural hot springs. For Alex and Iggy, however, the spa was a slaughterhouse by the rail yards, not very exotic but extremely therapeutic.

Ever since Iggy had figured out Moriarty's secret to transferring life energy from pigs, they'd gone back three times. The first time was to restore Alex's lost life energy. It had worked so well that Alex hadn't needed to go back in almost two years. Since then, they'd tried a toned-down version of the life transference construct on Iggy. At his age, they had worried he wouldn't be physically able to tolerate the transfer. Once the first one worked, however, they'd gone back six months later with a slightly more powerful version. After each experience, Iggy felt better than he had in years.

The problem with small life infusions like this, however, seemed to be that they wore off more quickly than expected, and Alex could tell Iggy was becoming impatient with the small steps.

"Are you sure you're ready?" he asked. When Alex had taken the risk of a large life energy infusion, it had been because he really didn't have any other option. Iggy, on the other hand, could keep using the smaller ones indefinitely.

His mentor gave him a hard look over the top of his bottle-brush mustache, daring Alex to object, then nodded with an air of both confidence and finality.

"I feel like each time we've managed to turn the clock back a few minutes," he said, "but then it just runs faster. It's time I took a larger step."

Alex wasn't sure he liked the idea, but it wasn't his life, and he'd learned a long time ago that when Iggy made up his mind, he was not to be dissuaded.

"I'll write up the construct and we can go on Saturday," Iggy went on, picking up a wicker basket that contained a half-dozen eggs. "How was your day yesterday?"

While Iggy cracked a few eggs into a hot pan, Alex recounted his experience with the stolen herbs and how he was out of leads already.

"Well," Iggy said, adding strips of cut bacon to the pan. "If these thieves are as proficient as the warehouse manager claims, this can't be the first robbery they've pulled off."

Alex nodded, catching his train of thought.

"Maybe if I find some other robberies done by the same crew, I can find some way to track them down," he said.

"Everyone makes a mistake sooner or later," Iggy said sagely.

"It's a place to start."

Iggy brought Alex a plate of eggs with two strips of bacon, then went back to the stove to fill a second plate.

"How late did you stay at the warehouse looking for your thieves?"

"I finished up at five, but I got another call," Alex said. "Say, do you know what a computer is?"

Iggy sat down across from Alex, setting his plate on the table.

"Someone who computes would be my guess," he said.

Alex explained about Alice Cartwright, her blackboards of unintelligible math, and Earnest Harcourt, the government man.

"Maybe she works for the Internal Revenue Service," Iggy guessed when Alex finished. "I'm sure the government wouldn't want their inner workings getting out."

"You'd think if Harcourt worked with money, he could afford a better hairpiece."

Iggy chuckled at that.

"Don't be so sure," he said with a twinkle in his eye. "A friend of mind looked into getting a hairpiece once, and a good one can cost over a hundred dollars."

Alex whistled at that.

Blood Relation

"In the end, my friend didn't go through with it," Iggy said with a grin. "He decided it was too much toupee."

Alex just stared at the old man as Iggy chuckled, amused by his own joke.

"Harcourt said he was with the War Department," he said, trying to pull the conversation back on course. "Plus, IRS math would be accounting. The stuff Alice was doing was, I don't know, more advanced than that?"

Iggy considered that between bites of egg, then he shrugged.

"If it's something scientific, you should ask Barton. He deals with that sort of thing all the time."

Alex chided himself for not thinking of that and he nodded. Before he could comment, however, the phone in his bedroom upstairs rang. According to the clock on the wall it was only seven forty-five, a bit early for calls.

Rising, Alex went to the phone mounted on the kitchen wall. A box with a metal plate on the front had been added above the phone. There were two wires running into the box and one wire running out to the phone. The metal plate on the box's front sported a lever with two positions, one marked 'Home' and one marked 'Alex.'

Reaching up, Alex turned the lever from 'Home' to 'Alex' and the phone on the wall began to ring.

"Hello?" he said after picking up the receiver.

"Mr. Lockerby, this is Stan Green down at the security desk," a man's voice greeted him. The phone in his bedroom was the same line as his office and the one in his apartment in Empire tower. Alex had run a connecting wire through his vault to the brownstone so that no matter where he was, he could answer his phone. Stan was calling from the security desk in Empire Station.

"What is it, Stan?" he said.

"There's a man here from the government," Stan said. "He's insisting we let him up to see you. His name is...uh."

"Earnest Harcourt?" Alex guessed.

"Yes, sir," Stan confirmed. "That's him."

Iggy looked up from the table with a raised eyebrow.

"The government man wants to see you at this hour?" he asked.

Alex nodded, then spoke into the telephone.

"Send him up."

"Did you make any copies of Miss Cartwright's incomprehensible math?" Iggy asked as Alex hung up.

Alex nodded, pulling his notebook from his shirt pocket.

"That'll be what he's after," Iggy said with a nod.

Alex was already ahead of him. He flipped open the spiral bound notepad and tore out the pages where he'd copied down the math from the blackboards, being careful to clear away any telltale bits of paper left in the wire. He thought about removing the first page, the one with Alice's name and his observations about the crime scene, but decided against it. Harcourt would know something was up if Alex didn't have any notes at all.

Tucking the torn pages in his trouser pocket, Alex shoveled a fork full of the scrambled eggs into his mouth and grabbed the remaining strip of bacon.

"Let me know how it goes," Iggy called after him as he hurried through the hall to the stairs and up to his room.

Grabbing his vest and suit coat, Alex opened his pocketwatch and passed through his vault back to his apartment in Empire tower. He was just shutting the vault's cover door behind him when he heard his doorbell ring. It rang again with an impatient insistency before he managed to get to the door.

"Mr. Harcourt," he said, pulling the door open. The skinny man with the immaculate suit and the bad toupee stood so close to the door that Alex felt the need to take an involuntary step back. While he took the step, Alex resisted the urge to laugh as Iggy's toupee pun came rushing into his mind. "What can I do for you at this hour?"

"You lied to me, Lockerby," he said, barging past Alex and into his apartment.

"I did no such thing," Alex protested as he closed the door.

Harcourt scanned the room and, once he'd assured himself that they were alone, he turned to confront Alex with his hands on his hips.

"You told me you were with the police," he said. "You can imagine my surprise when I called on them this morning and they told me that you are, in fact, a private detective."

"I told you I was a detective, and I am a detective," Alex said, pulling one of his business cards from his shirt pocket and holding it up. "It even says so here on my card."

"You led me to believe you were with the police," Harcourt went on, not losing any steam.

"Mr. Harcourt," Alex said, patiently but firmly. "I cannot control your assumptions, especially when I'm not privy to them. I am a consultant, I work with the police and Detective Nicholson, whom you no doubt remember, asked me to consult on the Cartwright case. Now, what is it I can do for you?"

Harcourt glared at Alex with what looked like naked hate, then he mastered himself.

"When my men went to remove Miss Cartwright's files, they found three of them out on her desk," he said. "They're all old files, dating back several years, so I'm reasonably sure that she didn't put them there."

"I removed them from her filing cabinet," Alex admitted. "I was about to go through them in the hopes of discovering Miss Cartwright's profession when you arrived."

Harcourt's glare didn't soften.

"Policemen keep notes," he said. "How about private dicks?"

Alex reached into his pocket and pulled out his spiral notebook. He opened it to the front and handed it to the government man.

"Are these all the notes you took?" he asked, scanning through the information Alex had recorded.

"Alice's name and address," Alex recited. "The method of her death, and the results of my search of the apartment. What did you expect me to write?"

"You didn't take any notes or her files?" he demanded. "Or the formulae on the blackboards?"

Alex almost grinned but that would have given away the game. Iggy had been right — whatever was on those blackboards was something the government didn't want getting out. He had a momentary thought of coming clean to Harcourt, but the man's officious, demeaning attitude bothered Alex. He decided to keep pursuing the Cartwright case on his own just to spite the man.

"As I said, Mr. Harcourt," Alex said, keeping his voice calm and even. "I hadn't even opened Miss Cartwright's files when you arrived. As for the blackboard, why would I bother writing that mess down? I barely recognized it as math in the first place."

"You write things down, *Detective* Lockerby, so you can figure them out later," Harcourt growled, putting particular emphasis on the word detective.

Alex laughed at that, not bothering to cover it.

"You do when it's your job to figure it out," he said as the government man fumed. "But that's Detective Nicholson's job. I was there to see if there was any magic involved in Alice's death."

"And?"

"As far as I can tell, there wasn't."

Harcourt held his gaze for a long moment, then he flipped Alex's notebook closed and reached up to tuck it into the inside pocket of his coat. Alex was ready for that and he snatched the notebook with a quick movement.

"I'll need that notebook," Harcourt said. "Everything about this case is classified."

Alex opened the notebook and tore out the page of notes relating to the Cartwright case.

"The rest of this regards my other cases," Alex said, offering the removed page to Harcourt. "So unless you have a warrant..."

He let the sentence hang and Harcourt turned red as a beet. Alex suddenly realized why the balding man had been so angry that Alex pretended to be a police detective.

"I'm guessing you do have a warrant," Alex said with a sly smile. "But your warrant specifically says that you can seize the police files. I'm betting it doesn't cover consultants, does it?"

Harcourt snatched the offered paper from Alex's grasp and stormed to the door.

"You haven't heard the last of this, detective," he said through clenched teeth. "I'll be back."

With that he threw open the door and stormed out, leaving it open behind him.

"Looking forward to it," Alex called after him. It was a childish thing to do and Alex knew he'd end up regretting it, but he just couldn't help himself. He did manage to wait until he'd shut his door before laughing out loud.

An hour later, Alex got off the skycrawler at the station across from the Chrysler Building and crossed the street. Once inside, he rode the elevator up to the sixty-fifth floor, home to the offices of Kincaid Enterprises. The last time he rode this elevator was five months ago when Andrew Barton's assistant had tried to make himself a god by channeling magical energy directly into his brain. Alex, Barton, and Sorsha had confronted him and managed to stop him, but just barely. They were all left a bit shaken by the incident. Especially its culmination.

Even now, Alex shuddered at the memory.

In the aftermath of that incident, he'd let his guard down with Sorsha. He'd called her 'doll.' She'd chastised him for it, but then she'd kissed him on the cheek. He could still see the slightly exaggerated sway of her hips as she'd walked away from that moment. It wasn't the first kiss she'd given him, but the previous one had been one full of fire and passion right on his mouth. She'd delivered it right before she'd informed him that she never wanted to see him again.

That had been back when he'd been dying from having burned through most of his life energy. She hadn't wanted to fall for him only to watch him fade away and die, and Alex didn't blame her. That said, things were different now — Alex could have as much life as he wanted and Sorsha knew it.

That kiss at the top of the Chrysler Building had been an invitation.

Unfortunately right after that kiss, Alex and Sorsha had formed the Arcane Irregulars, a group dedicated to seeking out and stopping magical troublemakers. Sorsha had maneuvered Alex into the leadership position in the group, something Alex objected to and later resented. It made things between them awkward. As a result, even though the Irregulars met twice a month to go over possible leads,

Alex hadn't been to visit Sorsha outside of these meetings. He kept thinking that he should see her, but things just got busy between working for Barton and moving his office.

He felt his hands shaking as the elevator slowed to a stop. Each time he'd failed to visit her in the past made it more and more difficult to face the possibility. Now he needed her help with a case, so he would have to confront Sorsha whether he wanted to or not.

The offices of Kincaid Enterprises occupied a corner space on the sixty-fifth floor. The exterior walls were made entirely of frosted panels made with slightly bluish glass. Large silver letters adorned the door next to a handle made of chromed metal.

Inside, a sumptuous waiting area was lined with comfortable leather seating and an art deco desk made of whitewashed wood, glass, and steel polished to a mirror shine. Alex knew from experience that the blonde, Scandinavian woman behind the desk was named Inge, and she smiled when she saw him. The smile quickly slid into a look of mocking amusement, as if she knew a secret about Alex. Ever since he'd met the girl, she made that face whenever she saw him. Clearly Alex's potential relationship with the boss was a topic of conversation around the office and Inge had opinions.

As Alex crossed the carpeted floor to the desk, Inge pressed a key on her intercom. A moment later Sorsha's voice emanated from the speaker.

"Mr. Lockerby is here to see you," Inge said, her knowing grin getting somehow wider.

There was a pause that made Inge raise the blonde eyebrow over her left eye, then Sorsha spoke.

"Send him back."

Inge started to rise, but Alex waved her back into her seat.

"I know the way," he said.

A set of double glass doors to the left of Inge's desk led to a hallway with even more doors. Alex knew from experience that a large conference room occupied the right side with offices on the left, Sorsha's being the first one. Alex knocked and went in.

The office was as he remembered it — Sorsha's desk in the center, with a massive window behind and comfortable armchairs in front. A door to the right side of the office led to a powder room, and it opened as Alex entered.

"Hello, Alex," Sorsha Kincaid said as she entered. Her platinum hair shone in the morning light, framing her delicate features and shading her face just enough to make her pale blue eyes stand out in contrast. Burgundy paint adorned her lips and her eyebrows had been darkened with eyeliner. There was a classical beauty about her that always reminded Alex of statues in museums, and he wondered if she cultivated that look on purpose. It had a way of reminding others that she was a very literal Greek goddess, at least in terms of her power.

"It's about time you came by," she went on, the shadow of annoyance passing briefly over her features. There was also a slight edge in her voice that made the hairs on Alex's arm stand up.

"We saw each other two weeks ago at the last meeting of the Irregulars," Alex said, attempting to put her at ease. That earned him a hard look.

"But you haven't come to see *me*," she said, clearly irritated now. "I suppose you've come to ask me for my help on one of your cases?"

She was exactly right, but her voice told Alex that this was the absolute wrong answer. Fortunately Alex had already decided to face her irritation head on.

"Of course I've come for your help," he said, pausing just long enough for Sorsha's features to harden. "It gives me the perfect excuse to see you."

She held his gaze for a long moment, as if weighing his remarks for any signs of deceit, then the ghost of a smile touched her lips. Alex took that as a good sign, but Sorsha wasn't the kind of woman to give up her pique without a fight.

"As you said, though," she said, her eyes flashing dangerously. "We saw each other just a few weeks ago. Why would you need an excuse to see me now?"

Pasting on his most charming smile, he shrugged his shoulders. He was an idiot. He should have come to her months ago and he knew it. She knew it too, but she wouldn't be satisfied until he admitted it.

"The last time I was seen in public with you, the newspapers printed pictures," he explained. "The way I remember it, they made some assertions you didn't like. I didn't want to put you through that again."

Her eyes narrowed down to slits and he could see the muscles in her jaw tightening. He'd boxed her in rather neatly, passing off his reluctance as courtesy, but she was far too smart not to suspect him of duplicity. If he didn't offer an olive branch to go with his declaration, she'd be sure to make him regret it.

"Of course if you're willing to risk it," he said in the most nonchalant tone he could manage. "I helped the head waiter at the Rainbow Room out of some trouble a while back. I'm sure he could get us a nice quiet, out-of-the-way table."

The only sign that the words had any effect on her was the arching of an eyebrow. After a tense moment, however, her lips melted into a languid smile.

"Why Mr. Lockerby," she said in a lilting voice. "Are you asking me out?"

"I believe I am, Miss Kincaid. Perhaps we could take in a show—"

Sorsha's eyes suddenly hardened again. Alex almost blushed as he realized her mind had jumped to Regina Darling, the Broadway star Alex had dated recently. He chided himself as his mind raced.

"There's a picture I've been wanting to see," he covered and Sorsha visibly relaxed. "Maybe we could see that first. You know, make an evening of it."

"I'm busy tonight," she said, her smile becoming more genuine. "But I'm free tomorrow."

"Pick you up at six for the show?"

"That would be lovely." she said.

Alex inclined his head and then turned to leave. He stopped as if suddenly remembering something and turned back.

"Yes?" Sorsha said, barely hiding a smile at his somewhat obvious tactic. "Was there something else you needed?"

"Since I'm here, you don't happen to know someone named Earnest Harcourt, do you? Snappy dresser, bad toupee. He claims to work for the War Department."

"The government is a big organization, Alex," she said. "I only work with the FBI."

Blood Relation

"Could you ask around? I need to know if he's on the level."

Sorsha promised that she would, and Alex turned to leave again.

"How did you come to know a man in the War Department this week?" Sorsha asked, causing Alex to stop. Something in her voice sounded a warning bell in his mind and when he turned back, the playful look she'd worn was gone. Her face now had a serious aspect that Alex knew meant she was thinking through a problem.

Alex told her about the death of Alice Cartwright and the appearance of Harcourt.

"I guess that makes sense," she said in a voice that clearly indicated she still had questions.

"Are you working with the War Department now?" Alex asked, hoping to catch her in an unguarded moment and get an answer. Instead she just gave him a sly smile.

"You ought to know that if I were working with the War Department, I couldn't tell you about it."

So, yes.

"You'll let me know if you find out anything about Earnest Harcourt?" he said.

Sorsha promised she would, and Alex showed himself out. She'd admitted that whatever she was currently involved in concerned the War Department, but that was all she could give him without compromising her own position. He'd have to do his own digging if he wanted to connect those dots. Still, if Harcourt turned out to be who he said he was, Alex might not need to bother at all.

He decided not to worry about that until he had to, pushing the whole mess with Harcourt and Alice Cartwright out of his thoughts. They were much better occupied with a memory from the spring — a dance he shared in the Emerald Room.

6

RUNES

Half an hour after leaving Sorsha's office, Alex rode the public elevator up from Empire Station to his twelfth floor office. Sorsha knew about his interconnected vault, so it would have been easier to return to his office that way, but when he opened his rune book, he found himself out of vault runes.

It had been more than a week since he restocked his red-backed book, and he was running low on several of his usual constructs. He'd have to spend at least a few hours this morning replacing the more important ones. To completely refill his book would take the better part of two days, and Alex wasn't looking forward to it. Writing runes used to excite and challenge him, but these days it had become a tedious task that occupied more of his time than he liked.

What he really needed was to figure out how Moriarty had opened his vault using only a key. Now that thought filled Alex with nervous energy; he loved figuring out new ways to use runes and, as much to his surprise as anyone else's, he was good at it.

The elevator slowed and Alex stepped off onto the twelfth floor. The reality that he wasn't going to play with new rune combinations brought a sigh from him, but there was no helping it. He was a runewright detective, despite having taken that slogan off his door, and that meant he needed the tools of his trade.

"What's that face about?" Sherry asked as he entered his office. Her usual smile shifted into worry before he could answer. "Marnie wasn't out of coffee, was she?"

Alex opened his kit bag and pulled out a heavy thermos, eliciting a relieved grin from his secretary.

"Anything needing my attention?" he asked, placing the thermos on Sherry's desk.

She shook her head as she unscrewed the top of the thermos bottle.

"I've got a few calls to return, but nothing active yet."

Alex nodded and headed for the back hallway.

"I've got to call Danny, then I'll be in my vault working on some runes," he said. "If anyone needs me...take a message."

Sherry assured him that she'd handle things, and Alex trudged down the hall to his office. Just like his previous one, this office had a desk with two comfortable armchairs facing it. Unlike his former office, this desk was polished oak with brass accents and a leather top. It was something Alex could have afforded, but would never have bothered with. Like the furniture in his apartment upstairs, everything in his office had been supplied by Andrew Barton. As Alex sat behind the massive desk, he had to admit that the Lightning Lord had style.

The top of the desk held a brass tray for his active case folders, a polished metal intercom box, a pen holder with a blotter, and a new, cradle-style telephone with an all-in-one receiver. Alex had a habit of leaving whatever folder he was working on open when he left for the day, but Sherry always came in first thing in the morning and tidied. She said that a clean workspace would keep Alex 'centered,' whatever that meant. Alex did have to admit that coming in to find a clean desk made him eager to face the day, so maybe she was on to something.

Picking up the phone, Alex dialed the number for the Central Office of Police and asked for Lieutenant Pak.

"I'm sorry, sir," the operator came back on after a minute. "Your party doesn't answer."

"Try Captain Callahan," Alex said. "Tell him it's Alex Lockerby."

This time the line was quiet for almost two minutes.

"What do I have to do to get rid of you, scribbler?" Callahan said when the line connected. "I figured now that I have the big office, you'd be Danny's problem."

Callahan's tone was gruff but there was no malice in his voice.

"I'm just like a bad penny," Alex said. "I always turn up. Besides, I've still got a whole book full of expensive runes you haven't used."

"I'll bet," Callahan said, a bit of an edge creeping into his voice. "I've got work to do, Lockerby, what do you want?"

"I'm on the trail of some burglars that knocked over a warehouse near Grand Central Terminal," Alex explained. "Real pros."

"And you want to know if they've hit anyone else recently?" Callahan guessed.

"You don't get good at stealing without practice," Alex said. "I figure this isn't their first job."

"You want to talk to Lieutenant McClory," Callahan said. "He's over division four, they handle robbery. Tell him I sent you."

Alex thanked the Captain and hung up, calling back for McClory. The robbery lieutenant wasn't thrilled with Alex's request, but he took down the information and promised to have one of his detectives call back with any information matching the warehouse robbery.

As he hung up the phone, Alex felt like there was something more he should do. Until he heard back on the robberies, though, he had no leads. Besides, he was just trying to avoid the work he needed to do.

With a sigh, he put his hands on the leather desktop and pushed himself to his feet. If he didn't restock his rune book, he wouldn't be able to do much even if he got information on the robberies.

"Off to work," he said, heading for the cover door to his vault.

Alex still wrote his runes at the large drafting table in his vault. He'd received the table years ago as payment for a case and he loved working at it. Unlike a desk, the drafting table had an angled writing surface that was four feet square. The angle of the upright surface was adjustable, as was the height, making it perfect for long writing jobs.

Next to the drafting table stood a three-foot-tall rollaway cabinet. It was wider than a standard filing cabinet with drawers in the front where Alex kept the various pens, papers, and ink bottles he needed for rune writing. On top of the cabinet sat a half-full bottle of single malt Scotch, an empty shot glass, an intercom box, and a telephone. The latter two items were connected to the ones on Alex's desk by running wires under the vault's cover door. A second set of wires ran from the phone, along the wall behind the drafting table, and ended in the brownstone.

As he sat down, Alex ignored the intercom and the phone; neither one would ring unless Sherry had something important to pass on, so Alex poured himself a Scotch, drained it, and set to work.

His book was low on pretty much everything, and he didn't have time to write all that he needed, so he had to prioritize. Most important were the finding runes. He still had three of those, but one good lead on Su Hi's missing herbs could use those up in a single afternoon. In the old days, it would take Alex half an hour to write a finding rune. Now he could do it in half that time.

Sitting at the writing table, Alex selected a bottle of emerald infused ink from the top drawer of the rollaway cabinet and set to work. Finding runes were elaborate constructs based on an octagon with runic symbols at each point. In the center, a sweeping, curved line went over the top of a straight, horizontal one with an angled end. When Alex first learned it, he thought of it as a dragon reclining on a chaise longue.

After an hour, Alex had written four of the all-important runes, setting them aside on the edge of the drafting board so the ink could fully dry. Next came vault runes. With his linked doors, Alex used his vault to get back to his office or the brownstone several times a day. Fortunately vault runes were fairly simple, just a triangle with circles on each point and rune symbols in each circle, rendered in silver ink. In the center went a symbol of Alex's own design that linked the rune to his specific vault. These were simple enough that Alex could knock out ten of them in an hour.

Once he had ten of the vault runes drying next to the finding runes, Alex weighed his options. He was out of restoration runes, purity runes, and unlocking runes, but all of those were elaborate and time consuming. Instead, he decided to restock the simpler runes from his book.

He'd barely made a half dozen minor barrier runes, however, when the intercom box on the rollaway cabinet chirped. Alex set aside his pen and pushed the key that activated the microphone.

"What is it?" he asked.

"Sorry to bother you, boss," Sherry's voice came through the speaker, "but Danny's on the line for you."

Alex had been hoping for a call from Lieutenant McClory or one of his subordinates, but he was always happy to hear from Danny.

"Put him through."

A moment later the phone next to the intercom began to ring and Alex picked it up.

"What's the good word?" he asked.

"How fast can you get uptown?" Danny asked, ignoring Alex's lighthearted question. "I've got a body for you to look at."

Alex consulted his pocketwatch and found it was just after noon. He hadn't eaten but something in Danny's tone told him to favor haste over nourishment.

"I can leave in about ten minutes," he said, glancing at all the drying runes he would need to put into his book. "Where are you?"

Danny gave him an address in north Harlem and Alex scribbled it in his notebook.

"Get here as quick as you can," he said. "And don't do anything tricky, just take a cab."

Danny knew about Alex's vault, but that was only useful for getting from a remote location back to the office or the brownstone. Alex could use his vault to go to the brownstone and catch a cab from there, but that would only cut ten minutes off the trip at best.

"You think I might be followed?" Alex wondered.

"I don't know," his friend admitted. "You need to see this crime scene. I don't want to talk about it over the phone, but...our friends might be involved."

Alex felt a chill. 'Our friends' was a code word they'd worked out to refer to the Legion. Since the Irregulars started looking for evidence of

Legion activities, they hadn't found anything they could confirm, but Alex knew it was just a matter of time.

"I'll grab my kit and a cab and see you in about forty minutes," he said.

The cab dropped Alex off in front of an outer-ring building that could only be called a shack. It appeared to be a one-room dwelling built before the turn of the century. The boards that made up the exterior were gray and splintering. Dried mud had been applied as chinking where gaps had appeared in an effort to keep the weather out. Clearly there had been some kind of structural damage, however, because the roof leaned to one side.

As Alex approached, the entire appearance of the little structure gave the impression that it was too old and tired to stand up straight. Only the presence of the police cars and Danny's green Ford coupe told Alex he was in the right place.

Mounting the creaking wooden steps in front, Alex reached out to knock on the door. Before he could, the door opened, and a slightly greenish policeman appeared. Alex didn't know the officer, and that usually meant he'd have to stall until Danny realized he'd arrived.

"Through there," the cop said, jerking his thumb over his shoulder as he stepped past Alex. With the door open, Alex could smell the aroma of sour sweat and the iron tang of blood coming from inside.

He took a deep breath of the relatively fresh outside air, then entered. The inside of the shack was just as run-down as the outside. A single bed stood in the corner, and like the roof, it was leaning a bit to one side. Next to it was a battered chest of drawers, with a rough table and two chairs in the opposite corner. A cast iron stove used for cooking and heating in the winter was the only other object in the room, though it seemed in relatively good repair.

Despite the dilapidated state of the house and the furnishings, there were signs that someone had taken the time to make the place a home. A chipped mason jar on the table held a mass of wildflowers above a faded tablecloth, and above the stove was a sort of mantel where a row of knick-knacks and curios were proudly displayed.

Only two things were out of place in the ramshackle dwelling. The first was an area rug that had been pulled off the floor and left in a pile at the foot of the bed. The second was the naked woman lying dead on the floor. Her body was gaunt rather than thin, with the telltale boniness that came from too little food. She had dark brown skin, with a mass of kinky hair that had been pulled back behind her head by a simple cord. From where she lay, Alex could see that the skin on her wrists and ankles had been worn raw and there was a long gash that ran horizontally across her neck where it met her lower jaw.

As disturbing a sight as the woman was, the floor around her was worse. She lay in the exact center of the room, occupying the space where the discarded rug should have been. It was clear why the rug had been removed, because beneath the body, a geometric shape had been painted in what looked disturbingly like blood. Inside the shape, a massive symbol had been painted. It looked like a rune, but Alex didn't recognize it.

The shape consisted of an outer ring of lines forming ten shallow points and a flowing ring of flower-like curlicues inside. Candles and some of the knick-knacks from the dead woman's shelf had been laid around the body at places where lines touched the tip of the curlicues. With ten sides, the symbol would be a decagon, but Alex didn't know of any runes that used such a complicated shape.

"What do you think?" Danny said. He and another detective stood on opposite sides of the body, looking down at the grisly tableau. The second man was broad-shouldered and fit, with black hair and a thick mustache that drooped over the ends of his mouth, giving the impression of a perpetual frown.

"I see why you called me," Alex said, stepping in and setting his kit bag next to the wildflowers on the table. While he opened it, Danny said something to the mustachioed detective, and the man withdrew outside.

"Meet Katherine Biggs," Danny said, indicating the dead woman. "She lived here alone, but one of the uniforms recognized her as a local prostitute. The blood," Danny indicated the symbol, "appears to be hers, as her body's been entirely drained. Whoever did this cut her throat and let her bleed out."

Alex looked around at the meager walls and furniture. There weren't any overt signs of blood spatter or any signs of a blood pool, only the painted symbol. Cutting someone's throat was a messy business, so Alex had expected there to be some sign.

"How did he collect the blood?"

Danny looked up at the ridge beam that ran across the top of the walls and helped hold up the roof. Alex could see a rope still tied around it, right over where the girl lay. The trailing end had been cut clean by a sharp knife.

"He hung her up, then used a bucket or a washtub to catch the blood."

Alex shivered as he pulled his lamp and oculus from his bag. He couldn't imagine what the dead woman's last moments had been like, trussed up like a Christmas turkey until her killer finally just cut her throat and watched her bleed out.

"I know," Danny said, noticing Alex's discomfort. "We're dealing with one sick bastard." He gave Alex an intense look. "I want this guy," he said. "What can you tell me?"

Alex lit the burner and shone silverlight around the room. As he expected, the symbol lit up like a neon sign. Silverlight reacted to bodily fluids like blood. As he stepped around the dead body, the light passed over her, and Alex stopped.

"You said she was a prostitute?" Alex asked. When Danny nodded, he went on. "There's bodily fluids all over her thighs," he said. "She had intercourse recently. Maybe one of her customers did this?"

Danny didn't say anything, but he jotted a note on his pad. Alex leaned down and touched the fluorescing blood. The moment he did, a sick knot formed in his gut and the smell of rotting meat filled the air.

Gagging, he stood up and backed away.

"What's the matter?" Danny asked.

Alex pulled out his handkerchief and scrubbed the blood from his fingertip. As soon as it was gone, the rancid stench disappeared, and his stomach settled.

"Something happened when I touched the blood," he said. "It was like being downwind from a rendering plant."

Danny shook his head and looked at the blood.

"Other guys touched that stuff, and nothing happened to them," he said.

Alex blew out the silverlight burner and switched it for ghostlight. When he shone that at the symbol, it lit up like Broadway. He had to close the aperture in his oculus to avoid being blinded by the glow. When he could see again, he went over the symbol meticulously, being careful not to touch it. The markings were definitely magical, but he couldn't tell if they had been imbued with power when they were painted, or if some alchemical substance had been added to the blood beforehand.

"What now?" Danny asked as Alex pulled off his oculus and blew out the lamp.

"The symbol is definitely magical," he said. "But it's unlike anything I've ever seen. You'd better call that guy with the mustache back in."

"Detective Wilson," Danny supplied. "Why?"

"We need to pick up the body and move it off that symbol," Alex said. "And we need to be careful not to smear it."

"Okay, then what?"

"Then I'll copy down the symbol and try to find out what it is and where it came from."

"You think this is the work of the Legion?" Danny asked.

Alex wished he had an answer for that question, but he could only shrug.

"Maybe," he admitted. "But killing prostitutes seems a bit low rent for them."

"I guess that depends on why Miss Biggs was killed," Danny said.

Alex walked around the blood symbol again.

"It's so outlandish," Alex declared at last. "Hanging the poor girl, collecting her blood, and then using it to paint all this. It's like some kind of primitive ritual."

"You mean like an occult ceremony?" Danny said. "Someone trying to commune with the spirits or something like that?"

Alex shrugged again.

"All right," Danny said, stepping to the door to summon Detective Wilson. "I'll look into Miss Biggs' known clients and associates, you run down what that symbol is and why whoever killed her painted it."

"All right" Alex said. "I'll talk with Iggy tonight; maybe he'll know what this is." It was a long shot — by now, Alex knew most of what Iggy knew about runes, but it was better than admitting to Danny that he had absolutely no idea where to begin.

7

CRACKS

It took Alex another hour to finish going over the scene of Katherine Biggs' murder, and by the time he got back to his office it was three o'clock. He wasn't convinced that the bloody symbol was the work of the Legion, but he took a cab back to his office just in case.

"Hi, Boss," Sherry greeted him with her usual enthusiasm as he walked in. "How did it go with Danny?"

"Bad," he said. He didn't plan to elaborate, but a thought made him pull out his notepad. "Do you recognize this symbol?" he said, holding out his drawing of the blood rune.

Sherry squinted at the drawing then shook her head.

"Sorry, Boss."

"Can you do a reading about it?"

She shook her head again, sending her waves of dark hair swirling around her face.

"I can only read people," she said. "Sometimes I get...premonitions about things, but nothing came when I looked at your drawing. Is it some kind of new rune?"

"I don't know," Alex admitted. "Did your...your former boss ever write runes in blood?"

Alex hadn't asked Sherry much about her former life since he learned she spent the better part of three thousand years as a mummy. The pain on her face when she described the Runelord, the man who'd essentially owned her, made Alex angry. It also made him reluctant to make her relive the experience.

A cloud passed over Sherry's face, but she recovered quickly.

"Back then runes were mostly painted on walls or stone tablets," she said. "I never heard of anyone using blood, but it's possible."

Alex sighed and flipped his notebook closed, returning it to his shirt pocket. Frustration bubbled up inside him, but he squashed it quickly. Asking Sherry about the blood rune had been a long shot, after all.

"Any messages?" he said, changing the subject.

Sherry's mouth crooked into a sly smile and she picked up a notepad from her desk.

"A Lieutenant McClory called from the Central Office," she said. "He said there were two other robberies this month that match the one you asked about."

Alex felt the knot of tension that had formed between his shoulder blades begin to relax a bit. He was overdue for some good news.

"Did he leave the names of the warehouses that were hit?"

Sherry tore the top page off the notebook and handed it over. Two businesses were listed on the paper; one was on the south side by the port, and another one was near Grand Central. The note didn't say what was taken, but Alex could get that information from the warehouses in question.

"This is great," he said with a grin. "If anything stolen was personal to the owner, I should be able to track the thieves."

"Which will lead you to Mr. Su's missing herbs," Sherry finished, nodding along with Alex's excitement.

"I'll go call them," he said, heading for the back office door.

"Boss," Sherry said with a note in her voice that stopped Alex short. "There is one other message."

That knot of tension between Alex's shoulders clenched again and he sighed.

"Barton?" he asked, dreading the answer.

Sherry nodded.

"He wants you upstairs," she said, holding out her hand. "I'll call those warehouses and find out who had merchandise stolen, then I'll run down the owners and find out what it was."

When Alex accepted the Lightning Lord's offer to be the runewright on his power distribution network, he figured it would be a once a month kind of job. Linking runes didn't require much in the way of maintenance. They would fade when the rune they were connected to degraded away, but when connected to a spell like Barton's, it was possible they would remain active forever. What he wasn't prepared for was the onslaught of ideas on which Barton wanted his opinion, once Alex worked for him. It seemed like he was up to Barton's office, or to one of his other workshops, at least three times a week. Alex liked the work, but it was making it difficult to resolve his cases. He had a suspicion that Barton was doing it on purpose to convince Alex to work for him full time.

With a heavy sigh, he handed the paper with the warehouse names on it to Sherry and headed back out in the direction of the elevator. A few minutes later he found himself in the vast lobby of Barton Electric. In former days he would have to wait for Gary Bickman, Barton's valet, to get approval to go up to the private office. These days he had his own key to the private elevator, and he only talked to Gary in the time it took the elevator to arrive.

When it finished its journey, Alex stepped out into Andrew Barton's massive office. The back wall was window glass from floor to ceiling, revealing a stunning view of the city and Central Park. Sumptuous leather couches and chairs were spread around the room, all encircling a massive desk with a marble top that had to be fifteen feet long. Pacing around behind the desk was the man himself. The Lightning Lord wore a red velvet smoking jacket with gold embroidery instead of a suit coat. An unlit cigar was clenched in his teeth and he moved with the nervous energy of a caged tiger.

"There you are," Barton bellowed when he noticed Alex. "It's about time, we've got a problem."

That snapped Alex's distracted mind back into focus.

"What problem?"

Barton waved him over to the desk where he leaned over a pile of blueprints and schematics.

"The Brooklyn tower has been fluctuating all day," he said. "Several of the breaker boxes keep tripping."

"It's not the linking runes," Alex protested. "We've been running power to the Bronx tower for almost four months without a hitch, and the Brooklyn tower has the exact same setup."

"Well, something's off," Barton said. "I've got a crew over there turning the breakers back on, but there's four of them that trip about once an hour."

"Are they on the same side of the system?"

Barton nodded. Since the power was distributed through a central plate to two daughter nodes, the fact that the problem was only on one side would make it easier to track down.

"They're all on the south side," he said.

"Maybe something on that end of Brooklyn is pulling too much power."

"That shouldn't be possible," the Lightning Lord said, pulling a note pad from under the stack of blueprints. "Yes," he said after running his finger down the topmost page. "I built that system with at least a dozen years of growth potential." He handed the pad to Alex. "Nothing in the city should be able to trip it."

Alex looked at the pad, but all it contained was a mass of incomprehensible mathematics.

"Hey," he said, setting the pad down and pulling out the torn page with Alice Cartwright's calculations on it. "Do you know what this means?"

Barton took the page and scrutinized it, then shook his head and handed it back.

"It's nothing I recognize, why?"

"The woman who wrote it was a computer for the government, whatever that is. Somebody killed her and I need to know if this is related to the murder."

"A computer is someone who checks math," Barton said distractedly. He leaned over his blueprints again, tracing lines with his finger. "People employ them when their calculations have to be right. If you want to know what the math means, head out to Columbia and ask Dr. Samuel Phillips. He's the head of applied mathematics there. If anyone will know what those formulae mean, it will be him. Now can we please get back to the problem at hand?"

Alex jotted the name down, then joined Barton at his desk. The schematics didn't mean much to him, but they really didn't need to. The Brooklyn tower was an exact copy of the Bronx tower, so he knew the system was solid.

"Could one of your linking runes be faulty?" Barton asked. There was no accusation in the question, just an honest request for information.

"No," Alex said. "Runes either work or they don't."

"Maybe the breakers are faulty."

"Four of them at once?" Alex asked. "That's beyond coincidence, you're talking about sabotage."

"I've had a security team on site during construction," Barton said. "No one could have gotten in and damaged the breakers."

"We know the system works," Alex said, somewhat frustrated. "If it didn't, we'd have the same problem at the Bronx Relay. Whatever is causing this must be coming from outside."

"It can't be," Barton said, thumping the page with the math on it. "I've checked and rechecked the city's power needs, there simply isn't enough demand to trip four breakers."

Alex sighed. Barton was one of those men who simply couldn't abide when something that should work, didn't. The situation was getting to him. Alex walked around the massive desk to the far side of the room where an ornate liquor cabinet stood. Taking out two glasses, he poured two fingers of fifty-year-old whiskey into each and brought them back.

"Drink," he said, passing one of the glasses to Barton.

The sorcerer glared at Alex for a moment, then sighed and accepted the glass.

"A friend of mine is fond of saying that if you eliminate the impossible, what you're left with must be the truth," Alex said as Barton drank the scotch.

"How does that help us?" Barton said, setting the glass aside. "We've eliminated everything, there's nothing left."

Alex gave the man an enigmatic smile that made Barton's expression sour.

"What?" he said.

"My friend went on to say that if you eliminate the impossible and then nothing remains, then some part of the impossible must be possible."

Barton sighed and leaned on the table with his head hanging down.

"Did your friend tell you what do to in those situations?" he asked. His voice shifted from irritated to weary.

That, at least, was a question Alex had an answer for.

"Well, you said the breakers couldn't be faulty and I said the linking runes couldn't fail."

"So we go to the Brooklyn Relay Tower and recheck everything," Barton said with a growl. Motioning for Alex to follow him, he made his way back to the liquor cabinet and poured another round. "Are you ready?" he asked when they'd both finished their drinks.

Alex made a sour face, but nodded nonetheless. He held out his arm and Barton grabbed him around the wrist. A moment later they vanished.

"Rough day?" Iggy asked as Alex came shuffling down the stairs of the brownstone. The grandfather clock in the corner of the foyer read six-twenty, but Alex felt like it might as well have been two in the morning.

"You have no idea," he groaned, slumping down into the reading chair on the near side of the little table with the lamp and the cigar box. Iggy's chair was on the far side of the table and he leaned forward, setting the pulp novel aside, as Alex closed his eyes and sighed.

"I can see you need a drink and dinner," Iggy said, getting up out of his chair. "And I'm thinking in that order."

Alex could hear Iggy moving to the liquor cabinet, then the clink of a bottle on the lip of a glass.

"Here you are, lad," he said, handing Alex what looked like a miniature wine glass, with a short stem and small cup. "A glass of port will settle your nerves until dinner's ready." Alex accepted the glass as Iggy pulled his pocketwatch from his vest pocket and flipped the cover open. "I have a stew on, but it won't be ready for at least half an hour. Why don't you regale me with the no-doubt harrowing tale of your day?"

Alex didn't usually drink port, so he just sat and sipped it. The wine had a fruity, sweet flavor and just as Iggy predicted, its warmth began to seep into Alex's tired body.

"Where to begin," he said after taking a second swig. "You were right about Harcourt."

"The government man?" Iggy probed.

Alex nodded.

"He wanted my notes on Alice Cartwright's math. Point of fact, he wanted my whole notebook, but I threatened to make him show me his warrant." Alex chuckled at the memory of Harcourt's smoldering anger.

"Antagonizing him might not have been the smartest move," Iggy said, trimming a cigar with a pocket knife taken from his jacket pocket. "Some of those government people can make proper nuisances of themselves if they've a mind to."

Alex gave him a sly grin.

"Well I tagged in my own government contact."

"Went running to Miss Kincaid for protection, did you?" Iggy said with a chuckle.

"Something about Harcourt just felt...off. I wanted Sorsha to make sure he's on the level."

"And what about Miss Kincaid?"

Alex let the question hang in the air for a long moment. He thought about playing dumb, but Iggy would put him on bread and water if he tried that.

"We're going out tomorrow night."

Iggy gave Alex a knowing grin, then puffed the cigar to life against the flame of his gold lighter.

"I'm surprised she let you off that easily," he said, blowing out a cloud of aromatic smoke.

"I dazzled her with my sincerity," Alex said, putting his hand on his chest with a wounded expression.

Iggy laughed.

"I'm not falling for that, and you can bet a sharp girl like Sorsha won't either."

"I guess I'll know tomorrow night," Alex said. Sorsha didn't seem too angry that it had taken him four months to follow up on her invitation. That alone was probably a giant red flag.

"I take it that your romantic life isn't what's weighing on you," Iggy said.

Alex sighed again.

"No, that's mostly the last four hours I spent with Andrew going over every rune and spell in the Brooklyn Relay Tower." He explained about the weird fluctuations and how, once they'd checked everything obvious, they'd discovered that the metal plate used to anchor the linking runes had a crack in it that was causing one of the linking runes to get an uneven flow of current. When the power fluctuated, it tripped the breaker, transferring too much power to the next one in line and tripping it too.

"All that work for such a little problem," Iggy said with a shake of his head.

"That was the tiring part of my day," Alex said, reaching into his shirt pocket. He pulled out his notepad and flipped to the page where he'd drawn the blood rune. "This is the disturbing part."

He passed the notepad across the table.

"Is this a rune?" Iggy asked after looking at it for a long minute.

"That's what I'd like to know," Alex said. He took another drink of the port and started in on the tale of Danny's murder victim. Iggy didn't interrupt, just sat puffing absently on his cigar as Alex wove the grisly tale.

When he was done, Iggy looked at the blood rune again.

"Do you know if this was drawn in the girl's blood?" he asked.

Of all the things Alex had expected his mentor and friend to ask about, that one hadn't made the list.

"Uh," he said, eloquently. "I guess, why?"

Iggy puffed on his cigar before responding.

"You might want to find out," Iggy said. "You'll have to collect samples, of course, but Dr. Wagner should be able to tell you if the blood is human or not."

Alex made a sour face at the idea of talking to the police coroner.

"Be sure you get samples from the outer shape as well as the symbol in the middle," Iggy went on.

"What are you thinking?"

Iggy leaned over the table, passing the notebook back.

"Have a look at the places where the inner symbol overlaps the surrounding geometry."

Alex scrutinized the image again. He hadn't noticed before, but the symbol at the center of the blood rune crossed the decagon in three places. Alex doubted the murderer was going for artistic style when he painted it, but if it had been a rune, those intersections would have fouled the magic. Symbols and shapes were simply not permitted to touch in rune magic.

"So it isn't a rune," he said at last.

"Don't be so hasty," Iggy said. "Look again."

Alex did as he was told, but other than the intersections he'd missed before, the blood symbol appeared to be a rune and he said so.

"It looks like a rune," Iggy said with a twinkle in his eye, "because I believe it is."

"You were right about this," Alex said, pointing to the drawing. "It definitely overlaps, and runes can't do that."

"You're not thinking laterally," Iggy chided. "Did you notice that the underlying geometry is done very precisely, but the symbol in the middle is sloppy by comparison?"

Alex checked the drawing again. Iggy hadn't suggested that Alex had drawn it poorly because they both knew that reproducing symbols accurately was a runewright's stock in trade. Alex had drawn the rune exactly as he'd seen it and Iggy was right, the decagon and its internal spiral pattern were made with a thin brush and laid down precisely. Alex had to go over the central symbol several times with the side of his pencil lead to capture the width of the symbol. Closing his eyes, he pictured Katherine Biggs' floor in his mind's eye. The symbol had definitely been made with a wide brush, and one that had uneven bristles that made the symbol appear sloppy.

"The symbol isn't part of the rune," he realized. "It was put down later to disguise what's underneath."

"Excellent deduction," Iggy said with a satisfied smile.

"So we are looking for a runewright."

"I don't think so," Iggy said with a shake of his head.

Alex's mouth dropped open at that.

"But you just…"

"I don't know of a single rune that used a geometry that complex," Iggy said, jabbing his cigar at the drawing in Alex's hand. "Do you?"

Alex was forced to admit that he didn't.

"Then what is this?" he protested. "If it wouldn't be recognizable, why hide it?"

"Maybe the symbol isn't there to hide what's beneath, but rather as a finishing step to whatever the killer was doing."

"So what was he doing?"

Iggy puffed his cigar for a moment, then turned to Alex.

"This whole thing puts me in mind of the kind of outlandish setup you get in a pulp crime novel," he said. "Murder committed by some voodoo priest seeking the blessings of the spirits or some such. You said the victim was a colored woman; maybe she was from Jamaica?"

"The crime scene did seem a bit overdone," Alex said. "Like it was staged. Now all I need is a voodoo priest I can ask about it."

Iggy chuckled.

"You can do far better than that," he said. "Such lurid murders aren't only the purview of the pulp novelist. They are just as often the stock in trade of the tabloid journalist."

Now it was Alex's turn to chuckle.

"Billy Tasker still owes me big for letting him in on the resolution of the Anderson murder," he said. "Maybe he can put me on to someone who knows about this occult stuff."

Iggy picked up his book and opened it again.

"Just make sure you're not twisting the facts to suit that theory," he said without looking up.

Alex finished his port and set the glass on the table.

"Is there another possibility I'm missing?"

"Of course," the older man said in a voice that implied it was perfectly obvious what he meant. When Alex didn't answer, he went on. "Your killer could be a vampire."

Alex rolled his eyes.

"You're not funny," he said in an annoyed voice.

"I've got over a million readers who would beg to differ," Iggy said without even the hint of a smile.

Alex leaned forward, putting his elbows on his knees and stretching his back. When he finally sat up, he caught sight of some dust clinging to the cuff of his trouser leg.

"I'm going to go change," he said, standing up. "I spent the last few hours crawling around Barton's new tower, and I seem to have brought back some of it with me."

"Alex," Iggy said before Alex could head for the stairs. There was a note of concern in his voice that made Alex turn back to his mentor's chair. "Have you finished your new escape rune?"

Alex had expended his most recent escape rune a few months ago when he yanked himself and Sorsha out of the path of a mad bomber. That rune had been fairly simple, one he put together quickly, and it wasn't as elegant as his first one. On the plus side, it didn't drain away huge chunks of his life energy either.

"I still have a few hours of work left to do on it," he admitted. "My last one almost got Sorsha killed, so I want this one to drop me back here like the original one did. That way if anyone needs medical attention, you'll be close."

Iggy nodded, clipping his cigar between his fingers as he stroked his thick mustache.

"A solid plan," he said. "One doesn't use an escape rune lightly, after all."

"Why are you suddenly interested in my escape rune?"

"Danny thought this killing might be the work of the Legion," he said, contemplating his cigar.

"You agree with him?" Alex asked. He was pretty sure this wasn't the Legion's style, but it never paid to be too rigid in your thinking.

"It's possible," Iggy said with a sigh. "There's a certain elegance to their work, but this killing seems more...theatrical. I'm worried about that blood rune though. You said it radiated magic?"

"So brightly I had to use a filter in my oculus," Alex said. "Whoever made it might have mixed the blood with some alchemical solution though."

"Or it might be something new," Iggy said. "Five years ago, I would have said that I understood magic better than just about anyone alive, but now..."

Alex knew what he meant. Since the appearance of Moriarty, it seemed as if magic was getting darker and more dangerous by the day.

"You think this blood rune is something new?"

"Or something old," Iggy said. "Very, very old. That seems to be the way of it these days."

"Moriarty did say that what was coming had happened before," Alex said. "Should we start poring over history books?"

"That's not a bad idea," Iggy said. "But leave that to me. I don't know whether this murder is a portent of things to come or just the work of a murderous sadist, but either way, I want you to keep your wits about you."

"Always," Alex chuckled, turning toward the stairs.

"And finish your escape rune," Iggy called after him.

8

COPS AND ROBBERIES

At Iggy's insistence, Alex spent the night in his vault poring over the delicate lines and intricate colors of his new escape rune. It was after midnight when he finished, and he'd retreated to the armchair in his library, intending to relax with a book for a few minutes before heading to bed.

When he woke the following morning, his back was stiff from having slept in the chair all night. Fortunately there was a bottle of single malt on the reading table along with a tumbler, so he poured himself two fingers' worth and drank it before attempting to rise. At thirty-four, he didn't feel old, but his body told him, in no uncertain terms, that he was too old to spend the night sitting up in chairs, no matter how comfortable they were.

Groaning as his back cracked, Alex shuffled to his drafting table. The completed escape rune sat on the angled surface, drawn on a heavy sheet of parchment paper and glittering in the magelights like a stained glass window. The rune was inscribed in a circle with arcs drawn inside, creating a dozen cells around the edge. Each of these had runic symbols in them with runic text running around the inside and outside of the main shape. In the center was a combination of three runes written so that they interlocked, joining their magic together.

Unlike the blood rune, however, none of the symbols touched the geometric lines.

It had taken Alex the better part of a month to write this rune and it functioned just like his first one, though he'd moved the first jump several miles away from where he'd dropped Sorsha's first castle, out of respect for its resting place. Sorsha had been quite angry about the loss of her home, even though that wasn't Alex's fault strictly speaking, and he had no wish to further antagonize her.

Since the creation of the intricate rune took such a long time, Alex had taken to keeping it in a picture frame that he hung on the wall near the drafting table. It was a piece of art, after all. Since he'd have to arrange for the rune to be tattooed on his body, Alex returned the rune to its frame and hung it back up.

When he returned to the drafting table, he saw the paper with the blood rune sitting to one side. He'd spent a frustrating couple of minutes last night trying to decipher it, but without any luck.

As he reached for the paper, intending to put it in his pocket with Alice Cartwright's math, his breath suddenly quickened and he turned to look at a shelf off to the right of the table. Several containers of powdered ingredients he used to make ink sat on the middle shelf, nothing special or expensive, but behind them was a removable panel and behind that was his secret safe. Alex had installed the safe because he reasoned that it was so difficult to get into a runewright's vault that any potential thief would never think to look for further concealment. The safe was where Alex kept his important papers, a few gold bars, a stack of ready cash, and a small mason jar.

It was the kind of jar women everywhere used to keep homemade jams and preserves. Alex's jar, however, was filled with a fine, lime green powder.

The thought of it made his hand twitch with anticipation. He wouldn't need much. Just a few grains dissolved in two fingers of Scotch would do it. With the Limelight he would understand what the blood rune was and what it did. He was certain of it.

"No" Alex said out loud, breaking the spell. He turned away from the wall that concealed his safe, breathing heavily, and focused his eyes on the blood rune. He didn't need a magical crutch to figure this out, he just needed to remove the obscuring symbol and he'd be able to see what lay beneath.

But how would he do that?

He laughed as the thought struck him. It was so simple. All he had to do was write a temporal restoration rune, cast it on the blood that made up the obscuring symbol and he could remove it without removing the shape beneath.

Pulling out the second drawer of his rollaway cabinet, Alex pulled out a fresh sheet of flash paper and set it on the desk. The rune would take a couple of hours to finish, but he'd let Sherry know what he was doing through the intercom as soon as she arrived in the office.

Feeling re-invigorated, Alex unstoppered a bottle of gold infused ink and set to work.

Alex stepped off the elevator on the fifth floor of the Central Office of Police just after ten and made his way down the side of the large open area to the hallway along the back wall that led to the offices. He'd wanted to talk to Danny first thing that morning, but there wasn't anything he could do until he finished the temporal restoration rune, so he'd taken the time to create it.

Now that Danny was a Lieutenant, he occupied Callahan's old office. It was the third one along the row, opposite the secure room where evidence was kept. All of the offices had large windows running along the upper half of the wall, and while most were shuttered, Danny usually kept his open.

"Get in here," Danny yelled when Alex waved through the glass. He had a look on his face that Alex hadn't seen since the time he walked in on Alex flirting with Amy right after they first met.

"What's up?" Alex asked, giving him a questioning look as he entered the office.

Danny picked up a newspaper from off his desk and held it up. The headline across the top read, Voodoo Killer Stalks Harlem. Below the banner was a picture of Katherine Biggs' room; her body was mercifully gone, but the blood rune was clearly visible.

"Is this your work?" Danny asked, a hard edge in his voice.

Alex refrained from rolling his eyes. He almost laughed. Callahan had grilled him more than once when case information leaked to the press. It was just too easy to believe it was the work of an outsider rather than someone inside the department. In that regard, Alex was a friend, but he wasn't family.

"You know I only leak police secrets to the Midnight Sun," Alex said with a grin.

A flash of anger washed over Danny's face, then he sighed and dropped the paper.

"Sorry," he said, slumping down into the chair behind his desk.

"You should be," Alex said, dropping his hat on the desk. "In the first place, I don't carry a camera in my kit, though it's probably not a bad idea. Secondly, I can't believe you thought I'd do that to you."

Danny pinched the bridge of his nose and shook his head.

"I've been on the phone all morning with Captain Callahan, Chief Montgomery, and even the mayor. If whoever gave that picture to the Chronicle had given them one with Katherine Biggs' body in it, the city would already be in panic. As it is, the Chief is telling the press that the picture isn't real."

Alex was surprised to hear that. The Chief's story wasn't likely to stand up to any level of scrutiny.

"Well, at least I've got some good news," Alex said. "I showed my drawing of the blood rune to Iggy and he suggested that the killer might have painted the big symbol to cover up whatever he was really doing. I can use a temporal restoration rune to remove the top layer so we can see underneath."

Danny sat back in his chair and sighed.

"That sounds like it might have worked," he said. "Problem is the house sort of...crumbled sometime last night."

That didn't make sense. Kathrine Biggs' home was little more than a shack, but it hadn't been in any danger of falling down yesterday.

"Someone destroyed it?"

"No." Danny shook his head. "I was out there this morning. All that's left is a pile of sand and dust where the shack stood."

Alex felt a sudden chill that raised gooseflesh on his arms.

"What kind of dust?" he asked. "White, like fireplace ash, or dark like soot?"

"Soot."

Alex took out his cigarette case to give himself time to think, and to calm down.

"Remember Jerry Pemberton?"

Danny cocked his head to the side.

"The guy who helped steal that German plague?"

"Remember the rune I used on his body? The one that restored the parts that had been burned?"

Danny pulled a crumpled pack of cigarettes from his pocket, shook it and, tugged one out.

"You said when the rune wore off that his body would crumble to dust. I remember it." He lit the cigarette and blew out a cloud of smoke. "When I went to Katherine Biggs' shack this morning, it looked just like Pemberton's body after your rune wore off. You told me there was some reason that happened, something to do with the magic involved."

"Temporal restoration runes turn back time," Alex said. "It isn't much and it doesn't last for long, but even so, there are some things magic just isn't supposed to do. When one of us crosses that line, the universe sort of...pushes back. Iggy calls it backlash."

"So whoever killed Katherine wanted to reverse time?"

"It's possible," Alex said. "But it might be anything. I need to get a look at that symbol."

"Which is now a pile of dust," Danny observed. "Is there anything you can do?"

Alex thought a minute, then he grinned and picked up his hat.

"Do you have another picture of the murder scene?"

Danny gave him a suspicious look.

"Why?"

"I'm on my way to talk to Billy at the Midnight Sun and it never hurts to bribe him."

"Get out of here," Danny scoffed.

Blood Relation

Alex might have been joking about wanting a photograph, but he'd been honest about his next destination. A crime as outlandish as this one was red meat for the tabloid industry. If anyone knew of a crime like it, it would be his friend Billy Tasker...or one of Billy's associates.

Twenty minutes later, a cab deposited Alex in front of the worn brick building that housed the offices and presses of the Midnight Sun. Laura, the receptionist, gave him her usual sneer, but she did call Billy right away rather than making Alex wait while she finished filing her nails. She was pretty enough, with bleached blonde hair that looked slightly unnatural, a voluptuous figure, and dark eyes. Alex met her when he had been dating Jessica, and Laura hadn't gotten over the fact that he didn't respond to her flirting. In hindsight, he probably should have encouraged her just a bit, enough to keep on her good side, but that ship had sailed.

"Alex," Billy Tasker called, emerging from a door that led to the tabloid's offices. He wore a better-quality suit than Alex had seen him in before and it made his boyish face look almost grown up. "What brings you to me?"

Alex didn't want to discuss the blood rune in the lobby, so he nodded in the direction of Billy's office.

"Not here," he said.

Billy looked intrigued and a predatory smile spread across his face as he motioned for Alex to follow him. After the Anderson story, Billy had moved into the corner office at the end of the hall. Alex wasn't sure how many papers that story had sold, but someone definitely appreciated it.

The office was just as cramped as Alex remembered it, overstuffed with papers, files, and books. This one had a bank of windows that let in much more light, which gave the room an open feeling despite the clutter.

"Pardon the mess," he said. "We're scrambling to catch up at the moment. Can you believe we actually got scooped by that rag, the Daily Chronicle?"

"The voodoo killer story?" Alex asked.

Something in Alex's question made Billy look up quickly from clearing a space on his desk.

"You don't know anything about that?" he asked. "Do you?"

There was a note of tantalized interest and hope in the question. Alex decided to milk that. He put on a disinterested expression and shrugged.

"Now what would a humble private dick like me know about such outlandish crimes?" he said, adopting a speech mannerism closer to Iggy's than his own.

Billy's grin got so wide Alex worried it would wrap around to the sides of his head.

"You do know something," he declared, leaning across the table in eager anticipation.

Alex sat down in the comfortable armchair opposite the desk, crossed his legs, and dropped his hat on his knee.

"I might have been in that house before those pictures were taken," he said. "I might even be looking for the killer."

"That's quite the hypothetical," Billy said, sitting down and folding his arms on the desk. "What would I have to come up with to get more...concrete information?"

"I need to know if anyone's ever heard of a crime scene like that one," Alex said.

Billy looked confused for a minute, then reached into the pile of papers on his desk and pulled out a copy of the Chronicle. Smoothing it out on his desk, he stared at the picture, then shook his head.

"Am I missing something?" he said.

"I don't know," Alex said. "What I do know is that tabloids write about this kind of sensationalized crime all the time. Any of those stories have crime scenes like this one?"

Billy's eyes widened and he looked down at the picture, then back up at Alex.

"You think this isn't the first victim," he gasped. "You think there's a maniac on the loose."

"Don't sound so excited," Alex chided. "But yes, I think this isn't our killer's first time out. In order to prove that, however, I need to find evidence of a previous murder."

Billy sat looking at the picture on the Chronicle's front page, then shook his head.

"I can't think of anything," he said, rubbing his chin with his thumb and forefinger. "But I know someone who might."

"I'll cut you in on the story," Alex offered.

Billy seemed to be thinking that over, but before he could counter, Alex went on.

"Nice office," he said. "Get that after the Anderson story?"

"All right, all right," Billy said, chuckling. "You win. I owe you big for that one."

"How many papers did that story sell?"

Billy's look shifted from amused to smug in an instant.

"Over a quarter million," he said. "It was a sensation."

Alex didn't tell him, but he had a framed copy of the front-page story hanging on the wall in his vault.

"So who do I need to talk to?" he prodded.

Billy opened a drawer in his desk and pulled out a worn leather book. Opening it, he ran his thumb along the edge and opened it near the front.

"His name is Theodore Bell," Billy said, jotting an address on a scrap of paper. "He's an expert in the occult, you know, spiritualism, voodoo, that sort of thing. He's one of my consultants for just this kind of story."

Alex accepted the paper, tucked it into his pocket and rose.

"Just make sure I'm there when you take this bastard down," Billy said.

Alex promised that he would be, then he put on his hat and walked out.

9

FORMULAE

The address Billy gave Alex led him to a small mid-ring bookstore on the East Side along Second Avenue. It was sandwiched in between a dry goods store and a cobbler's shop, with a wooden sign hanging from an iron support. The name, *Bell's Book & Candle*, had been painted across a maroon field in large white letters, but it had been some time since the sign had been touched up. Now it was so gray and faded that Alex had to get close before he could read it.

The windows of the shop were dirty, but Alex could see several stacks of books in the display boxes inside. From the amount of dust on them, it was clear they hadn't been attended to recently, either.

He pushed the door open, and the bell hanging above it jingled, announcing his presence.

At least something in here is in working condition.

The inside of the shop was basically an open room with shelves lining the side walls and the back. Several tables filled the space in the center, some piled with books while others held an odd assortment of unusual objects like Ouija boards and candles. A podium-like high table stood in the back of the room, near a curtained door, with a cash register sitting on top and a punk of incense burning in a brass holder.

The whole place was filled with the musty smell of old books, cheap candle wax, and burnt pine needles.

"Hello there," a pudgy man in a maroon vest said as he emerged from the back room. He had a round face with rosy cheeks and an affable expression. The hair on his head was thin, barely more than clinging wisps, but he'd compensated with a prodigious pair of graying mutton chops. A pair of spectacles was perched on the tip of his pointed nose, and his mouth was drawn up in a smile.

"And how can I help you today?" he said, approaching Alex with his hand out to shake.

Alex accepted the hand and gripped it firmly.

"Are you Theodore Bell?" Alex wondered.

"I am," the man said, his smile widening. "I am, indeed."

"My name's Alex Lockerby," Alex said once he'd extracted his hand. "Billy Tasker over at The Midnight Sun gave me your name."

Bell looked confused for a moment, then nodded.

"Yes, I've advised him on several stories in the past," Bell said. "What is it you are looking for?"

Alex had bought a copy of the Chronicle on his way over and torn out the story about the voodoo killer. He pulled the clipping from his jacket pocket and unfolded it.

"I'm a private detective," he said handing over the paper. "I'm also a runewright, so the police asked me if I could tell them anything about that."

Bell glanced at the photo, then sighed.

"Terrible business," he said. "I saw the story this morning."

"Can you tell me anything about it?" Alex said. "I don't recognize that symbol on the floor. I don't think it's rune magic, so I wondered if maybe it was something occult."

Bell looked at the picture again, this time focusing intently.

"Given the shape, I had assumed it was a rune of some kind," he said.

"Do you know a lot about rune magic?"

"Certainly not as much as you do," he said with a chuckle. "But I do carry books on all kinds of magic, so I'm familiar with the basics."

"Well I'm pretty sure that's not a rune."

Bell didn't seem to hear Alex. He turned and walked toward the back corner of the store, muttering to himself. He stopped when he reached the farthest bookshelf, then ran his finger across one row of books, moving to the next and the next until he found what he wanted.

"Here we go," he said, pulling a thick, leather-backed volume down. Carrying it over to one of the many book tables, he set it atop a stack of paperbacks and began flipping pages. "Whoever wrote the newspaper story thought the symbol on the floor was from voodoo," he said as he searched the book. "But I don't think that's right. It has some of the form of a voodoo ritual, especially with the objects laid around the symbol, but…" His voice trailed off as he began reading.

"Find something?" Alex asked when Bell didn't speak for several minutes.

Bell shook his head and headed back to the shelf without explanation. He returned the book to the space from whence he'd pulled it, then headed back across the store to another shelf and pulled down two more.

"I was right," Bell said as he set the books down and began flipping through the top one. "This symbol," he tapped the newspaper in Alex's hand, "is similar to voodoo, I think because they have a common origin."

He found the page he was looking for and Alex saw the strange, flower-like spiral he'd noticed inside the geometric shape.

"That looks about right," he said.

"Yes. This is a symbol of protection used by native shamen in the Congo region of Africa," Bell said.

"So whoever made this was trying to do what?" Alex chuckled. "Invoke the spirits to protect him?"

"Don't scoff, young man," Bell chided. "Just because we don't know how something works, that doesn't mean it's nonsense." He stuck his stubby finger in Alex's face. "It wasn't all that long ago, after all, that a man with your particular skill set would have been burned at the stake."

That was, in fact, several centuries ago, but Alex took the man's point.

"As for what he was trying to do," Bell said, then he shrugged. "I can't tell from just this picture. You said you're working with the police, can you get me in to see this symbol in person?"

Alex explained about the rune being destroyed, though he left out the crumbling to dust part, implying instead that it had been the result of fire.

Bell sighed and closed the book from which he'd been reading.

"Well, without more information, I don't think there's anything more I can tell you," he said.

"You seem very well informed about the occult world," Alex said. "Can you think of any case like this one happening before?" He tapped the article for emphasis.

Bell rubbed his chin for a moment, then shook his head.

"Can't say that I do," he admitted. "But I can look through my files if you like. I keep records on any mysterious happenings that make the papers."

It was a long shot, but Alex was grateful for it.

"Thanks," he said, sticking out his hand for Bell to shake. He fished one of his business cards out of his shirt pocket with his left hand and held it out. "Give me call at this number if you find anything."

"The runewright detective," Bell read off the card. "You're the one who caught the Ghost. I ought to slug you for that." Despite the resolve in his words, there was no malice in the man's voice. "I really wanted that one to be real."

The idea that an actual vengeful spirit had returned, bent on murder, wasn't the kind of thing Alex would wish to be real. The idea was terrifying. Still, he knew what Bell meant. The old man had probably spent his whole life looking for signs of things stranger than mundane magic and had come up empty.

"Sorry," Alex said.

"Whatever happened to him?" Bell asked. "The Ghost, I mean. I didn't see anything in the papers. Shouldn't he have been put on trial by now?"

"He died in prison about six months after he was captured," Alex said.

The Ghost had been a man named Duane King who'd used escape runes to enter and leave his victim's homes unseen. The price of that power was that runes burned up his life energy, leaving him almost nothing in the end. Alex had been surprised he lasted as long as he did.

Bell seemed to have run out of steam with his questions, so Alex took the opportunity to excuse himself and stepped back out onto the street. The September air was cool, despite its being just after noon, and Alex headed to the street to hail a cab. The news that the blood rune had some basis in reality was encouraging. If he could find out more about it, he might figure out the killer's true motive. That would put him one step closer to catching the man. Unfortunately, all Alex really knew was that the strange symbol might have come from a vast region of trackless jungle in Africa. It wasn't exactly a solid lead, but it was all he had.

The mathematics building at Columbia University was a three-story brick building with rows of tall windows, spaced at regular intervals, that ran its entire height. As Alex approached, he could hear the sound of lessons being given in the large lecture halls and the small classrooms courtesy of the open windows. With the cool weather starting to supplant the heat of New York in the summertime, everyone was taking advantage.

A large pinboard in the lobby of the building contained the name, Dr. Samuel Phillips, Dean of Applied Mathematics, and gave the number for an office on the third floor. When Alex reached it, the door opened into a waiting area, much like his own office, and a perky student intern told Alex that Professor Phillips was preparing to teach a class in room three-fifteen at the end of the hall. Alex thanked her, and a few moments later he entered the designated classroom.

The room wasn't large, maybe big enough for twenty students, but it did have three tiers leading down to a well at the bottom where three enormous blackboards hung on the wall. These boards were on weighted cables and could be raised up to the top of the room, or lowered so the teacher could write on them. All of the upper boards were covered with the kinds of mathematical gibberish Alex had seen on Alice Cartwright's rollaway boards.

A slender man with bushy gray hair and rounded shoulders stood squinting at the center blackboard. He wore a white coat, like a doctor, presumably to keep chalk dust off his clothes. As Alex approached, the man checked the writing on the board, comparing it with a book of notes he took from his pocket, then went back to chalking symbols.

"Professor Phillips?" Alex asked.

The man held up a cautioning finger, then consulted his book again. He went back to the board and wrote another two lines before he sighed and dropped the piece of chalk in the wooden tray below the board.

"I've told you not to bother me during prep time," he growled, still scrutinizing the board. "If you have questions about an assignment, I have teaching assistants who can help you."

"I'm afraid there's been a mistake," Alex pressed on. He took out a business card and stepped up next to the man. "I'm not one of your students, I'm a private detective."

Phillips looked at the offered card, then at Alex, before turning back to the board.

"Then I definitely don't have time for you," he said. "I have a class in ten minutes, and I have to make sure these calculations are correct."

"Please, Professor," Alex said, pocketing his card and taking out the pages with Alice Cartwright's math on them. "A woman was murdered two days ago."

"I can assure you," Phillips said in an irritable voice. "I had nothing to do with that."

"That isn't what I mean, Professor," Alex pressed on. "I believe she might have been killed over some math."

That got Phillips attention. He whirled on Alex with the look of a man who'd just heard a profanity during Mass.

"That's absurd," he said.

"Can you just take a look at this, please," Alex said, pressing the paper with the central calculation from Alice's board against the front of Phillips' coat.

The Professor hesitated, then snatched the papers out of Alex's hand.

"Since it's clear you won't go away until I see this," he said, unfolding the paper. He looked for a moment, then handed it back. "This is Fermat's Conjecture," he said. "No one would kill over it."

He started to turn back to the board, but Alex grabbed his arm.

"Why do you think that, Professor?"

"Because, Fermat's Conjecture isn't a secret, it's one of a dozen or so proofs that mathematicians all over the world are trying to solve. There are probably hundreds of people working on it as we speak."

"So it's like a puzzle that people are trying to figure out?" Alex asked.

"Essentially," Phillips confirmed. "It's a formula proposed by Pierre de Fermat in the early sixteen hundreds. He wasn't able to prove that it was true, but generations of mathematicians since have made the attempt. Eventually someone will figure it out."

"Will that someone make a name for themselves?" Alex asked. "Maybe secure a high paying job?"

"Of course. Whoever solves Fermat's Conjecture will be famous."

"Well, Professor," Alex said. "In my business, that sounds a lot like motive."

Phillips looked at him for a moment as if he hadn't understood the words Alex had spoken, then he shook his head.

"No, no," he scoffed. "First of all, the person who solves Fermat's Conjecture will only be famous to other mathematicians. There are only a handful of people capable of making a serious attempt to solve it, so it's not exactly the Nobel Prize. Secondly, as I said, mathematicians capable of working at the level of Fermat's Conjecture are a very small fraternity. Anyone in that group will already have a good paying job. They have skills that are in demand."

Alex held out the second sheet where he'd copied the rest of Alice's calculations. Phillips glared at Alex then took the paper. As his eyes moved over the math, his eyebrows got gradually higher and higher.

"This is good work," he said at last. "Very impressive. I'd say that whoever did this is more than capable of attempting Fermat's Conjecture. Whose work did you say this was?"

"I didn't," Alex said. "Her name was Alice Cartwright."

A look of profound shock washed over Professor Phillips face and he leaned against the blackboard for support.

"No," he gasped.

"You knew Miss Cartwright?" Alex probed.

Phillips nodded, unable to find his voice for a moment.

"She was my student," he said in a wistful voice. "Years ago, of course, but I'd never forget her. She had a great mind, the kind of intellect a teacher yearns for but only finds if he's lucky. It was an honor to teach her."

Based on the Professor's reaction Alex was pretty sure he could cross the man off the list of potential suspects.

"And you're sure no one killed her over this Farragut's Conjecture?"

"Fermat's Conjecture," Phillips corrected absently. "And no, no one would have killed her over that."

"She worked as a computer," Alex said. "Could that have involved something worth killing over?"

Phillips took out a handkerchief and mopped his forehead before nodding.

"Unfortunately, yes," he said. "Computers are private contractors who check people's math," he explained. "When architects design buildings, they usually hire a computer to make sure their math is correct. It wouldn't do to have the building fall down, after all."

That made sense, but Alex couldn't see Alice being killed by a rogue architect. If she'd found errors in the math, he'd want them fixed. Architects whose buildings fell down tended not to get much work after that.

"Apparently she worked for the government," Alex said. "What kind of work with Uncle Sam would need a computer to do?"

"The secret kind," Phillips said. "If the Navy wants to build a carrier, someone has to check the math. If the runway is a few feet too short, people can die. If the guns on a battleship are too light, recoil could literally knock them off the deck. There are lots of things Washington might want a calculator to check."

Now that sounded like motive. It also sounded dangerous. The Germans had already proved that they were willing to cause trouble in America, and this could be real trouble. He'd have to ask Sorsha about it when he saw her that evening.

"Thank you, Professor," Alex said, flipping his notebook closed and returning the scraps of paper with Alice's math to his pocket. "I'm sorry to have bothered you."

He turned to go, but before he reached the door, Phillips called after him.

"Young man?"

Alex turned to find the Professor staring intently up at him from the well of the room.

"When you find out who killed Alice, would you come by and tell me about it? I...I'd like to know."

Alex didn't have a clue what all the scribbles on the boards meant, but this he understood. The man had loved Alice in a way, cherished her as a student. He wanted closure as much as any blood relative.

"Sure thing, Professor," Alex said in a gentle voice. "I'll let you know."

10

THE HOME OFFICE

Since Alex had restocked his red-backed book, he decided to skip the cab and just open his vault. The hardest part turned out to be finding a quiet place to open his vault. Not everyone knew about runewright vaults, but those who did understood that a runewright shutting himself inside his vault was committing suicide. It wouldn't do for word of his new abilities to get out, so he always had to find a place where he could open his vault unobserved. In this case, he finally located a large janitorial closet with enough room on the back wall to draw the chalk door.

It actually took Alex longer to find the closet than it did to actually get back to his office. When he arrived, he headed straight for the front room to check in with Sherry. Before he could traverse the hallway, however, the door to the map room opened and Mike Fitzgerald stuck his head out. When he saw Alex, his bushy mustache turned up in a way that reminded Alex of a fuzzy caterpillar.

"I thought I heard you, Mr. Lockerby," he said.

"Mike," Alex said. "And call me Alex, you've got the job."

Mike chuckled and nodded, a little embarrassed. He was in his forties and was raised to always observe propriety in the workplace.

"Sorry," he said. "I wanted to let you know that I had eleven successful cases over the last two days."

"That's great, Mike," Alex said, clapping him on the shoulder. "Keep it up."

"Well, I also wanted to let you know that I also did two other cases."

That got Alex's attention. Clearly Mike was unsure how he would react to that.

"Tell me about them."

"One was a couple who misplaced the deed to their home," Mike said, tugging his mustache nervously. "Turns out one of them put it in a book of poetry for safekeeping. The finding rune led me right to it. The other one was a wife who thought she lost her diamond bracelet."

Alex could tell by the change in Mike's voice that the other shoe was about to drop.

"Let me guess, her husband got in with his bookie and hocked it."

"Not exactly," Mike said. "He did hock it, but it was because he lost his job and was trying to keep it from his wife while he looked for another one."

Just when you think you've got people figured out, they surprise you.

"How did the wife take that?" Alex asked.

"She was upset," Mike said with a shrug, "but it was because the husband didn't tell her. She did pay her bill."

The way Mike said it, he expected Alex to be worried about the money.

"Go back when you have a break and give her the money back," Alex said. "Times being what they are, we don't take money from people who just lost their income."

These days twenty-five bucks wasn't a lot of money for him and he could afford to make such decisions. In the old days Alex would have done the same, but it would have been much more painful.

"You sure about that, Mr. Lockerby?"

"Alex. And yes, I'm sure."

Mike visibly relaxed at that.

"On the other hand," Alex went on. "You got lucky this time. This case could have gone bad fast. The last place a detective wants to be is between a feuding husband and wife."

"I see what you mean," Mike said. "I guess I won't take any more of those."

"I didn't say that. I just want you to think it through if someone comes to you looking for lost things. Use the finding rune here and if it shows an unexpected location, bring me in."

Mike relaxed and grinned.

"Thanks. Mr. — Alex. I will. One other thing," he said when Alex started to turn. "I'm almost out of finding runes."

Ales suppressed a sigh. He only had six of those himself and he didn't want to take the time to write more. He would need at least one if he located a clue to the missing herbs in the list of other items stolen by the thieves, two would be safer.

"Here," he said, opening his rune book and carefully tearing out four of the six runes. "I'll try to write some more sometime today, but I might not be able to get to it until tonight."

"What do you want me to do if I run out of runes?"

Alex thought about that for a moment. Mike wasn't proficient enough at rune lore to make advanced finding runes or any other standard runes, but his work with minor runes was excellent. Alex still hadn't managed to fully restock his rune book, and he needed about fifteen minor runes of various kinds.

"If I get you a list of runes I need done, along with flash paper and ink, can you write them for me?"

Mike nodded.

"Of course, assuming I know them."

"I'll get you the list as soon as I'm done with Sherry," Alex said. "Do the ones you can in any spare time you have."

Mike promised to take care of it and withdrew back to the map room.

"Hey boss," Sherry said as he entered the waiting room. She sat behind her desk with at least three notepads in front of her and a stack of case folders in the far corner. This time Sherry was not alone in the waiting room. A plump, morose-looking woman in a purple dress sat on one of the couches clutching a beaded handbag. She had the look of someone who always thought of themselves as 'put-upon'.

"She's waiting to see Mike," Sherry said before Alex could approach.

"I just spoke to him, so I imagine he'll be out in a minute. Any luck with those robberies?"

Sherry gave him her version of Leslie Thompson's million-dollar smile. She didn't quite have it down, so it was more of a hundred-grand smile, but for most guys that was plenty.

Selecting one of the notepads in front of her, she tore off the top two pages and handed them to Alex.

"I got a hold of each warehouse and got a list of the people who had items stolen in the break-ins," she said. "Then I called them and made a list of everything taken. I hope it helps."

Alex took the papers with a grin. Whether it helped or not, Sherry had just saved him hours of work, and with the deadline to find Mr. Su's herbs looming, Alex needed every second. He'd promised Mr. Su that he'd let him know his progress by today. With any luck, he'd have something to report.

"Thanks, Doll," he said., beaming at her. "I owe you."

"I take flowers, chocolates, and preferably, expensive lunches."

Alex promised to take her somewhere nice for lunch next week and withdrew to his office. He wanted to get started on the property list, but he still needed to call Detective Nicholson and let him know about Alice Cartwright, so he set the list aside and picked up the telephone.

"I'm sorry, sir," the operator at the Central Office said a moment later. "Your party doesn't answer. Is there someone else I can transfer you to?"

"No," Alex said, "I'll call back later."

He hung up and sighed. He'd have to brief Nicholson sooner or later, but it wasn't his job to go tracking the man down. He'd call again as soon as he'd finished with Sherry's list.

He picked up the two notebook pages and read through them quickly. Nothing jumped out at him as being a better candidate for his finding rune than the rest. He was going to have to call each of the victims and get the story on their stolen items.

"At least they'll know what the call is about," he said with a chuckle. The longest part of calls like these was explaining who you were and why you were calling.

Alex reached for the telephone, but before he could pick it up, the intercom on his desk buzzed. It made a clicking noise, then Sherry's voice came out of the little speaker.

"Alex, there's a Detective Nicholson here to— Hey! You can't go back there."

The intercom cut off and Alex rose with a sigh. Clearly Nicholson was in a hurry. When he walked around his desk and opened the office door, however, he found himself face to red face with Earnest Harcourt, the government man.

"There you are, you thieving rat," he fumed, trying to push Alex backward into his office. At six foot one, Alex was no lightweight and he just stood his ground.

"Mr. Harcourt," he said, putting on the most insincere smile he could manage. "It's a pleasure to see you. What brings you to my office this fine day?"

"Don't you give me that, you charlatan. I'll have your license for this."

Alex looked past the unintelligible G-man and found Detective Nicholson coming along behind him. The Detective looked irritated, but not with Alex.

"Lockerby," he said, nodding.

"Well what are we standing out here for?" Alex said, as if it hadn't been him blocking the door all along. "Come in. Make yourselves comfortable."

He finally stepped back, and Harcourt barged in, followed by Nicholson. They each took a chair in front of Alex's desk while Alex made a show of checking the hall as if he expected there to be more in their party. Satisfied that he'd let Harcourt steam long enough, he closed the door and walked back around his massive, leather-topped desk.

"What's all this about?" he asked Harcourt as he sat down.

The government man had been quivering with rage and he popped out of his seat as if he'd been burned.

"You know very well why I'm here," he fumed. "You were alone in her office and now they're missing. You're the only one who could have taken them."

Harcourt was so mad he wasn't speaking in complete sentences and Alex had to pinch his thigh to keep from smiling.

"I assume you're talking about Miss Cartwright," he said. "I already told you I didn't take anything from her apartment."

"Then where are they?" he raged, getting spittle on Alex's desk. "The police don't have them, I checked."

Since Harcourt had mentioned Alex being alone, he must be referring to Alex's time in Miss Cartwright's office. Obviously some of her files were missing.

"Mr. Harcourt," Alex said with the exaggerated patience usually reserved for toddlers and drunks. "I told you that I hadn't had a chance to go through Miss Cartwright's files."

"Well, files are missing, and you're the only one left who could have taken them."

Alex resisted the urge to pinch the bridge of his nose and sigh.

"Has it occurred to you, Mr. Harcourt, that Alice Cartwright was murdered? Most people are murdered for a reason," he went on. "Maybe the killer was looking for the missing files. Maybe that's why they're missing...because he took them."

Harcourt looked stunned for a minute, then shook his head.

"You said Miss Cartwright was killed over the math on her blackboard," he said.

"That is a possibility," Detective Nicholson spoke up. "But it's by no means definite, as I tried to tell you back at the station. And in the cab ride over here."

Alex almost smirked at the wounded tone in the Detective's voice.

"Actually," Alex said, "I'm pretty sure Miss Cartwright wasn't killed because of the math on her board."

"Oh," Harcourt and Nicholson said together.

Alex pulled the pages he'd torn from his notebook out of his pocket and tossed them on his desk.

"I forgot I wrote these," he lied. "But when I found them in the pocket of my suit coat, I showed them to the head of the mathematics department over at Columbia."

"What!" Harcourt shouted, snatching the papers off the desk. "This could be top secret government information. Giving it out is treason, Lockerby."

"Relax, Mr. Harcourt," Alex said, raising his voice for emphasis. "It's not secret anything." He stood and pointed to the main equation, the one Alice Cartwright had written large in the center of her musings. "That is called Fermat's Conjecture, it's a kind of mathematical puzzle that's been around since the sixteen-hundreds. Professor Phillips, who runs the math department, assured me that no one would be killed over this."

"Then what—" Harcourt began but Alex cut him off.

"It's far more likely that Miss Cartwright was killed because of that top secret work you just mentioned, the work she was doing for the government. Unless she's got a violent lover," Alex added. "Then my money's on him."

"No relations of any kind," Nicholson said. "Miss Cartwright was quite the homebody. According to her neighbors, she never went out after work and only to church on the weekends."

Harcourt sat down heavily with a stunned look on his face.

"I have to call my office," he said. "Let them know the files are no longer secure."

"I don't think you need to do that yet," Alex said.

Both men across the desk stared at him.

"Why not?" Nicholson said. "Unless you have the files, they aren't accounted for in Miss Cartwright's house."

"I don't have them," Alex assured him. "But I think I know where you can find them."

"I don't see how," Nicholson replied.

"You said it yourself," Alex said. "Miss Cartwright was a woman of regular habits who never went out after work."

"Why is that important?" Harcourt demanded.

"Because," Alex said, "she never went out *after* work. We assumed Alice worked from home because of her blackboards, but what if those boards were for her private musings on Fermat's Conjecture?"

"Then she must have been going out somewhere to do her work," Nicholson said, nodding.

"What!" Harcourt exploded. "Are you telling me she has an office somewhere? And you didn't know that?"

"I only just met the woman," Alex said. "Actually, come to think of it, I've never met her; the coroner removed her body before I even arrived."

"So?" Harcourt pressed. "You're supposed to be a detective."

"Me too," Nicholson said with a growl. "And my keen detective skills are telling me that the man she worked for, who brought her math to work on for who-knows-how-long, should damn well know where she works."

Harcourt sat with his mouth open like a fish.

"I was wondering that myself, Mr. Harcourt," Alex said. "Why is it that, by your own admission, you gave Miss Cartwright sensitive government information without knowing where she took it?"

"I..." Harcourt started, but his voice cracked, and he had to start again. "I work in Albany," he managed. "I have to take the train to get into the city, so I would always meet Alice on the weekends."

"When she was home," Nicholson said. He shook his head and rolled his eyes.

Alex agreed with the sentiment. As much as he hated to admit it, though, Harcourt simply wasn't smart enough to cook up a lie that convincing on the spot. Most likely he was telling the truth.

"Well, Mr. Harcourt," Alex said. "I wouldn't be calling in your superiors just yet."

"Don't tell me what to do, scribbler," he snapped.

Alex shrugged at that.

"Well, if you do call them, do me a favor and make sure I'm in the room when you tell them you don't know where Alice Cartwright was working on their super-secret government math. That ought to be a hoot."

Harcourt turned green at the thought.

"What am I going to do?" he asked, before he thought better of it.

"I'd suggest you start playing ball," Alex said, leaning across the desk. "Cooperate with Detective Nicholson and go through Miss

Cartwright's apartment with a fine-toothed comb. There must be a reference to her office somewhere; a lease agreement, record of a rent payment, check her key ring, maybe you can get a room or building number."

"Yes," Harcourt said, leaping to his feet. "We need to get over there right away."

With that, he turned on his heel and left the office without even waiting for Nicholson to stand up.

"I don't envy you this case," Alex said, as the Detective stood and put away the note pad he'd been using during the meeting.

"Are you kidding?" Nicholson said with a predatory grin. "He's terrified. He'll do anything I tell him now."

Alex stuck out his hand and Nicholson shook it.

"If you run across any magical problems, you know where to find me."

Nicholson thanked him, then picked up his hat and headed out into the hall after Harcourt.

11

STOLEN PROPERTY

Alex waited a few minutes before digging into Sherry's list. Truth be told, he wanted to make sure Harcourt and Nicholson were actually gone. To pass the time, he opened the polished oak drawer in his magnificent desk and pulled out a bottle and a tumbler. Just like former days, he always kept something to drink handy. Unlike former days, this was a bottle of twelve-year-old single malt.

Alex poured out two fingers' worth of the amber liquid in the tumbler, then leaned back in his chair and sipped it. Cheap Scotch always reminded Alex of cough medicine, but the good stuff had a taste that made him think of fine wood, oiled leather, and beautiful women. It was worth what he paid for it.

Closing his eyes, Alex just sat, enjoying the experience of the whiskey. It was something he could do for an hour if he let himself, but he had work to do, so he inhaled deeply, then finished his drink and sat up.

Sherry's notes had a list of all the warehouses she had called, to whom she spoke, and the names of the businesses that had property stolen. Further down she had listed the property owners, the address of their businesses, to whom she spoke, and what had been stolen. It was all laid out perfectly in neat, orderly rows.

Iggy would have been proud.

At the bottom of the page, Sherry had compiled her results into a list of everything that had been stolen. As Alex read it, he couldn't help thinking there must have been a mistake. Of the four entries, only one was decently valuable, and none of them would be used together. He'd assumed the thieves were looking for specific items for a specific buyer, but this made no sense at all.

According to Sherry, the stolen items were Su Hi's alchemy ingredients, some surgical tools manufactured in Belgium, and several bottles of oil from Italy.

With nothing on the list standing out, Alex picked up his telephone and dialed the first number on the list, Fransson Medical Instruments. The owner, one Hans Fransson, told Alex that he received shipments of specialty surgical tools about once a quarter, and they weren't exactly hot sellers. Most of the buyers tended to be new doctors setting up practices. Nothing about the shipment was special or important to Hans, so the tools were a dead end.

Next on the list was Enzo Romero, who made a name for himself creating perfume for the fashionable ladies of the Core. Sherry's notes indicated that she'd spoken with his secretary and she hadn't known much beyond the fact that what had been taken were 'oils from Italy.' Alex didn't know much about perfume, but he imagined it was similar to alchemy and that meant some of those oils might be expensive or even rare. He resolved to call and find someone at the perfume company who could give him a better answer.

That turned out to be easier said than done. Enzo Romero's secretary seemed to exist solely to prevent anyone from talking to Enzo, or anyone else of any importance at the company. Frustrated, Alex hung up.

If he was going to have a shot at finding Hi Su's missing herbs, however, the perfume oils were probably his only chance.

Glancing at the address, Alex contemplated going down to the office and taking his chances that he wouldn't be thrown out. Fashion people tended to be eccentric and picky.

There was something interesting about the address, though. It was only half a block from the House of Leone. Alex had met famous fashion designer, Maybelle Leone when he was investigating the decade-old murder of Broadway starlet Dolly Anderson. She had been friends with Dolly and had been eager to help once she understood what Alex was doing.

It presented an interesting opportunity, so Alex fished out his address book from his center desk drawer and dialed the number for the House of Leone. The secretary who answered the phone didn't sound familiar, but if the tabloids were to be believed, turnover was a fact of life in the fashion industry. It took almost ten minutes to explain what he wanted to the woman, but once she understood, Maybelle herself came on the line.

"Alexander," she said, as if he were an old friend she hadn't seen in ages. "How are you? I recognized your friend from the police in the newspaper story about Dolly, and I know you helped him with that. I can't tell you how grateful I am that you finally got justice for my dear friend."

She said all of that with the air of someone giving a speech to a crowded theater, but Alex didn't mind, since he wanted a favor. He spent another ten minutes recounting the events leading up to the arrest of Ethan Nelson, Dolly's old lover who murdered her out of jealousy. When he finished, he didn't give Maybelle any room to brush him off.

"I'm calling because I need to talk to Enzo Romero about a case. I can't get past his secretary, so I was hoping you knew him."

"Well of course I know him, darling," Maybelle said with a smile Alex could hear. "I'll give him a call and let him know to expect you in an hour. I have to go now, darling. Don't be a stranger."

With that she hung up, leaving Alex chuckling in his seat. Maybelle was a force of nature, and he had no doubt that when he showed up at Enzo's business, the man himself would be there to greet him.

Since the fashion district was only a twenty-minute cab ride away, Alex was tempted to refill his whisky glass. After a moment's hesitation he decided against it. He had at least half an hour for lunch before visiting Enzo and he intended to take advantage of it. Grabbing his hat, he said goodbye to Sherry and headed out. Since the Core was near the fashion district, Alex stopped at an upscale cafe for a Reuben sandwich and a coffee.

As he perused the paper and ate, he couldn't help reflecting on the early days of his career. Back then he always seemed to be running from one place to another, chasing down whatever cases he could get. Stopping for lunch back then usually involved a stale sandwich from an automat, eaten while Alex waited for a crawler.

Dropping a dollar on the counter for his meal, Alex was amazed how far he'd come from his basement office in Harlem.

The office of Enzo Romero was only a few blocks away, but Alex was running a bit late, so he caught a cab and made it just in time. Like many of the businesses in the fashion district, Enzo's offices had a sales floor on the ground level. Racks of decorative bottles, some with fully formed glass figures on top, were scattered around the room on polished chrome shelves. Among all this sparkling opulence, immaculately dressed ladies browsed. Occasionally they would request one of the many attractive young salesgirls to spray some concoction or other on their wrists as they went. Alex asked a perky young brunette behind the counter where the offices were and was directed to a staircase behind a door tucked into an alcove.

When he reached the offices, he was greeted by a sturdy-looking woman with her dark hair up in a tight bun who sat behind an equally sturdy-looking desk. Alex introduced himself to the spinsterly woman and found she was a totally different person than she'd been on the phone. Clearly Maybelle Leone had made an impression.

"Mr. Romero is expecting you," she said, indicating a large set of double doors at the end of a short hallway.

Alex thanked her and made his way to the doors, knocking politely before pulling one open. Based on the rest of the building, Alex expected Enzo's office to be full of wood paneling with a massive desk made of mahogany. What he found was a workshop that was only a little fancier than the basement where Dr. Kellin had her lab. Rows of tables lined the walls, with all kinds of equipment and glassware on them.

Alex recognized evaporators and distillers, and there were several jars over open flames, bubbling away. If he hadn't expected the sight of the room, Alex simply wasn't prepared for the smell. It was like a truck carrying pastries had crashed into a flower shop, leaving a sickly sweet, cloying odor that assaulted Alex as he entered.

In the center of this mess stood a thick, blocky man with large hands, a square jaw, flat nose, and a well-coiffed mass of gray hair. As Alex entered, he turned from where he had been making notes in a blank book.

"Are you the person dear Maybelle told me about?" he said in an Italian accent that was just a bit too thick to be credible.

"I'm Alex Lockerby," he said, holding out one of his cards. "I'm a private detective."

Enzo Romero waved the card away with a look of disinterest.

"I don't remember needing a detective," he said. "Does Maybelle think I have some skeletons in my closet that need the airing out?"

"No, sir," Alex said. "I'm here about your missing oils, the ones you ordered from Italy."

Enzo gave him a penetrating look.

"I am familiar with my missing supplies," he said, not bothering to hide his irritation. "I have already requested another shipment, so the matter is done."

"That will take months to get here," Alex said. "It might be possible for me to find your missing supplies."

That got Enzo's attention.

"How?" he asked after a pause.

Alex explained about his finding rune and asked if Enzo had any particular attachment to any of his missing supplies. Since both the supplies and Enzo came from Italy, Alex had high hopes.

"Most of them are typical enough," he said with a dismissive gesture. "But the benzoin comes from bushes in my family's vineyard. I tended the plants myself as a boy."

Alex couldn't help the grin that spread across his face.

"That sounds like something you'd be connected to," Alex said. "With your help, I'm pretty sure I can get your oils back for you."

"I am intrigued," Enzo said. "Show me."

For the third time in a week, Alex headed to Brooklyn. It had only taken him a few minutes to set up his map and use the finding rune. At first Alex thought the rune hadn't worked, but the map he used for his rune casting only showed Manhattan. When he picked up the compass, however, the needle pointed unwaveringly toward the southeast.

Taking his leave from Enzo and his perfume research, Alex caught a skycrawler and crossed the East River. When the compass needle started to swing around, he got off and hailed a cab. He was already well past Barton's new tower and heading south into the more rural part of Brooklyn.

"Stop here," Alex told the cabbie when the needle suddenly whipped around.

The cabbie gave him a surprised look in the mirror, but he pulled over to the curb. The place wasn't the best neighborhood. With the economic depression, many businesses had closed, and half a dozen of the structures in either direction were boarded up. On the corner was a derelict gasoline station and the compass pointed right to it.

"Thanks," Alex said, handing the cabby a dollar for the ride.

"You sure this is the right place?" the man asked. It wasn't a very good neighborhood and out here, Alex's suit screamed money.

Alex assured the man he'd be fine, then got out and crossed the street as the cab drove away. He wasn't too worried since there was almost nobody on the street, despite it being early afternoon. The more concerning thing was the abandoned, boarded-up garage. There was a large bank of windows along the front, but they were so encrusted with filth that he couldn't see inside.

What he could see was the dirt in front of the main door. It had been disturbed recently, leaving a clear track of footprints going in and out. Having seen that, Alex walked along the edge of the road as if he were continuing down the street. The tracks he'd seen looked to be a few days old, but there was no sense taking chances. If the gang of thieves was using this garage as a hideout, they might still be in there.

Alex had no desire to take on a group, especially without his 1911, or better yet the Thompson.

Turning the corner, Alex walked along the windowless side of the building. Confident he was out of view, he moved to the wall and pressed his ear against the cold brick. He held his breath for a moment, listening intently, but all he could hear was his own heartbeat.

Moving around to the back of the building, Alex found a row of small windows high up in the wall. They were just low enough for him to peer through them, so he took a chance, wiping away a line of grime with his finger. Leaning forward on his tip toes, he shielded his eyes and peered inside.

The garage was mostly empty. He could see random garbage strewn around and the pile of empty bottles and cigarette butts in one corner suggested that someone had taken shelter there in the past. The thick layer of dust and grime covering everything told Alex that whoever it had been, they hadn't been back in some time.

The only thing out of place in the derelict station was a lump in the middle of the floor covered by a tarp. It was too small to be a person and had a squarish shape.

Satisfied that the place was empty, Alex went back around to the front of the station and tried the main door. There were still several boards across the frame, but they had been nailed to the frame rather than the door itself. When Alex pushed the door, it swung open with a creak.

Ducking under the remaining boards, Alex stepped carefully over the threshold. Dust caked every surface, except for a clear path of footprints from the door to the tarp in the center of the garage area. From the size of the shoe prints in the dust, Alex could tell that two different men had entered once, then left the way they'd come.

There wasn't anything else to be deduced from the footprints, so Alex walked around the dust path, being careful not to disturb it, and made his way to the tarp. It was a heavy sheet of canvas, dark green in color, and looked relatively new and mostly free of dust. He doubted it had been there more than a day or two.

He took the compass linked to the finding rune out of his pocket. As he suspected, the needle pointed unwaveringly at the tarp. Putting the compass away, Alex picked up the corner of the heavy tarp and carefully lifted it. As he expected, it concealed three medium-sized boxes.

Taking the lid off the boxes, Alex found all of the merchandise missing from the warehouse thefts. From the look of it, the thieves hadn't even opened them.

"What did they steal this for?" he wondered aloud.

His first thought was that the thieves had been paid to steal these items by someone else, someone who instructed that they be left here. If that were true, however, why hadn't the buyer showed up to collect his prize?

Unless he's on his way now.

The thought inspired Alex to action. He'd have plenty of time to work though the motivations of the thieves later. Standing, he walked to the nearest wall and chalked the outline of a door. Once he had his vault open, he carried each of the boxes inside, then folded up the canvas tarp and added it to the pile.

That done, Alex took a moment to survey his surroundings, making sure he was unobserved, then shut himself inside the vault. Usually vault doors resembled the kind of door one might find on a bank vault, but when shut from the inside, the heavy steel door just vanished into the plain gray stone that made up the bounds of his extra-dimensional home.

Now that he was sure to be uninterrupted, Alex picked up two of the boxes and carried them to one of the workbenches along the wall near his drafting table. When he'd added the last to the pile, he grabbed the closest one and tore open the brown paper packaging. Inside he found the medical equipment intended for the Hans Fransson company. The other boxes yielded the remainder of the missing goods, including Mr. Su's alchemy herbs.

Something about the way he'd found all this still bothered Alex, but safe in his vault, he decided not to look a gift horse in the mouth. Picking up the box of herbs, he made his way back to his office and put in a call to Lung Chen.

He answered the phone in a language Alex assumed to be Chinese, but switched to English when he recognized Alex's voice.

"You said you would call today," Chen said. "I'm guessing you didn't have any luck."

"Don't be so quick to write me off," Alex chuckled, chiding the man gently. "I'm holding in my hand a box with a painting of a crane on the side with a bunch of herbs in it."

"That's it!" Chen exclaimed. "I'll tell my uncle, and we'll come over right away. How did you manage it?"

"I'll tell you the whole story when you get here," Alex said.

12

RESTITUTION

"Lieutenant McClory, please," Alex said once the Central Office switchboard operator came on. With Su and Lung on their way in to pick up their herbs, Alex had to deal with the rest of the recovered property. He could return them himself, of course, but if he let the detectives in charge of the various cases do it, he'd gain some goodwill with the robbery division.

A private detective could always use goodwill at the Central Office.

"McClory," the lieutenant's voice came on a moment later.

"This is Alex Lockerby," Alex began, but before he could continue, McClory cut him off.

"What is it, scribbler?" he growled. "I answered all your questions, and I don't have time to hold your hand, or your Nip friend's hand."

Alex stopped for a moment, unsure he'd heard the lieutenant right. Danny had faced a lot of prejudice coming up in the department, but he'd more than proved himself. He hadn't been made Lieutenant because Callahan liked him, he'd earned that. To hear this pompous ass of a lieutenant call Danny a Nip made Alex wish that his rune book included something that would let him reach through the phone and deck the man.

"Don't worry, Lieutenant," Alex said, forcing himself to relax. "I just needed to know who has these cases in case I turn up something."

"After you called, I transferred all three to the same detective," McClory said.

Of course you did, Alex thought. *After I pointed out the similarities to you.*

"They're being handled by Detective Arnold," he said, then he hung up on Alex.

Alex just sat there for a long moment, staring at the receiver in his hand. He had a good mind to skip Detective Arnold and just take all the stolen property back himself. It would be satisfying, but Alex's pragmatic side reasserted itself almost immediately. It was clear he wouldn't get anywhere with McClory, and he might need an in with the Robbery Division in the future. With a sigh, he pressed down the pin on top of the phone body that would disconnect the line, then let it go and dialed the Central Office again.

"This is Detective Arnold," a pleasant voice announced when the line connected.

Alex explained what happened and how he'd found the stolen property relating to Arnold's case.

"And you want me to deliver it back to the owners?" Arnold said, suspicion and disbelief equally evident in his voice.

"It is your case, isn't it?" Alex said in his friendly, helpful tone of voice. "I do want to go with you to Enzo Romero's place, though. I promised him I'd find his oils and I want him to know I made good."

"That's mighty considerate of you, Mr. Lockerby," Arnold said. "It never hurts to make a new friend, at least that's what my wife is always telling me. When are you available to go by Mr. Romero's shop? I bet he'll be very happy to get his oils back."

Arnold made it clear he knew exactly what Alex's ulterior motive was, but he didn't care. Alex was doing him a favor, he knew it, and he wasn't afraid of owing a private dick.

Alex decided he liked the man.

"How soon can you come by Empire Tower?" Alex asked, checking his pocketwatch.

"I've got a few things to wrap up here," Arnold said. "Is half an hour okay?"

"That'll do fine. I'll see you then."

Alex hung up, then went to his vault to get the stolen goods and carry them to the waiting room.

"Good day's work," Sherry said when he finished. "Are we getting paid for any of those?"

Alex shook his head and explained. Leslie would have berated him for not getting something, but she'd come to work when Alex couldn't afford his own cigarettes. Sherry just took the information to mean that she didn't need to produce a bill for the owners of the missing properties. In this era of hard times, Alex had done exceptionally well for himself.

Never forget that hard work pays off, but that blessings come from Heaven, Father Harry's voice echoed in his head. *That's why you have to work like success is in your hands, and pray like it's in God's.*

It was one of the many lessons the pious man had taught him in his youth. He felt a pang of guilt; it had been several months since he'd visited the Father's grave, and he made a mental note to remedy that. At least he hadn't missed a Mass in months. Father Harry would approve of that.

"I'm expecting Mr. Su and Mr. Lung soon," he said, offering Sherry a cigarette. "Then there's a Detective Arnold who will be by for that stuff," he indicated the three boxes on the floor behind her desk. "Once he gets here, I'm going out with him to deliver some of it."

"Are you going by Enzo Romero's shop?" she asked in a far too disinterested voice.

"You want me to buy you some perfume?" Alex joked.

Sherry's grin told him it hadn't been a joke to her.

"That's what I like about you, boss," she said, lighting her cigarette. "You know how to take care of your people."

Alex rolled his eyes, but promised to pick up something for her.

"Are you going to come back after that?" Sherry asked, a little too eagerly.

"Not to work," he said. "I'll swing by on my way upstairs, but I've got a date tonight and I need to talk to Dr. Bell before I go."

Sherry gave him a penetrating look, followed by a sly smile.

"Sorsha," she said. It wasn't a question.

"You *know* something?" he asked, putting emphasis on the word 'know.' With Sherry's gift she could be privy to all kinds of information, and Alex didn't want her holding out on him.

"Nothing," she said coyly, taking a drag off her cigarette. "But I've got eyes."

Before Alex could ask what that meant, Lung Chen opened the outer door and held it open for his uncle. They were just as mismatched a pair as they had been before, the younger Mr. Lung in a dark suit with a blue tie and his uncle in a traditional Chinese coat. Alex had to admit, Su Hi's coat was something to behold. It was basically red, but there were patterns of colored embroidery running down the front and over to the back depicting various figures and Chinese hieroglyphs.

As they came in, Alex walked behind Sherry's desk and picked up the painted box with the herbs inside. The box was very reminiscent of Mr. Su's coat.

"I believe these are yours," Alex said, handing the box to Su Hi.

The older man opened the box and his craggy face split into a broad grin. He said something very fast to his nephew, then bowed to Alex.

"My uncle thanks you for this," Chen translated. "He says that if you are ever in need of alchemy, you must let him serve you."

"I'll do that," Alex said with a grin.

"Please do," Chen said, speaking for himself now. "I'm sure you're familiar with western alchemy, but in China we do things a bit differently. Come by and you'll see."

Alex promised that he would, and then excused himself, turning the two men over to Sherry, who would settle their account. Just as he turned to head back to his office, the front door opened and a short man in a blue suit came in. Despite his lean build, the man had a round, pale face, made more so by the mop of red hair atop his head. He had an athletic build with a broad chest and narrow hips, and he moved with the grace Alex associated with physical competence. It was something usually seen with bouncers at nightclubs and mob enforcers.

Immediately Alex's eyes were drawn to the front of the man's coat, looking for the telltale bulge of a weapon. He couldn't see one, but professional gunmen tended to have their suits tailored specifically to hide such evidence.

Alex slipped his thumb inside his palm until it made contact with the flash ring on the ring finger of his left hand. As he did, the little man turned to close the door behind him, opening his coat a bit and revealing the butt of a revolver under his left arm.

With his back turned, Alex could rush him before he could draw his weapon, but as the man reached for the door Alex saw that the right elbow of his suit was shiny from wear.

"Detective Arnold," Alex said, stepping forward with his hand out. "I wasn't expecting you for at least another quarter hour."

The man looked confused for a moment, then accepted Alex's offered hand.

"I got finished quicker than I thought," he said. "Say, that's a pretty good trick, how did you know I was a detective?"

"You're carrying a gun on your left side, so you're right-handed," Alex explained. "And the elbow of your right sleeve is shiny from wear, meaning you spend a great deal of time at a desk."

Arnold's eyebrows went up at this and he nodded.

"You must be a good detective to notice things like that," he said with no trace of sarcasm or mockery. "A real-life Sherlock Holmes. My wife keeps telling me that I have to be more observant. She wants me to make Lieutenant."

"And you don't?"

"Nah," Arnold said with a wave of his hand. "Robbery lieutenants just sit back at Central and push papers around. I don't want that. Division Four is pretty boring as it is. Now if I could transfer to Homicide, that'd be much more interesting."

Alex smiled at that. Chasing burglars all the time didn't sound very exciting. He led Detective Arnold over to where he'd piled the remaining boxes of stolen property, only asking belatedly if Arnold had a car.

"Detectives have to have a car," he said, picking up two of the boxes and leaving the last for Alex. "If we don't have one, we get a patrolman to drive us around, but I don't like that. That's why I've got my own."

As Alex headed for the door following Detective Arnold, Sherry called out to him.

"Don't forget to pick up something for me!"

"Yes, mother," he called back. He'd never really understood the whole perfume thing, but the thought of something from Enzo's shop seemed to have Sherry very excited. As he rode the elevator down to the street, he thought about that. Sorsha was a woman who was literally in a class by herself, and he was sure she could buy whatever perfume she wanted, whenever she wanted. That said, she was still angry with him for taking so long to make this date and an exclusive, expensive peace offering might go a long way toward smoothing out the evening.

Detective Arnold's car turned out to be a Model A sedan that looked like it had been through the war. Once they had deposited the boxes in the back seat, Arnold cranked her up and they headed for the fashion district. As they drove, the engine popped and coughed as if it would die, but never quite managed it. To take his mind off the spluttering engine, Alex turned his attention to Detective Arnold, who had been regaling him with stories of cases he'd solved and the folksy wisdom of his wife, which he seemed to take very seriously.

"Here we are," he said at last, maneuvering his rattletrap of a vehicle to the curb in front of the building. He pulled up behind a gleaming Rolls Royce and when he killed the engine, it backfired with a bang that made several people on the sidewalk jump.

"Do you mind waiting a minute?" Detective Arnold asked as Alex reached for the door handle. He pointed at the corner of the block where a blue police call box hung on a power pole. "I just remembered that I didn't tell my Lieutenant where I was going. Let me check in before we go."

"I was planning on picking up something for a friend anyway," Alex said, indicating the shop on Romero's ground floor. "Grab the oils when you're done and meet me inside."

Arnold gave him a smile and a nod and headed up the street toward the corner. Alex got out of the car and headed for the shop. The word 'Romero's' was emblazoned above the door with absolutely nothing to explain what was sold inside. Alex guessed the Italian must be famous enough that no other words were needed. He started to understand Sherry's excitement and he imagined he could hear his wallet groaning in response.

Inside, he found the dazzling array of chrome and glass shelves with their display of colorful, elaborate bottles. There weren't any price tags on the items and as soon as Alex picked one up to look on the bottom, a pretty blonde salesgirl appeared at his elbow.

"Looking for something special?" she said. She had a midwestern accent with a slight rural twang, large blue eyes, and freckles on her nose.

"Just something for a friend," he said, giving her his sincere smile.

"Then I'd suggest these shelves over here," she said, leading Alex to one side. The bottles on the two shelves she indicated were smaller and not as decorative, but they were still impressive.

"These are twenty dollars," the girl said, indicating the rack on the left. "And these are forty."

Alex about dropped his hat. When he'd first hired Leslie, the rent on her apartment was only forty dollars a month. Alex could afford to buy one of these expensive bottles these days, but the frugality of former times still had a firm hold on his wallet. Paying that much for perfume seemed ridiculous.

"How good a friend are we talking about?" the girl asked.

"It's for my secretary," he said.

Immediately her smile went from helpful and sincere to conspiratorial.

"Oh," she said in a manner that spoke volumes. "And what kind of relationship are we talking about?"

Alex cleared his throat.

"Professional," he insisted.

The girl nodded her head, seeming to take his words at face value.

"Then I'd contain your attention to the left-hand shelf," she said, indicating the cheaper perfumes. If a twenty-dollar bottle of oil and water could be called cheap.

"Why?" he asked before realizing he probably didn't want the answer.

"These say that you're proud of your secretary's work and value her as an employee," the girl explained. "While these," she indicated the right-hand shelf, "might be taken to mean that you're interested in... more than a professional relationship."

Alex nodded his head, understanding.

"What do those say?" he asked, pointing back at the shelves of elaborate bottles where he'd been standing before.

The girl smirked.

"Those would be considered an indecent proposal," she said.

Alex reached up and took a dark blue bottle from the left-hand shelf. He had no idea what scent it contained, but he doubted it would matter, and the bottle's color matched Sherry's eyes.

"I'd better take this one then," he said.

Alex was back at his office in less than an hour, but it felt like a lot more time had passed. Enzo Romero had thanked him profusely and repeatedly, and the time seemed to crawl by at the same lackadaisical pace as the last horse he'd bet on.

"Boss?" Sherry said, catching sight of the large gift bag with the word *Romero's* stenciled on the side. The look on her face told him she hadn't really expected him to get her anything.

"How could I disappoint the best secretary in the world?" he said, reaching into the bag and pulling out the dark blue box wrapped with silver ribbon. It was, without a doubt, the fanciest gift Alex had ever given anyone.

Sherry set the elaborate box down on the desk with the same kind of reverence that demolition experts reserve for sweaty dynamite. It was so fancy she didn't even want to untie the ribbon.

Alex set the bag down on her desk with a thump and dropped his hat next to it. Sherry looked up from her prize and gave the bag a suspicious look.

"What else did you buy?" she asked, trying not to hide a smirk. "Something for your evening with Miss Kincaid?"

Alex rolled his eyes, then pulled a somewhat larger, sky blue box out of the bag. It had alternating stripes of dark and light blue around the sides and the whole thing was bound in a glittering silver ribbon. The name *Stardust* was printed in a blank oval on the front of the box and Sherry's eyes went wide when she read it.

"Wow," Sherry said. "She must really be mad for you to drop that kind of cash."

"It was a gift from Mr. Romero," Alex explained. "He gave a bottle of perfume to Detective Arnold, for his wife, and then asked me if I was married."

Sherry nodded sagely, understanding blooming across her face.

"You mentioned you were going out with New York's preeminent sorceress?" she guessed. "And he insisted on giving you something fancy?"

Alex chuckled.

"How'd you know?"

"That's Stardust," she said, nodding at the label on the light blue box. "You wouldn't know, of course, but it's Enzo Romero's new fragrance. There are ads for it in all the magazines, and absolutely no one can get it."

Alex considered that for a moment. He hadn't known about the perfume being hard to get, but it made sense. Enzo wanted Sorsha wearing his perfume. If she liked it, and kept wearing it, word would get out and that would be good for Enzo's bottom line.

"Think Sorsha will like it?" he asked, suddenly unsure. Sorsha was an amazingly attractive woman, but she had certain modern sensibilities, wearing men's clothes and such. Would she even wear a fancy perfume?

Sherry read the expression on his face and laughed.

"Don't worry about that," she said. "Just don't tell her Mr. Romero gave it to you."

Now it was Alex's turn to laugh.

"Don't worry about that," he repeated her admonition. "I was born at night, but not last night."

"Well, I'm going to take this home and open it there," Sherry said, standing and heading to the coat rack for her hat.

"And I need to see Dr. Bell before I meet Sorsha," Alex said, picking up the Romero's bag and putting on his grey fedora. "May I walk you out, Miss Knox?"

He offered her his arm and she took it.

"Why Mr. Lockerby, I thought you'd never ask."

13

THE RAINBOW ROOM

Iggy was out in the greenhouse tending his orchids when Alex came down the brownstone stairs a few minutes later. Normally at this hour the air would be thick with the smell of cooking, Iggy's other passion. Today, however, the kitchen was dark and empty of pots, pans, and utensils.

"I figured that since you were going out, I'd take the night off," Iggy answered Alex's questioning look. "I think I might even go down to the Lunch Box. I haven't seen Mary in quite a while."

"Say hi for me."

Alex pulled out one of the heavy oak chairs from the kitchen table and moved it near the open door. The greenhouse had been added to the back of the kitchen when Iggy bought the house, and it was really only big enough for a small growing table down each side and one at the end. A narrow aisle ran down the center with enough space between the end of the rightmost table and the back table for a small padded chair.

After tending the plants, Iggy would sit and read during the daylight hours, enjoying the heady fragrance of the flowers.

"I assume that since you have a date that you're not getting ready for, you have something you wish to discuss," Iggy said, closing his book and setting it aside.

Alex paused, attempting to order his thoughts on the day's events.

"How did it go with the blood rune?" Iggy asked, attempting to prod the discussion. "Were you able to remove the symbol painted on top?"

"Turns out someone did that for me," Alex said. "They went a bit overboard, though."

Alex explained about the demise of the shack where Katherine Biggs had lived and his suspicions. When he finished, Iggy just sat, stroking his mustache with his thumb.

"Iggy?" Alex asked when a minute had passed.

"I want to tell you to drop this case," he said with a sigh. "That much backlash...whatever your killer was doing, it must have been immensely powerful."

"And equally dangerous," Alex added.

Iggy nodded sagely.

"He's lucky the construct didn't explode."

"What was he trying to do?" Alex asked. "What would require that kind of power?"

"Nothing good," Iggy said, then he got up and made his way out of the greenhouse. "You need to be careful." He put a hand on Alex's shoulder. "The next time he kills, the crime scene could crumble at any time. If you're there when that happens..."

He didn't finish the thought, but he didn't have to. Iggy had used a temporal restoration rune on the remains of a chicken when he first explained the concept of backlash. Alex vividly remembered Iggy touching the crumbling bird with a pencil and watching the corruption swarm up the pencil until it threatened to engulf Iggy's hand. With something as small as a chicken, the backlash wouldn't have gone very far, but if Iggy had let it touch him, he might have lost a finger. Alex got the message — backlash wasn't something a runewright should take lightly.

"I've got to warn Danny," Alex said. "He and his men need to stay clear of any new crime scenes."

"You be careful too," Iggy said, squeezing Alex's shoulder hard. "I know you're going to want to figure out what the blood rune is, but if you feel the magic starting to give way, you get out of there. Understand?"

"Yes, sir," Alex said. If the blood rune was actually a rune, Alex would be able to feel it as its power began to unravel. "What if it's not a rune, though? What if it's something else?"

Iggy thought about that for a second, then released Alex's shoulder.

"Well, it's not alchemy, so that only leaves sorcery," he said. "Why don't you ask your date about it?" He pulled out his pocketwatch and flipped open the cover. "Speaking of which..."

"Right," Alex said. He still needed to shower and change into his tuxedo. The Rainbow Room didn't require black tie specifically, but he knew Sorsha would be dressed to the nines, and she'd be upset if he didn't make an effort.

"I'll do some reading in the Monograph," Iggy said as Alex turned to head back to the stairs. "Maybe there's something about backlash in there that we've missed."

Alex grunted noncommittally. He'd been through the Archimedean Monograph enough to know there wasn't anything in there Iggy had missed, but he needed all the help he could get, so better safe than sorry.

Alex arrived at the door to Sorsha's high-rent office promptly at six forty-five. That gave him plenty of time to catch a cab to the RCA building and still make their seven o'clock reservation. He needed to meet Sorsha at her office, since her home was floating over the East River, and so far no one had started a floater-based taxi service.

Since he had arranged to meet her there, he wasn't surprised to find the lights on in the front office of Kincaid Enterprises. When he opened the door, however, he found three men in identical dark suits waiting inside. Alex didn't have to be a detective to recognize them as Feds, probably part of Sorsha's FBI detail.

As Alex came in, the nearest man rose and stepped in front of him. He wasn't as tall as Alex, but the man had the kind of broad shoulders and heavy arms usually associated with wrestlers. From what Alex could see of the man's hands, they were thick and calloused, with stubby fingers and scars across the back. Clearly this man was used to fighting with his hands.

"And just who are you?" the brawler demanded.

Alex introduced himself, plastering a friendly smile on his face. He'd been to Sorsha's office before, even when FBI agents were present, but he'd never been stopped at the door. Still, it was after business hours, so maybe the brawler was just being careful.

"Stand down, Agent Hill," the voice of Agent Aissa Mendes came from off to Alex's left.

He turned to see the curly-haired Agent emerge from the back hallway. Mendes was a little taller than Sorsha, with olive skin, dark eyes and an exuberant attitude that Alex attributed to her youth. She was part of a pilot program that let women become FBI agents and she had a fierce desire to prove herself.

"Is this the guy?" Agent Hill asked, jerking his thick thumb at Alex.

Mendez gave Alex a smile and nodded.

"He's harmless."

"You and I both know that's not true," Agent Redhorn disagreed, coming through the door after his partner. "But he is the one Miss Kincaid is waiting for."

Redhorn was Mendes' trainer and the one who would decide whether or not she got the recommendation that would make her a full-fledged agent. The man had always been a paradox to Alex. Outwardly, he was the epitome of control. He spoke in a gruff but non-threatening voice, dressed in pressed shirts with creased trousers, and exuded the kind of professionalism that the Bureau would be proud of. That said, something about the man just made Alex wary, like if that façade of pleasant neutrality ever cracked, it would release a raging beast.

As the pair of them came into the office lobby, Alex noted that neither moved with their usual energetic stride. A quick look around at the other agents in the room confirmed that they all appeared to be on the brink of exhaustion.

"What's the good word, Redhorn?" Alex asked, deciding to fish a little for information.

"Mind your business," Redhorn retorted, slumping down onto one of the leather couches that surrounded the empty desk where Sorsha's receptionist normally sat.

Alex was about to push a little when the hall door opened again and Sorsha emerged. She was breathtaking in a cocktail dress that was so deeply purple that it was almost black, which clung to her modest curves exquisitely. A necklace of heavy gold links supported a teardrop-shaped ruby that was dark, like the dress, and she wore high heels to bring her up to a decent height next to Alex. Her makeup was as subtle as ever, though Alex noticed her eyebrows, which she drew in on account of her platinum blonde hair, had been done in a more approving style than usual. The only excess she wore was her usual burgundy lipstick, though in keeping with the outfit, she appeared to have darkened it as well. A wrap of some dark fur completed the ensemble and she stood for a moment, framed in the doorway so Alex could take her in.

"You look lovely this evening, Miss Kincaid," Alex said, deciding a formal address went better with her attire.

"You clean up well yourself," she shot back with a sultry half-smile.

She crossed the space and took Alex's arm, sweeping him along with her toward the door.

"What do you want us to do while you're out?" Redhorn asked, standing as Sorsha passed.

"Send everyone home. We'll pick it up in the morning," she said. "That includes you," Sorsha added. "Everyone spend time with your families, and get a good night's sleep."

Redhorn looked like he wanted to argue, but Sorsha kept moving, and he just nodded.

"What was all that about?" Alex asked as they rode the express elevator down to the street to catch a cab.

Sorsha's expression soured and she sighed.

"Nothing that concerns you," she said, patting him on the cheek as one might a child. "I'm sure you've got plenty to keep you busy without butting into my affairs."

Alex raised one eyebrow comically high as he regarded the sorceress with a smirk.

"Wow, it must be a very interesting case for you to be trying to get rid of me this early."

Sorsha smirked in return, then let out a genuine laugh.

"I wish it were," she said. "I'm just putting together a security detail for some Washington officials who are visiting."

That revelation was puzzling, to say the least. Sorsha was far too intelligent and savvy to have difficulty with something as simple as a security detail.

"It's not the security, it's all the government rules and red tape," she admitted when Alex protested. "Every time I think I've got things nailed down, the government types come up with some new wrinkle." She sighed and leaned against him. "It's exhausting."

"I hadn't heard that Roosevelt was coming to town," he half-joked.

Sorsha looked up at him, her smirk firmly back in place.

"He's not," she said. "And I told you to stop nosing in."

Alex was enjoying sparring with Sorsha, but at that moment the elevator chimed and the door opened. He led her across the vast lobby of the Chrysler Building and hailed a cab out front. Ten minutes later they were riding the elevator to the roof of the RCA Building where the famous Rainbow Room nightclub waited for them.

"Alex," a slender man in a silk tuxedo called when he and Sorsha entered the crowded waiting area. The man's name was Benedict Faulkner and Alex had helped him break up the impending marriage of his sister to a no-good lowlife. Benny had promised to get Alex into the exclusive club and as the Maitre D', he had that kind of pull.

"I have your table prepared," Benny said, smiling and nodding as he directed Alex and Sorsha into the massive open space that formed the nightclub. "Right this way."

The Rainbow Room had windows on three sides with a breathtaking view of the city. Tables radiated out from a circular dance floor in the center of the room, with the most exclusive tables being the ones along the windows. Occasionally the nightclub would have performers in to dance, sing, or both, and then the best tables were the ones near the dance-floor-turned-stage.

Blood Relation

Benny led them to a table in the right-side corner and held out the chair for Sorsha.

"I'm going to go find the cigarette girl," Alex said once Sorsha was seated. "Give me a minute."

Instead of looking for cigarettes, Alex headed to the restroom and quickly chalked a door on the back wall. He'd decided not to give Sorsha the perfume right away, so he left the decorative blue box from Romero's sitting on a little table he kept just inside his vault door. Moving quickly, he used a vault rune to open the door, reached in and grabbed the present, then shouldered the door closed. Relieved that he hadn't attracted any unwanted attention, Alex headed back to the corner table.

Sorsha was sitting with her back to him so she could look out at the city through the massive windows. In the distance, he could see the shining spire that was the Chrysler Building gleaming like a tower of fire in the last light of the setting sun.

"That's the strangest pack of cigarettes I've ever seen," she said as Alex placed the box on the table.

"I might have lied about the cigarettes," he admitted. "Open it."

She gave him a penetrating look, as if some part of her expected there to be a rubber snake inside, then picked up the box and deftly untied the silver ribbon. When she removed the lid from the box, however, her expression changed.

"Alex," she gasped, reaching in and removing a sky-blue bottle with a winged fairy of glass on top of the stopper. The detail was exquisite. The fairy's wings were made of different pieces of glass, making them appear to shimmer and change color depending on which way Sorsha turned it.

With a smile of delight, Sorsha tipped the bottle upside down, then righted it and removed the stopper. She touched the bottom of the stopper to her wrist, then breathed in the fragrance.

After a moment of reveling in the aroma, she replaced the fairy bottle in the box and put the lid back. When her eyes moved up to Alex's, he would have sworn they were sparkling with an inner light.

"I'm very impressed," she said. "You really went all out. First you found out my favorite table and arranged for it and this," she nodded at the box. "Stardust isn't supposed to be available for weeks."

She reached up and touched her neck with her perfumed wrist, then held out her hand to him.

"It's been a while since we danced," she said, "and I like this song."

Alex hadn't been aware that music was even playing for the last few minutes but the mention of it sent the sound rushing in to fill his awareness. He didn't know the song, but it was something he could dance to, so he took Sorsha's hand and led her to the floor.

When he took her in his arms, her eyes had gone from shining to smoldering.

"Tell me about your latest case," she said as he pulled her close.

Alex blinked. The change from dancing to work made him stumble for a second.

"You're being too adorable," Sorsha said, the smoldering look in her eyes dying back to an ember. "I think I'd better keep a clear head, and nothing focuses my mind like work."

Alex chuckled, but didn't argue. He told her about the warehouse thefts and how he'd recovered the stolen property.

"What I can't figure out is what the thieves really wanted," he concluded. "Obviously the thefts were cover for something else, but according to the foreman at each place, nothing else was taken."

"Maybe they wanted access to the warehouses themselves," Sorsha said. "A dry run for another theft."

It wasn't a bad idea, but Alex shook his head.

"If that's it, they made a mistake," he said. "At least two of the warehouses have changed the way their night watchmen patrol as a result of the thefts."

"You said that the thieves broke open a bunch of shipping crates looking for what they eventually stole," Sorsha observed. "Maybe what they were after was in those other crates."

"Then why didn't the owners report something stolen?"

Sorsha chewed her lip in a way that made Alex want to kiss her.

"Maybe they didn't need to steal anything," she guessed. "Maybe they just needed access to whatever it was."

Alex thought about that for a long minute, then slowly nodded.

"I need to find out what was in the other crates," he declared. "I bet those were mostly a diversion too. Only one crate in each warehouse held their intended target."

Now Sorsha nodded.

"They must have had to open the crate they wanted to get at what was inside, so they broke open others to hide it."

"And stole something easy to carry to make it look like that's what they were after all along," Alex concluded.

She beamed up at him and this time the urge to kiss her was almost overwhelming. Clearly she felt it too, because she let go of his arm and quickly stepped back.

"That's enough dancing for now," she said. "Let's order dinner."

Alex escorted her back to their table where they found a waiter and a bottle of champagne waiting for them.

"Compliments of the house," the man said, pouring the champagne into glasses for them. Since Sorsha had been to the Rainbow Room before, Alex let her order for him and the waiter withdrew. Once he was gone, Sorsha picked up the perfume box and made a motion as if she were setting it on an invisible shelf. When she withdrew her hand, the box vanished entirely.

"That always amazes me," Alex said. "How you make that look so easy."

Sorsha laughed.

"It is easy," she said, sipping her champagne. Right after, she made a face. "Must be domestic," she said, setting it aside.

Alex took a drink, but he'd never had champagne before, so it seemed okay to him.

"Do sorcerers have a problem with backlash?" he asked, remembering the vanishing box.

"That's an odd question," Sorsha said.

Alex explained about the blood rune and the crumbling crime scene.

"You had a case like that and you told me about your warehouse robbery instead?" she asked, her eyebrow quivering on the brink of her annoyed expression.

"Bloody crime scenes didn't seem like good dance conversation," he responded.

"Well, sorcerers don't really experience backlash," Sorsha said, a lazy smile spreading across her face. "With us, we either can do something, or we can't. There are stories of sorcerers who just disappear, and some say that it's because they tried some great magic that was beyond their power."

"So it's possible?" Alex asked. "Backlash, I mean."

Sorsha shrugged.

"I guess," she said, losing interest in the topic. "But I...I doubt it. It's like moving things in and out of a dimensional pocket," she said, reaching out and miming picking up the perfume box. "We just think about what we want to do and..."

Sorsha's jaw dropped open and she stared at her empty hand in shock.

"What is it?" Alex demanded. Sorsha's hand seemed to move and twist as he looked at it.

"I can't use my magic," she said at last. Her eyes snapped to his with a look of panic. "I can't use my magic."

It took Alex a moment to understand what she'd said and, now that he thought about it, his head seemed fuzzy. By the time he realized why, he figured he was almost too late.

He stood and offered Sorsha his hand.

"Pretend we're going dancing again," he hissed.

"But Alex," she said in a strangled voice, her eyes still wide as saucers.

"We've been drugged," he said, fighting to keep his balance. "We need to get out of here fast, now stand up and take my arm."

She wavered for a second, then seemed to regain some of her faculties. Grabbing his hand, she got to her feet.

"Follow my lead," he said, as he grabbed the champagne bottle out of the ice bath.

Walking slowly, Alex made his way along the back wall, then turned and headed toward the bar behind the dance floor. As he went, he spotted at least two men that seemed to be moving with them. Neither were remarkable and he was having trouble focusing on them, so he focused on leading Sorsha instead. She stumbled and he had to get a good grip under her arm to keep her upright.

"I can't teleport us away, if that's what you're thinking," Sorsha said, her speech slurred and halting.

As they drew even with the hall that led back to the kitchens, Alex turned, dragging Sorsha inside. At the end of the hallway on the left was the men's room and Alex ran for it, pulling Sorsha along with him.

"What are we doing in here?" she said with an amused laugh. She sounded drunk.

Alex pulled out his rune book and fumbled for a vault rune. Fortunately he'd been in such a hurry before that he'd left the doorway chalked on the back wall of the restroom.

"I'll check the kitchen," he heard someone say, then the outer door was pushed open and one of the men he'd noticed came in. He had his hand inside his coat, no doubt gripping a pistol, but when he saw Alex and Sorsha, he turned to call out to his companion.

Alex slammed the heavy champagne bottle into the man's jaw, and he crumpled to the floor.

"That was amazing," Sorsha purred, leaning heavily against him.

It took Alex a minute to find a vault rune. It would have gone faster had the book not been swimming from side to side in his hands.

"That won't work," Sorsha giggled as Alex licked the rune paper and stuck it to the wall. "You won't be able to use your magic."

"That's the...the great thing about runes," Alex managed to say as he reached for his lighter. "You only need magic...to write them."

He touched the flame of his squeeze lighter to the paper and it burst into flame. A moment later he felt the smooth metal of his vault door as he leaned against it, struggling to stay awake for just a few moments more.

14

HANGOVERS

Alex shivered, reaching out to grab his blanket but not finding it. For some reason, his side hurt and his jaw ached. He tried to wake up, but couldn't seem to manage it. The cold began to seep into him in earnest and he felt the first stages of real panic. He was asleep, and he knew he was asleep, but so far, he was powerless to change that.

The creeping cold finally managed to pull him up to a groggy awareness. Somewhere above him a light was shining brightly. Not with the warm, yellow color of sunlight, but with the more amber shade of a magelight. Squinting, he finally managed to focus his eyes, revealing a ceiling of plain gray stone with a simple magelight suspended from it. Since magelights received electricity through Barton's power projector, there weren't any wires on the ceiling, just the light.

Alex recognized the ceiling, of course. He'd dug it out of solid rock with his own hands. Rolling painfully onto his side, Alex found himself lying on the bare floor of his vault, in the aisle between his work area and his library.

The vault was naturally cool, like being underground, and the floor was cool to the touch. Alex had offset this by using rugs under his drafting table and the comfortable chair in his library. A boiler stone in the fake fireplace would heat the vault if it got too uncomfortable, but Alex only used it when he wanted to read in the library.

Shivering again, Alex pressed himself up onto his elbow, which took far more effort than it should have. He was about to try sitting up when a hand grabbed his shoulder and pulled him onto his back again.

"-n't go," Sorsha's voice slurred from his right. "S' cold."

She lay on the carpet just beyond the bare floor. She was curled up on her side with her arm now across Alex's chest. Her hair fell in a white-blond curtain, obscuring most of her face, and it shifted and moved with her breath.

"S' better," she mumbled, pulling herself close.

"Sorsha," Alex said, a bit more forcefully than he intended.

The sorceress' head shot up and she looked around in confusion.

"Alex?" she began, but as her eyes found his face, she blushed to the roots of her hair. "Wha-what happened?"

Alex forced himself to sit up over his body's protestations.

"This," he said, reaching for the heavy champagne bottle that lay a few feet away. "You didn't like it, remember?"

She looked confused, then nodded.

"Someone drugged it," she managed. "Kept me from using my magic."

Alex had a rush of memories involving dragging Sorsha into the men's lavatory at the Rainbow Room and managing to make it into his vault. The blank wall where his door would appear was only ten feet from where he lay, a mute testament to how close they'd both come to being grabbed by whoever drugged the champagne.

"You got us in here," Sorsha said, putting it together. "Good work. Now help me up."

Alex wasn't sure he could get up himself, but after a couple unsteady starts, he managed it. He pulled Sorsha to her feet, but she immediately lost her balance and he had to grab her to keep her from falling.

"Someone wanted you pretty badly," she said, leaning against him until she got her balance.

"I don't think so," Alex said, his head finally beginning to clear.

"Whatever they spiked our drinks with was designed to stop a sorcerer from using magic. That suggests they were after you."

"How did they know I'd be there? Did you tell your friend who you were bringing?"

"No," Alex admitted. "But somebody knew. Remember our table? You said it was your favorite, but I didn't know you had a favorite. I just told Benny to get a good table. What are the odds he chose your favorite without knowing it was you who was coming?"

"Makes sense," she said, pushing away from him and standing on her own.

"That government official that you're supposed to be protecting," Alex said. "Just how important is he?"

"You think this is about my security detail?"

Alex shrugged at that.

"Trying to grab a sorceress out of a crowded restaurant takes guts," he said. "It's the kind of thing desperate people would try."

"That still doesn't explain how they knew I'd be there," she said.

"I bet one of your FBI minders was worried about you going out," Alex guessed. "That Agent Hill fellow comes to mind. He didn't seem very happy about me being there, but maybe he was worried you were exposed. Maybe he called the Rainbow Room just to make sure I actually had a table there?"

Sorsha shrugged, then nodded.

"That might explain how the nightclub knew, but it would be one heck of a coincidence if whoever tried to grab us just happened to work at the Rainbow Room. How did they find out?"

"You've got a leak inside the FBI," Alex said. It was the only answer that made sense.

"I vetted everyone on my team personally," she said, her brows dropping into an angry scowl. She'd never gotten over being betrayed by Agent Davis.

"But the FBI keeps track of you," Alex pointed out. "That means there's some kind of schedule or calendar somewhere. I bet whoever verified your evening out, called it in to the official schedule in case they had to find you in a hurry. Whoever the bad guys are, they've got someone at the New York FBI branch with access to that calendar."

Sorsha scowled and tapped her teeth with her fingernail as she thought.

"That makes sense," she said, sounding unsure. "There are too many Agents in the field office here to figure out who the leak might be. I'll have to cut communication with them." She reached out and took the heavy champagne bottle from Alex, holding it up to the light.

"Good work bringing this," she said, sloshing the bottle from side to side. "There's still some champagne in here, enough for the FBI to test it. The main office in D.C.," she added hastily.

Alex looked around but couldn't find his hat, then he remembered that he'd checked it at the Rainbow Room, along with Sorsha's fur wrap. Sorsha seemed shorter than when they'd been dancing, and he noticed that her shoes were missing as well, lost during their flight from the nightclub table. He tried to picture what it must have looked like, him drawing Sorsha through the club and into the men's room only to vanish.

The tabloids are going to have a field day.

"Is that the time?" Sorsha asked, a note of alarm in her voice.

Alex followed her gaze to the clock on the library wall that read nine-fifteen.

"Yes."

"I need to call my team," Sorsha declared, taking a deep breath and standing a bit straighter. "Agent Redhorn is probably at your office as we speak, demanding to know where I am."

"Why would he go there instead of my apartment?" Alex asked. He was being deliberately provocative and Sorsha blushed slightly.

"He...uh," she stammered.

"This way," Alex said, heading over to his drafting table. When he reached it, he pressed the call key on the chrome intercom box.

"It's about time," Sherry chided him when her voice emerged from the little speaker. "I've had people calling for you all morning." She sounded stern, but then her voice became amused and conspiratorial. "Apparently you and Miss Kincaid made quite a scene last night."

Sorsha groaned and put her head in her hands.

"Is that...Is Miss Kincaid with you?" Sherry asked.

"Long story, but yes," Alex said.

"I've had a few calls looking for her as well. Mostly from that cute Agent Redhorn. He said if I heard from either of you, I was to have you call him right away."

"Thank you, Miss Knox," Sorsha said.

"When will you be coming in to work, boss?" Sherry asked without even sniggering.

Alex was about to answer that he'd be right out, but Sorsha spoke first.

"He'll be with you in five minutes," she said, then flipped the key that turned off the microphone.

Alex raised an eyebrow but Sorsha just picked up the telephone next to the intercom.

"Can I call my office from this?" she said.

"Yes," he said.

"While I do that, you need to wash up," she said, not making eye contact. "You have lipstick on your..." She waved her hand in his general direction. "Face."

Alex remembered how red Sorsha had blushed when she opened her eyes next to him. He could guess what he must look like, and he made his way through the brownstone door to his little bathroom. The one in his vault was closer, but it didn't have hot water.

When he stood in front of the mirror, he saw why Sorsha didn't want him going out into his office. Along his cheek and all around his mouth were the remnants of Sorsha's burgundy lipstick. Clearly she hadn't just kissed him, she'd been all over him. He started to laugh, but the sound died as he clenched his fists in sudden anger. He had no memory of those obviously passionate kisses thanks to his drink being drugged.

"When I find the bastard who did that, I'm going to loosen his teeth for him," he growled at his reflection.

Ten minutes later Alex and Sorsha emerged from the vault in Alex's office. Sorsha had tried to teleport to her home, but every time she tried, she developed a massive headache. The hangover from the drug was something else. Since that option was off the table, an FBI car was on its way to pick her up and bring her a spare pair of shoes. She decided to wait in Alex's office rather than risk being seen, shoeless, in his waiting room.

In the time it had taken Alex to clean up and change into one of his regular suits, she'd managed to repair her face and brush out her hair. Apparently she kept supplies for that in her dimensional pocket.

"I'm going to start carrying extra shoes and a change of clothes too," she said as she opened the door to Alex's office. "Tell Miss Knox to call in when the FBI detail gets here."

Alex promised that he would and started to turn, but Sorsha grabbed his arm. She stood up on tiptoes and placed a chaste kiss on his cheek.

"Thank you for the perfume," she said, then she stepped into the office and closed the door.

Whistling to himself, Alex made his way along the hall and emerged into the waiting room. Sherry sat, smirking behind her desk and Alex chuckled.

"It wasn't like that," he said.

"I'm sure," Sherry said, in a voice that clearly communicated that she didn't believe a word. "I've got several messages for you, but I think you'll want this one first." She handed him a note with a southside, outer ring address on it. "Danny wants you to meet him there, said you'd know what it's about."

Alex looked at the note in confusion for a moment, then swore.

"When did you get this?" he demanded.

Sherry looked taken aback for a moment, but rallied quickly.

"About half an hour ago," she said.

Alex opened the door to the back hall, then ran to his vault and retrieved his crime scene kit.

"If Danny calls, tell him I'm on my way," he said as he returned to the waiting room. "And tell him to stay away from the blood rune."

Sherry nodded and Alex headed out the door and down the hall to the elevator.

This time, Danny's address led Alex to a crumbling pile of an apartment building lined with dirty windows. Pieces of the façade had broken free of the eves and a litter of shattered brickwork lay piled against the side, making Alex look up nervously as he hurried along the sidewalk from where the taxi had dropped him.

The building had no lobby, just a bare stairwell that led upward through its three floors. A uniformed policeman on the main level pointed Alex up and toward the back.

"Second floor," he said as Alex mounted the stairs.

When Alex reached the second floor, he found Danny, two officers, and a detective he didn't know waiting in the hall. Several items seemed to have been removed from the apartment and were lined up against the wall in the hallway. If Alex had to guess, they were the ritual bric-a-brac that the killer had positioned around the body.

"Good," Alex said when he saw his friend. "I wanted to warn you keep away from the blood rune. No telling what would happen if it started collapsing with you inside the room."

Danny gave Alex a flat look.

"Gee, I never would have figured that out on my own," he said.

"Point taken," Alex chuckled.

"Can you tell if that thing's going to crumble away anytime soon?"

Alex looked in through the open door. The apartment appeared to be two rooms, a front room with the kitchen in it and the bedroom beyond a door on the far wall. This place was furnished better than Katherine Biggs' shack, but not by much. A table with two chairs stood near the stove, with a sink and a half-height ice box beyond. A broken-down sofa slumped against the opposite wall along with an end table supporting a radio.

In the center of the room, a hole had been cut through the plaster of the ceiling, revealing the beams that supported the floor above. Alex wasn't surprised to see the remains of a rope hanging down through the hole. Beneath the hole and rope was another blood rune. This one didn't appear to be the same as the previous one, which gave Alex pause until he realized that the only thing different was the obfuscating symbol on top. From what he could see, the geometric shape underneath looked like the same one as before.

Taking a deep breath, Alex stepped into the room. Remembering what happened the last time he'd touched a blood rune, he held his hand over it without making contact.

"It's degrading," he reported, feeling the magic ebb and flow, rising and falling like a heartbeat. He knew from experience that the beat would get faster and faster until it felt like one, long, continuous pulse. That was when the magic would fail and the backlash would set in.

"How long do we have?" Danny asked.

"At least a half hour, I would guess," Alex said. "Maybe longer but I can't be sure."

"What happens when the rune runs out?" Danny asked. "Will it eat the floor and the walls?"

Alex just shook his head. He'd never experienced a construct this unfocused before, so he had no frame of reference. He'd used magic that was powerful, probably much more powerful than whatever had been done here, but that magic was refined, controlled. This magic was just raw magical force being used as a blunt instrument. Which, now that he thought about it, explained the backlash.

"If you've got anything else to do in here, you'd better do it," Alex said.

"I thought you wanted to try to reveal the blood rune under all that mess," Danny said, indicating the bloody writing.

"I do, but it might accelerate the backlash," Alex explained. "Or just trigger it immediately."

Danny turned to the detective and the cops in the hall.

"All right, move in and look around," he said. "And make it fast."

One of the policeman knelt down and took a camera out of a thick leather bag on the floor. As he screwed a flash bulb into it, Danny grabbed his shoulder.

"If a picture of this crime scene shows up in tomorrow's paper, I'll have your hide," he growled.

"I develop my own film," the man said. "No paper is going to get these."

Danny just grunted as the man filed into the crime scene and began taking pictures.

"Nicely done," Alex complimented his friend.

Danny laughed humorlessly at that.

"I'm starting to understand why Callahan was angry all the time."

"So what's the story here?"

Danny pulled out his flip notebook and scanned it.

"This place is rented to two women, a Miss Linsey O'Day, that's our victim, and Miss Phoebe Green. Phoebe works nights, and when she came home, she found Linsey hanging from the rafters."

Alex could just imagine the shock and horror poor Phoebe must have gone through in that moment.

"Did Linsey have a sweetheart?" Alex asked. "Maybe someone she just started seeing?"

Danny shook his head.

"Nothing like that, but..." he hesitated, and Alex turned to regard him. "According to Miss Green, Linsey was a clerk at a general store a few blocks down. With business being slow, she wasn't getting as much work as she used to."

Alex nodded, seeing where this was going.

"And she supplemented her income by bringing gentleman callers home," he guessed.

Danny nodded, flipping the pad closed.

"With her roommate at work, she had the place to herself."

"That's the second prostitute," Alex observed. "It's starting to look like this sicko has a pattern."

"Lucky us," Danny said without any enthusiasm. "Do you have any idea what the papers are going to say about this? They'll start a panic."

"Maybe you should leak it yourself," Alex said. He hurried on when Danny gave him a dirty look. "Seriously, think about it. This guy appears to be targeting prostitutes. If you put the word out, the girls on the street might be more careful."

"Which will make it more difficult for our killer to hunt his victims," Danny said. "Then what happens if he decides to move to easier prey?"

Alex nodded. Danny had a point; as long as the killer stuck to ladies of the evening, outrage would be minimal. But if some nice housewife got killed, people would be calling for Danny's badge...and his head.

Blood Relation

Alex sensed a change in the steady background beat of the magic.

"The rune is degrading faster," he said. "Better pull your boys back." He glanced up at the ceiling, remembering that this was the second of three floors. "Did you evacuate the people upstairs?"

Danny nodded as he waved his men out.

"And the one below, and on either side."

As soon as Danny and the others were back in the hall, Alex pulled out his rune book and tore out one of the temporal restoration runes he'd written. Being careful not to touch the blood on the floor, Alex folded the rune and set it gently on the symbol covering up the rune.

Taking a deep breath, he squeezed his lighter to life and touched the flame to the paper. The rune flared to life in a burst of red and orange, sparking and popping like oil poured into a hot pan. Instantly the bloody mark on the floor began to fade, rising up off the floor in a red vapor.

Not waiting for it to finish, Alex took out his notepad and stood back in the doorway where he could get a good look at the floor. When the burning rune disappeared and the vapor finally cleared, Alex almost dropped his pencil.

"What is that?" Danny asked, looking at the construct that had been revealed.

It was definitely a construct. More than that, it was something Alex recognized.

"What does it mean?" Danny prodded when Alex didn't answer him.

"It means," Alex said, sketching quickly, "I have to catch a train upstate."

"To where?"

"Sing-Sing," Alex responded.

15

DEMONS

One long train ride later, Alex found himself at the gates of the Sing-Sing penitentiary. Danny had called ahead so no one gave him any trouble, and within a few minutes of arriving, he had been shown to a small, windowless visiting room.

"Someone will bring him out in a minute," a bored guard said before leaving Alex alone in the bleak little room. A rough wooden table sat in the middle of the space, and Alex took the chair on the far side so he could face the door. He wasn't too worried about the man he'd come to see, but Alex did put him in prison, so it never hurt to be careful.

As the minutes stretched on, Alex took out his notebook. But before he could review any more than the first page, the door opened and a prison guard who appeared to have no discernible neck brought in a large man with bushy black eyebrows.

"I'll be right outside the door," the no-necked man said, pushing his charge down into the chair opposite Alex. "Holler if this one makes trouble."

Alex waited until the guard withdrew before addressing the man across the table.

"Hello, Jimmy," he said.

"Alex Lockerby," Jimmy said with a chuckle. "I haven't seen you in a couple years. You didn't give up on me, did ya?"

Jimmy Cortez had been the floor manager for Andrew Barton's manufacturing facility on the West Side. He was a large, friendly fellow with olive skin, dark hair, and a Jersey accent you could cut with a knife. Alex had liked the man, right up 'til he discovered that Jimmy was the leader of a gang that kidnapped a young engineer and forced him to tunnel into the American History Museum in order to rob it.

None of that was why Alex was in a visiting room at Sing-Sing, however. That had to do with Jimmy's other profession as a runewright of the heretofore unknown glyph school. In the months after Jimmy's incarceration, Alex had visited him multiple times in an effort to learn about glyph runes. Each time Jimmy had told him, politely, to pound sand.

"You told me not to come back," Alex said with a shrug. "I know when I'm licked."

Jimmy gave Alex the once over and chuckled.

"Nice suit," he said. "Tailored. Not like those Sears catalogue numbers you used to wear. Looks like life's been good to you."

"I've kept busy," Alex said.

"So what brings you back to me?" Jimmy said, his curiosity finally getting the better of him. "You want to go another round about rune magic? I gotta warn you, I'm a bit rusty. They don't exactly let me use magic in here."

That was a joke. Runewrights could make basic runes with ink, mud, charcoal, or even blood. Fortunately, the kind of runes available without specialized inks were weak and basic. Not what a desperate convict would need to mount an escape.

Alex pulled out his notepad and flipped to the drawing he'd made in Katherine Biggs's apartment. It had the geometric shape he'd been able to see before, but inside, where runic text should be, was a Mayan glyph. It looked like a blocky snake's head, but with some kind of hood along the back, like a cobra. That was what brought Alex to Sing-Sing and Jimmy Cortez.

"I might have run into a friend of yours," he said, tossing the notepad onto the table.

Jimmy glanced at it, but didn't move to pick it up.

"What's that?" he asked with a sardonic smile.

"A glyph rune," Alex answered. "Found on the floor in a dead girl's apartment."

Jimmy's smile disappeared and he glanced at the notepad again. This time when he looked up at Alex, there was suspicion in his eyes.

"You think whoever wrote this," he pointed at the pad, "murdered the girl?"

Alex shook his head.

"I don't think it," he said. "I know it. The glyph was written using the dead girl's blood."

Jimmy reacted like he'd been slapped. His eyes went wide, then he seized the notepad and held it up into the light from the overhead bulb.

A moment later he cursed and threw the notepad back at Alex.

"El Diablo," he spat. "Incubo."

"I take it you've met," Alex said, leaning down to pick up the notepad from the floor.

"No," Jimmy said, seeming to get ahold of himself. "I never met that guy."

"But you know him," Alex pressed.

"Only stories," he said. "When my family came to America, they brought me and my grandmother. She had stories, tales of a guy who came to their village when she was a young girl. He was like you."

"Like me?" Alex protested.

"He wanted to learn about glyph runes too, but back then we weren't smart enough to keep our mouths shut."

"So your people taught this man?" Alex asked. "What was his name?"

Jimmy shook his head and leaned in, lowering his voice as if he were afraid of being overheard.

"My grandma just called him, El Diablo. The Devil."

"What happened to make her call him that?"

"He lived with the villagers for a while, but he wasn't what you would call a good guest. Apparently he was quite the charmer, and he didn't consider married women off limits."

"Ah," Alex said. "So the men ran him out of town?"

Jimmy shook his head.

"Some of the husbands challenged him, but he beat them, even killed a few."

"Didn't the women complain about that? I doubt many of them wanted their husbands dead over a dalliance."

"That's the strange part. They all seemed…unaffected. My grandmother said he'd cast some kind of spell on them."

Visions of the Legion and their mind control rune flashed through Alex's mind, and he kept his face deliberately blank.

"What happened then?" he asked, leaning forward over the table as well.

"Everything quieted down for a while, but the women who kept company with the stranger all began to get sick. Finally the village elder, my great grandfather, had enough and rallied the men to throw him out. When they got to his house, they found three of the women dead and that symbol," Jimmy pointed at the notebook in Alex's hand, "painted on the floor in blood."

Alex thought about that for a long moment. There was definitely some connection between this new killer and this El Diablo.

"That's some bedtime story," he said at last. "Why did your grandmother tell you that?"

"She saw what El Diablo did," Jimmy said, lowering his voice even more. "She said that one of the men from her village, an experienced hunter, tracked down El Diablo and shot him, but he didn't die. He got up and killed the hunter. My Grandma didn't believe he could be killed, so she warned me what to look for." Jimmy paused, looking from side to side as if he expected someone else to be in the little room with them. "I don't know what this is about, Alex, but do yourself a favor — drop it. Nothing good comes from dancing with the Devil."

Alex put the notepad back on the table and pointed to the decagon around the glyph.

"This looks like a geometric rune, but no rune I know uses this shape," he said. "Do you have any idea what this hooded snake glyph is?"

Jimmy didn't look, but he nodded.

"That's the feathered serpent," he said. "It's a Mayan symbol, but as far as I know it isn't used in glyphs."

"So I've got magic being made from two different schools, but with elements that neither school uses," Alex summarized.

"I'm serious, Alex," Jimmy said, leaning in again. "You're a decent guy. Let this one go."

Alex stared at him for a long moment before nodding.

"I'll see what I can do," he said.

Jimmy sat back and shrugged.

"Don't say I didn't warn ya," he said.

Alex tucked his notebook into his pocket, but then paused as a thought stuck him.

"Did your grandmother say what happened to that house? The one where the dead women were found?"

Jimmy looked shocked but then he laughed.

"She said that spirits came and took the bodies," he said. "That's how they knew the stranger was really El Diablo. Why did you ask that?"

"Because," Alex said, picking up his hat. "The apartment where I drew this," he held up the notebook. "It dissolved. Melted right out of the building it was in. Collapsed part of the roof and everything."

"Like I said, Alex," Jimmy said as Alex banged the door for the guard. "Let it go. You'll live longer."

Alex closed the heavy steel door to his vault and it melted away into the wall of gray stone leaving no sign that it had ever existed. The sight always gave him a chill, but he watched it anyway. The thought that if his other doors weren't open his vault would be his tomb was both thrilling and terrifying at the same time.

This time, however, Alex didn't give it a moment's thought. Resisting the urge to run, he forced himself to walk around his library, then turn down the hall toward the office door. It had taken half an hour for the authorities at Sing-Sing to process him out of the visitors

Blood Relation

area. He'd been so tempted to just open his vault in one of the many corridors, but that would have caused a lockdown, and led to the inevitable questions about how he'd managed it. He wished he'd brought Sorsha to explain him vanishing, but she had other problems. So he'd been forced to wait until he could get back to the train station and open his vault in a broom closet.

Taking out his pocketwatch, Alex opened the cover door leading to his office, revealing the back hallway. Passing by the door to his private office, Alex made his way to the end of the corridor and entered the waiting area.

"Afternoon boss," Sherry said. She wore her usual smile, but there was something about it that gave Alex pause, like she was privy to a joke Alex hadn't yet heard. A stack of paperwork was arranged in front of her with several folders stacked to the side, cases she thought Alex should take.

"No time," he said as she reached for one of the folders. "I'm on my way to see Dr. Bell, then I'll be out for an hour or so. Is there anything critical I need to know?"

"Mike is out of finding runes," she said.

Alex suppressed a curse, pulling out his red backed book. He only had two finding runes left, so he tore one out and put it on Sherry's desk.

"I'll try to write some more tonight," he said. "In the meantime, have him slow down."

She nodded, picking up the rune and dropping it into the center drawer of her desk. Before shutting the drawer, Sherry withdrew a thick envelope made of heavy paper.

"In case you were wondering, Miss Kincaid got off okay," she said, holding the envelope out to Alex. "She told me to give you this."

Alex was torn between his need to talk to Iggy and the desire to open the envelope, but he tucked the latter into the inside pocket of his suit jacket.

Business before pleasure.

It was one of Iggy's favorite maxims.

"Anything else?"

Sherry's subtle smirk returned, and she reached under one of her stacks and withdrew a folded newspaper, holding it out for Alex to take. It was a copy of *The Midnight Sun* and on the front page was a picture taken at The Rainbow Room. Alex could clearly see himself, striding along the back wall, dragging Sorsha behind him. The caption read, Runewright PI Chaperons Drunk Sorceress.

Alex closed his eyes and sighed. Sorsha would not be happy when she saw this.

He experienced a moment of panic as he checked the headline, but the story wasn't by Billy.

Thank God for small favors.

"Thanks," Alex said, sarcasm dripping from his voice. "I'll call in when I'm done with Dr. Bell."

With that, he turned and headed back toward the cover door to his vault. This time he walked across the great room that contained his work area and library, heading down the opposite hallway toward the brownstone door. Using his pocketwatch, he released the protection runes, passed into his bedroom, then headed downstairs.

"Iggy?" he called when he reached the ground floor.

"You're home early," Iggy said, opening the door to the vestibule. He wore his tweed suit and flat cap, taking the latter off as he came in. "I was just out at Linda's, helping with her brewing. She's got most of the recipes in her mother's book down pretty well, but I was able to show her a few refinements to her apparatus."

Linda Kellen was Andrea Kellen's daughter. Andrea had spent her life trying to find a cure for her daughter's polio. She'd succeeded, but at the literal cost of her own life. Linda had inherited her mother's shop, following in her footsteps.

"Helping?" Alex asked. Iggy was a runewright, not an alchemist, after all.

"You forget that I was trained to work closely with alchemists," he said, with a twinkle in his eyes. "I was around them most of my youth. I know a thing or two about the mechanics of the art."

"How's she doing?"

Iggy gave him a penetrating look.

"She's doing well. I daresay she's stepped into her mother's shoes quite well. You should go by and see her."

Alex nodded, but without much enthusiasm. Going by Andrea's shop always brought back memories, the kind Alex didn't want to deal with.

"So why are you home at this hour?" Iggy persisted, passing Alex and heading into the library. "I'm parched," he said, rolling up the cover to the liquor cabinet. "Care for a belt?"

"Sure," he said, following Iggy into the library. "I think I need one."

"I'd think you'd swear off after last night," Iggy said in an unamused voice. "Linda pointed out the story on you in the tabloids."

Alex quickly outlined the events of the previous evening while Iggy poured him some of his port.

"Sounds like Sorsha needs to be more careful," he said, handing Alex a glass. "If you hadn't been there, who knows what would have happened. I'm guessing, however," he went on, taking his usual seat by the window, "that your misadventure last evening isn't why you're here now."

"No," Alex said, walking to the hearth and leaning against the heavy mantle. He took a sip of the port and started in on the story of the blood rune and its connection to the glyph runewrights.

"So you thought the killer was one of James Cortez' friends, but he wants nothing to do with this," Iggy summed up. "Assuming your killer is the same man as this El Diablo Jimmy's grandmother knew."

"You and I both know that it is possible," Alex said. "And the details are almost exact. The question is, why is he here?"

Iggy nodded sagely, then drained his glass of port.

"I doubt he's here for the glyph runewrights," he said. "If this is the same man from before, he already has what he needs from them."

Alex nodded.

"The way I see it, there are three possibilities," Alex said. "One, it's a coincidence. Whoever this guy is, he's just passing through."

"And you know how I love the idea of coincidence," Iggy said.

"Possibility two, this is Jimmy's El Diablo and he's here for the same reason Jimmy and his pals came to town."

Iggy nodded, following Alex's train of thought.

"The so-called Entropy Stone."

Alex nodded, holding up three fingers.

"And last," he concluded. "Now that El Diablo has the knowledge of the glyph runewrights, he's here for the Monograph."

Iggy didn't answer. He sat back in his chair and stoked his mustache.

"I don't think your Devil could know about the Monograph," he said at last. "We've been careful and Sorsha told the government that the New York lead was a dead end."

"So that leaves coincidence or the Entropy Stone," Alex said. "Did you ever find out anything about it?"

Iggy shook his head. Since they first heard of the stone, Iggy had been digging into history books and writings on magic, looking for any mention of it.

"Not that or anything even remotely like it," he said. When Alex didn't respond, he looked up with suspicion in his eyes. "What are you thinking?"

Alex finished his port, then set the glass down on the mantle.

"The only thing I can think of is to try to pick up the trail of the Entropy Stone," he said.

"The museum," Iggy nodded, understanding. "I'd say you're setting yourself an impossible task. The last time we looked for it we came up empty. That said, when you're out of hot leads, all you can do is pick up a cold one."

Alex chuckled as he headed for the door.

"I have a feeling that, after all this, I'm going to need a cold one."

16

BREAD CRUMBS

The American Museum of Natural History was on the West Side, just across the street from Central Park. A skycrawler station ran right in front of the building, so Alex went through his vault, back to his office, then down to Empire Station to catch one. At this time of day, a cab would have taken at least half an hour to get uptown from his office. Even with all the stops it made, the skycrawler beat that by ten minutes.

Alex found Weldon Swain in the Curator's office in the museum's basement. Despite being in the basement, Swain's office looked like something out of a magazine. His desk wasn't as large as Alex's new one, but it was impressive. Made from mahogany, it glistened black like a patch of midnight. Along the walls were display cases with various little exhibits in them ranging from a display of Indian arrowheads to the skeleton of some aquatic animal. All were properly illuminated by overhead lights, and there wasn't a speck of dust anywhere.

"Alex," Swain said, rising to greet him and extending a friendly hand. He was average height and thin with an immaculate gray suit and a pencil mustache.

The last time Alex had come, he'd received a very different greeting. Swain had associated the disappearance of one of his mummies with Alex's search for the Entropy Stone. Alex had found the mummy, but when it turned out to be his secretary, literally returned from the dead, he couldn't exactly return her. Still, Alex had mended fences, making sure that Billy Tasker's story about the Dolly Anderson murder mentioned that the actual murder weapon was in the museum. The exhibit with the candlestick telephone had been a sensation ever since.

"You haven't found another mystery in one of my displays, have you?" Swain wondered as Alex shook his hand.

"Sorry," Alex said. "Actually, I wanted to ask about the Almiranta exhibit."

A cloud of confusion washed over Swain's face, then he chuckled.

"Oh, we haven't had that for over a year," he said. "It moved on to Chicago, then St. Louis, Salt Lake, Sacramento, and I believe it's in San Francisco now."

Alex frowned at that. He knew that Swain had struck a deal with Philip Leland, the man who'd found the treasure of the Almiranta, but he hadn't heard that anyone else had. That pretty much shot his theory that El Diablo had come to New York looking for the Entropy Stone. Still, Alex wasn't one to give up without a fight.

"Has anything unusual been happening around here in the last few weeks?"

Swain rolled his eyes.

"You have no idea," he said. "We got a new dinosaur skeleton from the dig site in Utah. People keep trying to sneak in to get a look while we're building it. Some of them are quite persistent."

As interesting as dinosaur skeletons were, Alex doubted they had anything to do with El Diablo, but he wasn't ready to surrender yet.

"Is there anything strange about the fossils?"

"No," Swain said. "But we've managed to find a complete Tyrannosaurus. When it's unveiled, it will be a sensation."

Alex had a vague memory of an enormous skull the museum had displayed for several years now, one with an impressive row of dagger-like teeth.

"Sounds like it," he admitted, trying to sound enthusiastic.

Foiled at every turn, Alex thanked the Curator and made his way back up to the main floor of the museum. A large crowd had gathered at the entrance to one of the halls where a security guard was keeping them back. As he passed, Alex could see a large drape covering something over a story tall. If that represented the height of the Tyrannosaurus skeleton, he was very glad they were extinct.

Before reaching the door, Alex stopped at the row of phone booths and dialed his office.

"Where are you?" Sherry asked once the line connected.

"The Museum," he said, "but it's a bust here. Is there anything I need to do before heading back?"

"Danny called," she said. "He wants an update on your trip to Sing-Sing, but he said to call when you get a chance."

"Anything else?"

"A man named Theodore Bell called for you," she reported. "He says he has some information for you and asked you to come by at your earliest convenience."

Alex brightened up at that. Any information on El Diablo would be welcome after the day he was having.

"Is he a relative of Dr. Bell's?" Sherry asked.

"No," Alex said. "He's an expert on magic and the occult, runs a shop on the East Side. I'll go see him on my way back."

Sherry wished him well and he hung up.

Since Theodore Bell's shop was north of the museum and on the other side of the park, Alex caught a cab to get there. The skycrawler ran that way, but he'd have to change cars twice to do it and that would make for a long trip.

As the cab made its way around Central Park, Alex reached for his rune book. He was running low on his important runes again and he wanted to take a quick inventory. When he put his hand in his pocket, however, he found the heavy envelope Sherry had given him.

Pulling it out, he found it to be made of a heavy paper that was slate gray in color. His name had been written across the face in what could only be called an elegant hand. In keeping with Sorsha's aesthetic, the ink was a deep, sapphire blue.

"She must have an entire stationary kit in that dimensional pocket of hers," he murmured as he carefully tore open the end of the envelope. The letter inside was on the same heavy, gray paper as the envelope and contained a short message in her flowing hand. As Alex opened it up to read it, he caught the aroma of flowers. Sniffing the paper, he confirmed that Sorsha had dabbed some of the perfume he'd given her on the paper.

Alex,

Thank you for last night. If you hadn't kept your head, that could have gotten bad. I'm sorry I dragged you into all this, though that's hardly a new experience for either of us.

I do regret our evening being ruined; it was lovely right up until we were drugged. I promise as soon as this protection detail is over, I will make it up to you. In the meantime, I want you to stay clear. I don't want to have to explain your presence to the government. The less they know about you the better.

Sincerely Yours,
Sorsha

"Sincerely yours," Alex read aloud. "How romantic."

He folded the letter and put it back in his pocket. Sorsha had promised to make the evening up to him, so at least he was out of her doghouse. As nice as that was, it didn't change the fact that someone had tried to kidnap her. She had an FBI detail and now they would be on the alert, but Alex felt like she would need his help too. Unfortunately Sorsha had thought of that, pointing out that the more he interacted with the FBI agents assigned to whatever security project she was working on, the more likely someone would mention him in an official report. That was something Alex simply didn't need. Already people were noticing that his skills far outstripped other runewrights. If someone in the government took notice, he might have to fake his death just like Iggy and go into hiding. Which would likely put an end to any relationship with Sorsha.

Alex shivered at the thought and pushed the whole affair from his mind. Sorsha was a big girl with lots of armed feds at her disposal and the mystic power of a Greek god — she'd be fine.

"Here you go, pal," the cabbie interrupted his thoughts as he came to a stop before the run-down bookshop.

Alex paid the man, along with a generous tip, and headed inside. It was just after five, but the shop showed no sign of closing. Alex reckoned that the kind of people who frequented occult bookstores were probably part of the after-hours crowd.

"Mr. Lockerby," Theodore Bell said as Alex entered. He was sitting in a chair next to the counter reading a thick book. The rest of the store was empty of customers.

"Call me Alex. Do you have something for me?"

"I think so," Theodore said, setting the book aside as he stood. "And if I'm to call you Alex, you must call me Theo."

"All right, Theo," Alex said with a smile.

Theo reached behind the counter and came out with a thin book with a dark cover.

"I thought I recognized some of the details of that crime," he said, paging through the book. "This was written a few years ago by Patrick Bastian, he's a dabbler in the weird and occult. Anyway, he chronicled the biggest stories at the time, and I think you'd do well to consider this one."

Theo handed the book to Alex, open to the spot where a new chapter began. The words across the top of the page read, *Terror in Paris*.

"It's the account of five murders that happened back in 'thirty-one," Theo continued as Alex skimmed the text. According to Bastian's account, five prostitutes had been murdered in a gruesome manner, trussed up like Christmas turkeys and drained of their blood. The perpetrator was never caught, but a French board of inquiry ruled that the killer must be a madman, since he painted the walls and floors of the dead girl's rooms with nonsense symbols.

As Alex read, he felt a chill run down his back. The details were sensationalized, probably by Patrick Bastion in an effort to sell more books, but the bones of the tale matched Danny's crime scenes exactly.

"Did anything ever come of this case?" Alex asked, skipping to the end.

"The French police tried for months to make progress," Theo said. "They called in magic experts, linguists, even a sorcerer, but no one could interpret the symbols or find the killer. The strangest thing is that the bodies and the symbols disappeared on their own and no one knew why. As far as Bastion knew, the French didn't even have a motive for the crimes. The women were from different parts of the city with different backgrounds. The only thing that united them was their profession."

"Prostitutes," Alex said.

"Just so. Some of the French newspapers were calling it the return of Jack the Ripper," Theo said. "It caused quite a panic, according to Bastion. He says that the story showed up in newspapers the world over."

Alex shut the little book and held it up.

"How much for this?" he asked.

Theo looked befuddled for a moment, then turned the book over in Alex's hands. A paper label on the back read forty cents, and Alex dug some change out of his pocket.

"I appreciate you finding this," he said, handing over the change. "If you think of anything else, call my office."

"I did have a question about magic, if you don't mind," Theo said, looking a bit apologetic.

Alex was in a good mood, thanks to the pudgy man's find, so he dropped the little book in his outside jacket pocket and smiled.

"Shoot," he said.

"I was wondering what it takes to be a really proficient runewright?" Theo asked.

The question caught Alex flat-footed and he stumbled for an answer.

"I mean, I've read extensively about rune magic," Theo went on. "But I've never been able to determine what makes one runewright good at the craft and another incompetent. With sorcerers they seem to be limited by their own native intelligence and imagination, but what makes one runewright better than another?"

Alex had to think about that for a moment.

"Well," he said, struggling to put his thoughts into words. "In the first place, a runewright has to be able to channel magic in order to be a runewright."

"So, some people just can't channel as much magic as others," Theo said, nodding as if he'd expected that answer.

"No," Alex said, rubbing his chin. As far as he knew channeling was just something a runewright did, a byproduct of the rune writing process. "I think it's more how good they are at writing the actual runes. Basic runes are simple, easy to write, where others are extremely complex, they can take days or even weeks to finish."

Theo looked perplexed at that.

"But if that's the case," he said, "why don't bad runewrights just get better?"

Alex shrugged.

"As far as I know, runewrights do get better, right up until they hit constructs that are beyond them. I don't know why it's that way, but that's the way it works."

Theo's eyebrows knit together, and he nodded.

"I suppose there must be some limitation that just isn't obvious," he muttered, more to himself than to Alex.

"Well, if I think of anything, I'll let you know," Alex said, clapping the shorter man on the shoulder.

Theo thanked him, and Alex put on his hat and headed back out into the evening air. Since the brownstone was closer to Theo's shop than Alex's office, he was tempted to just head there and call it a night. He still needed to check with Sherry and see if she found out anything from the burgled warehouses, so instead of just grabbing a cab, Alex crossed the street and made his way to a five and dime at the end of the block. The neon nickel hanging over the door buzzed as he passed under it and went inside. This shop was a bit better kept than Theo's bookstore, but not by much. One look at the grease-laden griddle and crumb-covered cutting board behind the lunch counter made Alex decide that he wouldn't eat in this establishment if his life depended on it.

The bored-looking man behind the lunch counter wore a stained, yellowed apron and he didn't even look up from the magazine he was reading when Alex came in. Just as well, because Alex was in no mood to exchange pleasantries. A wooden phone booth stood against the wall on the far side of the lunch counter, and Alex stepped inside and shut the door behind him. Dropping a nickel into the slot, he dialed his office number.

"Hi boss," Sherry said before he even spoke. Her gift of foresight didn't work all the time, but when it did, Sherry could come across as a bit unnerving. "How did it go with Mr. Bell?"

"I think he may have given me a solid lead," Alex reported. "I need you to run over to the library archives in the morning and see if there are any mentions of a string of murders in Paris in nineteen thirty-one that match our voodoo killer."

There was a pause on the line while Sherry wrote the information down.

"I'm still not through calling those warehouses for you," she said. "Which of these do you want me to focus on?"

"Take the library," Alex said. "Just leave what you've got on the warehouse thefts on my desk, and I'll finish calling them in the morning. If there's nothing else, I'm going to head home and write more runes for Mike."

"I do have a message for you."

Alex resisted the urge to sigh.

"Let me have it," he said, pulling his notebook from his shirt pocket.

"Detective Nicholson called," Sherry reported. "He said that he needs your help at Alice Cartwright's office as soon as you can make it."

Alex did sigh this time.

"Did he leave an address?" Alex asked. The last time he'd spoken to Nicholson, the police still hadn't found Alice's office.

Sherry rattled off the address of a relatively new inner ring office building and Alex wrote it in his book.

"Don't forget those runes for Mike," she admonished when he was done. "I already had to turn away two cases."

Alex promised that he'd remember, then hung up and dropped his notebook back into his shirt pocket. Exiting the phone booth, he headed back through the five and dime to the door. A light rain had begun to fall while he was inside, and he hesitated in the doorway for a moment.

Flipping his rune book open, Alex found he still had three minor barrier runes.

"Thank God for small favors," he muttered, tearing the rune free and sticking it to the brim of his hat. Taking out a cigarette, he lit it, then touched the lighter's flame to the flash paper containing the barrier rune. He felt a prickly sensation wash over him from his head down to his feet as the magic activated, then he took a drag from his cigarette and headed out onto the rainy sidewalk.

17

NUMBERS

What had started as a gentle rain turned into a full-fledged downpour by the time Alex climbed out of a cab in front of a very modern white brick and glass office building. His barrier rune was still in place, causing the rain to avoid him as he crossed the sidewalk toward the building's extended portico. The image of the building blurred as the torrent flowed around the invisible shield as if it were being bent by a magnetic field.

He expected to find an officer in the lobby, but there wasn't one. He knew Alice's office was on the eighth floor, and fortunately the building had an elevator.

"It's about time you showed up," Nicholson growled when Alex stepped off the elevator. He was standing outside an open doorway just down the hall, his suit rumpled and his hair in need of combing. Both states were common to the man, but the sour expression was not, and it gave Nicholson the look of a man having a very bad day.

"Came as soon as I could, Detective," Alex said. "What is it you wanted me to look at?"

"Not much anymore," the Detective said, motioning for Alex to follow. As Alex approached the door, he saw the name Alice Cartwright engraved on a brass plate next to the frame. No company name or type of services offered were listed, just Alice's name. That probably meant that her work was either by referral only or exclusively for the government.

The inside of Alice's office was neat and modern. A row of six blackboards formed a semicircle against the left-hand wall with an angled drafting table like Alex used opposite. The desk's adjustable top had been lowered so that it was inclined but not enough to obscure the blackboards. A short filing cabinet stood next to the table, reminding Alex of the rollaway cabinet he had next to his own work desk.

There weren't any chairs for visitors in the space, just a sturdy chair behind the desk and a metal stool next to the blackboards. Clearly Alice was used to working alone and she didn't receive regular visitors here. Based on how hot under the collar Harcourt, the government man, was to locate his missing files, Alex wondered if Alice's lack of accommodations for visitors was due to being a private person, or for security reasons.

The thought of Harcourt stopped Alex's musings and he took a hard look at the room. All six of the blackboards were empty but not clean. They'd been erased, but not washed. Also, the little file cabinet next to the drafting table was sitting askew. Alex could see the impression in the area rug where it had obviously stood for some time.

Putting those things together, he understood Detective Nicholson's frustration.

"I see Harcourt's already been here," Alex said. "How much did he take?"

"Everything," Nicholson fumed. "He took all the files here and the ones in the back, his goons erased all the boards, and he even took the damn pencils from the desk."

Alex nodded, looking around. Alice Cartwright hadn't been killed here, and it seemed like whoever killed her either didn't know about this office, or didn't care. It wasn't very likely that any evidence of the killer would be here, but his professionalism would not let him leave it at that.

"Well you got me out here," he said. "The least I can do is take a look around." He nodded in the direction of the hallway that led into the back. "What's back there?"

"Another office," Nicholson said. "There's a desk and a row of now-empty filing cabinets. Seems like that's where she did her bookkeeping."

"Anything else?"

"There's another office, but all that's in there is a table with a hotplate, a coffee pot, and a cot."

"In case she worked late," Alex said with a nod. There were many times he'd slept on one of the couches in his waiting room at his old office, at least until he put a bedroom in his vault.

"Where are your men?" Alex asked, just noticing the lack of uniformed officers.

"That jackanapes Harcourt conscripted them to help his men clean this place out," Nicholson fumed.

"Of course he did," Alex said. "Well, I don't need them here to have a look around."

He started on the left side, walking around the blackboards, but Harcourt's men had been thorough and erased the back sides as well. The desk and the little filing cabinet were empty, but Alex checked inside and under their drawers just be sure nothing had been hidden there.

Moving on to the back rooms, Alex found them similarly cleaned out. Only the furniture remained. The offices themselves were much more luxurious than the furniture, with gilded crown molding and wainscoting with chair rail along the walls. Alice's furniture was brutal in its utilitarianism, no frills or decoration, just solid, well-built efficiency. Even the cot in the spare room was just that, a wood and canvas cot like one might find in a military surplus sale. It revealed a great deal about the woman, but precious little about her killer.

"Anything?" Nicholson asked when Alex emerged back into the front room.

"No," he admitted. "But I'm not licked yet." Alex pulled out his rune book and flipped to the back where he kept runes he didn't use often, but that were good to keep on hand. There were only three of the ones he wanted, so he tore them out, then went to the empty blackboards. The construct he had in mind wasn't powerful enough for one rune to extend over all the boards, but with three he figured he could make do.

"What are you doing?" Nicholson asked as Alex pulled the second blackboard over to touch the first.

"Do you have a photographer?" Alex asked, repeating the process with the next two boards.

"Sure," Nicholson said. "But not 'til my men get back from helping that weasel Harcourt."

Alex pulled the last two boards together, then licked the first rune and stuck it to the pair. Moving down the line he stuck the others to the other groups of boards, then picked up two of the chalk-filled erasers. Giving Nicholson a mischievous grin, Alex took out his lighter, ignited the rune paper, and then began clapping the erasers together.

Initially a cloud of chalk dust billowed out from Alex, but as the magic took hold the dust began to drift toward the board, drawn to the places where there had been writing before Harcourt had erased it.

"Revelation rune," Alex explained, moving on to the next board. "I usually use it to show pencil impressions on paper," he explained.

"Neat trick," Nicholson said as incomprehensible equations filled in on the boards. When Alex was done, all six boards had been restored to the way they were.

"If Harcourt had washed the boards, it wouldn't have worked," Alex admitted. "Have your photographer get pictures of this and then erase it again. You might need whatever this is."

Nicholson nodded approvingly.

"It's not nothing," he admitted, "but if that's all you can do, I think I'm still at square one."

Alex pulled out his chalk and held it up.

"Have a little faith, Detective," he said, heading out into the hall. Alex hadn't wanted to use a vault rune since he was running low on them, but he needed his crime scene kit, and it was currently in the vault. He drew a door on the hallway wall, then burned a rune to expose the door and its brass keyhole.

"That's the damnedest thing," Nicholson said as Alex pushed the vault door inward. His old doors used to open out, like every other vault Alex had ever seen. The way the construct was put together made it that way. The problem Alex had was what to do with the massive steel door when he wanted a more permanent opening. It was much easier to hide the door if he could open it inward, rather than outward. He'd played around with it for a solid month, but eventually he'd figured out how to rewrite the construct so the door opened inward. It made it much less obtrusive to open his vault in public spaces, like the hallway, and it made it possible for him to use the external cover doors that, once magically secured to a wall, protected the open vault from being entered by anyone but him.

Alex had taken to keeping his kit on a tall table that he'd put next to the spot where the vault door appeared. This way he didn't have to open his vault all the way to reach in and get it. That kept prying eyes, like those of Detective Nicholson, from seeing into his vault.

Once Alex had his kit, he pulled the vault door closed and headed back into Alice's office. Nicholson just watched as Alex took out his multi lamp and oculus. Alex started with ghostlight. He didn't think anything in Alice's life was magical, but with her files and other things removed from the office, any magic residue would have already begun to fade.

"What's that supposed to do?" Nicholson asked as Alex swept the room with the faint green light emanating from the lamp. Alex explained about ghostlight as he went. When he finished with the back offices, he even checked the little bathroom, but to no avail.

Undaunted, he changed to silverlight. As expected, the blackboards and writing desks were covered in fingerprints, but nothing that indicated anything other than regular use. There was no blood or other fluids anywhere to be seen.

He moved on to the spare room and checked the cot for fluids. If Alice had a lover, her death would make more sense. Crimes of passion were the stock in trade of detectives investigating the murders of young women. Again he was disappointed. The only evidence of fluid his lamp revealed was a stain on the rug where Alice had spilled what Alex guessed was coffee.

Lastly, Alex moved to the office. He swept the desk and the filing cabinets without success. He was about to give up when a group of fingerprints on the wainscoting caught his eye. It looked like Alice was in the habit of touching the wall in one place. That wasn't terribly unusual; if her desk had been by the wall for any length of time, she might have touched the wall when closing drawers or getting up out of her chair. The strange thing was that the fingerprints were all over one board, but completely absent from its neighbor. When Alex knelt down for a closer look, he found another cluster of fingerprints diagonally down from the first set. It was as if someone had pulled out some of the boards, turned them upside down, then put them back.

"Detective," Alex said, taking out his chalk and drawing lines on the suspect boards. "I think I've got something."

Alex took off his oculus as Nicholson arrived.

"I think there's a removable panel here," Alex said. "Do you have a jackknife?"

Nicholson nodded and produced a folding knife from his pocket. Alex opened the blade and carefully worked it in between the two boards where the fingerprints vanished. After a few moments of gently wiggling the blade, a section of the paneling about a foot and a half wide popped out. Alex set the knife aside and tugged the panel free from the wall. Behind it was a cavity that held a small safe, much like the one hiding behind a similar panel in Alex's vault.

"I'll be," Nicholson said. "That was hidden really well. I'll have to get someone up here to drill it out before Harcourt shows up again."

"I don't think so," Alex said, pointing to the large dial in the center of the door.

"You know the combination?" Nicholson asked.

Alex nodded.

"And unless I miss my guess, so do you."

Nicholson looked startled, then nodded.

"Nineteen, seven, and eleven," he said. "The numbers Alice wrote in her own blood."

"Told you it sounded like the combination to a safe," Alex said with a self-satisfied grin. He gave the dial on the safe a spin, then dialed it around to nineteen, then back to seven, and finally to eleven. Taking hold of the locking handle, Alex twisted it and the safe door popped open.

"So what does a woman like Alice Cartwright keep in a safe?" Nicholson mused as Alex peered inside.

"Looks like about a thousand dollars in cash," Alex said, pulling out a medium sized stack of wrapped bills and handing them to Nicholson. "Here's a couple of files, a stack of letters, and a box of..." Alex opened the little box. "Looks like receipts."

Checking to make sure he hadn't missed anything, Alex carried the files, letters, and the box to the desk.

"You take these," Alex said, passing the folders to Nicholson. "I'll take a look at the letters."

Nicholson sat in the single chair in front of the desk while Alex sat behind it. The letters had been folded in thirds, as they would be if they'd arrived in envelopes, and a strand of orange ribbon was tied around them, keeping them together. Removing the ribbon, Alex picked up the first letter and began to read.

Or rather he would have, if the letters had been written in English.

At first he thought the language was German, but while the letters were the standard alphabet, they weren't in any order that made sense. He quickly moved to the next and found it similarly unintelligible.

"I hope you're having better luck than I am," Nicholson said. "This," he held up one of the folders, "is Alice Cartwright's will. This one," he picked up another, "is the lease agreement for this office. One for her apartment, one with her bank records, safe deposit box information." He dropped the folders back on the desk. "Nothing that gives any clue to why she might have been murdered. What have you got?"

Alex just shook his head and handed over the letter he'd been looking at.

"I have no idea," he said.

"What's this?" Nicholson said after giving the letter the once over.

"It's a code of some kind," Alex said, picking up another letter.

"Who writes to someone in code?"

"Someone who doesn't want their letters intercepted," Alex said.

Nicholson sat up straight at that.

"Do you think she was a spy?" he asked, holding up the letter Alex had given him. "And these are her orders from whatever government she worked for?"

"I doubt it," Alex said. "I don't know much about spies, but I doubt they're in the habit of keeping coded messages that could prove their guilt. Secondly, these letters all have names on the bottom."

Alex pointed to the bottom of the note where four letters stood alone on the last line.

"That's someone's name?" Nicholson asked.

"Probably," Alex said, picking up several more of the notes. "There are four random letters on the bottom of each of these."

Nicholson looked at his letter, then at the ones Alex was holding up.

"They're all different though."

"I'm guessing the code changes with each letter," Alex said. "What it does tell us, though, is that someone with a four-letter name was writing to Alice." He dropped the letters and picked up the orange ribbon, holding it up. "And she not only kept these letters, but wrapped them up like a keepsake."

"She had a beau," Nicholson said. "One that didn't want anyone to find out that he was writing to her."

"Could be married," Alex guessed. "Or maybe the code is some kind of math puzzle, something Miss Cartwright would enjoy."

"Beats me," Nicholson said, tossing his letter on the pile. "So far we haven't been able to find any men in Miss Cartwright's life."

He was about to continue when there was a knock at the office door.

"Alice?" a man's voice called out. "Is everything okay?"

Alex and Detective Nicholson exchanged glances, then they both rose and headed for the front room. A slender, good-looking man with short brown hair and an expensive suit stood in the open door with a look of concern on his face.

"Who are you?" he demanded. "Where is Miss Cartwright?"

"I'll ask the questions," Nicholson said, flashing his badge. "Just who might you be?"

The well-dressed man hesitated a moment, then he got hold of himself.

"My name is Matthew Crabtree," he said.

"Matt," Alex whispered. "Four letters."

"What are you doing here, Mr. Crabtree?" Nicholson asked.

"My office is down the hall," Crabtree said. "I saw Alice...I mean Miss Cartwright's door open and thought I'd better look in on her. She never leaves her door open. Now," he said, drawing himself up to his full height. "I must insist you tell me where Miss Cartwright is."

Alex exchanged a meaningful glance with Nicholson. If Crabtree murdered Alice Cartwright, he was a damn good actor. His concern for her welfare seemed genuine.

"I'm sorry to inform you, but Alice Cartwright was murdered in her home four days ago," Nicholson said.

Crabtree seemed to crumple at the news, and he sagged against the doorframe.

"That's terrible," he said, recovering himself quickly. "What happened?"

"Right now, it looks like a crime of passion," Alex said. "Did Miss Cartwright have a romantic interest? Maybe someone she was close with?"

Crabtree shook his head.

"As far as I could tell, Alice...Miss Cartwright didn't have any interests outside of her work. She loved math. Well, math and pictures, she went to the theater at least once a week."

"Did you ever ask Miss Cartwright out to a picture?" Detective Nicholson asked.

Crabtree nodded.

"Once," he said. "And once to hear a lecture on the life of Lewis Carroll. She turned me down both times."

"Lewis Carroll the author?" Alex asked.

"Yes," Crabtree said. "He was also a mathematician. I thought Miss Cartwright might find it interesting."

"Do you work with math, Mr. Crabtree?" Alex said.

The man laughed and nodded.

"I do, but not like Miss Cartwright," he explained. "I only do boring math. I'm an accountant."

"Did you ever see anyone come in or out of this office?" Nicholson asked. "Other than Miss Cartwright, I mean."

Crabtree thought about that for a minute then shook his head.

"Never."

Nicholson thanked the man and sent him on his way.

"What do you think?" the Detective asked once Crabtree had boarded the elevator outside.

"I think Alice Cartwright had a lover," Alex said. "Not Crabtree. He seemed genuinely shocked to hear of her death, but someone. Someone well versed in mathematics and codes."

"So how do we find this person?"

"Find a codebreaker," Alex said with a shrug. "The sooner you crack that code, the sooner you'll know the name of the four-lettered man."

Nicholson chuckled darkly at that.

"There are a lot of men with four-lettered names, Alex," Nicholson said. "Like Alex, for example."

"I have an alibi," Alex said with a grin.

"And what's that?"

"I hate math."

18

LORE

Just like the night before, Alex slept in his vault. This time he woke up in his spare bed, but he felt even less rested than when he'd been unconscious on the floor in a drug-laden stupor. After finishing up with Detective Nicholson, he'd returned to his office and spent the rest of the evening writing runes. He'd managed to replace many of his important ones, but there were still a few holes in his book. At least he had a dozen finding runes for Mike.

By the time Alex had finished, it was well after midnight and he was exhausted. He'd barely made it to his vault bed, to say nothing of returning to the brownstone or his apartment.

Since there was no bedside clock in the vault bedroom, Alex fumbled for his pocketwatch, forcing his eyes to focus on it once he managed to push in the crown and flip the cover open. Predictably, he'd overslept, but it wasn't yet nine o'clock, so he could still make it into the office at a decent hour.

Groaning, he rolled out of bed and carried his clothes through to his brownstone bedroom. After a quick shower and a shave, Alex put on a clean shirt, his dark suit, and headed downstairs.

"Another late night," Iggy said as he sat at the table reading the morning paper. It was a statement rather than a question.

"Business is good," Alex said, heading for the coffee pot. "I'm constantly out of runes and Mike is taking lost pet cases like he's getting paid by the rune."

"Why didn't you say something?" Iggy said, setting the paper aside. "I can take an hour or two during the day to help out."

"I appreciate that," Alex said, sitting down opposite his mentor and blowing on his coffee. "But at some point, I've got to be able to supply myself. Besides, aren't you getting a life transference rune ready for tonight?"

"Tosh," Iggy said with a dismissive gesture. "I've had that ready for a week now, and I've already made arrangements with Silas Green."

Silas was the owner of the slaughterhouse where Alex and Iggy purchased the pigs they used for life transference.

Alex shrugged and sipped his coffee.

"Was there something else you wanted to discuss?" Iggy went on. "You're late for work and you haven't asked for a plate of eggs, so I deduce you have a question."

"Are there eggs?" Alex asked, looking around.

Iggy chuckled and rose, moving to the stove to turn on the gas.

"A few fried eggs will take about two minutes once the iron heats up," he said, taking three eggs from the icebox. "So let's hear your question."

Alex hesitated a minute, not sure how to ask what he wanted.

"When you first met me, selling runes on the street, how did you know I had any potential?"

Iggy chuckled as he applied lard to the large iron griddle he'd placed on the burner.

"It was the efficiency of your barrier runes," he said. "Your line work was excellent, but that could have just been artistic flair. No, what impressed me was how your line work flowed through the construct. I could tell immediately that you had a strong connection to your magic."

Alex thought back to his early days living in the brownstone and learning the craft. He'd spent many hours in the basement office writing and rewriting runes. Simple ones at first, then gradually more and more complex. Each time it would be the same — he'd struggle just to get the form down, then once he knew it, he could begin to feel the magic flow through him and onto the paper. Each time he'd fail and fail until he got it. After that, he almost never botched a rune that he knew. Once he understood a construct, it was like the magic inside him remembered it and would push his pen along as he drew.

"So my talent is what made it possible for me to learn what I've learned?" he said. "Does that mean that if I'm not talented enough, I'll never be able to write life restoration runes?"

He expected Iggy to reply right away, but the old man just stood at the stove flipping eggs.

"No," he said at last. "I never really thought about it, but I suspect that as long as you keep pushing yourself to write more and more complex runes, your ability will continue to expand."

"So the reason most runewrights can't manage advanced constructs is that they just don't know them?" Alex postulated.

"Quite possibly. If a runewright had access to a decent sized lore book, I expect he could master the whole thing with enough time."

"And assuming he had the talent to begin with," Alex said.

"Well that's a given," Iggy said, scooping the cooked eggs onto a plate. "If a person doesn't have the magic, then runes are just fancy pictures."

Alex thought about that as he ate his fried eggs. The fact that he had been incredibly lucky to meet Iggy and win the man's favor was not lost on him. The lore book Alex inherited from his father was anemically thin with only a dozen useful runes, none of which would sell for more than a quarter on the street. Without access to more complex runes to lead him forward, Alex would never have developed his talent beyond that.

"Why all these questions about magic?" Iggy asked.

Alex shrugged.

"No reason," he said. "That occultist fellow, Theodore Bell, he wanted to know."

"I have no stomach for spiritualists," Iggy said, turning back to his paper. "In my youth I sought them out, but it always turned out the same. Con men, the lot of them."

Alex finished his eggs and excused himself.

"Don't forget we're going to the spa tonight at nine," Iggy called after.

"I'll be back before then," Alex promised, then headed upstairs. He entered his vault, but instead of proceeding through to his office, he stopped in his workshop. Taking two large jars of powdered components off one of his shelves, Alex removed the panel behind it, revealing his secret safe.

With deft twists of the dial, Alex unlocked the safe and pulled out a leather-backed book about an inch thick. This was his lore book, the repository of all his runic knowledge.

Or rather all he knew up to about three years ago.

It had been a while since he had added to it and he needed to bring it up to date. That wasn't why he'd retrieved it this time, though. Leaving the safe open, he moved to his writing desk and opened the book. The old runes from his father's book were first, and he smiled at the memory of them. When he'd first seen them as a child, they'd seemed impossibly complex and arcane. Now he could write any one of them in less than three minutes, most in less than one.

Turning the pages reverently, he found the spot where his father's runes ended and his began. These were the runes Iggy had taught him in the beginning. Even they seemed simple and basic to Alex now.

Alex took out three sheets of plain paper from the top drawer of his rollaway cabinet, then quickly wrote out a minor binding rune, a quick-dry rune, and a minor purity rune. These were all fairly simple, but still above the skill level of most runewrights.

Once Alex was done, he jotted down the notes he'd taken about each rune, including the order of symbols when writing it and the effect it was supposed to have. When he finished, he took out another sheet and wrote out a list of needed equipment and ingredients for making the runes.

Satisfied he was ready, Alex returned his lore book to the safe and replaced the concealing panel and the ingredient jars.

It was almost ten when he finally emerged from his vault into the back hallway of his office. Figuring he'd better check in, he made his way down to the waiting room door and pulled it open. He was surprised to find Mike Fitzgerald sitting at the desk instead of Sherry, but his tired mind caught up quickly, reminding him that he'd sent Sherry to the library in search of stories about the Paris murders. She must have tapped Mike to fill in as receptionist.

"Morning, Mr. Lockerby," Mike said, rising as Alex came in. Mike had spent the better part of the last fifteen years selling runes for cash on Runewright Row and he was grateful for the job Alex had given him. He made significantly more than he had before, and he did most of it without having to stand out in the weather. All of that conspired to make Mike very keen to be a model employee.

Alex didn't want to laugh, but he did.

"First of all, Mike, sit. I'm not the Duke of Ellington."

Mike got a sheepish look for a second, but then he sat down.

"Second, call me Alex. Sherry and I are a family, now you're part of that family too."

"Sherry calls you 'boss,'" Mike pointed out.

"You can call me boss if you want," Alex said. "You just don't have to, and neither does Sherry."

"Yes, Mr...boss."

"Third," Alex continued. He pulled a stack of rune papers out of his pocket and put them on the desk. "Here are a dozen finding runes, but try not to use them all today."

"We're not quite that busy," Mike said, picking up the runes and tucking them into his inside jacket pocket. "But I do have a client anxiously waiting. I'll call her to come over now that I have these."

Alex reached into his inside pocket and took out the paper that contained his shopping list, dropping it on the desk.

"That's a list of runewright supplies I need," Alex said. "Call over to Vanderwaller and Sons and have them delivered today."

"Yes sir, boss," Mike said, sliding the list over by the phone. "Anything else?"

"As a matter of fact, there is," Alex said, taking out the three pages he'd copied from his lore book. "After Sherry gets back and once you've seen to your client, I have a job for you."

He handed over the pages. Mike's eyebrows went up when he unfolded the papers.

"I've never seen anything like this before," he said.

"I know," Alex said. "But I'm confident you can master them. I want you to take the supplies on that list and set up in the spare office. When you're not working on a case, I want you to practice writing those. When you think you've got one right, come show me."

Mike paged through the three runes, examining them and the instructions Alex had written.

"Are you sure about this?" he asked. "I mean are these even useful for a detective?"

"I've used versions of all those runes in cases before," Alex said.

Mike folded the papers reverently and then tucked them in his inside pocket with the rune papers.

"I won't let you down, boss," he said with an eager smile.

"Great," Alex said. "Now, I've got some calls to make so—"

Alex could see from Mike's face that there was something more.

"I should have said this right off," he said with a chagrined look. "Mr. Barton wants to see you right away."

"Of course," Alex said with a sigh. "If Sherry gets back before I do, tell her to finish those warehouse calls for me."

"Yes sir, boss."

"How is it that whenever I need you, you're off on some case?" Andrew Barton asked irritably when Alex stepped out of the private elevator. The Lightning Lord wore a pair of thick work trousers with a white shirt and no tie. An apron of thick leather protected his clothing, and he had a pair of heavy gloves tucked into the front pocket.

"It is my job," Alex pointed out.

Barton sneered at that.

"I can pay you ten times what you make finding people's dogs and helping the police catch purse snatchers," he grumbled. "If you'd just take the cursed money."

Alex just shrugged at that. He and Barton had this discussion before. In fact, Barton had offered him quite a sum to work for him exclusively just the other day.

"What can I say?" Alex said. "I like my job."

That, at least, was something Barton understood, even though he didn't like it.

"What's the emergency this morning?" Alex continued.

Barton beckoned Alex over and handed him a notepad.

"The breakers in the Brooklyn tower are tripping again," he said. "I don't think that crack in the metal plate was the problem."

"Is it just the ones on the south side again?"

Barton nodded and muttered a curse.

"Are you sure your runes are solid?"

"You asked me that last time," Alex said. "They were solid then and they're still solid now."

Barton gave him an annoyed look and Alex just shrugged.

"This is why you don't want me working for you, remember?"

"You said that last time," he mimicked Alex. "Come on," he said sticking out his arm for Alex to grab. "Let's go see if we can figure it out."

"Maybe it's something on this end," Alex protested. He hated teleporting — it always left him nauseated for hours afterward.

"Then all the breakers would be tripping, not just half of them," Barton growled. "Now gut up, Lockerby, we've got work to do."

Alex sighed and grabbed the offered forearm. A moment later he felt as if his insides were being squeezed into a new shape while the sensation of rushing through a tiny, enclosed space overwhelmed him. An instant later there was ground under his feet again and he staggered forward, grabbing one of the breaker boxes that surrounded the transfer core of the Brooklyn tower.

A very surprised workman jumped back with a cry of alarm, but he was quickly shushed by a thick-bodied man in coveralls.

"Mr. Barton," the coveralled man addressed the Lightning Lord.

"We've had to pin the breakers to keep them from tripping, but that's not going to work long term."

"I'll check the breakers," Barton said to Alex. "You check the magic."

Barton headed over to the ring of malfunctioning breakers with the man in the coveralls while Alex opened the hinged top of the glass case that held the three transfer plates. The one on the south side of the case was a slightly different color than the other two, having been replaced when the previous one had a flaw. According to Barton, that hadn't helped.

The linking runes on the central plate led to the two side plates, and other linking runes then ran to the breaker boxes. They were invisible to the naked eye, but Alex could feel them. He walked around the pedestal supporting the glass case, sensing each linking rune individually. All of them felt exactly the same. If one had been weak or improperly made, he would have known it. Still Barton wouldn't be satisfied until he'd checked absolutely everything, so Alex closed the protective lid and went into the stairwell to open his vault. The chalk door he'd drawn the last time was still there, so he tore out a vault rune and opened the door with his key.

After retrieving his bag, Alex set it on top of the glass case and used his ghostlight burner to examine the transfer plates and the runes connecting them. As he'd known they would be, all the runes were solid and working as intended.

"Well?" Barton said, coming over as Alex blew out the burner in his lamp.

"Everything looks good," Alex reported, grabbing his kit bag to begin repacking his gear. "If there's a..."

"What?" Barton asked when Alex's voice just trailed off.

"It's wet," he said, pulling his hand back from his bag.

Barton took hold of the top of the bag, then looked up at the ceiling. Alex followed his eyes, but couldn't see anything amiss. Just as he was ready to give up, however, a shimmering drop of water detached itself from the seam where the ceiling met a large support beam and splashed on the back of Alex's hand.

Moving his kit, Alex followed the path the drop would have taken if his hand hadn't been in the way.

"Here," he said, pointing to the corner of the glass case. "The water's hitting this corner and seeping inside where the glass panels come together."

Barton bent down to look then moved to the far side and opened the case. Reaching inside with no fear of being electrocuted, he ran his finger down the inside corner. When he reached the bottom, Alex saw the base ripple. There was a small amount of water covering the bottom corner of the case.

Barton slid his finger along the tiny puddle, then splashed the water up onto the transfer plate. Enormous sparks leapt up and there was a crack like a gunshot; at the same moment all the unpinned breakers on the south side of the room tripped.

While the man in coveralls and his associate scrambled to reset the breakers, Barton looked up at the ceiling and swore.

"That's a brand-new roof," he fumed.

"There must be standing water up there," Alex said. "It rained last night, but it's been dry all morning."

Barton nodded in agreement.

"I'll call my crew over to fix that roof right away," he said. "In the meantime, I'll need something to cover the case. You wouldn't happen to have a tarp in your vault, would you?"

Alex grinned and pulled out his rune book.

"I can do better than that." He tore out a standard barrier rune and dropped it on the transfer plate near the puddle. "Would you mind?"

Barton stuck his finger down by the paper and lit it with a tiny spark. Alex felt the familiar caress of energy as an invisible bubble spread out from the rune, forming a waterproof sphere around the plates and most of the case. As it went, the water in the bottom of the case was pushed up against the glass and finally through the gap in the corner.

"Don't those runes only last an hour?" Barton asked.

"Minor barrier runes do," Alex confirmed. "That one was its big brother, it will last a whole day."

Barton looked at Alex like he'd said something ridiculous.

"Then why don't runewrights sell those on rainy days?"

"Because they're too expensive and too hard to make," Alex said. He indicated the water running down the back side of the pillar that held the transfer plates up. "Besides, it expels any exposed water inside the bubble, so how would you drink anything?"

Barton chuckled at that thought. "That could be dangerous," he said. "I don't remember regular barrier runes doing that."

"They don't," Alex said. "Now if you don't mind, I've got one of those annoying cases to get back to. If you need me to come back tomorrow with another barrier rune, let me know."

Barton nodded, then turned to the man in the coveralls and began giving orders. Alex went back to the stairwell and, once he was sure Barton was fully engaged with the problem of the leaking roof, he slipped into his vault and closed the door behind him.

19

KEEPSAKES

It was almost noon by the time Alex finished with Andrew Barton. He hadn't eaten yet, but his stomach was still a bit queasy from the earlier teleport, so he made his way back to his office instead of stopping at the brownstone for a sandwich.

"Hi'ya boss," Sherry said when he came into the waiting room.

Alex smiled, grateful to see her. If she was back, that meant she was done at the library and maybe he could get somewhere on the blood rune case.

"Where's Mike?" he asked.

Sherry shrugged at that.

"He got a delivery right as I got in and went running into the back."

"Good," Alex said. The sooner Mike got up to speed, the sooner he could take some of the rune writing duties off Alex's plate.

"How'd you do?"

Sherry picked up a notepad from the desk and handed it over to Alex. It was full of her tight script.

"There were murders matching the voodoo killing in Paris in thirty-one," she said. "As far as I can tell, though, the only reason they made the papers was because of the reaction to them. Apparently there was a panic in Paris as a result."

"Did the papers say why?"

Sherry nodded.

"There was a decent sized community of Russian immigrants in the city," she said. "Most had fled the revolution and they believed the murders were the work of Grigori Rasputin."

"The mad monk?" Alex asked.

"The very same."

"But he was killed ten years before the murders."

"Fifteen," Sherry corrected. "The problem was that the Russians believed that Rasputin couldn't die, that he saved his body from death with dark rituals."

Alex had heard those stories before, of course. Rasputin's political enemies had tried to kill him several times before they got the job done and those events inspired rumors and legends of his alleged immortality.

"But what does Rasputin have to do with the Paris murders?"

"According to the immigrant Russians, there were a string of similar murders in Moscow back in nineteen-seventeen. That was the year after Rasputin was supposed to have died. During those murders, Moscow was in a panic because the people believed it was Rasputin reviving himself, returning from the grave."

"So when similar murders happened in Paris, the Russians thought Rasputin had followed them?"

"The story doesn't say that," Sherry said. "But it certainly seems that way."

That didn't make a lot of sense, but superstition and ghost stories rarely did.

"All right," he sighed, scanning the notes on the pad Sherry had given him for any other information. "I don't think we're dealing with a mad monk, Rasputin or otherwise, but the Paris killings and the ones in Russia seem connected to ours. Was there any information on the Russian murders?"

Sherry shook her head.

"Thanks anyway," he said. "I'm going to call on those warehouse break-ins, so if you need me, I'll be in my office."

He left Sherry to her work and headed through the back hallway to his private office. The knowledge that the blood rune had appeared at other murder scenes, possibly going back twenty years, was tantalizing, but Alex didn't have any real information on those killings, just rumors and second-hand reports. It was a lead, just not much of one.

"Maybe Theo will remember something else in another book," he said as he sat behind his desk.

Pushing thoughts of blood runes and Russian monks from his conscious mind, Alex picked up the folder Sherry had labeled Warehouse Burglaries. Inside was a page for each of the three warehouses that contained the names of the people who had property stolen and what was taken. Alex knew this, and he knew it for the misdirection it was. Whoever broke open all those shipping crates was after something else. Now all Alex needed to do was find out what.

On the top of each page, right below the name of each warehouse, was the name of a contact person. Two were warehouse foremen and one was a clerk. It wasn't much, but it was a place to start.

With a sigh, Alex reached for the telephone on his desk. Before he could grab it, however, it began to ring.

"Lockerby," he said once he picked up the handset.

"It's Danny," his friend's voice came through the speaker. "Please tell me you've got something on our voodoo killer. I've got a half-dozen city councilmen calling me for updates after half of Linsey O'Day's apartment building fell down. I'm running out of things to tell them."

"What's the story?" Alex asked.

"We're saying it was a structural defect, but they're not buying it. The Captain says that I am not to tell them what really happened under any circumstances."

"It would start a panic," Alex agreed.

Like the one in Paris.

"Do you have any contacts with the police in France?" he asked.

"No," Danny said, in a voice that suggested Alex should know that. "Why?"

"Because five years ago there was a string of murders in Paris that were exactly like these," Alex explained.

There was a pause on the line, then Danny came back on.

"I'll see if Captain Callahan can find out anything," he said. "In the meantime, however, I need you to come over to the morgue. According to Dr. Wagner, the bodies of Katherine Biggs and Linsey O'Day are decaying at an accelerated rate, even in our cooler."

Alex clenched his teeth. Ever since Dr. Anderson had retired and moved out west to care for his sister, the morgue had been functionally off limits to Alex. The new coroner, Dr. Wagner, didn't like private detectives in general and Alex in particular. Every time Alex went to the morgue, he ended up verbally sparring with the man.

"All right," Alex said, rubbing his forehead. "I'll catch a cab and be right over."

He hung up with a sigh and stared at the paperwork from the warehouse robberies. As boring as calling a bunch of surly warehouse foremen looking for what hadn't been stolen sounded, an afternoon at Wagner's morgue would be worse.

Forcing himself to close the folder, Alex stood. He picked it up, put on his hat, grabbed his kit, and headed back out to the waiting room. When he got there, Sherry was holding her hand out expectantly for the robbery folder.

"I've got to go see Danny at the morgue," he said, handing the folder over.

"Have fun," Sherry said with a smile that indicated she knew very well he wouldn't.

The morgue that served the Manhattan Central Office of Police was in the basement of an unassuming five-story building just inside the mid ring and a few blocks south and west of the Central Office. The morgue was in the basement since building a refrigerated cold room was cheaper if it was underground. The upper floors held the support staff that kept the police department running.

A dark stairwell led down to the morgue, but it was always locked at the bottom, so Alex had to take the freight elevator. The morgue itself was tiled all around with white tiles on the floor and green ones running up the walls. The hallways weren't lit especially well, which always made Alex think of it as a dungeon. Bright lights did shine out from the office windows and through the operating theater doors, but the dark hallways seemed to soak up the light, not letting it pass along the corridors.

"Alex," Danny's voice called out of the gloom to his right.

Alex had already turned that way since the chiller was at the right-hand end of the hallway with the operating theaters to the left.

"Okay, I'm here," he said as he approached.

"Thank the heavens," the sarcastic voice of Dr. Wagner drifted out from behind Danny. "Will you please do whatever it is you're going to do so I can send these bodies to the crematorium," he went on. "They're stinking up my chiller."

Alex chuckled humorlessly as Danny rolled his eyes. Wagner was a big man, almost as tall as Alex, with a squarish jaw and a handsome face that was a big hit with the ladies. That had gotten him in trouble in Chicago and he'd had to move to New York and take the coroner's job to preserve his advantageous marriage.

"Dr. Wagner," he said, giving the man a nod. "As always, your compassion and professionalism are an example to the rest of us."

"Get going, scribbler," he growled. "Before I lodge a formal complaint against your friend, here."

With that, Wagner stormed off in the direction of his office. As he went, Alex picked up the faint aroma of putrefaction coming from the direction of the chiller.

"What is it you want me to do?" Alex asked as Danny turned and led the way around to the heavy, insulated door. As they approached, the smell of rot got thicker. "That's really bad," Alex observed.

Danny nodded and pulled a handkerchief from his pocket, pressing it over his nose and mouth as he reached for the door.

"Hang on," Alex said, setting his kit down and opening it. The kit was an old doctor's valise and it had mounting straps for tools under each side of the fold-down top. One side held a row of jars that had various inks and powders Alex might need at a crime scene. The other side held his oculus and a little-used face mask made of sturdy leather with a rubber seal around the edge. Alex slipped it free of the strap that held it in place, then placed it over his face, securing it around the back of his head with an elastic band.

As he did this, Danny gave him a quizzical look. The mask had holes in each side where paper and cloth filters were mounted. It didn't look effective for protecting against anything but, like most of Alex's gear, appearances were deceiving. Taking his lighter from his pocket, Alex lit a tiny wick sticking out of the front of the mask. It burst into flame and vanished, leaving a modified purity rune hovering over the mask. As soon as the rune appeared, the rank aroma of decomposition vanished.

He gave a thumbs-up. and Danny pulled the door open. From the look on his friend's face, Alex could tell that the smell was much worse inside. He saw immediately what the problem was. Two bodies on nearby gurneys were partially uncovered, or rather what was left of them was uncovered. The skin of both women had a greenish cast and was starting to slough off, exposing bone beneath. A puddle of noisome fluid was pooling in the metal pan that ran beneath the gurney top to catch fluids during autopsy. Both women were too far gone for Alex to perform any meaningful investigation.

"I don't know what I can do," Alex said. "What did you want me to try?"

"Can you do that thing where you reconstitute the body?" Danny asked. "Like you did with Jerry Pemberton?"

Alex had a temporal restoration rune in his book, but he didn't bother to reach for it.

"That's a bad idea," he said, pointing at the bodies. "The decay is a residual effect of the magical backlash from whatever magic our killer did."

"What's the worst that could happen?" Danny asked.

"You remember Linsey O'Day's apartment building? I'm pretty sure my rune made that way worse than it otherwise would have been. There's no mention of decaying buildings in any of the other cases."

"What about Katherine Biggs' house?"

Alex shrugged at that.

"It was pretty far gone to begin with. I don't want to try it in here, in any case."

Danny looked up at the roof overhead, probably imagining the five more floors of people and equipment above it.

"It might even explode," Alex continued. "I've seen improperly written runes blow up in runewrights' faces, and this would be way more destructive."

"Okay," he said. "I guess I got you over here for nothing."

He turned and headed out into the hall again, motioning for Alex to follow. As soon as Alex was clear, he shut the door and headed back down the hall.

"Okay, Doctor," he said, opening the door to Wagner's office. "You can send those bodies out."

"Finally," Wagner said, picking up his phone. "If you want their property," he said, dialing, "it's in those boxes."

He waved in the direction of a line of boxes on a gurney in the hall, then began speaking to someone on the other end of the phone.

"Come on," Danny said, still pressing the handkerchief over his face. He led Alex back into the hallway and picked up one of the boxes, then passed it to Alex. Picking up the second one, he headed for the elevator. "I want to do this up in the lobby."

One elevator ride later, Alex and Danny stood at the counter where Charlie Cooper, the retired officer who served as the building guard, sat. He was used to all kinds of strange things going on in the building, so he gave Danny and Alex an appraising eye, then went back to reading his paper.

Alex looked into the box marked, *Linsey O'Day*. It was filled with an eclectic mix of small objects. There was a salt shaker with the word Dublin stamped into the top, a wooden disk with a relief carving of a shamrock, a porcelain leprechaun, a glass frame with a pressed flower in it, and other green or Irish themed bric-a-brac. Nothing in the box seemed particularly important. There weren't any clothes in the box, but Alex remembered that Katherine Biggs had been naked when her body was discovered. It was probably the same for Linsey.

"Is this the stuff the killer positioned around the body?" Alex asked.

Danny nodded, picking up a cheap pocketwatch and a chipped mug from the other box. Like the things in Alex's box, they were personal items that likely had meaning to the murdered women.

"It all seems like such junk," Danny said.

"Neither of these women were well off," Alex pointed out.

"I don't mean that," Danny said, picking up a worn hairbrush from his box. "I mean why bother with this stuff at all?"

That actually was a pretty good question, and Alex considered it before answering.

"If I had to guess, our killer was trying to create a connection between his victim and whatever his blood rune was supposed to do."

"The same way you need an object of significance to make a finding rune work?"

"Exactly."

"That doesn't sound like it would work very well," Danny said, pulling a tiny replica of the Eiffel Tower from the box. "I mean some of this stuff is useful," he held up the hairbrush, "and our victims probably used them every day, but that doesn't mean they were particularly connected to them. I mean I use my razor every day, but if I broke it, I wouldn't think twice about replacing it."

Alex nodded. Danny had a point. If the killer was trying to establish a link between the victims and his rune, using random objects from their home wasn't a very efficient way to do it.

"And the rest of this stuff is just keepsakes," Danny went on. "They might not even belong to the victim; maybe they found them, or they were left by the former occupant of their apartment. I don't see Katherine Biggs owning something like this, do you?" He held up the Eiffel Tower.

Alex just stared at it as his brain made several rapid connections.

"You're right," he said. "That's not something Katherine would own."

Alex dumped out Linsey O'Day's box on the counter and began sifting through the items.

"I know that look," Danny said. "You've figured something out."

Alex nodded and kept sorting.

"I don't think that Eiffel Tower belonged to Katherine Biggs at all," he said. "I don't think she even saw it until just before she died."

"You think the killer brought it? Why?"

Alex explained about the murders in Paris as he sifted through Linsey's belongings.

"Why would the killer bring something from Paris when he murdered Katherine?"

"Don't know," Alex admitted. "But I know I'm right."

He picked up a small curio from the counter. It was an oval frame, about an inch high with glass in the front, like a tiny picture frame. Inside was a curling purple flower that had been pressed.

"Katherine Biggs wasn't from New York," he said. "Was she?"

Danny gave Alex a skeptical look, then pulled out his notebook.

"No," he said after flipping a few pages. "According to her previous arrest record she was from South Carolina, but how would you know that?"

Alex held up the flower.

"Because this is kudzu," Alex said, setting the curio down on the counter. "It's a Japanese flower that's been planted in the South to prevent soil erosion. It's also not something that Irishwoman Linsey O'Day would be likely to have. Green's her color, not purple."

"You think the kudzu belonged to Katherine and the killer took it, then left it at the scene of Linsey's murder. Which means that this," he held up the Eiffel Tower, "came from the last murder he committed in Paris."

"That's exactly what I think," Alex said.

A fierce grin spread across Danny's face.

"If you're right," he said, "then that was a sentimental thing to do. It means the killer was emotionally attached to this." He set the tower down on the counter. "And that means you can use it as the basis for a finding rune, right?"

Alex matched Danny's grin and nodded, pulling his chalk from his pocket. As a founding member of the Arcane Irregulars, Danny knew about his vault.

"We'll use the map room in my office to make sure we get a good connection," Alex said, drawing a door on the wall. "You call up your boys and have them meet us at Empire Tower. By the time they get there, we'll know where to find your killer."

20

THE APPRENTICE

Alex knew something was wrong the moment the elevator door opened on the seventh floor of the Hotel Astor. His finding rune had located the blood rune killer using the Eiffel Tower keepsake, pointing Alex, Danny, and a dozen uniformed officers to the single most expensive hotel in the city.

Using the trick of turning the compass sideways, Alex had ridden the elevator up until the needle was level.

"What's the matter?" Danny whispered from behind him when Alex didn't move. "Is this it?"

"Yes," Alex whispered back. "Does something feel wrong to you?"

"No. Is there some kind of magic on this floor?"

Alex nodded. He couldn't say what it was, but the very air seemed greasy and heavy. It was as if Alex could detect a sour smell, like rot or decay, but it wasn't physical, he was sensing it on a magical level.

"Is it some kind of defensive magic?" Danny asked. "Does he know we're coming?"

Alex wasn't sure, but there was some kind of corrupt magic happening on this floor, he was certain of that.

"I don't think so," he whispered. He turned the compass flat on his palm and the needle pointed down the hallway to the left. Alex tentatively stepped out of the elevator, but the feel of the tainted magic didn't change. He moved carefully down the hall with Danny and five officers in tow, all of them unnaturally quiet.

"Go down and bring up the rest," Danny told the lone officer remaining in the elevator before the door closed.

As Alex made his way carefully along the hall, the strange feeling made him jumpy. He had an unshakeable feeling that any sudden moves would disrupt whatever spell or rune was operating, and he was absolutely sure that would be bad. As he neared the end of the hall, the needle pivoted, pointing toward a single door on the right-hand side.

Looking back to catch Danny's attention, Alex turned and pointed toward the door. That was Danny's cue to take his men and surround the door. Since his part was done for the moment, Alex would wait until the suspect was secured, then he would go in and check the room with his oculus.

That was how these things usually went. As Alex stood aside so Danny could pass, however, he heard the sound of glass breaking. Not a large piece of glass, like a mirror or a window, but something small. It made a tinkling sound almost like a bell.

Before Alex could wonder what it was, a blast of magic slammed into him. He felt as if a wave of filthy water had engulfed him, and he staggered against the opposite wall from the physical impact. The initial blast faded quickly, and Alex didn't seem to have been harmed by it, but when he looked up, he found Danny and the policemen frozen in place, like living statues.

He felt a moment of raw, primal fear. This was magic like a sorcerer would use, though he never would have felt the power a sorcerer would employ. Alex's 1911 and his knuckle duster were safely locked away in the gun case in his vault, but he still had options. Danny and all the policemen were armed.

Alex grabbed the butt of an officer's service revolver, but his hand had barely wrapped around it when he was interrupted.

"I wish you wouldn't do that," a voice said. "I'd hate to have to shoot you after I went through all this trouble so we could talk."

Alex looked up and found a man standing outside the door the compass had indicated. He was average height with a thin, athletic build and dark, intense eyes. An expensive red velvet smoking jacket covered his torso, and his trousers and shoes were of the highest quality. He had a swarthy, Mediterranean complexion, though his accent was American, upper Midwest if Alex had to guess. His dark hair was wavy and longish, and he wore it combed back and parted on the left.

The man was smiling. It was an open, affable smile, the kind one reserved for a dear friend, though the effect was somewhat lessened by the revolver in his hand.

Alex slowly took his hand away from the patrolman's gun, raising it and the other in a gesture of submission.

"Excellent," the man said, his smile never wavering. "Come in." He stepped back from the door and swept his left hand up in a grand gesture of welcome. "I have so wanted to meet you."

Alex's mind was running overtime. Whatever spell had frozen time must be immensely powerful, and therefore power hungry. It couldn't last very long, five or ten minutes at most. If he could keep the smiling man talking long enough, the spell would break, and Danny and the policemen would be free to act again.

"If you wanted to meet me," Alex said, stepping forward, "my number's in the book and I have an office downtown."

The man laughed at that as if he were actually amused.

"Oh, you are a pistol," he said. "I should have known they wouldn't choose just anyone."

Alex turned and walked into the room. This being the most opulent hotel in the city, the rooms did not disappoint. Gold painted molding covered the ceilings and the walls were covered in textured paper. The front area was a small sitting room with elegant furniture, and the smiling man directed Alex to one of the overstuffed chairs.

"How is it you know me?" Alex asked as he sat. The smiling man took the chair opposite, just a couple feet too far away for Alex to make a lunge for the gun.

"You mean they haven't told you?" the other man said, then he laughed another genuine laugh. "Oh, this really is too good. What is your name, if I may ask?"

With the gun pointed at Alex, it really wasn't a request, so Alex introduced himself.

"Well, Alex," the man said, his amused smile never slipping. "My name is Diego Ruiz, and I am your brother."

Now it was Alex's turn to laugh.

"I'm an only child," he said. "And even if I had a missing sibling, I'm pretty sure they'd know my name."

"Don't be ridiculous," Diego said, crossing his legs casually. "I knew you were my brother the moment your finding rune broke through my protections. No ordinary runewright could have done that; only my brother would have such power."

Alex had no idea what the man was talking about, and it must have showed on his face.

"You're not thinking big enough, Alex. I am your brother in magic. Your elder brother, to be precise."

That didn't make any sense, but Alex needed to keep the man talking; so he plowed on.

"You said that 'they' didn't tell me about you. Who did you mean?"

"Oh, come now, Alex, don't be coy. I know the Immortals are supposed to be a secret, but they aren't secret from me. You see, they chose me before they chose you. That's what makes you my brother."

"And who are they again?"

Diego's smile slipped for the first time, and his eyes became calculating.

"You really don't know," he said, astonishment plain in his voice.

"No," Alex admitted. "I really don't."

Diego's eyes darted back and forth, and he mumbled to himself for a moment.

"Ah," he said, his smile of delight suddenly returning. "You have the notebook."

That raised gooseflesh on Alex's arms.

"What are they calling it this time," Diego went on. "The Book of Thoth? The Black Grimoire? Well, whatever they're calling it, it's their training manual. They make sure it falls into the hands of up and coming runewrights. Runewrights with talent. Runewrights with agile minds. Runewrights like you, Alex."

Now Alex knew exactly what Diego Ruiz was talking about.

Moriarty.

Moriarty had said that he had allowed Iggy to find the Archimedean Monograph, that he'd expected great things from Iggy once he learned what was in it. How he'd later transferred those expectations to Alex. He'd told Alex about the quote on the front page of the Monograph, about using a lever to move the world.

You're going to be my lever, Alex, he heard the man's voice in his head. *You are going to be my lever.*

"Yes," Diego said, reading the expression on Alex's face. "I can see it now. You found their notebook. You studied it, drinking in its secrets and believing that you were the only one in the world privy to such knowledge. But trust me, Alex, that book isn't the gift you believe it to be. It's a pact with the Immortals. One where they give you a peek at their power, then offer you more, provided you're willing to dance to their tune."

"Who are these Immortals?"

"If they haven't contacted you yet, they will," Diego said. "Soon, unless I miss my guess. Your skills seem well developed."

Diego's affable grin never slipped, but there was a note in his voice when he spoke of the Immortals. It was a note of pure hatred.

"You don't seem to like these Immortals very much," Alex said. "If they really did pick me for some reason, I would think that would make us enemies, not brothers."

"You must believe me, Alex," Diego said, his voice earnest and open. "I bear you no ill will. I was once like you, chosen by the Immortals to be their apprentice."

"But something changed," Alex guessed. "Didn't it? These Immortals, they kicked you out of their club."

Alex wasn't surprised at that thought. Despite his pleasant smile and easy manner, Diego Ruiz was a psychopath who availed himself of prostitutes and then murdered them.

"Yes," he admitted easily. "They cast me out. And do you know why?"

Alex wanted to suggest a reason, but he also wanted Diego to keep talking.

"Because I grew too powerful," he explained. "I was starting to exceed them. You must understand, Alex, the Immortals are old and stagnant in their thinking. The modern world is changing at a breakneck pace and modern minds must adapt to it."

"Minds like yours?"

"Like ours," Diego corrected. "I can tell by how quickly you found me that your mind is agile, Alex. You think new thoughts, in new ways. Soon you will outshine the Immortals too."

That thought didn't make Alex feel any better. Just seeing Moriarty enter his vault and close the door behind him had made Alex pursue that magic. Now his vault could do what Moriarty's had done. He still needed a vault rune to open it, but that was the only difference. What would happen if Alex began to make more complex constructs than Moriarty?

"What happens then?" he voiced his thoughts.

Diego gave him an intense look, not one of anger or intimidation, but the kind of look an earnest friend might give when delivering a dire warning.

"Let me show you," he said.

Using his left hand, Diego unbuttoned his smoking jacket, revealing a blue silk shirt. Without stopping, he unbuttoned the shirt and pulled it open. Across the left side of his chest, radiating out from a spot over his heart, was the most complex rune Alex had ever seen. The escape rune he'd finished a few days ago was nothing compared to this. It was etched into the skin of Diego's chest, but Alex could tell it was no tattoo. The lines were too perfect, the colors too bright. Whoever had done this has used some kind of magic to bind the construct into the man's flesh.

Alex's eyes tried to trace the interlocking symbols but every time he thought he'd followed one to its end, it doubled back into another shape.

"Mesmerizing," Diego said. "Isn't it?"

Alex could only nod his agreement.

"I've never seen anything like it," he admitted. "What is it?"

Diego chuckled.

"This is the Immortal's punishment for failure," he said. "Or in my case, for success. It's called the rune of damnation and it forever shuts me out from rune magic."

That couldn't possibly be true, and Alex knew it. Whatever rune he'd used to stop time was incredibly powerful, something Alex had believed only a sorcerer could do.

"Your magic seems to be working now," Alex said.

Diego smirked and closed his shirt.

"I'm sure that you are aware that runes aren't the only kind of magic," he said. "Let's just say that I've found that drawing magic from the universe isn't the only way to power a construct."

Alex was about to ask him to explain that, but he felt a sudden pulse of magic that pushed against him like a wind. He turned toward the place the power had come from and found a shattered glass globe about the size of a baseball on the hardwood floor.

"Alas," Diego said in a voice that sounded genuinely disappointed. "Our time grows short. What you need to know, Alex, is that sooner or later the Immortals will come for you. First they'll tell you how important you are. How there is great evil in the world, and they need you to be their agent."

That bit sounded very familiar.

"Alex," Diego continued, then he paused. "Brother, hear me. No matter what they promise, they will turn on you. As soon as you are no longer useful to them, this is what awaits you." He pulled on his shirt again, revealing the damnation rune.

Alex felt another pulse from the broken globe.

"In addition to being unpleasant," Diego said, "the methods I've had to use to stay alive are quite dangerous." He stood and moved to the other side of the room, grabbing a few things out of a portmanteau trunk and stuffing them into a leather valise. "When the time suspension rune fails, the backlash will be quite severe," he continued. "I enhanced this construct with that little trick you did at dear Linsey's apartment. I really must thank you for showing me that; the backlash now will be several times more destructive. I'd suggest you start running immediately." He dropped the pistol into the pocket of his smoking jacket and moved around to the room's large window. "And don't forget what I told you, Brother. The Immortals will turn on you, sooner or later. When they do, you're welcome to come find me."

Another wave of the decaying spell hit Alex and he noticed the fragments of the glass globe, that had been suspended in the air by the rune, were beginning to move.

"Good luck," Diego said, then he threw open the window and leapt out into the night.

Alex was torn between the desire to run to the window and the desire to just run. He quickly mastered himself. As soon as Diego's construct failed, this room and maybe more were going to dissolve into nothing from the backlash. Diego told him to run, so it was quite possible that backlash would be much larger than Alex originally thought. With Danny and the policemen still frozen in the hall, there was nothing Alex could do to keep them from being consumed.

"You're supposed to be smart," he growled out loud. "Iggy thinks so, Moriarty thinks so, even that psychopath Diego thinks so, so think! How do you stop an explosion of backlash? What can you do that will stand against..."

He tore at his suit coat, ripping out his rune book and paging frantically through it. There was a chance, but it wasn't good. If he was wrong, it might destroy the entire hotel and him along with it. Still, he had to try.

"This is so stupid," he said as he tore out a temporal restoration rune. Not bothering to fold it, he dropped it on the slowly expanding pile of shattered glass from the globe and flicked his lighter to life.

Praying that he wasn't about to kill himself and everyone else in the building, Alex touched the flame to the flash paper. It caught, burning in slow motion as Diego's construct failed. The shattered glass began to expand quickly as time returned to normal. Alex began to hear sounds out in the hall, but before anyone could move freely enough to enter the room, the shards of the glass globe slowed and stopped. It hovered in place for a moment, then moved backward, collapsing in on itself until it solidified into a glass ball sitting on top of a round metal base. Inside was a model of the cathedral at Notre Dame, and white paper shapes swirled around it like birds.

Alex picked up the water-filled orb with a trembling hand. As he touched it, he could feel the magic inside, straining to burst forth but held in place by his own rune.

The door behind him burst open and Danny and the policemen rushed in.

"Alex," Danny said, taking in the room. "How did you get in here?"

"Never mind," Alex said, standing up and holding the glass ball at arm's length. "In ten minutes this thing is going to explode and destroy the hotel."

Danny opened his mouth in confusion and then shut it again.

"Trust me," Alex said. "You've got to get everyone out."

Alex needed to figure out how to get the ball out of the hotel, but the only thing he could think of was his vault, and that might expose his office or the brownstone to the backlash. Neither of those would be a better place for the ball to explode. He could shut it in his vault and just leave it there, but he had no idea what that kind of backlash would do in the extra-dimensional space the vault occupied. It could become even more dangerous for all he knew.

"You," Danny said, pointing at one of the officers. "Go activate the fire bell. The rest of you take a floor and get everyone out of the hotel. Now! Move!"

The officers scrambled to obey, and Danny joined Alex.

"Can you use your escape rune?" he asked. "Dump it in the north Atlantic like you did with Sorsha's castle?"

It was a good idea, but his latest escape rune was currently hanging on his vault wall where it wouldn't do him any good. He opened his mouth to explain that when he realized what Danny had said.

"You're a genius," he said, running to the writing desk in the room and scooping up the gilded telephone. "I need to talk to Sorsha," he said when the line connected.

"I'm sorry," the voice of her secretary said on the other end. "She's not available right now. Can I take a message?"

"This is Alex Lockerby. Tell Sorsha that if she doesn't get to room eight-seventeen of the Hotel Astor in less than ten minutes a lot of people are going to die."

21

THE GOLDEN ARROW

"What's the plan?" Danny asked, striding back into the room as the fire bell began to ring.

Alex put down the telephone, still holding the glass ball out at arm's length. He knew that if his rune were to fail in that moment, the reaction of the double backlash would completely destroy him, but holding it away from his body just felt like the sensible thing to do.

"I called Sorsha," he said. "Her secretary took a message."

"What about Barton?" Danny asked.

Alex shook his head.

"He's out at the Brooklyn relay tower overseeing repairs. By the time anyone got him a message, it would be too late."

Danny gave him an encouraging look.

"But you have a plan, right?"

Alex tried to think of something. His vault was still an option, but he had to save that as a last resort. Vaults existed in an entirely different dimension and there was no telling what the backlash would do in there. The magic could fizzle without its connection to the real world, or it might destroy Alex's entire vault. For all he knew it could destroy the entire dimension where vaults existed. He didn't think that was likely, but he didn't really know, and he didn't want to find out.

"You'd better get out of here," Alex said, not taking his eyes off the little representation of Notre Dame inside the glass.

"Like hell," Danny said. "You don't have a plan and two heads are better than one."

Alex opened his mouth to argue but the feel of the magic in the glass ball changed.

He was running out of time.

"What about the roof?" Danny said. "Hold on to that thing until right before it cuts loose, then throw it. That should keep it away from any people, right?"

"Unless it falls all the way to the ground before anything happens," Alex said. "We're running out of time, but I don't know exactly how much is left."

"That's not true," Danny said. "I remember Jerry Pemberton. You knew when the rune was down to about a minute left."

"Yes, but this thing could fall to the street in a minute."

"Can you make it fly?"

Alex shook his head. As far as he knew there wasn't an anti-gravity rune.

"I still think the roof is our best option," Danny said. "If that thing does dissolve a chunk of the building there's nothing above it to fall down."

"Right," Alex said with a nod. It wasn't a great plan, but it was better than anything he'd come up with.

Danny headed out into the hall and turned right toward the stairwell.

"Elevator," Alex called, turning the other way. "There's at least ten floors above this one, that'll take too long."

As Alex moved carefully down the hall, Danny pushed past him and ran to hit the elevator button. Before he reached it, however, the floor bell chimed and the door opened.

"Sorsha!" Alex gasped as the sorceress emerged into the hall.

"What's going on here?" she demanded. "Is there a fire?"

"This thing," Alex said, raising the glass ball to her eye level. "In a couple of minutes it might explode."

"A snow globe?" she said, unimpressed.

Alex had never heard of snow globes, but now wasn't the time to wonder why anyone would make such a thing.

"Who cares what it is," Alex said. "You've got to get it out of here."

Sorsha looked genuinely confused.

"Why? Is it filled with nitroglycerine?"

"An evil runewright used it to stop time and the backlash could blow up half this hotel," Alex explained.

"Or more," Danny added.

Sorsha's eyebrows furrowed and she stuck out a finger toward the snow globe. When she was still several inches away, there was a crack like thunder and she pulled her hand back like it had been burned.

"What did you do?" she gasped, looking at Alex with wide eyes.

"I stopped it from killing me, Danny, a dozen policemen, and most of the guests on this side of the hotel," Alex said. "Now I need you to teleport this somewhere it won't kill anyone when the rune I used to contain it fails."

Sorsha's face slackened and her mouth opened in an expression of helplessness.

"Alex," she stammered. "I can only teleport to places I've been, you know that."

"Did you ever visit Antarctica?" Danny asked.

"No," she said, "and before you ask, I've never been to the Grand Canyon or the Bermuda Triangle either."

Alex felt the temporal restoration rune begin to unravel, pulsing like an accelerating heartbeat. He had less than a minute. No time to reach the roof and even if Sorsha could make the snow globe float it might not clear the building in time. The only option was to teleport it somewhere.

Somewhere Sorsha had been that was far away from any people.

"Your castle," he said in a moment of pure clarity.

Sorsha gave him a hard look.

"I fail to see how blowing up my home and raining debris all over the city is better than just losing this hotel."

"Not your new castle," Alex said. "The original."

Sorsha held his eyes for a moment as she processed the information, then she nodded grimly.

"Give me a moment to find it," she said, closing her eyes and taking in a deep breath. "When I tell you, throw the snow globe straight up in the air."

"But don't hit the ceiling," Danny added.

Alex forced himself to relax his grip on the glass ball and took a breath himself. The thumping heartbeat that heralded the end of his rune was racing now, faster and faster.

"Almost got it," Sorsha said. She was sweating now, and her breathing was fast and shallow. Alex thought she'd be able to find her castle easily; after all, she'd teleported to it many times before. Of course, it was now under a mile or two of the North Atlantic, so that might complicate things.

The pulsing energy of the dying rune thumped one last time and Alex heard a tone like the ringing of a bell. As he watched, the glass ball cracks spread across its surface and it began to break for a second time. He felt the greasy air of corruption erupt from the ball and it stung his fingers where he held it.

"Sorsha!" he yelled, tossing the globe in the air. Foul magic burst from it as it flew and Alex grabbed Danny, dragging him along as he threw himself to the carpeted floor of the hallway.

As he fell, Alex could feel the pressure of the expanding wave of corruption behind him. When it reached him it would vaporize him, going right on through to get Danny, the floor, and whatever else stood in its way.

He hit the floor hard, rolling onto his back. Above him the glass globe was already in pieces, expanding outward just as they did when Diego shattered it to activate his time-stop rune. A ball of roiling black energy formed in the center where the glass used to be and suddenly burst forth.

Alex threw up his hands, more out of instinct than any belief that they would stop the inky wave of death, but after a few seconds, he was still there. Daring to peek around his arms, he saw the churning energy contained inside an invisible sphere. It flowed and moved like a living thing, seeking a way out. The suspended shards of glass stopped expanding and were slowly moving back, flowing into the shape of the snow globe again.

Standing on the opposite side of the retracing globe, Sorsha stood rigid with her hand extended and her splayed fingers bent. She was chanting in the guttural voice Alex always associated with sorcery and her eyes glowed as if lit from inside. Sweat was rolling off her face and her hair moved like she stood in a strong wind. Her outstretched hand looked as if she was trying to grip a baseball and, as her fingers slowly closed, the snow globe came back together.

Trembling, Sorsha raised her closed hand and suddenly brought it together with her other hand in a clapping gesture. When her hand opened, the ball tried to expand, but before it could do any more than quiver, a silver light enveloped it and it vanished.

Alex just lay on the floor, staring open mouthed at the spot where the snow globe of death had been a moment earlier. He'd felt the power coming off it like waves of heat from a furnace. It was more than enough power to level the Hotel Astor and maybe some of the surrounding buildings as well.

And Sorsha had stopped it with one hand.

"Sorsha," he gasped, turning to her. "That was incredi—"

As he looked, her eyes rolled back in her head and she collapsed, falling forward. Alex lunged and managed to catch her against his chest before she slammed into the floor.

"Sure," Danny said in a voice dripping with sarcasm, "sacrifice your body to keep *her* from hitting the floor." He pushed himself up to his knees and Alex could see a knot already forming on his forehead. Danny must have felt it because he reached up and touched the spot, then winced.

"Sorry," Alex said, trying to shift Sorsha enough to sit up. "That thing was about to eat both of us."

Danny got his feet under himself and stood.

"Is she going to be all right?" he asked, grabbing Sorsha under her arms and pulling her off Alex. "Where did she send that thing?"

"If we're lucky, the North Atlantic," Alex said, standing and looping one of Sorsha's arms around his neck. "Let's put her on the bed in Diego's room."

"Diego?"

"Evil runewright," Alex supplied.

They carried the unconscious sorceress back to the open door, then laid her gently on the made bed.

"What now?" Danny asked, looking around at the room and the open portmanteau trunk. "There must be plenty of things in here that you can use on another finding rune."

Alex thought about that, but Diego had known when the finding rune connected to him. He'd allowed it so that he and Alex could talk. He'd take steps to prevent that, going forward.

"I don't think that's going to work again," he said, explaining what had happened. "We should look around though. Maybe we can figure out his next move the old fashioned way."

"Alex," Danny said, putting a restraining hand on his friend's shoulder. He nodded in the direction of the bed.

Sorsha seemed to be breathing normally but there was a drop of blood oozing from the corner of her left eye making its way slowly down her cheek. Alex didn't know much about first aid, but he knew bleeding from the eyes was a bad thing.

"You call down to the desk and tell everyone it's okay to come back, while I go get Iggy," he said, pulling his chalk from his pocket. "Then call Captain Callahan and get him over here."

"You sure about that?" Danny asked, picking up the room telephone.

Alex nodded as he began to draw a chalk door on the immaculate wallpaper of the room.

"This is going to be all over the evening papers," he said. "If you don't warn the Captain before that happens, he'll have your head."

"True," Danny said in an unsure voice. "But will he believe any of this?"

"We'll have Sorsha explain it to him."

"All right," Danny said, dialing the number of the front desk. "Hurry up and get Iggy, because I want Sorsha fully awake when the Captain gets here."

Iggy pulled a small flashlight from his pocket and touched the rune carved into a flat spot on the little tube's side. Inside, a second rune began to give off a bright light and he pointed it into Sorsha's left eye.

Reflexively she turned her head, but he grabbed her by the chin and pulled her head back into place.

"Now be a good girl and I'll give you a lollipop when I'm done," he said in the same voice one might use on an unruly toddler.

Sorsha ground her teeth loud enough for Alex to hear, and he smirked.

"You're not helping," she growled at him.

"I don't see any permanent damage," Iggy said, releasing the rune on the side of the light causing it to die. "You burst a blood vessel but it's not serious, just take it easy the next couple of days."

"Thank you, Doctor," Sorsha said, swinging her legs off the side of the bed.

"Take it slow," Iggy said as she leaned forward to stand. "You overexerted yourself, and standing too quickly might make you dizzy."

Sorsha wobbled as she stood, but quickly gained her equilibrium.

"I need to call my team," she said, pressing a hand to her forehead. "I'm not up to teleporting at the moment." She started across the room toward the desk but stopped to give Alex a penetrating look. "That's becoming a regular occurrence around you."

"I could add a vault door to your office," Alex said with a smile. "Then I could walk you home whenever you like."

"Yes, and have you drop by whenever you need some magical information," she said. Her tone was chiding but she wore a half smile.

"Don't forget those times he needs you to stop something from blowing up," Danny added.

Alex tried to elbow his friend, but Danny stepped back too quickly.

"In either case," Sorsha said, trying and failing to hide her amusement. "I think things are fine the way they are. It will only take Agent Mendes fifteen minutes to get here. I'll go wait for her in the lobby."

"Before you go," Alex said, taking her by the arm. "There's something you all need to hear." He looked at Danny. "How long until the Captain gets here?"

Danny looked at his wristwatch and thought for a moment.

"I'd say ten minutes."

Alex took a deep breath and outlined his conversation with Diego Ruiz. When he finished, Iggy shook his head.

"I've never heard that name," he said. "And as far as I know, the Archimedean Monograph was lost for at least one hundred years before I found it."

"And I don't remember seeing any notes by Ruiz in it," Alex added.

"So," Sorsha said. "His story about being trained by a group of immortal runewrights is probably true. We know that immortality is possible, but the only way Diego would know about it is if he actually knew someone who was able to replenish their life energy."

"Do you think he was telling the truth about being thrown out?" Danny asked. "About the damnation rune?"

Alex hesitated for a moment, but then he nodded.

"That fits with the story I got from Jimmy Cortez. Diego lost his ability to use runes, so he went looking for different forms of magic."

"That makes sense," Sorsha said, "but if I understand correctly, glyph runes are just a different way of writing constructs. The magic comes from the same place. So how is he powering his runes?"

"I'm afraid that's where the blood comes in," Iggy said. "The ancient Maya and Inca Indians used to practice human sacrifice, sometimes on a massive scale, all to draw power from blood."

"Does that work?" Danny asked.

"Obviously," Sorsha said. "Otherwise Alex's new brother wouldn't be able to use magic at all."

"You're assuming that the damnation rune works as advertised," Alex offered. "Maybe the blood gives him the power to break through whatever seal the rune put on him."

"Occam's Razor," Iggy said.

Alex knew this one, it was a principle of science suggesting that if you had two equal possibilities, the simplest one was most likely right.

"You think the rune is solid so Diego is using the blood of his victims to power his constructs," Alex guessed.

"Just so."

"Why is the simplest solution that the Immortal's rune is infallible?" Sorsha asked.

"Because Alex met one," Iggy said. "And his power was undeniable."

Alex felt a chill. Iggy had come out and said something he'd been avoiding. He'd thought of it, of course, he just didn't want to consider it.

"Moriarty," he confirmed.

"He is undoubtedly an Immortal," Iggy said, "and I doubt there are two such groups in existence."

Sorsha nodded at that.

"They wouldn't allow it," she said. "They'd either join together or kill each other."

"So what does that do to all the talk of Alex being Moriarty's lever?" Danny asked. "To say nothing of that whole 'move the world' stuff."

Alex had gooseflesh on his arms. This was the thought he didn't want to consider. What if Moriarty hadn't been helping him when he restored a year of his life? What if he did that to give himself time to manipulate Alex, use him to work some great evil? Diego had certainly believed the Immortals had a plan for him.

"It means nothing," Iggy said as the silence between them stretched out. "So far all Moriarty has done is to show us a few tricks. He hasn't asked Alex to actually do anything."

"What if he does?" Danny said.

"If that happens, we tread carefully," Iggy said. "We keep everyone informed, trust each other, and trust our instincts."

"Agreed," Sorsha said. "I doubt these Immortals could pull the wool over all of our eyes."

"All right," Danny said, nodding. "It sounds like we have a plan, such as it is."

"Now we need to catch the Immortal's apprentice," Iggy said. "He used a great deal of magic tonight, so I imagine he'll be in need of more power very soon."

"Any ideas where to start on that?" Danny asked. "He knew we were coming so we won't be able to use a finding rune to locate him."

"I think we should start over there," Alex said. He pointed to the desk where the elaborate hotel telephone stood next to a box of hotel stationary. Above the desk, hanging on the wall was what appeared to be a framed handbill or maybe a magazine illustration. Alex had noticed it earlier, but as he stood talking to his friends and fellow conspirators, his eyes kept being drawn to it.

"Trust you to notice that," Sorsha said in a sardonic voice.

Her irritation was deserved. The illustration was a detailed drawing of a nude young woman. She was slender and athletic, with toned arms, small breasts, and a trim waist. A cloth of some blue fabric was draped over her shoulder and wrapped around her hips, giving her the illusion of clothing but covering nothing. Her hair was in a short bob, like Sorsha's, but it was jet black and it framed her pretty face perfectly. Her left hand was brought forward at her waist level and held an apple with a bite missing from it. Her right arm was raised over her head, and she held a gold arrow that pointed in the direction she was facing.

"That doesn't look like it belongs here," Alex said, taking the picture off the wall.

"No," Iggy agreed. "I suspect your brother apprentice brought it with him."

"His name is Diego," Alex said, irritably. He was really disliking the comparison of Diego to himself.

"Whoever he is, why would he hang this on the wall?" Danny asked.

"Look closer," Iggy said. "Note how the woman's body isn't idealized."

Alex hadn't noticed but now that he looked, he realized that the woman had a large nose and that her hips looked a bit too big for perfect proportions.

"It's like this was drawn from life," Sorsha said.

"Or a photograph," Danny agreed.

"Look here," Alex said, turning the frame on its side. There were bushes at the woman's feet and Greek columns behind her. Alex tapped one of the bushes where a word had been written in ink. The bushes were a light green and the ink was black, making the word hard to see.

"Maria," Danny read. "The girl who posed for this, maybe?"

"Almost certainly," Iggy agreed. "And look on top of that column."

"Confrerie de la Flèche d'Or," Alex managed. "That's not English."

"It's French," Sorsha said. "The Brotherhood of the Golden Arrow, but I don't know what that is."

From down the hall, the elevator chime announced the arrival of the car, and most likely Captain Callahan.

"You'd better make yourself scarce," Alex said to Iggy. They didn't want to have to explain how he'd arrived before the Captain.

"What about Maria and the Brotherhood of the Golden Arrow?" he asked, picking up his medical bag.

"I don't know what they are," Alex admitted with a grin. "But I'm pretty sure I know someone who does."

22

BOOKS & BULLETS

The door chimed as Alex stepped into the musty interior of Bell's Book and Candle. Unlike the previous times he'd been there, five customers were in various stages of browsing the stock of books and oddities. They were a strange lot, three middle-aged women with the look of bored housewives and two men, one short and portly with a dark, scraggly beard, and a tall, athletic man in a wool suit. All of them gave Alex suspicious looks before turning back to their own business.

"Alex!" Theo said with a large grin. "What brings you by?"

Alex shot a quick glance around the room and found all the other patrons watching him surreptitiously. Instead of answering Theo, Alex put his arm around the little man's shoulders and led him over to an empty corner.

"I need to know if you've ever heard of something called the Brotherhood of the Golden Arrow?" he said, keeping his voice low.

Theo chewed his lip for a moment, then shook his head.

"Doesn't sound familiar," he said. "Where did you hear it?"

"Read it on a handbill," Alex said. "Over a picture of a naked woman. She might be named Maria."

Theo shook his head again.

"No," he said. "It sounds like something I'd know, but I don't think I've ever heard of your Brotherhood."

Alex sighed. Billy Tasker had said that when it came to the magical or the occult, Theo's knowledge was unmatched. If he didn't know the Brotherhood of the Golden Arrow, it might actually be some kind of secret society.

But then why did the drawing of the naked woman look like a handbill? That's not a very good way to keep a secret society secret.

"Was there anything else on the picture of the naked woman?" Theo asked, a bit too loudly. Several of the other patrons cast reproving looks his way and the athletic man in the wool suit turned and left the store.

Alex looked back to Theo and shook his head.

"Nothing," he said. "Just the words Brotherhood of the Golden Arrow written in French."

"French?" Theo said, his eyebrows crawling together like fuzzy caterpillars. "That would be…Confrerie…de la Flèche…d'Or," he said.

"Is that different, somehow?"

"No," Theo said, "but that does ring a bell."

He moved over to one of his shelves and began running his finger along the spines of the books, eventually pulling one down. Opening it, he flipped through the pages, pausing occasionally to read before shaking his head and moving on.

"Ah," he said at last, a wide smile lighting up his face. "Here it is, Confrerie de la Flèche d'Or. It was an occult society started in Paris back in 'thirty-two. According to this, it was led by Maria de Naglowska."

"Most likely the Maria from the handbill," Alex said. "Do you know anything about her?"

"Oh, yes," Theo said. "Maria was quite well known in occult circles."

"Was?" Alex said, picking up on the past tense verb.

"Yes. She passed away just last year. Before that though, she was active in the occult community. She was a mystic and wrote extensively on channeling magic through the body."

"Was she a runewright then?" Alex asked.

Theo looked around, as if taking care not to be overheard, then leaned in close to Alex.

"She was a proponent of magical intimacy."

Alex raised an eyebrow at that. He'd heard romantic encounters described as 'magical,' but never literally.

"Is there such a thing?" he asked.

"If you mean, does it exist?" Theo shrugged. "I couldn't say. It has been a field of study for occultists for some time, however. The first known proponent of such theories was P.B. Randolph. Maria was a devotee of his, and translated many of his writings into French."

"Is this Randolph guy still alive?"

"No," Theo said. "He died shortly after the Civil War, if I remember correctly."

Alex chewed his lip. This seemed like a solid lead, but he couldn't connect Maria or Randolph or any of it to Diego Ruiz, beyond the strange framed handbill he'd hung up in his hotel room.

Maybe he just likes pictures of naked girls.

"All right, Theo," Alex sighed. "I guess I wasted your time."

Theo frowned a little, and his eyebrows drooped.

"I'm sorry I couldn't be more help," he said, closing the book he'd been consulting. "I'm not really well versed in Russian occultists."

Alex had started to turn, but he stopped.

"Maria was Russian?" he said. "I thought she was French."

Theo shook his head.

"She was born in St. Petersburg, but she moved around quite a bit. Spent her last years in Paris though. That's where she did most of her writing."

"Are there any writings on her life? You know, where she grew up and where she lived."

Theo drew in a deep breath and considered the question for a long moment.

"I don't think so," he said at last. "There are articles and papers on her, of course, but most of those deal with her philosophy and teachings. I suppose you could look at one of her books though. As I recall, most include a short biography of the author in the front."

"Do you have one of Maria's books?"

"I think I still have a copy of her most recent work," he said, replacing the reference book on the shelf before heading across the store to a shelf on the far side. Alex watched as he abandoned that shelf and crossed to another. As he went, he passed behind one of the women in the store, a plump woman with a pleasant face, dark eyes, and jet-black hair. When Alex noticed her, she gave him a sultry smile and winked. Apparently she'd heard the subject of his conversation with Theo.

Clearing his throat nervously, Alex looked away to where Theo was perusing another shelf. As he did, the woman smirked.

"Here we are," Theo said, returning to hand Alex a slim leather-bound volume. The title was *The Hanging Mystery* and it had Maria's name on the bottom.

Alex took the book and opened to the front. There was a fairly detailed biography of Maria de Naglowska in the front, so Alex closed the book and took out his wallet.

Five minutes later, Alex stepped outside into the afternoon sun with Maria's book sticking up from the outside pocket of his suit coat. It was almost three, so he turned left and headed for the grubby five and dime where he knew there was a public phone.

Time to check in with Sherry.

The little shop was just as he remembered it, with the same disinterested man in the dirty apron behind the lunch counter. The only difference this time was the customer sitting at the end of the counter having a sandwich and a cigarette.

As before, Alex ignored the cook and headed to the booth.

"Did you get the voodoo killer?" Sherry asked when the line connected.

"Yes and no," Alex said. He explained what had happened with Diego and his subsequent trip to Bell's Book and Candle.

"Is there anything I need to know about?" he asked when he

finished. "I want to run everything by Dr. Bell, see if there's anything I missed."

"I'm afraid that's going to have to wait, boss," Sherry said. "Mr. Barton wants you out at the new tower. He said you need to renew your rune on the transfer plate case."

Alex closed his eyes and rubbed his forehead.

"I need to put a vault door in that tower," he grumbled.

"What's that, boss?"

"Sorry," Alex said. "It's nothing. I'll grab a cab south until I can pick up the skycrawler, so if Andrew calls, tell him I should be there by four."

"Will do," Sherry said. Alex was about to hang up when she went on. "I also have that warehouse information you wanted."

Alex sighed and set the phone's earpiece down on the shelf in the booth.

"Hold on," he told Sherry as he dug out his notebook. "Okay," he said once he'd picked up the earpiece again. "What was in the crates that were broken open?"

"I could tell you that," Sherry said. "Or I could just tell you what they were looking for."

"If you can do that, I'll buy you a nice lunch on Monday."

"In each of the three warehouses, one of the opened crates contained radio parts."

Alex furrowed his brow as he wrote that down.

"Why would someone break open a box of radio parts?" he wondered out loud.

"I wondered that too," Sherry said. "So I called the radio stations where the parts were delivered. According to the secretary at each station, the parts were to upgrade their existing equipment."

Alex felt his headache getting worse.

"So this could just be someone trying to sabotage their competitors," he said. "Give me the addresses of these radio stations."

Alex wrote them down as she gave them to him, then thanked her and hung up. He was tempted to call Iggy and get him started on Diego and Maria de Naglowska but he didn't have time to explain it all with Barton expecting him out in Brooklyn.

With a sigh of resignation, he put away his notebook and picked up his hat from the little shelf. Turning, he opened the booth door and came face to face with the man from the counter. Alex realized, a moment too late, that it was the athletic man in the wool suit he'd seen in Theo's shop. The man smiled at him — a look of immense satisfaction — then he raised his arm, bringing a snub-nosed revolver with it, and fired three times.

Alex staggered back as the bullets hit him in the chest and upper arm. It happened so quickly that he hadn't had time to activate his flash ring or turn his back. He slammed into the back of the phone booth and dropped unceremoniously to the floor, not sure if his shield runes had stopped the bullets or if one of them had hit him where his jacket didn't cover. Even if the shield runes had stopped the bullets, the revolver still had three left and Alex only had two remaining shield runes. If he moved or tried to get up, the athletic man would just keep shooting.

Alex did the only thing he could think of. He played dead.

Above him the gunman hesitated, then he turned and ran out the front of the shop, slamming the door open and sending the bell above it flying.

Alex waited a full fifteen seconds before opening an eye. The only thing remaining of his assailant was the swinging door and the broken bell on the floor.

"Mister?" the terrified voice of the cook called. "Mister, are you okay?"

Alex wondered just what the man thought had happened that would leave him okay. The gunman had been a pro. He waited until Alex was in an enclosed space, with nowhere to go, and had shot at point blank range.

Looking down, Alex found that his white shirt was still pristine. The gunman's bullets had hit his left lapel and shoulder. Closing his eyes, he said a silent prayer of thanks and crossed himself.

"Mister?" the cook called out again. From the sound of it, he was still hiding behind the lunch counter.

"I'm all right," Alex said, climbing to his feet. "Guy must have been nervous. He missed me."

As Alex exited the booth, the cook peeked up over the counter, his eyes the size of saucers.

"Wow, Mister, you was really lucky," the man said, finally standing up.

"Yeah, that's me," Alex said, not bothering to hide the sarcasm. "Mr. Lucky." He nodded in the direction of the vanished gunman. "You ever see that guy before?"

The cook shook his head.

"He just came in and asked for a sandwich."

"That's all?"

"Well, he bought a bunch of cigarettes, too," the cook said. "Then he stood over there by the door while I made the sandwich. He only just came back when you came in."

Alex nodded. The man had been watching for him and used the five and dime for cover. It was a good plan, one Alex had used himself.

Knowing that the would-be assassin was long gone, Alex turned back to the counter. Moving down to the end, he found the plate with a half-eaten ham sandwich and an ashtray with a still-smoldering cigarette in it.

"You said the man bought cigarettes from you?" Alex asked the cook.

The cook nodded, his eyes still bulging.

Alex picked up the cigarette and sniffed it, then he turned it over in his hand. It was shorter than a normal cigarette and the aroma was strange.

"Is this one of the cigarettes he bought," Alex asked. "Or did he already have an open pack?"

"He...he bought that one," the cook said.

"That's what I thought," Alex said, taking out his own silver cigarette case and flipping it open. He crushed out the gunman's cigarette and dropped it into an empty spot in his case.

Snapping the case shut, Alex returned it to his pocket and made his way to the still open front door.

"Hey," the cook called out. "Shouldn't you wait for the cops? I mean, we should call the cops, right?"

Alex looked back at the man with a shrug.

"And tell them what? That someone neither of us ever saw before took a shot at me and missed?"

"Uh," the cook said. From the look his face, he was certain there was something wrong with Alex's statement but wasn't able to work out what.

"Tell you what," Alex said, taking one of his cards out of his shirt pocket and dropping it on the lunch counter. "If that guy comes back to buy more cigarettes, you call me. Understand?"

"He won't," the cook said. "He bought out all the packs I had."

Alex nodded, more to himself than the cook, and walked out, shutting the swinging door behind him.

The skycrawler ride out to Brooklyn took half an hour and it gave Alex plenty of time to think. He'd been lucky, very lucky, and he knew it. If the gunman had aimed for Alex's tie, Dr. Wagner would be scraping what was left of him out of that phone booth.

With a great deal of personal satisfaction, no doubt.

He needed to figure out a better way to deploy his shield runes, something that would cover the center of his chest. He'd thought about putting the runes on his vest, but then they wouldn't protect his arms. Of course, if he was shot where his suit coat didn't cover, it wouldn't matter if he could use his arms. Like most magic, it was a trade-off, and he'd have to spend some serious time thinking about it before he changed anything.

By the time he arrived at Barton Electric's Brooklyn Relay Tower, his watch showed just past four. He waved at the security guards, who knew him by sight, and headed up in the elevator to the top floor. As the door opened, the noise of workmen and the sounds of construction greeted him.

"Right on time," Barton called over the din as Alex emerged from the elevator.

"Came as soon as I could," he said, looking up. In the space where the roof had been there were only the wooden joist beams. "What's all this?"

Barton looked up as one of the workmen walked across the joist, sending a shower of sawdust and dirt cascading down. The Lightning Lord made a shooing gesture with his hand and the dust shifted away from his navy-blue suit.

"I was going over the blueprints last night and I realized that I can extend the tower's range another half-mile if I replace the roof with one made of steel and make it slightly convex. The problem is, it will take three days to do the work, so I'll need you to keep putting those waterproofing runes on the transfer plate case until they're done."

Alex grinned at that. It was about time he got an easy request. He'd started using rune engraving to fix the roof at the old Brotherhood of Hope when he was a teenager. For the glass case he could scribe the rune into a brass plate and just mount it on the top of the glass. That would last at least a month, well past when the new roof should be done.

He explained the process to Barton, who nodded enthusiastically the whole time.

"How long will it take to make that plate?" he asked.

"I have a piece of brass that will work," Alex said. "But I'll need to prepare it for the rune and that will take a few hours. I'll work on it tonight and have it ready for tomorrow."

Barton looked up at the sky through the hole in the roof.

"Do you have another of those fancy barrier runes?" he asked. "I have other projects I need to work on, but I don't want to leave if it might rain."

Alex nodded. Of course a sorcerer could keep the transfer plate case dry; his magic was far more powerful than Alex's, but while sorcerers could create powerful and near-permanent spells, utility magic required them to focus on the problem. If Barton wanted to use magic to keep the transfer plates dry, he would have to stay on site.

Alex pulled out his rune book and flipped to the back where he kept the runes he didn't use much. After a few moments of searching, he tore out his remaining standard barrier rune, mentally adding it to the growing list of runes he needed to write to restock his red book.

"This'll hold through tomorrow," he said. "I'll come by after church and mount the brass plate on top of the case."

Barton smiled and the lines of stress bled out of his face. Alex didn't wonder about that; with the power fluctuating in Brooklyn for the last couple of days, it was a sure thing Barton was getting an earful from the city.

"The Jersey City Tower won't be this much trouble," Barton said, leaning wearily against the glass case. "I promise."

Alex didn't trust himself to respond to that. When he stepped up to stick the barrier rune to the top of the glass case, however, thoughts of Barton's woes and the upcoming tower across the river were driven from his mind. His skin prickled as he felt the protective bubble of the still active barrier pass over him.

The rune he'd cast yesterday should have expired by now. It was possible for runes to last longer than anticipated, little things about how they were written could affect that. The problem here was that, as barrier runes decayed, the bubble of protection they created became weaker and weaker.

The bubble Alex had just passed through when he approached the case felt as it were near full strength.

"Something wrong?" Barton asked, noticing Alex's confusion.

"No," Alex said, sticking the new rune to the top of the glass. "It's just the previous rune hasn't fully decayed yet."

"But that's not a problem," Barton said, his worry lines creeping back onto his face. "It's not going to interfere with the new one, right?"

Alex nodded his assurance.

"Most runes can occupy the same space without interfering with each other," he said, lighting the flash paper with his lighter. Rune interference would cause runes and their effects to decay quickly. It was the principle reason he couldn't have more than five shield runes on his suit coat at one time.

That reminded Alex, he'd need to put new shield runes on his coat to replace the ones used up that afternoon.

Alex sighed as he added that to the list of things he had to do before he could sleep.

"Is it working?" Barton asked as the glow of the barrier rune faded away.

Alex could feel the fresh power of the new rune and he nodded.

"Good," Barton said. "Get that brass plate done and then get some rest. You look like hell."

Alex chuckled and nodded, then, before he could protest, Barton grabbed his shoulder and they both vanished.

23

NIL

"You look like five miles of bad road," Iggy greeted Alex as he came into the kitchen at the brownstone. "Did you manage to track down the apprentice?"

Alex shook his head as he slumped down into one of the heavy kitchen chairs. Iggy was cooking something, which smelled wonderful, but Alex was just too wrung out to care.

"Well, you know about the first part of my day," he said. "After almost getting blown up by an insane runewright, I went to look into that illustration of the naked woman."

"Any luck with that?"

Alex pulled the thin leather book he'd bought from Theo from where it stuck up out of his jacket pocket and dropped it on the table. Iggy wiped his hands on his apron and came over to examine it.

"The Hanging Mystery," he read the title with interest.

"I wouldn't," Alex said as he opened the front flap. "It's by the woman in the picture, Maria de Naglowska. It's her treatise on how the suspension of an intimate partner can allow people to gain magic powers."

Iggy rolled his eyes and shook his head.

"Not this nonsense again," he said, dropping the book on the table.

"You know about this stuff?" Alex asked, sitting up.

"Such theories have been pursued and practiced throughout history," he said, stirring something on the stove. "Every few decades someone with enough charisma manages to gather followers to go dancing around naked in the woods practicing free love and such. It's a vulgar perversion of both magic and human intimacy."

"So there's nothing to it?" Alex asked.

"Of course not," Iggy said, sounding as if the question should have been self-evident. "If that worked, I guarantee you would have heard of it before now."

"But you said that blood magic works," Alex countered. "And I hadn't heard of that until this week."

"That would seem to be obvious as well," Iggy said. "When we draw life energy, we don't use humans, we use swine. So why is the apprentice killing people, something that's bound to attract attention, instead of just using animals?"

"You think it has to be human blood for him to use it as a source of magic?"

"His behavior thus far supports that conclusion," Iggy said.

"Not necessarily," Alex said, looking at the book on the table. "So far, Deigo has killed prostitutes, ones that he's been intimate with, and he's suspended their bodies, just like Maria advocates in her book."

Iggy nodded, stroking his mustache.

"If he believed what Maria was selling, he might think the blood and the sex are linked," he said at last. "Each one making the other stronger."

"That would explain why he uses human blood," Alex said. "Unfortunately it doesn't help Danny and I catch him."

Iggy didn't respond as he took the pan he was stirring off the stove.

"Is there any way to modify the finding rune so Diego won't know it's found him?" Alex asked.

Iggy shook his head.

"You've already got the best finding rune I know how to make," he said, then added, "I suppose I could give it some thought. Maybe something will come to me."

Iggy picked up a plate and brought it to the table while Alex moved

Maria's book further down. The plate had a baked potato and a slab of meat on it, and both were covered by a reddish-brown sauce. Once Iggy put the plate down, Alex's appetite came roaring back.

"So what else happened today?" Iggy asked, returning to fix a plate for himself.

"Someone tried to kill me," he said, listening to his stomach growl. "They almost managed it too."

Iggy returned to the table, setting down his own plate, then gave Alex a penetrating look.

"I see you weathered the attack well enough," he said, sitting opposite Alex. "Now say grace for us, and don't forget to thank the good Lord that you're alive."

Alex did as he was told and, once he'd finished, Iggy began questioning him about the attack in the phone booth.

"Maybe you should split up your shield runes," Iggy said when Alex finished the story. "Put two on your vest and the rest on the coat."

"What I need is a way for a shield rune to cover my whole body," he said. "Could I tattoo them on my skin like the escape rune?"

"Yes," Iggy acknowledged. "But you'd have to have them redone every time one got used."

Alex didn't like the sound of that.

"Maybe put two on my body and the other three on my coat," he said. "That'd protect me if someone tried to shoot me in the head."

Iggy prevaricated, weighing the idea.

"For now that's a workable solution, but I want you to get that escape rune put on first."

"I'll go see Joe Mamoru tomorrow," Alex said. Joe was a second-generation Japanese who was probably the best tattoo artist in the city. When Alex first approached tattoo artists to do his original escape rune, most of them hadn't even wanted to try it. Joe took it as a challenge.

"Good," Iggy said. "Do you think the shooter is the same person who sent you and Sorsha that bottle of drugged wine?"

"No," Alex said, though he had to admit, it wasn't a far-fetched idea. "Whoever sent the wine was after Sorsha, not me. The drug removed her power, remember?" He reached into his vest pocket and took out his silver cigarette case. Opening it, he took out the stub of the cigarette the gunman had been smoking and passed it across the table.

Iggy took the stub and turned it over in his hand, then sniffed it.

"Nil," he said, setting it down again. "An uncommon brand but not unknown."

"According to the cook at the lunch counter, the gunman was very excited to see them and bought his entire stock."

Iggy considered that for a long moment, then nodded.

"You think your Teutonic friends are back," he said.

Alex nodded.

"Nil is a German brand of cigarette," he said. "And the gunman's reaction to seeing them means they are likely his favorite brand. As you said, Nil is an uncommon brand in the States, so it follows that the shooter is German."

"It's not an airtight case," Iggy said with a frown, but then he nodded. "But it seems the most likely explanation. The question bothering me is why? It's been four years since you foiled the Nazis' plan to start a civil war here in the U.S. Seems like a long time to wait for revenge."

"True," Alex admitted. "But as far as I know, I haven't had any other interactions with Nazis."

"Maybe it's about something entirely different," Iggy said. "Just because the gunman hails from Germany doesn't mean he's an agent of their government. Maybe the gunman is connected to one of your current cases."

Alex had considered that idea, but Diego didn't seem like the type to have others do his dirty work, and he wasn't even close to catching the gang who broke into the warehouse. As far as he knew, they didn't even know he was after them. When Alex expressed these doubts, Iggy gave him a steady look.

"What?" Alex asked, trying not to be defensive.

"What about the murdered girl?" he said. "The calculator for the government."

"That's not my case," Alex said, though he saw how whoever killed Alice Cartwright might not know that.

"She has access to government secrets," Iggy pointed out.

"And she's been communicating with someone in a highly complex code," Alex finished. "Detective Nicholson was right, Alice Cartwright was a spy."

"It's certainly possible," Iggy said with a nod. "Even probable. You need to break that code to prove it, though."

Alex thought about that. He'd left the details of the code to Detective Nicholson. Nicholson was a decent enough sort, but his abilities as a detective were mediocre at best. Harcourt, the government man, had insisted Alice Cartwright was in possession of top secret information, but Alex had considered that to be self-important hot air.

What if it wasn't?

Stifling a curse, Alex stood up.

"Excuse me," he said. "I need to let Detective Nicholson know that those coded messages might be correspondence with a Nazi agent. If they went after me, they might go after him too."

"Surely he's not carrying them around on his person," Iggy said as Alex made his way to the phone.

"No," Alex acknowledged, "but killing Nicholson would be a great way to sideline his investigation."

Alex picked up the phone and dialed the Central Office. It was just after five, but he managed to catch the Detective before he left.

"I'm not having any luck with those love letters," he said when Alex got him on the line. "Nobody has any idea how that code even works, much less how to crack it."

"You need to call Harcourt," Alex said. "The government is bound to have a code cracker that can figure it out."

"I'm not turning my case over to that jackass," Nicholson fumed.

Alex took a deep breath and told Nicholson about the shooting in the five and dime and its possible connection to Alice Cartwright's murder.

"I thought you said that if Miss Cartwright was a spy, she wouldn't keep the letters," Nicholson shot back. "She would've burned them, right?"

"People do stupid things," Alex said. "Maybe that's why she was killed, her collaborator found out she hadn't destroyed them. In any case, a German man tried to kill me today and I don't have any other cases that involve Europe or potential spies."

"So how will bringing Harcourt in help?" Nicholson growled. "He'll just take the coded letters and disappear."

"Probably," Alex admitted. "But if you keep them, whoever came after me might come after you. And, if you don't turn them over and Harcourt finds out…"

"He could level a treason charge at me," Nicholson said, then he swore. "All right, I'll call him first thing Monday morning."

"Why wait so long?"

Nicholson laughed.

"You don't know these government types, do you, Lockerby? It's ten after five, he's gone home, and he won't be back till Monday. So has anyone who might be able to tell me where he lives or his phone number."

Alex hadn't considered that, but Nicholson had a point, the government kept banker's hours. Since tomorrow was Saturday, Harcourt wouldn't be back to his office for two days.

"Just make sure those documents are locked up somewhere safe," Alex said. "And keep your eyes open."

Nicholson promised that he would, then he hung up.

"You don't sound convinced," Iggy said as Alex came back to the table.

"Nicholson reminded me that I thought Alice Cartwright's coded letters were from a lover," Alex said. "Because if she were a spy, she would have burned them."

"Possibly," Iggy said. "I guess it depends on what the letters really say."

"I still think I'm missing something," Alex said. Iggy wasn't a big believer in intuition, but Alex had learned to trust his gut over the years.

"Take your time and think it through," Iggy encouraged him. "Just don't take too long. We've got an appointment at the spa and since you're home early, we might as well go over right after dinner."

It was after nine when Alex and Iggy got back to the brownstone. The life transfer rune had performed exactly as expected, and Iggy recovered from the experience in less than half an hour. Alex had wanted to use his vault to go home, but Iggy had felt so good that he insisted they go to a nightclub and have a belt. One turned into a few, which turned into a few more, and now the old man was feeling a bit more jovial than usual.

"I haven't had that much fun in years," Iggy said, hanging his hat on one of the pegs in the hallway.

Alex followed him, shutting the vestibule door and hanging up his hat as well. His night hadn't been quite as enjoyable. Since someone had already tried to kill him in a public place, Alex was wearing his 1911 in its shoulder holster, and he'd only had two drinks.

"What say we have a cigar and I'll tell you about the book I've been thinking of writing," Iggy suggested.

"Is that wise?" Alex asked. "What if someone recognizes your style?"

"Tosh," Iggy said. "Lots of writers these days use the same style. I'm going to put on my smoking jacket," he declared. Then before Alex could say anything, his mentor ran up the stairs, two at a time.

Alex laughed at that and opened the humidor on the reading table, taking out two of Iggy's finest Cubans. He'd just finished trimming them when Iggy returned, resplendent in his embroidered jacket.

"You look ten years younger," Alex said, passing him a cigar.

"I feel twenty years younger," he said, sitting down to light the cigar.

Alex moved to the liquor cabinet, setting out two tumblers and a bottle of Iggy's best twenty-year old Scotch.

"So what will you do with it?" he asked, as he poured two fingers of the amber liquid into each glass.

"With what, dear boy?" Iggy asked, blowing out a plume of fragrant smoke.

"Eternity."

Alex passed his mentor a tumbler, then took his seat on the far side of the reading table. As he sipped his Scotch, Iggy just sat, considering Alex's words.

"Do you really think I look younger?" he asked after a long pause.

"Maybe not ten years," Alex admitted, "but yeah. I suspect next time it will be even more. Give it a few years and you'll look my age."

Iggy furrowed his brow and contemplated his Scotch for a long time while Alex puffed on his cigar.

"It is an interesting question," he said. "I'd be a young man again."

"We could both work at the agency," Alex said.

Iggy chuckled at that.

"I think I'll leave that to you," he said. "But I could open a medical practice or start a new writing career. It certainly fires the imagination. Although I suspect that the Immortals will have something to say about it. I doubt Moriarty revealed the possibility of immortality to you without some kind of long-term plan."

Alex felt the muscles in his jaw tighten and he nodded.

"Diego said pretty much the same thing," he said.

"Don't let it bother you, lad," Iggy said. "We'll deal with that when it comes. Right now, let's just enjoy this moment."

"I'll drink to that," Alex said, holding out his glass. Iggy reached across the table and clinked his glass against Alex's.

The next moment Alex was thrown to the floor as a massive explosion rocked the brownstone. The sound seemed to roll on like echoing thunder, long after the floor stopped shaking.

Alex pushed himself to his feet. Iggy lay on the floor by the window, rolling slowly onto his back. The windows were cracked in spiderweb patterns, but the glass was still intact, because the runes that protected the house had kept the shards in place. Dozens of books had been thrown from the shelves and covered the floor. Luckily the weather was still warm because if there had been a fire in the grate, embers would have been scattered all over the fallen books.

Reaching down, Alex took Iggy's hand and helped him to his feet. His lips were moving, but all Alex could hear was a ringing in his ears.

Realizing Alex couldn't hear, Iggy pointed toward the vestibule.

Alex stepped over the ruin of his broken tumbler and the fallen books. As he rounded the corner into the foyer, the glass sidewall and door of the vestibule were shattered but still held in place by the magic. He couldn't see well through the spiderweb patterns of cracks, but as he pulled the vestibule door open, the front door beyond was completely gone.

All Alex could do was stare. The door to the brownstone could withstand a crew with a battering ram, but now it was entirely missing. One of the brass hinges hung, twisted from the remainder of the frame, clinging vainly to a tiny sliver of the vanished door. Beyond the gaping hole where the door had stood, the paving stones of the stoop were fractured and broken, radiating out from a central point a few feet away from the threshold.

Alex jumped as something hit his shoulder and he whirled around to find Iggy yelling at him. Reaching up, Alex tapped his ears and the ringing subsided a bit.

"-reful," Iggy's voice finally came to him. "You don't know what's out there."

Alex turned back to the gaping hole, but he couldn't see much beyond the stoop as the outside lights had been blown out as well. What he could see was tiny shards of what looked like glass in the very center of the blast radius. He reached up under his left arm and pulled his 1911 free from its holster.

Taking a tentative step out through the door, Alex looked around, keeping the gun low. Already lights were appearing in the brownstones across the street and heads were appearing in windows. Feeling like it would be safe enough, he took another step and crouched down where he'd seen the glass. There were several curved shards of thin glass lying in a rough circle in the exact center of the spiderweb cracks in the masonry of the stoop.

"What the devil is that?" Iggy said, looking over Alex's shoulder.

"Unless I miss my guess," Alex said, holding the glass up so he could see its curving surface, "it's a piece of a snow globe."

"What does that mean?"

Alex stood up, his eyes sweeping the streets to the right and left, trying to penetrate the darkness.

"It means Diego Ruiz just tried to blow our house down."

Iggy glanced around as if he expected Diego to suddenly appear.

"Is he after you?"

"I doubt it," Alex said. "He seemed genuinely pleased to meet me earlier."

"Then why do this?"

"He wants to find a way to circumvent the damnation rune," Alex said.

Iggy nodded, catching Alex's train of thought.

"He thinks you have the Archimedean Monograph," he guessed.

Alex stood and tossed the bit of glass away.

"And he just tried to come in and take it."

24

EXPROPRIATION

"Long night, son?"

The voice pulled Alex from a fitful sleep and he startled awake. His neck hurt, along with his back, and the air smelled cool and musty.

"What?" he muttered as his eyes tried and failed to focus.

"I asked if you had a long night," the voice came again, this time tinged with amusement. "But I can tell you must have."

Alex's vision finally cleared and he found himself in Saint Patrick's Cathedral, sitting in an empty pew. A man in a black cassock and white collar sat in the next row up, looking back with a grin on his face.

"Oh, hi, Father di Francesca," Alex said, sitting up straight and rubbing his eyes. "Sorry. I didn't mean to fall asleep in the Mass."

The Father laughed. He was a thin man with bad skin, dark eyes, and a ready smile. He'd emigrated from Italy when he was a young man, but he still had a bit of the old country in his accent.

"God will forgive you," he said easily. "I hope you weren't out carousing, though."

Alex shook his head.

"You hear about that gas explosion over on the East Side?" he said.

Gas explosion was the official explanation for the damage on Iggy's block.

Father Di Francesca's face blanched and he took hold of Alex's arm.

"Was that near you?" he gasped. "Was anyone hurt?"

"It was right outside Dr. Bell's house," Alex said, "but it happened after ten so there wasn't anyone on the street."

"Praise God," the Father said with a relieved nod.

Alex nodded in agreement, then sighed.

"Dr. Bell and I were up most of the night, writing mending runes to fix the broken windows at our neighbors' homes."

"That's a very Christian thing to do," Father Di Francesca observed. He patted Alex's arm and stood up. "Now, you need to go home and get some rest. Even the Savior rested now and again."

"Thank you, Father," Alex said, grabbing the back of the pew in front and pulling himself to his feet. "And thanks for the Mass. What I heard was great."

He shook the Father's hand and headed out to the street. Tired as he was, Alex had a lot to do before he'd be able to get any rest. He and Iggy had managed to patch up the neighboring houses with several hundred dollars' worth of standard mending runes, but the brownstone was still a wreck and in need of a front door. Add to that the fact that Alex promised Andrew Barton that he'd install a long-term barrier rune in the Brooklyn tower, and Alex had plenty to keep him occupied.

Since it was Sunday, there wasn't anyplace to get a decent cup of coffee, so Alex just got on the skycrawler a block from the church and headed south and east. He had to change lines near City Hall, but then it was a straight shot across the river and out to Brooklyn. The view as the crawler crossed the East River was still amazing, but Alex had seen it so many times in the last weeks that he didn't even notice, dozing as the crawler zipped along the steel beam that supported it.

A few minutes later, Alex knocked on the door of the Brooklyn Relay Tower until the surly weekend guard let him in. The guard gave Alex a look that spoke volumes, but the man knew better than to offer an opinion to someone who was often in the company of his sorcerer boss.

Alex rode the elevator up to the top floor and smiled when the door opened and he saw the chalked outline of a door on the wall opposite. He crossed to it and opened his vault immediately. The knowledge that his vault bed, the bed in the brownstone, and the one in his apartment in Empire Tower were easily accessible sent a wave of weariness cascading through him, but Alex had a job to do.

"Miles to go before I sleep," he quoted, shuffling to one of the two heavy workbenches on the right side of his workspace. On top of the bench, a plate of bronze sat on a drying rack, glistening with now-hardened lacquer. Alex had painted it over once he'd finished engraving the rune and filling the lines with the prepared inks that would allow it to work. Since this was a standard barrier rune, the ingredients in the ink were more exotic than for a minor rune, which only required pencil lead. The lacquer would protect the plate from corroding, which could interfere with the rune.

Alex picked up the plate, feeling the magic in it, waiting just below the surface. Closing his eyes, he let the sensation bombard his senses. He'd learned, early on in his career, that runes, even uncast ones, would give off energy that he could feel. If the rune was done right, the feeling was like a musical chord, everything in harmony. A bad rune felt more like nails on a blackboard.

The rune on the plate hummed with his touch, all the energies in line, ready to be activated. Alex sighed with satisfaction. He was so tired, he hadn't been completely sure he'd done the rune correctly until that moment.

"All right," he said out loud to jar himself into action. "Let's get you in place."

He left his vault and headed toward the pillar that held up the transfer plates in their glass case. Above him, the trusses that held the ceiling up were still visible, but he could no longer see the doughnut-shaped projection antenna above. The workmen already had the metal sheeting in place that would make up the new roof.

Barton must be paying very well to get the job done this fast.

As he stepped around the cement pillar that held up the transfer plates, he felt the bubble of the energy from the rune he'd put on the night before pass over him. Just like last night, it felt stronger than he expected it would, but there were a few hours left before it would fade completely, so that wasn't anything to be worried about.

Setting the brass plate on top of the glass case, Alex took a minor binding rune from the pocket of his shirt and dropped it onto the plate. Igniting it with his lighter, the paper flared and vanished, locking the plate to the glass it sat on. With that done, Alex touched the rune etched into the plate, activating the magic within it. He could still feel the remnant of the previous rune, but the power of the new rune quickly eclipsed it.

Alex leaned against the case for a long moment, just reveling in the simple act of checking something off his list. Finally he sighed and pushed himself up. The lure of his vault was even more tempting, but he walked purposely back to the little hall by the elevator and pushed the call button. While the door opened, he crossed the hall and pulled the heavy door of his vault shut. Waiting until the door melted away into the wall, he entered the elevator car and headed back down to the ground floor.

Sunday was usually Alex's day to not worry about his cases. He respected the Sabbath, but beyond that, most things were closed on Sunday, which prevented any serious investigation. This time, however, he had a stop to make.

Something about the warehouse thefts still bothered Alex. At first it had seemed like some competitor had wanted to sabotage his competition, but that theory fell apart when Alex learned that the radio parts had been ordered by different stations in different areas.

Something else was at work here and he needed to know what.

Fortunately for Alex, radio stations operated on Sunday, and one of them was only a few blocks away from the Brooklyn Tower. That meant the problem of the warehouse thefts was an itch Alex could scratch.

The offices of WGRM radio were in a tiny building in a nondescript Brooklyn neighborhood. The only thing that gave it away was the large antenna rising above the back of the building. Stepping up to the door, Alex knocked. A full minute passed before he knocked again. Finally, when Alex was ready to knock a third time, the door was pushed open by a short, rotund man in shirt-sleeves and suspenders with the stub of a cigar clenched in his teeth.

"What are you, lost?" the man demanded.

Alex held out one of his cards and introduced himself.

"I got about a minute until I have to change the phonograph," the man said. "What's a private dick got to do with me?"

"Can I come in and ask you a few questions? It's about some equipment you ordered."

"We order equipment all the time, so what?"

"I think some of your gear might have been sabotaged."

The man chewed his cigar for a second, then he stepped back, allowing Alex inside.

"I've got to change the record, but then we can talk," he said. "Wait here."

The inside of the building had a lounge room just beyond the door with broken down couches and chairs arranged in a rough circle. A small desk, probably for a receptionist, stood by the entrance to a narrow hallway where the cigar-smoking man had gone. The wall behind the desk had windows running its length and revealed a studio where microphones had been set up. Just inside the glass was a row of instruments and dials along with several phonographs.

As Alex watched, the fat man spun up a record on a phonograph just as the song on a second phonograph was ending. With precision born of experience, he effortlessly switched the microphone over to the new phonograph, then he stood and made his way back out to the lounge area.

"That's an overture," he said, still chewing on his cigar. "We've got about ten minutes, so what is it you want to know?"

"You got a shipment of parts a few days ago," Alex said. "I was wondering if you noticed anything wrong with them?"

The man looked confused and shook his head.

"Like what?" he demanded. "As far as I know everything is working properly. I have to check the signal and frequency at least once an hour and everything is fine."

"Look, Mr.—"

"Wilkerson," the fat man said. "Aaron Wilkerson."

"Mr. Wilkerson," Alex began. "There was a break-in at the warehouse where your parts were stored and the thieves broke open the crate with your parts, but they didn't take anything."

"Sounds like the crime of the century," Wilkerson said, rapidly losing interest.

"I think they sabotaged your parts," Alex explained. "Could there be something wrong with what you got and you not know about it?"

Wilkerson thought about that, chewing on his cigar the entire time.

"I suppose," he admitted finally. "I don't remember anything being worked on this week, but I'm not here all the time. Let me look at the maintenance log."

He went back into the booth behind the glass and pulled a clipboard out of a drawer. When he returned, he was flipping through the pages.

"Here it is," he said. "We ordered some new transmission equipment. With Andrew Barton's new tower just up the street, we need more power to cut through the static. Our system uses an old Alexanderson rig, it just doesn't have the juice of the new ones with the vacuum tubes."

"So is it working like it's supposed to?" Alex prodded, not really understanding what Wilkerson was talking about.

"Don't know," he said, shaking his head. "It wasn't installed."

"Can I see it, then?"

Wilkerson shook his head.

"The reason we haven't installed it is that it was expropriated," he said.

"Ex...what?" Alex asked, wondering if his tired mind had missed something.

Wilkerson raised an eyebrow, flipping the paper down on the clipboard.

"Expropriated," he said again. "Means the government came in and took it."

"The government can do that?" Alex asked.

"Sure," Wilkerson said. "If the feds want something, they just show up with paperwork and take it. They're supposed to pay us for it, but I'm not going to hold my breath."

Alex's tired brain snapped into focus as he processed that information. Why would the government take radio equipment? The obvious answer was that they needed it for something right away and didn't have time to order one for themselves. So what did they need it for?

Wilkerson needed that equipment to cut through the static put out by Barton's new tower. Did the government need it for the same reason?

"Anything else?" Wilkerson asked. "I need to get back to work."

"Who took the equipment?" Alex asked.

"I told you, the government."

"But who from the government?"

"I don't know," Wilkerson protested. "I wasn't here when they came."

"Who was here? Would they know who picked up the equipment?" Alex pressed.

"I guess," Wilkerson said. "But if you really want to know, come back tomorrow and talk to Martha, she's our receptionist. Whoever expropriated that equipment would have brought paperwork. The government runs on paperwork, and they don't do anything without it. Martha can show you the form they brought and that will tell you who took it."

Alex thanked Wilkerson and headed back to the street. His mind was working overtime and he didn't even notice he'd walked two blocks until he reached the skycrawler station near the transmission tower. The phony thefts at the warehouses were starting to make some sense. If someone knew in advance that the Feds needed radio parts, and if those parts were hard to come by, then whoever it was could intercept the parts and alter them. Then, when the Feds showed up and took said parts, they'd be getting sabotaged equipment. It was a brilliant scheme, but there were an awful lot of 'ifs' involved. Whoever it was would have to have knowledge of whatever the Feds were doing, and they'd have to know what parts the Feds would need. That might make whoever was behind this easy to identify, assuming Alex could find out what federal agency needed the parts and why.

Why was the real question.

What could the saboteur have done that would really matter? If Alex could figure that out, it might tell him why the government needed a new vacuum tube transmitter.

"But if all they needed was the transmitter," he mumbled out loud as he waited for a skycrawler, "why sabotage three orders of parts?"

The obvious answer was that the saboteur didn't know which parts the government would expropriate. They had to sabotage every transmitter that arrived in the city during their window of opportunity. And that meant that the other radio stations might have the sabotaged parts. If Alex could find out what had been done to them, it might tell him what the saboteur was after.

Feeling more energy than he had had in hours, Alex opened his notebook and checked for the address of the closest radio station.

25

KIDNAPPING

Alex was up early the next morning, despite still being tired. Iggy had worked most of Sunday writing mending runes to fix the damage Diego's explosion had done to the brownstone, so Alex dressed quietly and let his mentor sleep. There still wasn't a front door, but the runes on the inner vestibule door were just as sturdy, so Alex wasn't worried. With Iggy sleeping, however, Alex was on his own for breakfast. Iggy had taught Alex a great many things, but thus far competency in the kitchen wasn't one of them. Fortunately, Empire Station opened at six, ready for the influx of working people traveling around the city to their various places of employment. And with the opening of the station, Alex had access to breakfast and, more importantly, Marnie's coffee.

He was excited to get started but Martha, the receptionist, wouldn't be in at WGRM until eight, so he ate at the Empire Station cafe, drank his coffee, and read the paper. The day before, he'd visited all three radio stations to ask about their new equipment. He'd assumed, after the first visit, that only WGRM's equipment had been taken by the government, but that turned out to be wrong. All the stations had ordered different parts, and all of them had been confiscated in the name of government need.

Alex had thought that whoever took the transmission equipment from WGRM had sabotaged multiple versions of the same equipment because they didn't know which one the government men would take. Now it looked like the saboteurs were working with a turncoat in the government, perhaps whoever authorized the expropriation.

He needed the forms the government men brought when they seized the parts. Those would tell him who had done the authorizing, and what agency they worked for. Fortunately, all he needed to do was to ride the crawler out to Brooklyn and meet WGRM's receptionist when she arrived.

When Martha Tourmaline, receptionist for WGRM Radio, arrived at the station promptly at eight, Alex was already waiting for her. He was properly fed and caffeinated, and wore his most ingratiating smile. Martha turned out to be a young woman, just out of her teens, with short chestnut hair and a pretty face. When Alex asked her about the paperwork, however, he found that her virtues were primarily her looks.

"I think it's this one," she said at last, handing Alex an official-looking paper from a large stack of the radio station's receipts.

Alex barely glanced at it before handing it back.

"This is a bill for water service to the building," he said, working very hard not to shout.

"Well, I'm sure it's in here somewhere," Martha said at last, her voice as vacuous as her expression.

"Can I have a look?" Alex asked.

"I told you," she said, holding the folder to her chest. "Mr. Zimmerman said I wasn't supposed to let anyone see company papers."

"I promise to only look at the one from the government," Alex said, holding out his hand.

Unbelievably, that worked, and Martha handed over the folder containing the receipts.

"No peeking at the others though," she admonished as Alex began to page through the receipts. Most of them were for the various goods and services that kept the station running, though there were a few that showed where the station had paid entertainers and live guests to come in and talk on-air.

Finally, Alex found a paper that looked crisp and new. It was filled with the kind of legalese he'd come to expect from official forms, so he pulled it out. Sure enough, the first few lines declared it to be an Order of Expropriation. Alex had to read all the way down to the bottom to find the signature of whoever approved the order.

"William Masters," he read aloud.

Underneath Masters' name was the name of his agency.

"The War Department?" Alex read, somewhat confused. The War Department was one of the Cabinet offices attached to the President. What were they doing in New York?

Something about that tickled Alex's memory. He'd heard something about the War Department recently.

"Harcourt," he growled. Earnest Harcourt, the meddling government busybody. He'd claimed that he worked for the War Department.

"Thank you, Martha," Alex said, folding up the expropriation order and tucking it into his inside coat pocket. "You've been a great help."

He handed her back the folder with the rest of the receipts, giving her his most charming smile, then headed for the door. It was tempting to go around to the side of the radio station and open a vault door there, but there wasn't any cover, and someone might see him. Instead, he walked briskly in the direction of the Barton Electric Power Projection Tower. He knew he could open a vault from inside the tower and not be observed. There was even a chalk door on the wall opposite the elevator.

When Alex reached the top floor of the tower, however, there was a great deal of activity. He'd forgotten about the workmen putting on the new roof.

"Are you supposed to be up here?" an enormous blond man asked when Alex got off the elevator. He had a barrel chest and thick arms, and he didn't look happy to see Alex. From his demeanor and the stub of a cigarette dangling from his mouth, Alex assumed he was on a smoke break.

"I'm here to check the runes on the glass case," Alex lied. He couldn't very well explain to the man that he'd come to use the chalk drawing on the wall, so he stepped around him and headed into the transfer room. The work on the roof was well underway and the construction crew had brought up crates of supplies that were strewn all over the place.

Picking his way through the various stacks of lumber and metal sheeting and boxes of nails and other gear, Alex moved to the case covering the transfer plates. The copper plate was right where he'd left it, stuck to the top of the glass case by a binding rune. As he reached the case, he felt the bubble of magical force that would keep water away from the transfer plates slide over him. It was strong and solid, just as he knew it would be.

Not wanting to appear to be hurrying, Alex touched the plate, then took out his notepad and jotted a line of nonsense. The big blond man was still watching him from the far side of the room, and it was putting Alex on edge. Looking around, he found several of the construction crew watching him surreptitiously.

Probably think I'm here to check up on them.

He continued fiddling with the plate until the big man finished his cigarette and went back to work. Once he was no longer occupying the elevator hallway, Alex tore a vault rune from his book and moved like he was leaving. He was certain someone would check to make sure he left, so he pushed the elevator button before opening his vault door. Once the elevator chimed and the door opened, Alex went inside his vault and pulled the door shut behind him.

Pushing the thought of the apprehensive workmen from his mind, Alex made his way to the candlestick phone that sat on the rollaway table by his writing desk.

"Detective Nicholson, please," he told the operator at the Central Office of Police.

"Yeah?" Nicholson's voice came on the line, sounding surly.

"Did you get hold of Harcourt?"

"Lockerby?" he guessed. "Yeah I did, and thanks for that. The little weasel spent the last half hour yelling at me and threatening to charge me with everything from jaywalking to treason. He's on his way in now to pick up the letters."

"Stall him," Alex said. "I'm on my way over and I think I've found something that'll make you happy."

"Will Harcourt like it?" Nicholson asked.

"I doubt it."

"Then I like it already. How long till you can get here?"

Alex checked his watch.

"About ten minutes. Just have him fill out a custody receipt for the letters, that ought to do it."

"With pleasure," Nicholson said, then he hung up.

Alex thought about stopping at his office, but he didn't want the inevitable distractions that would come with that, so he exited his vault in his apartment and rode the secure elevator down to Empire Station. From there he took the stairs to the ground level and caught a cab to the Central Office of Police.

"And here's your co-conspirator," Harcourt yelled when he saw Alex approaching across the open room where the detectives had their desks. Clearly he'd been shouting for some time, because a crowd of detectives and other officers had gathered around to watch.

"You ought to be careful, Harcourt," Alex said, louder than he needed to. "You needed Detective Nicholson to find Alice Cartwright's office, despite the fact that you knew she worked with government secrets, then you missed her hidden safe and those coded letters." Alex pointed to the folder Harcourt had clutched in his hand. "If someone made an anonymous call to your supervisor, he might wonder about your competence."

Grins spread through the onlookers, most hidden behind hands and coffee cups. Harcourt glared at Alex, then seemed to realize that people were listening and shifted his glare to them. The crowd broke up quickly.

"I ought to have you brought up on charges," Harcourt hissed, getting right in Alex's face.

"For what?" Alex scoffed back. "Making you look bad? Well in that case you'd better take notes, because I'm about to add to the charges."

"You are interfering in Federal matters, scribbler," Harcourt fumed.

"I'm pretty sure that's not a crime," Nicholson piped up.

Before Harcourt could shift his attention to the detective, Alex held up the paper he'd taken from the offices of WGRM.

"Someone from the War Department ordered the expropriation of radio equipment from three different radio stations last week," he said. "You work for the War Department if I remember correctly, right?"

Alex was looking straight into Harcourt's face when he mentioned the radio equipment and there was a flicker of recognition in the man's eyes. He covered it quickly, but Alex had seen it.

"I don't know what you're talking about," Harcourt lied. "I didn't order the removal of any radio equipment."

"I know you didn't," Alex said, unfolding the paper. "This was signed by someone named William Masters." Alex shifted his gaze to Detective Nicholson. "What do you want to bet Harcourt here knows Masters?"

"No bet," Nicholson said.

"Of course I know him," Harcourt said. "We work in the same office, but what do radio parts have to do with you and your cop friend," he jerked a thumb at Nicholson, "hiding coded letters from me?"

Alex smiled sweetly.

"I'm glad you asked," he said. "You see, I found out about those radio parts because someone broke into the warehouses where they were stored during shipment, and opened the crates they were in. They tried to hide what they were doing by stealing some random stuff, but they dumped that in an abandoned garage in Brooklyn. The only reason to do that is if the thefts were cover, a distraction from what the burglars were really after."

"And what might that be?" Harcourt demanded.

"To sabotage that radio equipment," Alex said.

"Why?"

"I assume to listen in on whatever top-secret things are being talked about over that radio," Alex said.

Harcourt scoffed at that.

"What makes you think anything that equipment would be used for would be some kind of secret?"

"Because Alice Cartwright worked on top secret things — for you," Alex said. "Well not you, strictly speaking. You said she usually dealt with someone else in your office. That wouldn't be William Masters, now would it?"

Harcourt opened his mouth to reply but Alex went on.

"So you've got a woman who was privy to government secrets, who's writing coded letters to someone, and then her contact at your department orders radio equipment expropriated for the government. Equipment that I'm pretty sure was sabotaged."

"That could all be a coincidence," Harcourt stammered. He seemed worried, but Alex got the distinct impression he was worried about his job, not the possibility of spies and saboteurs in his office.

"There is one more interesting fact," Alex said. "Several people saw me at Alice Cartwright's office, then the next day somebody took a shot at me. That shooter smoked a German brand of cigarette."

That got Nicholson's attention.

"So Alice gets information from Masters, then passes it on to some Nazi?"

Alex shrugged and nodded at Harcourt.

"As he said, it might just be a coincidence. But that's one hell of a coincidence."

"This is paranoid nonsense," Harcourt declared. "Now if you don't mind, I have to get someone working on this code right away."

He turned to go, and Alex stepped up close to Nicholson.

"Stall him for a couple minutes," he whispered.

"Just a minute, Harcourt," the detective said, giving Alex a discrete nod. "You need to fill out the property receipt for those documents."

Alex didn't wait to hear Harcourt's response; he quickly walked away, heading for the row of offices along the back wall. When he reached the one belonging to Danny, he ducked inside.

"Alex," Danny said, surprised to see him. He sat behind his desk filling out paperwork with a bored expression on his face. "Anything new on our mutual friend?"

"Later," Alex said, making for the desk. "I need to use your phone."

Danny chuckled but pushed the phone across the desk in Alex's direction. Picking up the receiver, Alex dialed the number for Sorsha's office.

"This is Alex Lockerby," he told her secretary. "I need to talk to Sorsha urgently."

"I'm sorry," the secretary said in a halting voice. "Miss Kincaid is out and I don't have any way to reach her."

"When will she be back?"

"Not until tomorrow," the secretary said.

Alex stifled a swear.

"If she calls in, tell her that her security job is compromised and that German agents are onto her."

The secretary read the message back and then Alex hung up.

"Nazis are after Sorsha?" Danny asked, a look of incredulity on his face. Going after a sorcerer was usually only the purview of the suicidal.

"Can't be sure, but it makes sense," Alex said. "Something important is happening and Sorsha has a top-secret protection job at the same time. It's a cinch they're connected, and if they are, the Germans know that Sorsha will be there."

"They'll bring spellbreakers," Danny said, following Alex's train of thought. "You need some help?"

Alex thought about it. Having someone he could trust back him up would make what he had planned safer, but it would put Danny's job at risk, so he shook his head.

"I need you on the outside to bail me out if this goes south," he said, turning and heading back toward the bullpen. "But thanks," he added.

Heading back toward Detective Nicholson's desk, Alex caught sight of Harcourt storming away toward the elevators.

"I don't think he believed you," Nicholson said as Alex stepped up next to him.

"No," Alex agreed. "And if he doesn't tell someone that the radio equipment has been compromised, people could die."

"You'll get no argument from me," Nicholson said. "Those

Germans wanted you out of the way pretty bad, and that means whatever is going on, it's big."

As Harcourt disappeared into the hallway, Alex turned to Nicholson, grabbing his arm in a firm grip.

"I need you to do something for me, and you're just going to have to trust me," he said.

Nicholson wavered for a moment, then nodded.

"If you're right, we need to do something. What do you have in mind?"

"I need you to go down to the motor pool and grab a squad car," Alex said. "Then you need to come meet me."

Two minutes later, Alex burst out of the stairwell into the lobby of the Central Office. He caught sight of Harcourt as the man pushed through the glass doors at the far end of the room, heading for the sidewalk.

Since running through the lobby of police headquarters was likely to draw the kind of attention Alex didn't want, he hurried across the vast lobby as quickly as he dared. When he reached the street, he found Harcourt waving down a cab.

Alex reached inside his coat as he moved up behind the government man, waiting until the cab had stopped and Harcourt opened the door. At that moment Alex stepped up behind him and jammed the muzzle of his 1911 into the surprised man's ribs.

"Don't do anything stupid," Alex whispered. "Just get in the cab like you're going to share it with your old pal Alex."

Harcourt spluttered for a moment, but Alex pressed the gun against him harder and he winced. Without a further word, he climbed into the cab and slid over so Alex could get in.

"Where to?" the cabbie asked as Alex awkwardly closed the door with his left hand.

"The Navy Yard," Alex said, keeping the 1911 under his left arm and pointed at Harcourt. "And step on it."

26

CODES & CONSEQUENCES

The guard at the Navy Yard took Alex's name along with Harcourt's and waved the cab through. A few minutes later, Alex was standing in front of the ramshackle building that housed the Admiral's offices. A bored Shore Patrolman stood beside the door, but he wasn't paying Alex or Harcourt any mind.

"You realize they're going to shoot you as soon as you go in there," Harcourt sneered.

Alex had thought about that, so he stepped behind Harcourt and prodded him forward with the barrel of his 1911.

"Just keep walking," he said.

As soon as Harcourt started up the path that led to the door, Alex dropped his 1911 into the outside pocket of his jacket. It would be found there once Harcourt raised an inevitable ruckus, but it wouldn't be pointing at anyone.

The waiting room in the office was much the way Alex remembered it. A small desk manned by a Lieutenant JG was to the right with an open area to the left. Several closed doors occupied the left-hand wall, with the admiral's door being straight past the Lieutenant at the desk.

"Is the Admiral in?" Alex asked the man at the desk. He was

younger than the last man had been, but he probably wasn't a murdering thief, either.

"The Admiral is quite busy today," the man said. "Do you have an appointment?"

"No, but he's going to want to see me. Tell him Alex Lockerby wants a few minutes of his time."

"I don't care who you are," the Lieutenant said in a gruff "go away" voice that his youthful throat couldn't quite manage. "The Admiral has asked not to be disturbed and that's what's going to happen."

Alex sighed. There really wasn't time for this. He had a fleeting thought of pulling his gun out again, but he remembered the armed Shore Patrolman just outside the door. He didn't want to get shot before he could explain himself.

"Is Lieutenant Commander Vaughn in?" Alex persisted.

"The Commander is busy too," the lieutenant said without looking up.

"Get him," Alex growled. "Or when I do finally get to speak with him, I'll make sure he puts you on kitchen duty for a month."

The lieutenant looked up with the expression of a man who was about to tell Alex where to go, but Alex just held his gaze until the young man looked away.

"Fine," he said, picking up the phone on his desk. "I'm sorry to disturb you, Sir," he said after a moment. "There's an Alex Lockerby out here who insists on speaking with you." The man's bored expression disappeared like a soap bubble on a needle and he sat up straight. "Yes, Sir. I'll let him know, Sir."

Alex suppressed a grin as the young man hung up the phone.

"The Commander said to wait here," he reported. "He'll be out in a minute."

Alex thanked the young man politely. No sense in making unnecessary enemies. He had enough of those already.

"And what will you do when the officer gets here," Harcourt mumbled over his shoulder. "Going to take him hostage too?"

"Shut up, Harcourt," Alex whispered back. "If you had an ounce of sense, we wouldn't have had to do this the hard way."

Well, maybe one more enemy.

"Alex," Commander Vaughn's booming voice emerged from his office a moment before he did. "It's good to see you. What brings you out here?"

Vaughn was Admiral Tennon's second in command and, despite his being overweight and soft, he had a brilliant mind and a spine of steel. He had a round face with large eyes that always reminded Alex of a basset hound he'd tracked down once. The only difference was that Vaughn's eyes could go from harmless to intimidating in a heartbeat.

"You look good, Dave," Alex said as Vaughn crossed the open reception area. "You've lost a few pounds."

Vaughn smiled and nodded.

"My wife wants me to get promoted," he started to explain.

"Are you in charge here?" Harcourt suddenly demanded in a loud voice. "Because this man," he bobbed his head in Alex's direction, "brought me here at gunpoint."

Vaughn's smile evaporated and he stopped dead in his tracks. Next to Alex, the young lieutenant at the desk stiffened as well.

"Are you armed, Alex?" Vaughn said in a carefully neutral voice.

Alex held up both his hands so that the Commander could see them, then he nodded.

"My gun is in my right-hand coat pocket," he said.

Vaughn nodded at the lieutenant, who stood and moved behind Alex before reaching carefully into his pocket.

"Gun, Sir," he said, pulling the weapon out.

At the same moment, Harcourt stepped away from Alex as if he'd received an electric shock.

"You see?" he said to Vaughn. "I demand you arrest this man immediately. In addition to kidnapping, he's been investigating government secrets."

Vaughn actually chuckled at that, eliciting a surprised look from Harcourt.

"Yes," the Commander said. "He has a habit of that."

Alex had met Vaughn when a secret Navy smoke machine had been stolen and turned on in the city.

"You want to explain all this, Alex," Vaughn said as the lieutenant passed him Alex's pistol.

Blood Relation

"You're not going to indulge this lunatic," Harcourt yelled.

"Please be quiet," Vaughn said, indicating one of the hard chairs in the waiting area. "You sit there while I get this sorted out."

Harcourt's face went from outraged to angry to chagrined in the space of a few seconds, then he slunk to the chair and sat down.

"Kidnapping is a serious charge, Alex," Vaughn said, dropping the pistol into the pocket of his uniform coat. "Maybe you'd better tell me what's going on."

"This is Earnest Harcourt," Alex said, indicating the government man. "He works for the War Department. Last week one of his contractors was killed and, when I investigated with the police, we found coded messages in a hidden safe."

"You think the contractor was a spy," Vaughn guessed.

"We don't know," Alex admitted. "The letters were coded using something the police have never seen."

Vaughn looked at Harcourt, who was still clutching the folder containing Alice Cartwright's letters.

"May I?" he said, holding out his hand to Harcourt.

The government man looked as if he'd rather chew off his own hand than relinquish the letters, but he did want Vaughn to arrest Alex, so he reluctantly passed them over.

Commander Vaughn opened the folder and flipped through the letters slowly.

"It looks like they used a different code for each one," Alex said.

"They didn't," Vaughn said, indicating the four-letter signature on the bottom of each page. "This is a complex shift cypher."

Alex exchanged a confused look with Harcourt.

"Whoever did this used a numerical sequence to shift each letter up or down the alphabet," Vaughn explained. "Each subsequent letter is shifted by a different number until the code repeats." He closed the folder and handed it back to Harcourt.

"So you can break it?" Alex asked, hopefully.

Vaughn shook his head.

"This kind of cypher would take a team months to break," he said. "The only reliable way to read them is to have the code. So what do you suspect this spy of doing?"

"I had another case," Alex continued his explanation. "I was investigating several warehouse robberies that I now believe were cover for an act of sabotage."

"What do you think was sabotaged?" Vaughn asked, his eyes going hard. Sabotage was a dirty word in the Navy.

"Radio equipment."

"So how does that connect to a dead government asset?"

"The radio equipment that was tampered with was also, coincidentally, expropriated for government use a few days later," Alex explained. "The orders came from one of Mr. Harcourt's underlings, the same man who was working with the dead woman who had the coded letters."

Vaughn rubbed his chin for a moment, then looked at Harcourt.

"Is what he says true?"

"I don't know anything about any radio equipment," Harcourt said. "But the expropriation order did come from William Masters, one of the men in my office, and he did have contact with Miss Cartwright, the murdered woman."

Vaughn looked as if he were exercising a great amount of restraint not to roll his eyes.

"Well that sounds like quite a coincidence, don't you think?"

"I suspect it's exactly that," Harcourt said. "My office doesn't choose what equipment the government takes. We get a call and then fill out the forms, but the orders come from higher up."

"But if this Masters fellow decided to write out that order himself, no one would know," Vaughn pointed out. "It'd be just another order coming from your office, right?"

"Well," Harcourt stammered. "I...I suppose."

Vaughn swore and shook his head.

"All right, Alex, I admit this thing stinks, but why grab him?" He jerked his thumb at Harcourt. "And why bring him here?"

"He knows what the radio equipment is for," Alex said with a shrug. "The only reason I could think of to sabotage a radio transmitter is to listen in on top secret radio transmissions, and I figured that might involve the Navy. Also a man who smoked German cigarettes tried to kill me right after I found the coded letters."

That got Vaughn's attention and he looked at Harcourt.

"What, exactly, was this dead spy working on?" he demanded.

"I can't tell you that," Harcourt said, some of his previous bluster creeping back into his voice. "Everything my office does is classified."

This time the Commander did roll his eyes.

"I'll get to the bottom of this," he growled, turning to the lieutenant at the reception desk. "Get me Charlie Thomas over at State," he said.

"There might not be time for that," Alex interjected as the young man picked up the phone.

"Keep going," Vaughn waved at the lieutenant, then turned to Alex. "Why not?"

"Because I happen to know that Sorsha Kincaid and the FBI have been busy all last week putting together a security detail for some bigwig. Now I can't get hold of Miss Kincaid, which probably means that they're with said bigwig right now. If some bad guys have been listening in on their communication thanks to the sabotaged radio..." Alex let the thought drift off, suggestively.

"Well you're wrong about the radio," Vaughn said. "Anyone with a receiver can intercept a radio transmission. That's why we don't send secret information that way. Secret orders here are delivered to our captains in person before they sail to prevent exactly that kind of listening in. The FBI is sure to take the same precautions."

Alex chewed his lip. He'd been so sure the radio parts had been tampered with, why else would their shipping crates be broken open? And whatever this whole thing was about, Sorsha was right in the middle of it, possibly with a compromised operation.

"I still think you're right," Vaughn said, rubbing his chin, thoughtfully. "But it all depends on who took those radio parts and what they wanted them for."

Harcourt shrunk back in his chair as if he expected Vaughn to press him, but instead, the Commander turned back to the lieutenant who was waiting on the phone.

"Hang that up," he said. "Is someone in with the Admiral right now?"

"No," the flustered officer said. "That is, no, Sir."

"Come on," Vaughn said, motioning for Alex to follow him. As he passed the chair where Harcourt was sitting, he grabbed the man by the back of his coat and hauled him to his feet. "You too."

The office of Admiral Walter Tennon was exactly as Alex remembered it, complete with the man himself sitting behind the desk, signing a stack of orders.

"Dave?" he said as Vaughn came barging in. When he saw Alex he smiled. "Nice to see you again, Alex. I'm guessing this isn't a social call."

Vaughn let go of Harcourt and then went over everything Alex had explained in the outer office.

"I know it's a bit light on the specifics, Admiral," Vaughn concluded. "But if there is someone targeting whoever the FBI is protecting, then we need to find out. I figure you could call that friend of yours on the President's staff."

"No need for that," Tennon said, steepling his hands in front of him. "I know exactly who Miss Kincaid and her FBI agents are protecting, Harry Woodring."

"Who?" Alex blurted out.

"He's the Secretary of War," Vaughn explained. "Part of Roosevelt's cabinet."

"And he's in the city," Tennon said. "I got a call from him this morning to let me know he'd be coming by tomorrow to do a little informal inspection. Said he couldn't come today because he had to go see something this afternoon."

Alex looked up at the clock on the Admiral's wall. It read eleven thirty-three.

Admiral Tennon stood up and walked around his desk, stepping so close to Harcourt that their noses almost touched.

"Woodring is your boss, Mr. Harcourt," he said. "How do you think it will look on your record if you let him get killed?"

"Uh," Harcourt stammered.

"Let me make this simple for you," Tennon went on. "I am an Admiral in the United States Navy. There are only a handful of men who outrank me in the entire service. Now, if you force me to, I'll pick up my phone and I'll call my boss, and he'll call his boss, and he'll call

Blood Relation

the President. By that time, whatever these Nazi spies are planning will probably have happened. Eventually, I'll get orders that tell you to tell me what I want to know. And when they're looking for someone to blame for missing an attempt on Harry Woodring's life," Tennon poked Harcourt in the chest so hard the man staggered back, "I'm going to give them you."

Harcourt's eyes darted back and forth as he calculated what the Admiral had said.

"Or," Tennon went on, not giving him time to think, "you can tell me what this is all about right now."

"It's a bomb," Harcourt squeaked.

The Admiral sauntered back to his desk and sat down.

"Go on," he said. "What's so special about this bomb?"

"It...it flies itself."

Alex exchanged glances with Tennon and Vaughn, then all eyes turned to Harcourt.

"The bomb is a plane," he said. "I mean it has wings and a motor, just no pilot."

"Then how does it fly?" Vaughn asked.

"When it takes off, it climbs to a certain altitude based on an altimeter inside," Harcourt explained. "Then it picks up a special radio transmission that tells it when it's flying too far one way. A second signal tells it that it's gone too far the other way. Basically the onboard radio just keeps the flying bomb between the two radio beams."

"So it will stay on course over a long distance," Vaughn said, nodding. "But how does this bomb know when it's over its target?"

"You set up the radio transmitters a few miles apart, then aim them just in front of the target," Harcourt said. "When the beams cross, the plane goes into a dive and hits the ground."

Alex snapped his fingers with sudden understanding.

"That explains the radio equipment," he said. "The engineer at one of the stations that was supposed to get the equipment said that they needed a new transmitter to cut through the static generated by Barton Electric's new tower."

"I don't see how that helps," Tennon said.

"Whoever expropriated the equipment probably needed it for the same reason. But if the transmitter was sabotaged in a way that reduced the power output..."

"Then someone with a stronger signal could redirect the bomb," Vaughn said.

"If there is a test of this flying bomb today, it's over at Fort Hamilton," Tennon said. "It's the only base in range of that new tower."

"I bet whoever is behind this is going to drop that flying bomb on the spectators watching the test," Alex guessed. His hands clenched into fists as he remembered that one of the attendees would be Sorsha.

"But how would they know how to do that?" Harcourt said. "There aren't more than a handful of people alive who know about this."

"You're forgetting Alice Cartwright," Alex said. "I'm sure you had her check the math for something this important. She would know about the radio signals." Alex jerked the folder of coded letters out of Harcourt's hands and pulled one out. "All she had to do was tell whoever was sending her these instructions."

"It doesn't matter who leaked the information," Admiral Tennon declared. "That test is happening this afternoon and I can't afford to assume it hasn't been sabotaged." He picked up the telephone on his desk, then ordered, "Get me General Blake over at Fort Hamilton," he said into the telephone.

Alex felt his muscles relax. He hadn't realized how tense he'd been, but now that someone finally took him seriously, the muscles in his neck unclenched. They weren't out of the woods yet, but there was motion in the right direction.

"What?" Tennon yelled into the phone. "All right, all right. Get my driver out front, I'll go myself."

"What's the problem?" Vaughn asked.

"That bomb is definitely being tested at Fort Hamilton," Tennon said, rising and putting on his hat. "Reggie Blake has the whole base on lockdown. No one in or out and no phone calls."

Alex looked nervously at the clock. It was at least a forty-five minute drive from the West Side of Manhattan to the south Brooklyn Army base, and he had no idea how much time was left before the test.

Admiral Tennon led the group out of his office into the waiting area.

Blood Relation

"I'm going over to Fort Hamilton," Tennon said to the lieutenant at the reception desk. "As soon as I'm gone, get on the horn to the State Department and tell them there's going to be an attempt on the life of Harry Woodring today while he's at Fort Ham—"

Three shots rang out, booming in the enclosed space of the office. Alex flung himself in front of the Admiral, not knowing where the shots had come from. Two more shots rang out, much closer, but Alex didn't have time to figure out who was shooting now. Tennon's eyes rolled back in his head and he crumpled to the floor. Alex grabbed him and eased him down. When he let the man go, there was blood all over the front of his suit coat.

"Admiral?" he said. "Walter!"

He felt for a pulse, but there was none to be found. Admiral Walter Tennon was dead.

27

STATIC

Alex leaped to his feet. His first thought was Harcourt. The man was a weasel and he hadn't wanted anyone looking into Alice Cartwright's death, but Alex never suspected him. Could he be the spy, now desperate enough to shoot the Admiral to stop him going to Fort Hamilton?

But Harcourt had been behind the Admiral, where he now stood, clutching the folder of coded letters to his chest.

Not him.

Alex turned. Beside him, Commander Vaughn was holding Alex's gun out, pointing it toward the door. Just inside the door lay the Shore Patrolman that had been standing outside. Two large red circles were spreading out over his white uniform and a smoking pistol lay on the ground next to him.

"Is he dead?" Vaughn demanded.

The young lieutenant rushed to check, kicking the smoking gun out of the man's reach. He knelt by the Shore Patrolman, then looked up and nodded.

"Sir," the Lieutenant gasped. "The Admiral."

"Get hold of yourself," Vaughn commanded in a voice that refused all disobedience. "Call the Sick Bay and have the surgeon report here on the double, then call Major Blanchard over at the Marine barracks. I want him and two dozen of his best men fully armed and over here on the double."

"Yes, Sir," the young man gasped, snapping out of his confusion.

"Lockerby," Vaughn said, grabbing Alex by the shoulder. "What can you tell me about that man?" He pointed at the dead patrolman.

Alex went and knelt over him. He appeared nondescript, average height with brown hair and blue eyes that stared eternally up at the ceiling. Turning out the man's pockets, Alex found a jackknife, a dollar twenty in change, a book of matches, and a pack of cigarettes.

Nil cigarettes.

"German brand," Alex said, holding up the pack. "Just like the guy who took a shot at me."

"Well this one wasn't shooting at you," Vaughn growled, looking down where the Admiral's body lay. "He was too close to miss you."

"He must be part of the attempt on Woodring's life," Alex guessed. "Put here to prevent anyone from stopping the test."

"That's convenient," Harcourt sneered. "He just happened to be on duty today."

"There are a dozen ways he could have arranged that," Vaughn said, finally kneeling down beside the body of Admiral Tennon. "He probably just traded shifts with whoever drew the duty assignment." Vaughn removed a set of keys from the Admiral's trouser pocket and a small black book from his shirt pocket, then he closed Walter Tennon's eyes.

"All right," he said, standing up. There wasn't time for grief; that would come later. "I'm assuming command of this base as of now." He looked at the lieutenant who was dialing the phone. "As soon as you're done, note that in the duty log. I'm going to Fort Hamilton. You're in charge of this scene until Major Blanchard gets here, then turn it over to him."

With that, Commander Vaughn set Alex's gun down on the lieutenant's desk and walked out, with Alex and Harcourt scrambling to catch up.

Outside, a long black car was just pulling up in front of the office.

At the same time a police squad car pulled up from the direction of the gate.

"Commander," Alex called as Vaughn opened the door to the black car. "I think I might be able to sabotage the Germans. Maybe give you more time to sound the alarm."

Vaughn thought about it, but only for a moment, then he nodded.

"Good luck," he said, then disappeared into the car, pulling Harcourt in after him.

"Where are they going?" Detective Nicholson said as he climbed out of the squad car.

"I'll tell you on the way," Alex said, climbing into the back of the car.

"On the way to where?"

"Barton Electric's new Brooklyn Tower."

"So, why are we here?" Detective Nicholson asked as the patrol car rounded a corner and Barton Electric's Brooklyn Relay Tower came into view.

"If I'm right," Alex said, leaning forward so he could see the doughnut-shaped power antenna on top of the building, "the Germans that Alice Cartwright was talking to are going to use a radio transmitter to disrupt a top secret military test at Fort Hamilton. They sabotaged the high output transmitter that the military is using so their signal will be stronger."

"So?" Nicholson griped. He was upset that Alex wouldn't tell him about the Army's top secret flying bomb.

"So, the Army needed that fancy equipment to cut through all the static that Barton's tower puts out," Alex explained. "If I can increase the amount of power the tower is projecting, I can increase the static."

"And disrupt the phony radio signal," Nicholson said, catching on. "But do you know how to do that?"

"Pretty sure," Alex said. He'd need to pin the breakers like Barton's crew had done so that would keep them from tripping, then he could use a few linking runes to draw more power into the south side transfer plate from the main. That should overload the system, but with the breakers pinned, the power would continue on to the projection antenna, blocking out the German radio broadcast.

I hope.

The policeman driving the patrol car brought it to a stop by the curb and then got out with Alex and Detective Nicholson. He had grey hair and a gray mustache, but his stride was easy and vigorous, and he caught up to Alex and the Detective easily.

"Shouldn't you call Barton about this?" Nicholson asked, as they crossed the lawn toward the front door.

"I'll have the security guard do that," Alex said. "We need to keep moving, I don't know how much time we have."

He took hold of the heavy metal door that was the building's entrance and pulled, stepping back so that the Detective and the officer could enter.

"I need you to call Mr. Barton right away," Alex said, coming in behind the other men. "There's an emergency and we need him here right..."

Alex stopped as he locked eyes with the guard. Alex recognized him, but he wasn't one of the regular guards. The last time Alex had seen this man, he'd put three slugs into Alex's chest.

The guard already had his gun and he raised it and fired in one smooth motion. Alex threw himself to the side, but the bullets weren't directed at him. He heard the policeman cry out as he was hit. Since he was the only one of them obviously carrying a weapon, the phony guard had targeted him first.

Alex started to push himself up from the floor when the guard swung his pistol around to point in his direction.

"Have the courtesy to die this time," the guard said, firing.

Alex rolled away from the guard and a bullet hit painfully in his lower back. The guard fired again and Alex felt the last of his shield runes fade from existence as the bullet hit his spine.

Another shot rang out and Alex flinched, but no burning impact came. Forcing himself to act, he rolled and pushed off the ground, getting his feet under him. Another shot boomed in the confines of

DAN WILLIS

the building lobby and Alex felt the slug tear a hole in his trouser leg, grazing his calf.

Two more shots came in quick succession, but these weren't aimed at Alex. Detective Nicholson had pulled his own service revolver and the barrel smoked as he fired a third time.

The German's .45 slipped from his hand as he staggered back against the wooden guard station. He wore a dazed expression as he looked down at the red circles spreading across his upper body. Nicholson might have taken his sweet time pulling his gun, but Alex couldn't fault the detective's aim.

Alex stood as the imposter guard slid slowly down into a sitting position. His eyes went to where he'd dropped his gun, but he couldn't seem to make his arm grab it.

"You all right?" Nicholson asked, giving Alex the once-over, looking for blood.

"Clipped my leg," Alex said, nodding at where the patrolman lay on the floor. "I'll be fine. Check him."

"John," Nicholson called, turning the man over.

The patrolman had blood on the left side of his uniform, just under his arm. He must have knocked his head on the floor when he fell, but he woke up gasping when Nicholson moved him.

"Got me in the ribs," he growled, clutching his side. "Doesn't feel too bad."

Nicholson pulled out a handkerchief from the pocket of his suit coat and pressed it against the wound, causing the man to grunt in pain.

"Hold this and don't move," he ordered the patrolman. "I'll call for an ambulance."

"Call for a squad of officers too," Alex said as Nicholson stood up. "This is the German who took a shot at me in the five and dime. If he's here, it's a cinch his pals are upstairs."

"Why?" Nicholson asked, picking up the phone at the guard desk.

"Power," Alex guessed. "He took a shot at me because they knew I was on to their scheme. They didn't know if I told the military about their sabotaged equipment, so they decided to connect their transmitter to a bigger power source . That way they could be sure their signal would override the Army's."

"Told them," the phony guard gasped. His white shirt was already soaked with blood and it was beginning to run down onto the marble floor. "You were too...too smart."

"Line's been cut," Nicholson said, holding up the cord that usually connected the phone to the wall. "Your car have a radio, John?"

The gray-haired man shook his head.

"I'll take the car and get help," Nicholson said, heading for the door.

"We don't have time," Alex said, pulling chalk out of his pocket.

"You..." the German gasped, making a wet wheezing noise, "...might as well...let him go. It's...already...too late."

Alex didn't bother responding to that. Since there was no way to know if the man was lying, he'd have to just assume that he was. Alex chalked a door right next to the elevator and tore a vault rune from his book.

His mind raced as he ignited the rune and unlocked the heavy door with the ornate skeleton key. The policeman, John, needed a doctor and sooner rather than later, and the German, too. Alex wasn't terribly concerned about the latter, but the government would want to interrogate him and that meant he needed to be alive. He could go through into the brownstone and get Iggy easy enough, but then the secret of his vault's multiple doors would be out. Nicholson and the policeman would know, and so would the German, if he survived.

What if the Government sends him back to Germany?

The risk was too great, so Alex opened the heavy door and went straight to the telephone on his rollaway cabinet.

"What the hell is that connected to?" Nicholson asked from the open vault door.

"It's a radio," Alex lied. "As long as the door is open, I can relay the signal to the phone in my office."

Nicholson raised an eyebrow at that, but didn't offer further comment.

Alex's first call was to Captain Callahan. He informed him about the saboteurs in the Brooklyn tower and the wounded policeman and spy. Callahan promised to get men out right away, but Alex knew the nearest help was likely to be half an hour out and that was time he didn't have.

Hanging up, he called Andrew Barton's private number. After a few rings, Gary Bickman's cultured voice came on the line.

"I need Mr. Barton out at the Brooklyn Tower," he explained. "There's trouble."

"I'm sorry, Alex," Bickman said. "But Mr. Barton got a call this morning from Washington. Apparently someone in the government wants to talk to him about wireless power transmission."

That was a ruse to get Barton out of town and Alex knew it.

"Can he be reached?"

"I can leave a message at his hotel," Bickman said. "And I'll give him your message should he call."

It was all Alex could do, so he thanked Bickman and hung up. He was about to call Iggy when Nicholson reappeared at the vault door.

"Your German's dead," he declared. "And I found the real guard. His body was stuffed in the broom closet."

Alex set down the phone and headed for his gun locker.

"How's John?" he asked.

"I'm fine," John's voice came from outside. "I got worse than this in the war."

Alex opened his gun locker and swore.

"What's the matter?" Nicholson asked.

Alex stood for a moment, his mind working overtime.

"We can stop the Germans if we burn out their radio transmitter," he said at last.

"That's quite the arsenal you've got, Lockerby," Nicholson said, suddenly behind him. "How about we just shoot them?"

Alex shook his head.

"The power room is big and open," he said, taking his Thompson sub-machine gun down. "They're sure to have someone watching the elevator, so they'll know we're coming in plenty of time to take cover."

He passed the gun to Nicholson, along with two loaded drum magazines. The last time Alex had used the Thompson, he'd had the straight, military-style magazine and he'd run out of rounds. The drums had a much higher capacity.

"So what's the plan?" Nicholson said, loading one of the drums.

Alex took down his Browning A-5 shotgun and a box of shells, pouring the shells into the left-hand pocket of his suit coat.

"I figure there are at least five of them up there," Alex said, remembering the strangely aggressive work crew that had been at the tower earlier. "All we need to do is get into the little hall where the elevator lets out. There's a pillar in the middle of the room that holds the metal plates that connect this tower to Empire Tower. If I can get the plates wet, it will send a power surge through the system and fry the German radio equipment."

I hope.

"How are you going to get to something in the middle of the room while five Nazi spies are shooting at you?" Nicholson asked. "And where are you going to get water?"

Alex turned toward his work bench. One of his side jobs was engraving runes in glassware for Charles Grier and Linda Kellin. He set down his shotgun, pulled out a drawer and removed five glass test tubes with rubber stoppers.

"Once we take the hallway, I'll use the shotgun to break the glass covering the plates." He held up the test tubes. "I'll fill these with water in the guard's washroom, and once the case is broken, I'll just throw these at the plates."

"And hope you get lucky?" Nicholson said with a raised eyebrow. "What about those five guys who'll be shooting at you?"

Alex shrugged as he picked up the shotgun.

"The wall is made of cement blocks," he said, "so we don't have to worry about them shooting through it. And I hope they'll be busy taking cover while you shoot at them."

Nicholson shook his head and sighed.

"All right" he said, pulling the charge lever on the Thompson to rack the first round into place. "Let's go."

"There are still two minor problems," Alex said, moving the secretary cabinet that stood next to his workbenches. He opened the top and pulled out a folder that contained a stack of pre-written runes.

"The glass case that covers the plates was made by Andrew Barton, so it's unbreakable."

"That's your idea of a minor problem?" Nicholson said, his voice going up a bit. "What's the other problem?"

"I put a rune on the case that will prevent water from coming anywhere near it."

Alex went back to his workbench and took out four of the shotgun shells. Working quickly, he wrapped each shell in one of the rune papers and lit them with his lighter.

"Spellbreakers," he explained.

"Aren't those illegal?" Nicholson asked.

"Completely," Alex said, loading the rune shells into the A-5. "I figure if I can hit the glass, the reaction will shatter it. Should knock my rune plate away as well."

"And if it doesn't?"

"Then we use your plan," Alex answered. He picked up the shotgun and racked a shell into the chamber. "Shoot 'em."

Nicholson just shook his head.

"Great," he said with mock enthusiasm.

Alex knew the elevator bell would chime before the door opened, announcing their arrival to anyone keeping watch. It would have been quieter to take the stairs, but the tower was ten stories high and he simply couldn't afford the time it would take to climb one-hundred and seventy steps.

"Kneel down," he told Nicholson, dropping down as the car began to decelerate. "If whoever's on guard shoots first, he'll probably shoot level with his arm."

The bell dinged and Nicholson dropped down.

The door opened on an empty hall. The block wall with Alex's chalk door looked just as it always had. Alex surged up, launching himself out the door. As he passed into the hall, Alex saw a startled man in a blue suit. The man raised a pistol and fired, but he hadn't expected Alex to leap out and he missed.

Slamming into the block wall, Alex raised the Browning and fired. Too late he remembered that the first four rounds in the shotgun were his spellbreakers. The blast caught the man in the side, but the buckshot made a mess of him and he went down like a puppet whose strings had been cut.

Ignoring him, Alex ran to the end of the short hall. In the power room around the corner, a chorus of voices began yelling all at once. Since it was all in German, Alex ignored it. Taking a deep breath, he ducked around the corner. The room was still strewn with construction supplies and several men were taking cover behind the breaker boxes. He could see heavy wires running from one of the boxes to the spiral stair that led to the observation platform. A bullet hit the wall just above his head and showered him with bits of broken concrete.

"How many?" Nicholson said as Alex jerked back his head.

"I saw three," he said, "but there's bound to be more."

"Could you see the case?"

Alex nodded.

"Cover me."

Nicholson backed up from the wall and took two tentative steps to the side. Shouldering the Thompson, he leaned forward and let off a blast from the machine gun. As he fired, Alex knelt and leaned around the corner. The glass case containing the power transfer plates was right where he expected, and he could see someone crouching behind it.

"Two birds," he whispered, then raised the Browning and shot the glass. It wasn't the most accurate shot he'd ever made, but it didn't really have to be. He felt a wave of magic slam into him just before the spellbreaker destroyed Barton's protection spell.

"Down," Alex yelled, retreating behind the wall.

In the room beyond, the case exploded, sending fragments of glass in all directions. Alex's ears rang from the sound and Nicholson took several steps down the hall despite being protected by the concrete blocks of the hall corner.

When Alex could hear again, the sound of screaming filled the air. He risked a quick check of the room and found that the men he'd seen before were scrambling for cover. All of them had cuts on their exposed skin, but the man who had been next to the case was covering his bloody face with his hands while he rolled on the ground. He was the one screaming.

Focus, he admonished himself.

The brass plaque with the barrier rune on it lay on the floor a dozen feet from where the glass case had been. It only had a range of about four feet, so it wouldn't interfere with Alex's plans.

Someone was shouting down from above and one of the less-wounded turned to look directly at Alex. Ducking back, Alex pulled one of the water-filled test tubes from his pocket. He stood and sidestepped like Nicholson had, keeping the corner between him and the gunmen.

Taking a deep breath, he cocked his arm back, stepped around the corner and threw. Almost immediately a shot clipped the cuff of his coat sleeve, tearing out a chunk of fabric. Alex didn't even notice as he watched the glass tube sail through the air. It arced perfectly, coming down right toward the open pedestal with the transfer plates.

And then it shattered.

As Alex watched, the water spread out and began running down the outside of an invisible barrier well away from the transfer plates.

28

THE PATH OF LEAST RESISTANCE

Fragments of concrete exploded from the block wall beside Alex's face and sharp bits cut his cheek. The pain pulled Alex out of his surprise and he jerked back behind the wall.

"What happened?" Nicholson said, reloading the Thompson with the second drum.

Alex shook his head, his mind scrambling to figure out how his barrier rune could still be working. He'd confirmed that the brass plate had been blown across the room by the shattering of Barton's protection spell, so how was there still a barrier?'

"I don't know," he admitted at last. "The barrier is still protecting the transfer plates."

"English, Lockerby," Nicholson said, leaning out to fire a quick burst. Several shots came back, shattering against the block wall.

"My plan won't work," he said. "The magic is still protecting the case."

Nicholson ducked out for half a second.

"I think they retreated," he said, then ducked out again, pulling back just as another shot rang out.

"Not far enough," Alex said.

"There's a guy on the staircase in the back of the room," Nicholson reported. "The one behind the case is down. I think he's dead. The others must have gone up the stairs."

"Their transmitter has to be up there," Alex said. "There's an observation platform with a view of the river."

"Fort Hamilton is right on the river," Nicholson confirmed.

"As long as they're up there they can sabotage the Army's weapons test," Alex said, trying to keep the details vague. "They can kill a lot of people if we don't stop them."

Nicholson ducked out around the corner, then quickly back. Two shots rang out, coming very close to hitting the detective.

"The guy on the stairs is looking down from above," he said. "I can't see very much of him, but he can see this entire corner. There's no way we can get to those stairs without getting shot."

"What if you cover me?"

Nicholson shrugged.

"I can probably make that guy keep his head down for a few seconds, but what are you going to do when you get there?"

He had a point. There were at least three people up on the observation platform, maybe more if they'd spread out to the new roof. Nicholson could cover him to the stairs, but what then? Even if Alex could reach the spiraling metal stairs, he'd never make it to the top without being cut down.

He needed a plan.

"Okay," he said, thinking quickly. "If you cover me, I can probably make it to the power transfer pillar."

"I thought you said that was out," Nicholson said.

"I put a rune on the glass a few days ago," Alex said, remembering how the first rune he'd used had lasted longer than he expected. "It's obviously still working, and the piece of glass with the rune on it must have fallen down into the box. As long as it's there, I can't use the water to fry the radio."

"So what do we do?" Nicholson asked. "Wait for the cavalry?"

Alex shook his head.

"No telling how much time we've got left. We have to kill that radio right now."

"Great," Nicholson said. "Do you have a new plan for how to do that?"

"Same plan," Alex said, stepping back so he could see the broken case but not the metal stair. "If I can get to the pillar, I can cancel the rune. Then the plan will work."

"You'll be exposed out there," Nicholson said. "I can cover you till you get there, but I don't know how much ammunition I've got left."

"Use short bursts," Alex said, tossing his hat onto the floor next to the shotgun. "Once I'm in position, I'll signal you to cover me while I cancel the barrier rune."

"For the record, I hate this plan," Nicholson said. "If I let you get yourself killed, I'll never hear the end of it from Lieutenant Pak or the Captain."

Alex laughed at that.

"Just tell them you couldn't talk me out of it," he said. "They'll believe that."

Nicholson moved up to the corner and held up the Thompson.

"Ready?"

Alex nodded, and the detective ducked around the corner, firing as he brought the weapon to bear. As soon as he moved, Alex bolted across the room. He passed inside the ring of breaker boxes and dropped down behind the pillar that held the power transfer plates. No sooner had he made it than shots rang out from the stairs, pelting off the pedestal and the nearest power box.

On the floor just beyond was the dead German who had been next to the glass case when it exploded. His face was turned away, something Alex was grateful for since there was a large puddle of blood under the dead man's head.

Being careful not to cut himself on the fragments of the broken case, Alex slid along until he was near the south end of the pedestal. As he moved, he felt the barrier rune pass over him. It had lost much of its energy, but was still plenty strong enough to push his jacket away when the water-filled test tubes reached it.

Muttering a curse, Alex pulled the tubes from his pocket and left them on the floor so he could move further inside the protective sphere of the barrier rune. Sweeping the broken fragments of the case away, he got to one knee so he could stand up and grab the shard with the rune on it.

"Go," he called to Nicholson.

A shot rang out from the stairs and a bullet caromed off the top of the pedestal, making Alex flinch. The detective fired in answer, sending a burst of rounds clattering off the metal stair. From that direction came a shouted word in German, which Alex took to be a curse. At least one of the detective's bullets had found a target.

Not pausing to think about that, Alex quickly rose up so he could see over the side of the pillar. The silver transfer plates were exactly where they should be and Alex reached out, trying to sense where the bit of case with the rune on it had landed. He felt it immediately, but when he opened his eyes, he didn't see a shard of formerly-shatterproof glass. The still-working rune was the one he'd put directly on the transfer plate last Friday. He'd heard of runes exceeding their normal time limits, but never by two whole days.

"Get down, you idiot," Nicholson yelled as he fired another burst from the Thompson.

A bullet hit the transfer plate just to Alex's left, leaving a white scratch behind. A second round caught him in the arm, tearing into his left bicep and forcing him back behind the safety of the concrete pedestal.

"You all right?" Nicholson called from behind the block wall.

"Yeah," Alex said, pressing his handkerchief to the hole in his arm. It was a lie, but not because of his aching, bleeding arm. In order to cancel the barrier rune, Alex would have to touch the spot where it had been cast. Unfortunately that spot was on a metal plate conducting enough electricity to power the south end of Brooklyn. If he touched it, the discharge would cook him in a split second.

His plan to generate a power surge by throwing water on the transfer plates was finished.

"Did it work?" Nicholson called.

Alex didn't answer. He needed a new plan and he needed it now.

Peeking out from behind the pedestal, Alex looked at the spiral stair. It was just a metal helix that ran up into the ceiling with solid metal steps winding around it. Located at the far end of the room, beyond the ring of breaker boxes, Alex doubted he could make it without being shot repeatedly.

Barton had taken him up onto the observation deck during the tower's final test, so Alex knew that above the stair was a metal balcony, and behind that was the roof. If he guessed right, the Germans had the radio set up on the observation deck. Whoever was operating it would be there, obviously, but it wasn't big enough for more than a few people. Everyone else would be on the new roof, just waiting for Alex to stick his head up from the stairs so they could blow it off.

Glancing up, Alex thought about trying to shoot through the roof. If he got lucky, he might take one or two of the Germans out. Of course, that was dependent on his having a gun.

Looking back to the dead spy, Alex grabbed him by the arm and pulled. With his left arm useless thanks to having been shot, he had to brace himself and heave. Finally, the dead weight of the body slid over a bit and Alex could see a silver semiautomatic pistol on the far side of his body. Risking exposure, he leaned forward and grabbed the weapon, pulling back right as another round of bullets hit on the floor just beyond him.

Raising the weapon, Alex aimed at the ceiling to the left of the stair and fired three times. He waited, but no sound of distress came from above, and there were no signs of sunlight filtering down through the spots where the bullets hit.

"What are you doing?" Nicholson called.

Alex ignored him as he cursed himself for a fool. Barton had the roof replaced with one made of metal because it slightly extended the range of the tower. Apparently the metal was thick enough to stop a bullet.

Grinding his teeth, Alex dropped the gun and pulled out his rune book. He paged through it one-handed, looking for something that might help. Any rune would do, one that could incapacitate the Germans or punch through the metal roof.

The metal roof.

Alex paged to the back of the book where the little pocket had been sewn under the back cover. He usually kept business cards or important loose papers here, but since he had to come out to this tower so often, he'd also taken the precaution of placing his two identical rune papers in there. Holding the book with his teeth, Alex pulled out the folded papers. Just as he got them free, he lost his grip on the rune book and it fell into his lap. Alex ignored it, fumbling with his thumb to open the folded papers. His left arm was beginning to throb in time with his heartbeat and somewhere south of the tower a flying bomb was about to fall on Sorsha.

He was running out of chances and time.

Dropping the rune papers in his lap with the book, Alex picked up the German's gun and thumbed the button that would release the magazine. Setting the gun aside, he picked up the magazine and popped out the remaining bullets with his thumb. Once it was empty, he set the magazine next to the pistol and put a rune on each one, lighting them with his squeeze lighter.

"Nicholson," he called, dropping the magazine into his coat pocket. "You still there?"

"For all the good I'm doing," the detective called back.

Alex pushed himself up to one knee, then picked up the gun.

"Cover me," he yelled.

A moment later the Thompson barked, and Alex leapt to his feet and ran. He was heading for the breaker box that was between the transfer pedestal and the stairs. As he ran, he held up the pistol and fired, using the lone shell remaining in the chamber.

The Thompson started up again but stopped almost as quickly. The detective had just run out of bullets.

Alex slid into the shelter of the breaker box like DiMaggio stealing second, trying his best not to roll onto his wounded arm. The German at the top of the stairs must have realized that Nicholson was empty because he opened up on the box, peppering it with bullets. Several of the rounds penetrated the flimsy metal of the box but none managed to hit Alex.

"Nicholson, get this guy off me," Alex yelled.

In response, Alex heard his shotgun boom and the rattle of buckshot peppering the staircase. Knowing the gunman above would have flinched from the blast, Alex leaned around the box and tossed the borrowed gun onto the bottom step of the spiral stair.

The German fired but missed as Alex pulled back into the shelter of the breaker box. Pulling the empty magazine from his pocket, he tossed it underhand. The magazine flew toward the power transfer pedestal, dropping down into the ruins of the glass case.

Alex didn't wait to see the results. He took off running for the center of the room. A single shot rang out from the stair...and then the magazine landed on one of the silver transfer plates.

A sound like thunder boomed through the power room followed by the sizzling sound of arcing electricity. From above came the sound of screaming men, a sound that was cut mercifully short, though it was followed by the nauseating smell of burning flesh.

Alex took shelter behind the transfer pedestal again. Above him, the metal magazine he'd thrown sizzled and popped.

"What did you do?" Nicholson said, stepping tentatively out from behind the shelter of the wall.

"I connected the gun to the empty magazine with a rune," Alex said, cradling his wounded arm as he stood. "The stairs, the roof, and the observation deck are all conductive metal, so once I threw the gun on the stairs and the magazine into the transfer box, all the electricity passing through this tower was diverted there."

The detective shouldered the shotgun and shook his head.

"You think that got the radio too?" he asked.

"Probably," Alex said with a shrug. "We'd better make sure though."

"How do we turn off the power?"

Alex looked around, but most of the construction debris had been removed.

"Shoot it off," he said, pointing to the dancing and crackling magazine.

"I'd rather you didn't," Andrew Barton's voice interrupted.

Alex spotted the man himself standing by the staircase wearing a gray suit with a bright blue tie. Clearly he had just teleported in.

"Did Bickman get hold of you?" Alex asked, relieved to see the sorcerer.

"No," Barton said, crossing the room and reaching into the transfer case. He pulled out the burned and twisted remains of the gun magazine. "I have spells on this tower that let me monitor the power flow.

Whatever you did with this," he held up the magazine, "caused a significant disruption." He leaned around Alex to look at the dead man on the floor, then looked up to where a burned and smoking arm hung down from the stairs. "I think you'd better catch me up to what's been going on."

"That's a German spy," Alex said nodding at the burned arm. "They're using a radio to disrupt a top secret military test at Fort Hamilton. They know that the Secretary of War is attending, and they probably have agents in place to kill him if their interference fails. Sorsha is there, but they know that, so they probably have spell breakers with them."

Barton took that all in stride as if such things were perfectly ordinary.

"Right," he said when Alex finished. "First thing is to warn Sorsha."

"What about the radio?" Nicholson asked.

"The amount of electricity Alex sent through my new roof would have fried it for certain," Barton said. "But it's safe now, so why don't you go make sure?" He reached into thin air like Sorsha did and pulled a large, full-length standing mirror into existence in front of him.

"Isn't that the mirror we used to trick Ethan Nelson into confessing to Dolly Anderson's murder?" Alex asked, recognizing the monstrosity.

"I liked it so much I bought it off the Schuberts," Barton said as he tapped the glass with his finger. "Sorsha darling?" he said. "I need to speak with you privately and I'm afraid it's rather urgent." He paused, then tapped again. "I don't want to alarm you, dearest, but your boyfriend has been shot."

"Hey," Alex protested. While it was true, Barton was making it sound worse just to get Sorsha's attention, something she would no doubt blame Alex for.

A popping sound emanated from the mirror and Sorsha's face appeared.

"Is Alex all right?" she demanded, and Alex was glad to hear the tone of worry in her voice.

"Thank you for confirming my suspicions about your relationship with my runewright," Barton said with a chuckle.

Sorsha's look went from worry to annoyance in less than a heartbeat.

"You are not amusing," she growled. "Is Alex all right or not?"

"Well," Barton said, looking at Alex. "It looks like someone winged him, but I imagine he'll be fine. The important thing is that he says someone is going to try to kill the Secretary of War during whatever test you're watching."

"How did..." she began, then just shook her head. "Alex," she continued. "Of course you know the top secret things I'm doing. That said, my charge is quite safe."

"No," Alex said, stepping up to the mirror. He quickly explained about the sabotaged radios and the Nazi spies. "I went to the Navy first," Alex went on. "Admiral Tennon believed me but when he called for his car, a Navy Shore Patrolman shot him dead. He had the same German cigarettes on him."

"You think the Nazis have an agent here as well," Sorsha said, following Alex's train of thought. "Either among the Army personnel or on my FBI team."

"Almost certainly," Alex confirmed.

Sorsha's face grew stony. She'd never really gotten over that her trusted confidant, Agent Phillip Davis, had been a German agent.

"All right," she said, looking up at something. "The test is happening now. I'll secure everything here, then I'll come to you."

Her image disappeared from the glass before Alex could reply and Barton touched the mirror, causing it to vanish.

"Everybody's dead up here," Detective Nicholson said as he made his way back down the spiral stairs.

"What about the radio?" Alex demanded. "Was it destroyed?"

"Not yet," Nicholson said with a grin. "But it is on fire."

29

CRIMES OF PASSION

Since there weren't any chairs in the power room, Alex sat with his back against the cement pedestal that held up the transfer plates. His arm was killing him, but the bleeding had slowed to a trickle. He was pretty sure that the bullet had removed a good chunk of his bicep because even though he was cradling it with his good arm, any time he shifted even a little bit, it exploded with pain. It hadn't hurt like that when he was trying to stop the Nazis, but adrenalin was good at masking pain.

"All right, Alex," Barton said, as he finished checking the breaker boxes. "Most everything is back up and running, so now let's get you to a hospital."

Alex shook his head, which, on reflection, was a bad move because his arm twinged with the movement.

"Sorsha said she'd be here as soon as she's done securing Woodring."

"Aw," Barton said with mock concern. "It's adorable that you want to cripple yourself to make sure your girlfriend is okay. She's a sorceress, Lockerby. She'll be fine."

"Go get Dr. Bell," Alex growled, mostly because of the pain in his arm. "He'll fix this up better than any hospital."

Barton sighed and shook his head.

"I guess if you weren't a stubborn ass, we wouldn't get along so well," he said. Then he closed his eyes and vanished.

"You sure that's the best idea?" Detective Nicholson wondered, sitting down next to Alex. "I could have sent Sorsha after you and I don't need you when the Captain gets here."

"I'm worried," Alex confessed. "I know she's an all-powerful sorceress, but so do the Nazis. Whoever they've got inside Fort Hamilton will have a plan to take her out."

"There's nothing you can do about that," Nicholson pointed out.

Alex grimaced as his arm throbbed, then he nodded.

"Did you ask about the code Alice Cartwright used when you spoke to the Navy?" Nicholson asked, attempting to change the subject.

Alex was grateful for the distraction. Taking a slow breath to keep the pain of his arm in check, he relayed Commander Vaughn's explanation of a complex shift cypher. When he finished, Nicholson just stared at him for a minute.

"So to figure out what the letters say," Nicholson said at last, "we need a master code."

"Yep," Alex said.

"And that code is just a string of numbers?"

Alex nodded again, then grimaced as his arm moved.

"And since Alice and her co-conspirator were spies, they wouldn't write this code down, would they?" Nicholson went on. "So it would have to be something they could remember."

"Probably." Alex said. The pain in his arm seemed more acute than before and he was regretting not going with Barton.

"Alex?" Sorsha's voice called out from somewhere behind the pillar.

At the sound, Alex felt the tension leaving his muscles. He hadn't realized how much they'd clenched, but it explained the increasing pain in his arm.

"Here," he called.

The sound of the sorceress' heels clacked on the floor and she came around the pillar. She wore an elegant suit and skirt of light gray, but the suit was marked by dirt and what looked like blood.

"You all right?" Alex asked, looking from the blood on her jacket to her face. There was a smudge of dirt or grease across her cheek and forehead.

She ran a critical eye over him, pausing at the sight of the blood leaking through his trouser leg and his cradled arm. Relief that he was all right and anger that he'd been wounded warred across her perfect face for a moment.

"Better than you," she said, giving him a thin smile. "You're supposed to use the coat with the shield runes on it."

"I did," Alex said with a laugh he regretted instantly.

"You need to be less careless," she admonished, squatting down to his level. "Now take a deep breath and I'll get you to Iggy."

"Barton went to get him," Alex said, with a small shake of his head. "They should be back any minute."

As if on cue, there was a popping sound and Barton and Iggy appeared a few feet away.

"Miss Kincaid," Iggy said, giving Sorsha a nod. "I'm glad to see you're here. I'll tend to you as soon as I've got Alex squared away."

Sorsha looked confused, then looked at the blood on the lapel of her jacket.

"None of this is mine," she said, standing back as Nicholson got up.

Iggy squatted down like Sorsha had done, running a practiced eye over Alex.

"How bad is your arm?"

"Bullet took a chunk out," Alex admitted.

Iggy's jaw clenched and he blew out an exasperated breath.

"Open up," he said, pulling a small vial of brown glass from his pocket. He pulled out the stopper and upended it over Alex's open mouth. As expected, it tasted vile, but as soon as the liquid hit his stomach, the pain in his arm lessened.

"I need my vault," Iggy said. He indicated Barton and Nicholson. "Get him up and follow me."

"There's a chalk outline in the hallway by the elevator," Alex called as Nicholson grabbed his good hand.

Barton reached out and touched Alex's shoulder and he felt his body begin to float as if he'd been suddenly immersed in water.

"Pull him up gently," Barton said, and Nicholson gave Alex's hand a firm tug.

Alex floated up and once he got his feet under him, Barton removed the effect. Moving carefully, he headed for the chalk door with the others in tow. By the time he arrived, Iggy had his vault open and he led Alex through his grand foyer to the room that contained his surgery.

"How long?" he growled as he helped Alex out of his torn and bloody coat.

"Twenty minutes," Alex gasped as the sleeve slipped over his arm. "Maybe twenty-five."

"That's cutting it close," Iggy said. "Lie down."

Regenerating wounds was a costly process involving a major restoration rune and some rare potions, but it wasn't really all that complicated. The real problem was time. After about thirty minutes, the effectiveness of a regeneration treatment began to go down quickly. By thirty-five minutes, it wasn't worth the bother. After that, all that could be done was to regrow the damaged tissue, which would take weeks and be fairly painful.

Alex knew this, of course, but he'd been more worried about Sorsha than he cared to admit. Sorcerers tended to think of themselves as invincible thanks to their magic, but they could be killed just like anyone else if the prospective assassin was determined enough. He'd seen Sorsha shot once before. When that happened, the pain kept her from accessing her magic, which left her helpless. Without her magic, the powerful, intimidating sorceress was just a pretty young blonde.

"Cut his shirt off," Iggy said from his workbench where he was setting out several potions in a line.

Barton picked up a pair of surgical scissors from an instrument tray and proceeded to cut the arm off Alex's shirt, then open it up for easy removal. When the wound in his bicep was exposed, Sorsha gripped his free hand tightly.

Alex hadn't realized that she'd taken his hand, but he wasn't going to complain. Whatever Iggy had given him was making his perception fuzzy and indistinct.

"All right," Iggy said, crossing back to the table. "Hold still."

Several hours later, Alex sat in the reading chair in his vault. His arm was done up in a sling, but that wouldn't be necessary for very long. The regeneration hadn't worked as well as Iggy would have liked, but it would be finished in another couple of hours and Alex's arm would be as good as new.

The potion he'd given Alex for pain had mostly worn off, but it left him tired and dozing as he sat. He hadn't wanted to sleep, so he'd insisted on sitting there. He'd wheeled the rollaway cabinet next to his writing desk over to stand beside his chair. The cabinet held his telephone and intercom, and both had a spool of wire that allowed them to be moved.

Iggy had put the boiler stone in the fake fireplace opposite the reading chair and it was giving off a very pleasant warmth that kept threatening to lull Alex to sleep. His mind, however, wouldn't allow that. While Iggy was patching him up, the police had arrived at the relay tower and Nicholson had to go and explain what had happened.

Barton's spell alarm had pulled him out of a meeting in Washington, so he had to leave as well. Sorsha had stayed until Iggy finished, but then she had to get back to her security detail and so she had vanished as well.

With no one to talk to, Alex sat, turning the day's events over and over in his mind. He kept trying to find a better way, something he could have done differently that wouldn't have cost the life of his friend, Admiral Tennon. If he'd noticed the suspicious workmen, maybe the security guard from the tower would still be alive.

You can't change the past, Iggy's voice came out of his memory, *all you can do is learn from it*.

But the only lesson he could glean from his experience was to be smarter, and he wasn't sure how to do that.

As he sat, lost in his circular musings, the phone rang. Since it was a candlestick phone and he only had one arm, he moved the phone over onto his reading table, then picked up the receiver and held it to his ear.

"Lockerby," he said, leaning down to the mouthpiece.

Blood Relation

"I just wanted to let you know that I just arrested William Masters," Detective Nicholson's voice came over the line.

"So it was him who told the Germans about the weapons test?"

"No idea," Nicholson said. "No one will tell me anything about that. I arrested him for murdering Alice Cartwright. Those letters she had in her safe were love letters. Toward the end he starts promising to divorce his wife, and it's clear Alice stopped believing him. From the context, I'm guessing she threatened to expose the affair, and he had to silence her."

"How did you decode the letters?" Alex asked, both impressed and confused.

"You said it yourself, Lockerby," the Detective said. "A sequence of numbers that Alice would remember."

If Alex had the use of both his arms, he would have slapped his palm on his forehead.

"The combination to her safe," he said. "That's why she wrote them in her blood. You could have drilled out the safe, but without the numbers you'd never have been able to decode the letters."

"And since the safe was hidden, Alice figured Masters wouldn't find it," Nicholson finished.

Something flitted across Alex's memory and he frowned.

"But what about the name at the bottom of the letters?" he asked.

"William Masters goes by Bill," Nicholson said. "I really appreciate your help on this one, Alex. Detweiler is going to love having this one in the solved column."

"I'll send you a bill," Alex said with a chuckle.

After he'd hung up, Alex felt more awake, so he picked up the paperback novel Iggy had left on his reading table. It was one of the pulp crime novels Iggy loved so much. Alex had read some of them before, and had come to the conclusion that he wasn't getting into enough fistfights or bedding enough dangerous women to make it as a pulp detective.

"Something to strive for," he joked as he picked up the book and awkwardly attempted to flip to the first page. Before he could manage, the phone rang again. This time it was Sorsha. She was still busy with the protection detail for Harry Woodring, but she wanted to check up on him and let him know she'd be free for dinner tomorrow. Alex asked about Agents Redhorn and Mendes and both of them had come through the assassination attempt relatively unscathed.

He drew out his conversation with the sorceress, just talking to hear her voice, until her FBI job interfered and she had to hang up.

Picking up the book again, he began to read. This time he made it through four pages of the novel before the phone rang. With a sigh, he set the book aside and picked up the phone's receiver.

"Grand Central," he joked.

"You're in a good mood, brother," Diego Ruiz' voice came through the earpiece. "You must have had an interesting day."

Alex sat up straight and he could feel his heartbeat pounding in his healing arm.

"Hello, Diego," he said, leaning back down to the phone's mouthpiece. "Or should I call you Rasputin?"

Diego actually laughed at that.

"You actually followed my trail all the way back to Russia," he said. "It's a good guess, of course. Grigori and I were...fellow travelers, kindred spirits if you will. But, no, I never assumed his identity. Truth be told, I wanted him to be my apprentice."

"What happened?" Alex asked, his mind racing. He would have bet a large sum of money that Diego had actually been Rasputin, especially based on some of the rumors about the man. He was very much in line with Maria de Naglowska and her strange obsession with alternative sources for magical power.

"Grigori and I didn't see eye to eye on several points," Diego said. He seemed perfectly willing to talk about the subject, but his voice betrayed a bit of irritation. "I learned a long time ago that it's difficult to be a leader. Leaders are always the ones out front. They get the glory when things go well, but they also take the blame for any failure."

"Rasputin wasn't a leader," Alex pointed out.

"No, but he positioned himself very publicly as the power behind the throne," Diego said. "It's one thing to be the one whispering in a leader's ear, but it's something else entirely when people see you doing it. So, when rivals had a problem with the Czar, they first removed Grigori."

Alex nodded, understanding.

"You want to be the one with the power," he said. "But rule from the shadows with the leader as your front man."

"You see, Alex," Diego said with a chuckle. "You and I understand each other. Grigori was an apt student, but he lacked the vision to see the bigger picture, whereas you have grasped it in only a few minutes."

"What are you saying, Diego?" Alex asked. "You want us to be friends?"

"Much more than that, Alex," Diego said, his voice full of fervor and passion. "I've lived a long time and I have never met a mind equal to my own. I admit, you might be stronger at runes than I was when the Immortals cast me out. Together, Alex, you and I could change the world."

"You mean rule it," Alex said.

"Yes, Alex," Diego said with no hesitation or shame. "I mean rule it."

"Sounds like a lot of work," Alex said, feigning boredom. "Why bother?"

Diego laughed at that.

"Don't try to pull the wool over my eyes, boy," he said, still chuckling. "I've read up on you. You view yourself as some kind of knight in shining armor, running around helping people and doing good."

"So?" Alex challenged him. "What's wrong with that?"

"Nothing," Diego said, almost yelling the word. "Nothing at all. But look at the world, Alex. It's a mess. Full of fear, want, pain, and death. Now, just imagine what you could do to help, what you could do to overcome these things. With a man like you at the helm, human ignorance could be eradicated. Drifting, rudderless souls could be given purpose, and with the two of us working together, the world would become a paradise."

It was tempting. Alex could almost see Diego's paradise in his mind's eye.

"That's a lovely thought," he admitted. "All it will cost the human race is their humanity, and their free will."

"Is that really such a high price to pay?" Diego said.

"Yes," Alex said. "I have enough trouble running my own life, I'm not arrogant enough to believe I can run everyone else's too."

There was silence on the line for a long time, then Diego sighed.

"I figured that would be your answer," he said. "But I hoped you'd surprise me. It's my own fault for not getting to you sooner. I must admit, I'm rather bad at spotting talent until it's too late to be shaped and molded."

The thought of Diego finding Alex on the street corner selling barrier runes in the rain instead of Iggy made him shiver.

"I'm sorry we won't be working together, Alex, I really am," Diego went on. "But your lack of vision isn't going to dissuade me from my goal. And to further my goal, I'm going to need the Immortal's book."

Alex had been wondering when Diego would get around to that. The only reason to try blowing the door off the brownstone was to obtain the Archimedean Monograph.

"No," Alex said simply.

This time the pause on the line was longer and the sigh at the end more pronounced.

"You're making a mistake, Alex," he said. "I need the knowledge in their training book to further my goals. It's been a long time since I learned anything new, and I crave knowledge."

"My answer is still no."

"I figured it would be," he said. "But I must have the book nonetheless. Unfortunately your surprisingly effective protection rune foiled my attempt to take it. It also left me in a weakened state, so I'm going to have to consolidate my power before we meet again."

"You mean kill more innocent women," Alex corrected, struggling to control his rising anger.

"We all do what we must to survive, Alex," he said. "To make a better world, sacrifices must be made. So, until we meet again, brother, I'll be watching you."

"I'll keep a lookout for you too," Alex growled.

"You do that," Diego chuckled. "And if you change your mind, put dear Maria's picture in your window. I'll call if I see it."

"Don't hold your breath."

"Goodbye, Alex," he said, his voice still full of amusement. "It's been a genuine pleasure meeting you."

With that, there was a click in the receiver and the line went dead.

Alex wanted to slam the earpiece back into the phone's cradle, but with one hand all he'd really do would be to knock the phone on the floor, and he wasn't feeling up to going after it. Diego had made it plain he would be killing again, soon. And there wasn't anything Alex could do to prevent it.

He'd been sure he was onto something with the Rasputin connection, but he could tell Diego wasn't lying when he'd denied being the mad monk.

Not wanting to throw the telephone, Alex turned to the reading table on the other side of the chair and snatched up the topmost book in his reading pile. He was about to throw it instead, when he recognized it. *The Hanging Mystery* by Maria de Naglowska.

"Dear Maria," he quoted, remembering what Diego had called her. "She meant something to him," he realized. "She was special to him."

That was why Diego kept an illustration of her in a frame and hung it in his hotel room.

Alex turned the book over in his hand and opened it to the front. The first section was a revised biography of Maria, added to the book after her death a year ago. It went on for several pages and detailed her life, her philosophy, and her writings. There was even a brief entry about the Brotherhood of the Golden Arrow.

Flipping to the biography, Alex began to read, not for information on Maria's life but for any clues to her relationships and the people in her life. She'd been married and had children, but Diego didn't seem like the type to settle down and raise a family. Besides, he knew enough of Maria and her ideals to know that she would have rejected monogamy.

Five minutes later, Alex snapped the book closed and got up, heading toward the brownstone door to find Iggy.

30

HUNTERS

"P.B. Randolph," Alex said as he reached the ground floor landing and turned into the library.

"Who?" Iggy said, looking up from the paperback he was reading.

"That's what I need to know," Alex said. "Diego called me—"

"What?" Iggy interrupted. "What did he say?"

"He wanted me to join him and give him the Monograph," Alex said, waving his hand as if the subject were unimportant. "What matters is that Diego wasn't Rasputin, but he admitted to being Rasputin's mentor."

"So who is P.B. Randolph?"

"Diego is," Alex explained. "Before he hung up, Diego referred to that handbill of Maria de Naglowska. He called her, 'Dear Maria'."

"So she was important to him," Iggy confirmed.

"Well, according to the biography of Maria in the front of her book, she was a devotee of P.B. Randolph. He was the source of her weird ideas about sex and magic, and she spent years translating his books into French. She worshiped him."

Iggy stroked his chin, considering the chain of events that Alex had laid out.

"From your description of Diego, he sounds like the kind of man who has a healthy ego."

"He sees himself as the man to rule the world because only he can make it a paradise," Alex confirmed. "I'd say he's got an ego."

"So," Iggy said, speaking carefully, "it stands to reason that, if a man like that learned of a beautiful woman who was enamored of his ideas, he would attempt to meet her."

"And Maria was a young woman in Russia when Rasputin was coming to power. It's entirely possible Diego knew her back then. I admit it's just a guess, but the timing lines up."

Iggy nodded and set his penny dreadful aside. Rising, he crossed to the bookshelf and ran his finger along the leather backs of the books until he came to a large, heavy volume. Pulling it from the shelf, he opened it just past the middle, then began turning pages.

"What's that?" Alex asked.

"Who's Who," Iggy said as he continued to page through the book. "Here he is," he said at last. "Paschal Beverly Randolph, born here in New York in eighteen twenty-five, reportedly died in July of eighteen seventy-five. According to this, he was an occultist and a medium who traveled extensively in Europe."

"Sounds like a fit for Diego," Alex said.

"According to this, Paschal was a mulatto," Iggy continued reading. "He was an educated man, and a medical doctor."

"Maybe that's where he got his theories about blood magic," Alex suggested. "Does it say anything else about him?"

"He wrote extensively, founded several occult societies, and was a descendant of William Randolph. Apparently he was very proud of his famous ancestor."

Alex paced to the grandfather clock in the hall, then back several times, going over the details about Randolph in his mind. Given what he'd said on the phone, Randolph would probably be out hunting for his next victim as soon as the sun went down. Alex could call Danny, but even the entire police force couldn't locate and protect every prostitute in the city. And, even if they did, Diego — or Randolph, rather — could easily find his prey in a bar or nightclub. Prostitutes were easier because he didn't have to woo them, but Diego was certainly handsome and well-spoken enough to seek prey the hard way.

"What are you thinking?" Iggy asked, watching Alex pace with his probing gaze.

"Diego was staying at the Astor Hotel," Alex said. "He's an educated man and a world traveler, so it stands to reason he likes high living."

"A reasonable assumption."

"He was using the Diego Ruiz alias, but that's not good anymore. He needs something he can fall back on until he can establish a new one."

"You're thinking he'll go back to something familiar."

Alex nodded.

"Do me a favor," he said. "Call every fancy hotel in the city until you find one with a guest named William Randolph."

"Or Will or Bill," Iggy said with an approving nod. "What are you going to do while I'm tilting at your windmill? From what we know of Randolph, he's powerful and dangerous. Do you have a plan to deal with him?"

Nodding, Alex headed for the stairs.

"I've got to write a couple of runes," he said. "Then, once we know where Randolph is hiding, I'll go pay him a visit."

An hour later, Alex got out of a cab across from the Biltmore Hotel. The sun had gone down, and darkness was starting to swallow the streets of the city.

The Biltmore was one of the city's most opulent residences. Iggy had started his search for Paschal Randolph by calling the most expensive hotels in the city first. As a result, it had only taken him twenty minutes to suss out Randolph's location. As Alex had guessed, he'd checked in under the name Bill Randolph. Iggy even described him to the desk clerk just to be sure.

It was him.

As Alex hurried across the busy street, he patted the shoulder holster under his bound left arm. His 1911 was still in the possession of the police, so he'd been reduced to bringing his back-up gun, a Smith and Wesson .38 revolver. It was a dependable weapon, but the boxy shape of the 1911 made it easy for Alex to put runes on the gun that helped with accuracy and recoil. The .38 didn't have a flat surface anywhere on the weapon. Even the sides and bottom of the grip were rounded.

In addition to the gun, Alex also had a few useful runes folded up under the front cover of his rune book. Having only one usable arm would make it difficult to tear runes out of his book, so he'd just folded them and stuck them inside.

Satisfied that he was as prepared as he could be, Alex turned toward the Biltmore's main door in the center of the block. The hotel was enormous, with two independent towers reaching up into the sky that held hundreds of rooms.

As he approached, the main door opened, and Paschal Randolph stepped out onto the sidewalk. Alex quickly turned away before he could be spotted, peering into a ground floor window and using the reflection from the brightly lit street to watch his prey. For his part, Randolph lit a cigarette and then approached the hotel doorman about summoning a cab.

Alex had a brief thought of approaching Randolph from behind and sticking the .38 in his back. It had worked with Harcourt, but this time Alex would have to do it under the nose of the doorman, and he was sure to be spotted. Even if Alex managed it, there was no way to know if Randolph was telling the truth about being out of magic. If he had one of his explosive snow globes, he could kill several dozen people on the street in an attempt to escape.

So Alex watched as the doorman hailed a cab, then he stepped up to the curb and whistled for one of his own.

"You see that cab right there?" Alex told the cabbie when he slid into the back of the taxi.

"I got eyes," the cabbie sneered back.

"Well keep 'em fixed on that cab and don't lose it," Alex said.

The cabbie looked like he wanted to ask questions, but Randolph's cab was pulling away from the curb, so he just put his foot on the gas and they pulled out into the evening traffic.

Almost an hour later, Alex climbed up the rickety stairs to the third floor of a disreputable rooming house. He'd watched Randolph pick up a prostitute from a street corner by the docks and then come straight here. The landlady downstairs had been only too happy to point out what room he was in, once Alex flashed a five spot at her.

Moving as quietly as he could, Alex went to the second door on the left, and gently gave the handle a push. He wasn't surprised to find it locked, given the fate Randolph had planned for his unfortunate partner. Alex, however, had come prepared.

Reaching into his jacket pocket, he took out his cigarette case and managed to open it one-handed. Holding it up to his mouth, he grabbed a cigarette with his lips and slid it free, snapping the case shut and returning it to his jacket. He transferred his hand to his trouser pocket and grabbed his lighter. Working with only one hand was a bother, but at least he hadn't been shot in his right arm.

Squeezing the lighter, it snapped open and Alex held the flame to his cigarette. Once it was lit, he got his rune book and pulled out one of the loose papers he'd put just inside the front cover. Awkwardly, he licked the rune paper while managing to not lose the cigarette, then he stuck the paper to the brass lock plate on the door.

He took a deep breath and blew out a cloud of smoke. He wasn't sure just how dead Paschal Randolph's magic was, but if he retained any of his natural abilities, he'd feel the unlocking rune the second Alex activated it. That meant Alex had to move quickly. Reaching over the sling that bound his left arm, Alex slipped his hand into his jacket, emerging a moment later with the revolver.

Since he couldn't hold the gun and the cigarette, Alex leaned down and touched the burning tip to the rune paper. He felt the unlocking rune flare to life and the lock clacked noisily as it opened. Without hesitation, Alex looped his little finger around the knob and turned it, hitting the door with his shoulder at the same time. It flew open with a bang and Alex held his gun at the ready.

Unfortunately, he wasn't as ready as he'd anticipated.

"Hello, Alex," Randolph said. "I've been expecting you."

The room was small, just a bed, a washbasin, a wardrobe, and a little table with a chair. Right now, the chair was positioned in the center of the room. The prostitute had been tied to it with thin rope that looped over and around her body. A gag of some kind had been forced into her mouth and the rope ran around her head, securing it in her mouth as well. The woman looked younger than Alex expected, probably still in her teens with dark hair and a fair complexion. Her face was beginning to show a large purple bruise, no doubt from when Randolph had subdued her, and she was completely naked.

Behind her stood Paschal Randolph. He was still dressed in his immaculate silk suit and wore a broad smile on his handsome face. With his left hand he held the prostitute by her hair, and with his right, he pressed a wicked-looking knife to her throat. Alex could see the red mark from where the blade touched her delicate flesh.

"Drop it," Alex said, leveling the revolver directly at Randolph's chest.

"Oh, I don't think so," he said, easily. "If you shoot me, I'll still have time to cut this lovely young lady's throat. Even if you were to shoot me through the heart, my body would spasm, and that would be enough to open her carotid artery. She'd be dead in seconds."

Alex resisted the urge to grind his teeth. Randolph was right. Alex might get him with a lucky shot, but if he didn't, the girl was dead.

"Drop your gun, Alex," Randolph said, pressing the blade into the prostitute's neck firmly enough to draw a bead of blood. "I'm not going to ask again."

Moving slowly, Alex took his hand off the trigger and leaned down to place the gun on the floor.

"Kick it over here," Randolph said. "Then close the door."

Alex did as he was instructed and when he turned back from the door, he found Randolph pointing his revolver back at him.

"There," he said, stepping out from behind the struggling, crying girl. "That's much better." He sighed, putting his free arm behind his back, as he considered Alex.

"So how did you know I was coming?" Alex asked, more to fill the silence than from any desire to know.

"You should really look into how the British are training their policemen to follow a suspect," he said. "You let your cab driver get too close, I could see he was following and let's face it, you were the only person who would do that in a cab. Then when I picked up Carmen, here," he stroked the girl's cheek and she pulled away as much as she could. "He left his headlights on. You might as well have put a blinking light on top the car."

Alex considered that. Most people who rode in taxis weren't paying attention to the road, so it never occurred to him to take precautions. He should have known, though. Randolph had been alive for over one hundred years, and you didn't live that long without learning to be careful.

"You know," Randolph went on, "this is the second time I've looked over my shoulder and found you there. How did you find me without using that powerful rune of yours?"

"William Randolph," Alex said with a shrug. "The ancestor you're so proud of. I figured that instead of taking time to work up a new alias, you'd just fall back on an old one for the moment."

Randolph looked genuinely surprised at that, then he laughed.

"You are too much, Lockerby," he said. "I always knew you were a dangerous opponent and still you keep exceeding my expectations. Are you sure you won't join me? With two minds like ours, there isn't anything we couldn't accomplish."

"Sorry," Alex said with a shrug.

Randolph looked genuinely sad, but then he smiled and shrugged.

"Oh, well," he said. "With that twisted sense of morality of yours, I would have had to kill you sooner or later anyway." He put his free hand around the bound woman's neck and grabbed her chin, forcing her to look at Alex. "I think before I dispatch you, I'd like you to see what you're giving up." He let her go and held the gun out toward Alex. "I've underestimated you for that last time, however. You're the kind of clever boy who will have drawn holdout runes on his body, just waiting for me to let my guard down. So let's take care of that right now." He cocked the .38. "Please remove your clothing."

Alex rolled his eyes, but he did as he was told, piling his jacket, trousers, shoes, socks, and eventually his shirt in a pile at his feet.

"All of it," Randolph said when Alex stopped.

Alex stripped out of his underwear, but had trouble unwinding the bandage around his wounded arm. When he finally got that free, the skin underneath was an angry red color with what looked like green veins running through it.

"Excellent," Randolph said. "I see you've been keeping up with your exercise, that's good for the health. Now, turn around."

Alex complied, showing that he had no runes drawn anywhere on his body. Randolph even made him show off the bottoms of his feet to be sure.

"I don't know whether to be disappointed or not," he said at last. "I really suspected you'd have a trick or two up your sleeve."

"Give me a pen," Alex said.

"I think not," Randolph said. He jerked the revolver in the direction of the lone window. A large radiator with peeling paint stood beneath it. "Get over by the radiator," he said, pulling a pair of handcuffs from the pocket of his suit. "I want you to have a good view."

Alex felt a bit sick that Randolph wanted him to witness the violation and brutal murder of the terrified girl in the chair. Any misgivings he had about Randolph disappeared entirely. He was a cruel and violent narcissist and he needed to be stopped.

"Sorry," Alex said, cocking his head to one side. "I'm afraid there won't be time for that."

"Don't be coy, Alex," Randolph said. "I can just as easily shoot you in the legs to make you stay put."

"You misunderstand," Alex said, moving over to the radiator. When he got there, he grabbed the window and pulled it up. The warped frame would only let it rise an inch, but that was enough. As soon as it opened, the faint sound of approaching police sirens became much louder. "I'm saying that you don't have much time until the policemen I called before I came up here arrive."

An expression of shock crossed Randolph's face, followed by rage, and then acceptance in quick succession.

"It seems I've underestimated you again," he said. "But all is not lost. There's still plenty of time for me to kill you and escape."

"No," Alex said, cradling his left arm to his chest and positioning his right hand over the left forearm. "I'd wanted to bring you in myself, or failing that, let the police take you, but I can't let you hurt anyone else, and I'm not keen on dying. So, if someone has to die, I vote for you."

"I have the gun, boy," Randolph almost shouted at him. "You have no weapons, no tools, and no runes. How do you propose to stop me?"

Alex stood facing him for a long moment before he let a wide grin spread slowly across his face.

"Just because you can't see something," he said, "doesn't mean it's not there."

With that, Alex touched the spot on his arm where he'd cast the invisible linking rune. Immediately he could feel the other end of that rune, the second link that he'd attached to a rune that hung on the wall of his vault.

His escape rune.

The instant the connection was made, Randolph felt it. Alex triggered the rune just as the other man raised the pistol and fired. Alex couldn't tell if the magic went first or if the bullet simply missed him, but suddenly the dilapidated room vanished. Alex's body was stretched and pulled until he felt like he could fit under a door, then everything twisted, and he rushed forward through a dark hallway. The experience was nausea-inducing, but before it could become overwhelming, the real world reasserted itself.

Which an audible pop, Alex found himself falling in a dark sky. From off to his left the poor confused prostitute was screaming through her gag. In front of him, Alex could see Randolph reflected in the light of a gibbous moon. He was staring down at the black expanse of ocean that was rushing up quickly to meet them.

Alex knew he only had a few moments before the second part of his rune engaged. He turned his body so the rushing wind pushed him into the woman. His escape rune had been specially tailored not to attach to furniture, so she was flailing as she fell, free of the chair but still wrapped in the rope that had been used to secure her. Alex grabbed her with his good arm, wrapping it tightly around her waist.

The impact spun him around and he caught sight of Randolph. The man glared at Alex with a look of pure hatred, raising the pistol for a killing shot.

And then everything vanished.

Alex popped back into existence in the library of the brownstone. He landed on the rug in the middle of the room, but unlike last time, he'd appeared mere inches above the floor, so it didn't knock the wind out of him. Since he had a hold on the prostitute, she had come with him and was now lying on the floor next to him, flailing hysterically.

"Hold still," Alex growled as she hit his injured arm.

He struggled to his feet and then pulled the naked woman up after him.

"Alex?" Iggy's voice came from behind him.

Turning, Alex found his mentor sitting in his reading chair, cigar and book in hand. He raised an eyebrow and Alex remembered that, like the bound woman, he was completely naked.

"Am I to assume you've decided to adopt Dr. Randolph's philosophies regarding magic?" The question was serious, but the tone of the old man's voice told Alex it was all Iggy could do to keep from laughing.

"Very funny," he growled. "Why don't you see if you can find our guest something to wear while I untie her?"

31

WHAT ISN'T THERE

It took Alex almost forty minutes to dress himself once he got upstairs. In the old days Alex only owned two suits, so with one covered in blood and needing repairs and the other still at the rooming house by the south docks, he would have been reduced to wearing a pair of dungarees and an undershirt. These days, however, Alex owned several suits, and he only had to enter his vault where he kept them.

Unfortunately, the pocketwatch that would open the seal on the vault cover door was also still at the ramshackle rooming house.

Cursing his security measures, he dug out a pen and a scrap of paper and wrote a vault rune for himself. His vault key was with his pocketwatch, but he had a spare in the center drawer of his dresser.

When he finally made it back downstairs, he found Iggy in the kitchen working his magic at the range. The prostitute was sitting at the massive table wearing a modest dress and devouring some kind of thin pancake that was rolled up with jam inside. Alex was about to ask where Iggy got the dress when Sherry came through the open door to the greenhouse.

"Your orchids are beautiful, Iggy," she said with a wide smile. "Hi'ya boss," she added when she saw Alex.

When Alex looked back at Iggy, his mentor just shrugged.

"I don't own any dresses," he said. "What took you so long?"

"My spare suits were in my vault."

Iggy's brows furrowed, then he nodded with understanding.

"That could be a problem," he admitted. "We'll have to give that some thought later. For now, I want to hear your side of what happened tonight. Carmen here," he nodded at the prostitute, "has already told us hers."

"Hi, Carmen," Alex said, moving around the table to sit opposite her. "I'm Alex."

She looked up from her plate as if she were unsure what to do. Alex tried to make eye contact with her, but she wouldn't.

"Carmen is a bit nervous around you, boss," Sherry said, sitting down next to the skittish girl. "Between you and the man who wants to kill her, she's a bit of a nervous wreck."

"It's all right, Carmen," Alex said in his soothing voice. "I'm sorry I frightened you."

This seemed to calm her, but she still wouldn't look up.

"Danny called while you were upstairs," Iggy said, putting a plate with a jam smeared pancake in front of Alex. "He should be here in a few minutes and he's bringing your things."

That was a relief. Alex felt naked without his rune book.

Figuratively.

"Let's wait until Danny gets here," he said. "I don't want to have to tell the story more than once." He looked at the pale pancake and his stomach rumbled as he remembered that he hadn't eaten anything since breakfast. "What is this thing?" Alex asked.

"It's a crêpe," he explained. "You roll it up and eat it."

Alex shrugged and did what he was told. As he ate, Sherry gave him a meaningful look, then nodded slightly in Carmen's direction. Alex really hadn't been paying much attention to her, probably leftover discomfort from having seen her naked. He pushed that aside and looked carefully at her. Since she refused to look at him, he didn't have to hide his appraising gaze.

His initial thought that she was young seemed to be correct. He couldn't be sure, but she looked about eighteen. Based on the way she was wolfing down the crêpes, and her almost bony physique, it was clear she didn't eat regularly.

A knock at the door interrupted Alex's musings. He got up from the table and made his way to the front door, which had been replaced sometime in the previous day. When he pulled it open, Danny gave him a probing look followed by an amused smile.

"You want to tell me why I found a pile of your clothes at that room you sent me to?" he asked, handing over a folded stack of Alex's things.

"That's a bit of a story," Alex admitted, stepping back so Danny could enter.

As they went into the kitchen, Alex dropped the bundle of clothes on his reading chair in the library, stopping to extract his rune book, pocketwatch, lighter, and cigarettes. Just having them made him feel whole again.

By the time he got back to the kitchen, Danny was sitting in his place, eating his last crêpe.

"All right," Alex said, sitting down next to Danny. He launched into a recitation of the night's events leading up to his encounter with Paschal Randolph and its conclusion with the man plummeting into the North Atlantic.

"You sure he's dead?" Danny asked.

Alex shrugged but he nodded at the same time.

"Water hits pretty hard when you fall from two-hundred feet," he said. "Plus at this time of year, the North Atlantic is very cold. A person can last about five minutes before their body starts shutting down."

"Could he have had an escape rune of his own?" Iggy asked.

Alex had thought of that, but he didn't want to give it serious consideration. The idea that Randolph might still be out there gave him chills.

"It's possible," he admitted. "But if Randolph survived, he's going to need to replenish his magic quickly. Wherever he ends up, there will be more killings and more blood runes."

"I'm not sure how to put that on a bolo sheet," Danny said, pushing his chair back. "But I'll think of something."

"I want to know how you managed to use your escape rune," Iggy said. "The last I heard it was hanging on the wall in your vault. It would have taken several weeks to have the tattooing done."

Alex explained about the barrier rune in the Brooklyn Relay Tower and how the linking runes had allowed it to connect to Andrew Barton's energy spell.

"I realized that the barrier rune was sharing the same linking runes that transfer electricity to the tower," he explained. "I could feel Barton's spell through the connection. Well, if that was possible, I ought to be able to connect to any rune through a linking rune."

"So you put one on your escape rune and linked it to your body," Iggy said, grinning with approval. "It was as if the rune were tattooed on you. Very clever."

Alex could tell from the look on his mentor's face that he was thinking of new and interesting ways that bit of information could be used.

"All right," Danny said, pushing the empty plate away and rising. "I'd love to stay, but I've got to go try to explain all this to Captain Callahan. Miss Knox, do you need a ride?"

"Why, detective," Sherry said with a bright smile. "That would be lovely, provided you have room for two."

Carmen looked up sharply at that. Her face flushed and she was squeezing her hands together to keep them from shaking.

She's afraid one of us will put the kibosh on whatever Sherry's got in mind.

"Carmen will be staying with me for a few days," Sherry went on easily.

Alex raised an eyebrow, and Sherry met his gaze.

"I have a feeling she has certain skills that might be useful to Charles Grier or maybe Linda Kellin," Sherry finished.

Alex knew better than to argue. Sherry could read people with just a touch, and if she thought Carmen had an affinity for alchemy, then she did. It was clear Carmen needed some direction in her life, and both Grier and Kellin could use the help.

Alex and Iggy showed the group to the door and watched from the stoop as they got into Danny's car and drove away.

"You got lucky," Iggy said as they headed back inside.

"What do you mean?" Alex asked. "I had everything covered with my brilliant plan." He wasn't being serious, but he wasn't taking Iggy's criticism seriously either.

"I mean that Randolph expected you to have a rune on your body," Iggy said, poking Alex's good shoulder. "That's why he had you strip down to your birthday suit. If you'd tattooed it on like normal, he'd have seen it and probably would have shot you right then."

Alex had to admit, Iggy was right about that.

"Thank goodness linking runes are invisible when you write them correctly," Alex said. "You should have seen the look on Randolph's face. He was so smug, thinking I was defenseless. I told him that just because you can't see something, it doesn't mean it's..." Alex hesitated as something brushed past his memory.

"It's not what?" Iggy prodded.

"Just because you can't see something, it doesn't mean it's not there," he repeated, feeling as if he'd just been struck by lightning. Without a word, he bolted for the stairs, running up two flights to his room. Pulling out his watch, he released the bindings on the vault cover door and ran past the vault bedroom and kitchen on his way to the main hall. Turning right he kept going to the place where his mobile door would appear when he opened it. Sitting on a narrow table nearby was his kit bag, and he scooped it up.

Alex stopped just long enough to grab something from the secretary cabinet where he kept his spare tools, then he ran back down to the brownstone's library.

"What is it?" Iggy demanded, looking affronted that Alex had run off without an explanation.

"Just because you can't see something, it doesn't mean it's not there," he repeated.

"Yes," Iggy said. "I heard you the first time."

"Sherry," Alex explained, a little out of breath. "She can read people when she touches them. Ever since I found out about her gift, she's only been able to read one thing from me."

Iggy nodded at that.

"*You aren't seeing what isn't there*," he repeated. "But that doesn't make much sense, does it? If something isn't there, you obviously can't see it."

Alex grabbed Iggy's shoulder with his free hand.

"What if we're coming at it backwards?" he said. "What if it doesn't mean that I'm supposed to see something that isn't there? What if it means that I haven't noticed that something that's supposed to exist...doesn't."

"You mean something that you should see is gone," Iggy tried to make sense of what Alex had said. "Like what?"

"Put this on," Alex said, handing Iggy his spare oculus.

"All right," Iggy sighed as he strapped the mini telescope over his right eye. Alex reached into his kit and took out his main oculus and strapped it on as well, then he took out his multi-lamp and fitted it with the ghostlight burner.

"Are you going to tell me why I'm wearing this?" Iggy said in a sardonic voice. Ghostlight, after all, revealed magical residue, something the entire brownstone would be covered in, especially after they used all those mending runes to repair the explosion damage.

"Moriarty," Alex said. "When he talked to me, he quoted Archimedes."

"The bit about the lever and the place to stand to move the world," Iggy said with a nod. "What of it?"

Alex didn't answer. Instead he went to the bookshelf and took down the Archimedean Monograph and opened the front cover. Holding it out so that Iggy could see, he pointed to the blank page just behind the cover.

"Moriarty chided me when I didn't know the Archimedes quote. He told me it was written on the first page of the Monograph."

"That page has never had anything written on it," Iggy said, leaning close. "It's definitely not there."

Alex took out his lighter and lit the ghostlight burner in the lamp. As soon as the light began to shine out through the main lens, Alex held the book into the beam. Instantly, glowing words sprang into existence, hovering over the page as if they were written in the air.

. . .

Give me a lever and a place to stand, and I will move the world.
　-Archimedes of Syracuse

"Mother of God," Iggy swore. His hand trembled as he reached out and turned the first page. Alex knew very well that this page dealt with how to focus a barrier rune to block different things than just water. It was a component of the purity rune in his breathing mask and one of the underlying principles of a shield rune. As the page opened, however, tightly packed lines of text erupted from the page, rising to float over the surface. They flicked and moved, making it difficult for Alex to read them, but they seemed to deal with alternate uses for linking runes.

"Bring that to the table," Iggy said, awe in his voice.

Alex carried the book and the lamp into the kitchen, and Iggy doused the overhead lights. For the next few hours they stood at the table, leaning over the book and reveling in each new page. There were runes for transmutation, changing one thing into something else. Other runes could allow someone to locate a marked object, much like a finding rune, though any object could be marked regardless of any personal link.

An entire section of the book dealt with how to build multiple constructs on top of each other in a technique the book called stacking. There were even designs for new kinds of equipment, including a more compact oculus. It would take months to get through it all, maybe even years.

When Alex closed the book and blew out the lamp, Iggy just slid down into one of the kitchen chairs.

"I can't believe it," he said in a weary voice. "All this time and it's been right under my nose. Your pal Moriarty must think me quite the dullard."

"Don't blame yourself," Alex said. "Why would we look for magical residue in a book about magic? Logically it's bound to be covered in residue, just not in any meaningful way."

"That's a frightening point," Iggy said. "It means that whoever wrote all that must have put some kind of protection rune on the book that keeps it from absorbing any new magical residue."

"A rune that's still functioning," Alex pointed out. That reminded him of the curiously long-lived barrier rune at the Brooklyn Tower. He made a mental note to look in on that if it was still active.

"This is too much," Iggy said. "I'm exhausted just from thinking about all of it. Let's get a good night's rest and go over this in the morning."

Alex wanted to refuel his lamp and start taking notes right then, but Iggy had a point. It was after eleven and he'd been up since the early morning.

"All right," he said, picking up his lamp and the book. The latter he returned to its place on the left side of the fireplace, the former went back into his kit bag along with his oculus.

"Thanks for the loan," Iggy said, handing back his spare. Then he headed up the stairs to his room.

Alex looked back to the bookshelf where the Monograph was doing its best not to be noticed. Hiding in plain sight. Now he knew that it was concealing more than just its presence.

"How many more secrets are you hiding?" he asked. When the book didn't answer, Alex turned off the light and headed up to bed.

32

AFTERMATH

The chapel at the Navy Yard wasn't terribly large, so Alex had to stand in the back during Admiral Tennon's funeral. He'd gone with Sorsha, but she, by virtue of her position of importance, had a seat up front. The service consisted of speeches by the Admiral's long-time friends and a eulogy given by Lt. Commander Vaughn. When it was finally over, Alex stood in line to pay his respects at the casket.

Walter Tennon was resplendent in his class A uniform. Alex learned during the service that he'd received a tombstone promotion, receiving a third star by special dispensation of the War Department. None of that really mattered, though. Alex had liked the Admiral even though they got off on the wrong foot initially. Tennon was a no-nonsense leader, but he was also cunning and intelligent.

And now he was dead.

"So long, Walter," Alex said as he passed the casket. "I'm sorry I got you into this." He clenched his fist, pressing the ends of his nails into the palm of his hand, then stepped away so the line could keep moving.

"Thank you for coming, Alex," Lt. Commander Vaughn said,

standing just beyond the casket. "I know Walter would have wanted you here."

Alex was tempted to say something sarcastic, but bit back the remark.

"Thanks," Alex said. "That was a swell eulogy you gave. What's going to happen now? They going to put you in charge?"

Vaughn laughed at that.

"That would be quite a promotion," he said. "I'm told a new Admiral will be coming in soon, and he'll be taking over. As for me," he held up his sleeve so that Alex could see the three stripes on the cuff. "I've been promoted to full Commander and I'm being given a command."

"Your own ship?" Alex said with an approving nod.

"She's just a cargo transport," Vaughn said, practically beaming, "but she'll be mine."

"I'm glad something good came out of this mess," Alex said, trying not to grumble. As far as he knew, the entire event, even Walter's murder, had been hushed up by the War Department. He looked back at the casket. "He died a hero, and people deserve to know it."

Vaughn put his hand on Alex's shoulder and turned him back.

"We know," he said. "For now, that has to be enough."

Alex didn't like it, but he understood, and he nodded.

They stood talking about unimportant things for a few more minutes until Sorsha found them. A few minutes later, Alex led the sorceress out to her waiting floater.

"You're very quiet," she observed once the car was in the air.

"Walter was my friend," Alex said. "One of the few."

She scooted over next to him and put her head on his shoulder.

"I know," she said. "But it wasn't your fault. If you hadn't interfered, it's quite likely I'd be dead now, and a lot of others along with me." She gripped his arm and he reached over to put his hand on top of hers.

"Father Harry hated funerals," Alex said after a long silence. "He said that they should be held in a music hall, and that instead of mourning the dead, we should celebrate them."

"I think that's a wonderful idea," Sorsha said, sitting up. "Tonight, you and I will put on our Sunday best and go dancing. We'll have cake and champagne, we'll toast the life of Admiral Tennon, and we'll celebrate that we were fortunate enough to know him."

"Sounds blasphemous," Alex said. Sorsha just stared back at him, one of her delicate eyebrows arching up into her forehead. "I love it."

"Good. Now I've got three meetings with various government officials this afternoon, so you be ready at seven sharp and I'll pick you up at Iggy's place."

"Yes, ma'am," he said.

"How was the funeral?" Sherry asked when Alex entered his office a few minutes later.

"It was good," Alex admitted. "How's your charge?"

He meant Carmen Harris, the hopefully-former prostitute. Sherry had found out that she was only seventeen and her father had been killed last year in an accident at the factory where he worked. After that she was taken in by a relative who put her to work selling her body. Alex resolved to pay that man a visit once Sherry had Carmen settled. According to Sherry's reading of the girl, she had a budding talent for alchemy, so she was trying to apprentice her to one of the alchemists Alex used regularly.

"Charles Grier doesn't have anywhere for her to live," Sherry said with a giggle. "Well, nowhere that wouldn't raise a scandal."

Grier was a bachelor and in his fifties, so bringing on a young, attractive apprentice would no doubt raise some eyebrows.

"Linda is willing to give her a try, though, and she's got the basement bedroom for her."

Alex knew that bedroom all too well. It had been Jessica's.

"Good work," he said, pushing those thoughts from his mind. "Let me know as soon as it's a done deal."

Sherry promised that she would, then told Alex that a stack of potential new cases was waiting on his desk.

"Right," he sighed. He wasn't particularly excited about getting back to work. He really wanted to hit his vault and join Iggy in the brownstone as he studied the hidden information in the Monograph. Still, he had bills to pay, and that meant work before pleasure.

He made his way along the back hall toward the door to his office, which was right next to the cover door to his vault.

Maybe I'll just check in on Iggy.

He pulled out his pocketwatch and opened the cover door, but before he could enter, the middle door in the hall opened and Mike Fitzgerald came hurrying out.

"Mr. Lockerby," he said, positively beaming. "I think I got it."

He pressed a square bit of paper into Alex's hands and stepped back. Alex held up the sheet, then turned it upside down. It was a rather crude purity rune. The line work was tentative and the symbols wobbled a bit, but Alex could feel the magic in it. While it wouldn't win any awards for beauty, it would work.

"This is great, Mike," Alex said with a genuine smile. This was a long way from a finding rune, but it was an important step.

Mike grinned, but then it faded.

"Can you come look at this other one, Mr...Alex?"

"Sure Mike," he said, following the man back into the spare room.

Half an hour later, Alex emerged back into the hall. He'd gone over all of Mike's work and given encouragement and suggestions. It had been a long time since he had to push his skills like Mike was doing, and he wondered if Iggy had to be as patient with him.

Probably more so, he admitted.

The door to his vault was standing open where he'd left it and he chided himself for not closing it. To be fair, he hadn't expected to spend so much time with Mike.

Alex glanced at the door to his office and pictured the waiting paperwork beyond. He really should get to it, but he just didn't want to. Resolving to look at it in an hour, he stepped through the cover door of his vault and this time, he shut it behind him.

With a spring in his step, Alex crossed the short hall that led from the office door to the main chamber of his vault.

"You really shouldn't leave your vault door open," Moriarty said, in his cultured British accent. "Anyone could just wander in."

He was sitting in Alex's reading chair perusing Maria de Naglowska's book with his legs crossed, casually. His dark hair was slicked back, and he was dressed in his shirtsleeves and suspenders.

"What are you doing here?" Alex demanded. He had a momentary thought of running to his gun cabinet, but he was out of ammo for the Thompson, and he'd lost both his pistols. The only thing he could use would be the Browning shotgun and in the time it would take to load it, Moriarty would be gone.

"You're here because I found the hidden text in the Monograph," Alex went on before Moriarty could answer, though how he could have known that was a mystery.

"That's what I like about you, Alex," Moriarty said, closing the book with a one-handed snap. "You're quick. Although," he added with a sardonic grin, "you did take your sweet time figuring out my clue. At least you learned to replenish your life energy. I would have been very put out if you'd let yourself die. Finding a replacement for you would have been the very devil."

"Then you need to try harder next time," Alex said. "I met my predecessor."

Moriarty chuckled at that and held up the book.

"You mean Pash," he said. "I wholeheartedly agree with you, he was not chosen well. I argued against his inclusion, but I was...overruled."

"By the other Immortals," Alex said. "How many of you are there?"

"Not as many as you might think. We're a rather exclusive club."

"So why didn't you want Randolph?"

Moriarty sighed and looked up at the ceiling for a moment.

"He had the opposite problem from Dr. Doyle. Whereas the good doctor treated power with such respect that he didn't want it for fear he'd misuse it, Paschal wanted as much power as he could handle, as quickly as he could get it."

"That's why he pursued blood magic," Alex guessed, then he nodded at the book in Moriarty's hand. "And sex magic."

"Just so," Moriarty said. "Truth be told, you can find magic in everything if you look hard enough. Paschal just wasn't willing to take his time and learn the proper way."

"You have to master the basics or you have no foundation to build on," Alex repeated the maxim Iggy had drummed into his head years ago.

"Exactly. When my colleagues wouldn't teach Paschal as fast as he wanted, he went looking elsewhere. Eventually he discovered that blood could be given more power if it was spilled in an act of murder. After that, we were forced to cast him out."

"The damnation rune," Alex said. "Does it really seal away a person's magic?"

Moriarty set the book back on Alex's reading table and stood.

"Yes and no," he said, as he began unbuttoning his shirt. He pulled it open so Alex could see the same elaborate rune that Randolph had shown him, right over Moriarty's heart. Unlike Paschal's rune, however, this one pulsed in time with the heart beneath it, changing colors with each beat and shifting like the image in a kaleidoscope.

"This isn't just a rune, Alex," Moriarty said. "It's a pledge, literally the oath we Immortals all take. It guides us and sometimes compels us to work for the good of humanity, but not to interfere in the world's development."

"Paschal broke his oath," Alex guessed. "When he did, the rune bound him with his own power."

"He took the oath willingly," Moriarty said, rebuttoning his shirt. "That's how the rune gained the power to damn him."

Alex had to admit, it was an elegant solution. Randolph didn't have access to his magic, because his magic was bound up in the rune.

"What if he decides one day that he's following his oath?" Alex asked. "Wouldn't that release his power?"

"A man can try to lie to himself, Alex, but deep down he always knows the truth. If Paschal ever regains his power, it will be because he's genuinely changed."

Alex thought about that for a moment, then pushed the whole mess to the back of his mind.

"I'm guessing you didn't come here just to tell me about Randolph and your oaths," he said.

DAN WILLIS

"No," Moriarty admitted. He reached into his shirt pocket and withdrew a pair of thick green spectacles. "Catch," he said, tossing them to Alex. "These will help you read the Monograph much easier."

"I thought you took an oath not to interfere," Alex said, holding the spectacles up so he could look through them.

"I'm doing no such thing," Moriarty said, pulling his vault key from his trouser pocket. "You found the hidden text all on your own, all I'm doing is giving you the ability to read it faster. That doesn't fundamentally change anything."

"Exactly how fast do I need to read the new text?" Alex asked as Moriarty pressed his vault key against the back wall of Alex's vault.

"Well, it did take you quite a bit longer than I'd anticipated to find that text," he said as his vault door appeared. He pulled it open and Alex once again had a view of his incredible vault. Through the opening he could see a stuffed mammoth and the bones of a dinosaur. Shelves and shelves of books occupied the back wall and there was a sitting area that was clearly for entertaining.

"Time is short, Alex," he went on as he stepped inside his vault. "Events that will affect the whole world are already in motion, and you are not prepared."

"You want to give me a hint?" Alex asked.

Moriarty smiled at him as he pulled his vault door closed.

"Get prepared," he said, and then the door to his vault faded away, leaving the gray stone wall of Alex's vault in its place.

"Great," Alex said.

THE END

You Know the Drill.

Thanks so much for reading my book, it really means a lot to me. This is the part where I ask you to please leave this book a review over on

Amazon. It really helps me out since Amazon favors books with lots of reviews. That means I can share these books with more people, and that keeps me writing more books.

So leave a review by going to the Blood Relation book page on Amazon. It doesn't have to be anything fancy, just a quick note saying whether or not you liked the book.

Thanks so much. You Rock!

I love talking to my readers, so please drop me a line at dan@danwillisauthor.com — I read every one. Or join the discussion on the Arcane Casebook Facebook Group. Just search for Arcane Casebook and ask to join.

And Look for Alex's continuing adventures in Capital Murder: Arcane Casebook #7.

ALSO BY DAN WILLIS

Arcane Casebook Series:

Dead Letter - Prequel

Get Dead Letter free at www.danwillisauthor.com

Available on Amazon and Audible.

In Plain Sight - Book 1

Ghost of a Chance - Book 2

The Long Chain - Book 3

Mind Games - Book 4

Limelight - Book 5

Blood Relation - Book 6

Capital Murder - Book 7

Hostile Takeover - Book 8

Hidden Voices - Book 9

Dragons of the Confederacy Series:

A steampunk Civil War story with NYT Bestseller, Tracy Hickman.

These books are currently unavailable, but I will be putting them back on the market in 2022

Lincoln's Wizard

The Georgia Alchemist

Other books:

The Flux Engine

In a Steampunk Wild West, fifteen-year-old John Porter wants nothing more than to find his missing family. Unfortunately a legendary lawman, a talented thief, and a homicidal madman have other plans, and now John will need his wits, his pistol, and a lot of luck if he's going to survive.

Get The Flux Engine at Amazon.

ABOUT THE AUTHOR

Dan Willis wrote for the long-running DragonLance series. He is the author of the Arcane Casebook series and the Dragons of the Confederacy series.

For more information:
www.danwillisauthor.com
dan@danwillisauthor.com

facebook.com/danwillisauthor
tiktok.com/@danwillisauthor
twitter.com/WDanWillis
instagram.com/danwillisauthor

Printed in Great Britain
by Amazon